THE TIME OF HER LIFE

Marjorie Eatock

ZEBRA BOOKS
KENSINGTON PUBLISHING CORP.

To Toots, BMW
(Best Mother-in-law in the World)

ZEBRA BOOKS

are published by

Kensington Publishing Corp.
475 Park Avenue South
New York, NY 10016

First printing: March, 1992

Printed in the United States of America

One

Harold, the postman, had often wondered about his brother carriers in the large cities. Did metropolitan mailmen get to know as much about the lives of people on their routes as small town mailmen? Sometimes, as he slogged along, he reflected on the passage of years and how much sorrow and joy he had delivered along with the junk. Today in particular he dreaded the stop at the big old white house on the bend of Sycamore Street. She was such a nice lady, Mrs. Cass. She had enough trouble with her husband in the nursing home not recognizing anybody and that no-good daughter in every bar in town. What Harold had in his battered leather pouch was a bank overdraft. He knew the envelope. He'd delivered plenty — but never to Evelyn Cass.

He dreaded it. He was conscious of hurrying a little as he went up the walk under the big, yellow-leaved trees. Brushing by the porch ivy — not as well-trimmed these days as it was when John was home — he dropped the mail in the box.

Damn, he thought as he trudged on to the next house, I sure do hate that . . .

As for Evelyn Matthews Cass, it was still a golden, sunshiny fall morning. She heard Harold's rattle at the front door. Coffee cup in hand, she hurried to the porch. She breathed the tang of smoky, crisp autumn air that rushed through the door with a skitter of leaves, and called cheerfully, " 'Morning, Harold!" to the retreating blue-gray figure.

The outside piece of mail was the retirement magazine John had subscribed to three years ago, before his stroke. Promising herself a pleasant hour on the back patio with it and a second cup of coffee, she left the door open. The living room needed airing. Two of her friends' husbands had put on her old storm windows last night, lingering for a beer and a smoke and the ten o'clock news.

It was strange. After thirty years of everybody puffing like chimneys as a way of life, now the acrid, stale smell of tobacco in the drapes and carpets bothered her. It didn't make her want a cigarette. It offended her nose — that facial appendage that had once happily snuffled three packs a day!

The guys still did. And John would, if they'd allow it at the nursing home. Smoking he remembered. Not his friends. Not his wife. Cigarettes.

Sighing, she stopped at John's desk to riffle

6

"I'M NOT GOING TO KISS YOU . . ."

"Bob . . . look!"

The deer stepped into view, ears up. Caught in crystal for a moment, she didn't move. Birds chirped drowsily in the locust trees. Bob and Evelyn held their breath, watching as the deer dissolved into the darkness of the trees.

Bob's arm had gone about her shoulders and was still there, warm and comforting. "It's been such a lovely day," she whispered. "I'm so glad I came."

His fingers had turned to clasp hers. "Will you come again?"

"I . . . I don't know." Her head was against the hollow of his shoulder. She felt warm, safe.

"Will you come again . . . if I tell you what I'm *not* going to do?"

She tried to answer, but couldn't.

"I'm not going to kiss you," he said softly. "I'm not." She felt his throat tighten against the back of her head, felt him swallow. "But God knows," he said, "I want to."

CATCH A RISING STAR!

ROBIN ST. THOMAS

FORTUNE'S SISTERS   (2616, $3.95)

It was Pia's destiny to be a Hollywood star. She had complete self-confidence, breathtaking beauty, and the help of her domineering mother. But her younger sister Jeanne began to steal the spotlight meant for Pia, diverting attention away from the ruthlessly ambitious star. When her mother Mathilde started to return the advances of dashing director Wes Guest, Pia's jealousy surfaced. Her passion for Guest and desire to be the brightest star in Hollywood pitted Pia against her own family — sister against sister, mother against daughter. Pia was determined to be the only survivor in the arenas of love and fame. But neither Mathilde nor Jeanne would surrender without a fight. . . .

LOVER'S MASQUERADE   (2886, $4.50)

New Orleans. A city of secrets, shrouded in mystery and magic. A city where dreams become obsessions and memories once again become reality. A city where even one trip, like a stop on Claudia Gage's book promotion tour, can lead to a perilous fall. For New Orleans is also the home of Armand Dantine, who knows the secrets that Claudia would conceal and the past she cannot remember. And he will stop at nothing to make her love him, and will not let her go again . . .

SENSATION   (3228, $4.95)

They'd dreamed of stardom, and their dreams came true. Now they had fame and the power that comes with it. In Hollywood, in New York, and around the world, the names of Aurora Styles, Rachel Allenby, and Pia Decameron commanded immediate attention — and lust and envy as well. They were stars, idols on pedestals. And there was always someone waiting in the wings to bring them crashing down . . .

through the rest of the mail. She was hoping for a postcard from their son Jack, who was directing his first cruise. When she caught sight of the bank envelope she opened it and tugged at the pink slip, frowning. What in the world was that?

Her glasses were shoved in a pigeonhole. She pulled them out, stuck them on her face, and squinted through her grandson's smeary finger-prints.

It took about twenty seconds for the dark meaning of the slip to sink in. She'd never in thirty-three years of marriage had an overdraft. Her initial reaction was anger.

How dare the bank send her such a thing? Of course there was money in her account! There was always money in her account! Someone had made a mistake. It was those awful, inhuman computers. To be one hundred and thirteen dollars overdrawn was the most ridiculous thing she'd ever heard!

Shoving her thick, silvery hair from her eyes, Evelyn put down her coffee cup so hard it slopped wet brown on the pristine blotter. She plopped into the oak desk chair, ignoring its familiar squeak, grabbed her shoulder bag from its hanging place on the chair back and dumped its contents helter-skelter next to the coffee. With exasperated but oddly nervous pawing, she scrabbled through the heap of cosmetics, tissues, lottery stubs, dead ball-point pens, tattered sales slips, earrings, aspirin, and antacid tablets until she found her checkbook lurking beneath her grandson Poo's I-Can-Read primer. Now she'd show those idiots!

Now, indeed.

Fifteen minutes later—having added and subtracted four times on her small pocket calculator that never made mistakes, she pushed it aside and stared at the oak paneled and polished wall behind the desk.

There was no mistake.

Evelyn Matthews Cass (Mrs. John) was overdrawn one hundred and thirteen dollars.

Further, she had learned from the pink slip that if she didn't quickly replace the overdraft (plus five dollars for the penalty) the bank was going to return both her check to Maples' Department Store and another casually scribbled at the supermarket.

Evelyn Matthews Cass felt her cheeks burning—partly at the embarrassment, of course—but mostly because of the awful, inescapable fact that she didn't *have* one hundred and thirteen dollars (plus five dollars penalty)!

Where had all the money gone? Why hadn't she foreseen the inevitable result of emptying their savings account, of authorizing bond cashing, transferring IRAs—how could she have been so stupid, so shortsighted, so obtuse? She'd even ignored her son's tentative warnings. Dad needs it, we have to have it, and that's that, she'd said—and deliberately ignored the reckoning day.

"Oh God," said Evelyn of the day that had just begun.

A one-hundred-and-thirteen-dollar day.

With cold fingers and the manual dexterity of a garden snail, she fumbled open her wallet and counted. Twelve dollars in bills. And sixty-four cents.

With a dull sense of total unreality, she swivelled in the chair. She looked at her comfortable living room with its thick carpet, ginger jar lamps, graceful Queen Anne chairs. The tall windows had leaded glass surmounts; through them the sunshine sent crimson, emerald and sapphire light to sparkle on polished walnut tabletops.

Beyond the windows in the neatly-surfaced driveway sat the long, ebony-black Lincoln Continental that John had loved so dearly. It was the last thing he'd bought before that ghastly seizure in the middle of the night. Six long weeks of trauma had put him where he was now: in the nursing home, physically recovered but thin, hesitant in speech, and brain damaged beyond repair. He lived in the past, excluding Evelyn, his children, and his mother who, in the forties, had been red-haired and heavy, not bone-slender and gray. He waited patiently for his young first wife to come to him, though she'd been dead thirty-six years. He was a courteous stranger. The nursing home bill for this stranger was like water gushing through a ravine.

Evelyn shut her eyes tightly, knowing it was not

John's fault. None of it. Certainly not this over-draft—that was hers. To whom could she turn for advice? Her stepdaughter Brenda's life was already a mess—widowed, alcohol-soaked and adrift; after years of trying, Evelyn had almost given up on Brenda. Her son Jack was aboard ship—far beyond reach. "Sure you'll be okay, Mom?" he'd asked, and how confidently she'd answered, "Of course. Have fun. See you in December."

The three other couples with whom she and John had spent most of their social life for thirty years had been touchingly supportive during John's illness—but this was different. This was embarrassing. Mortifying. Mary Lou DeKalb, Jane Nixon, and Liz Swan had been casual with money; they'd always had plenty of it. She hadn't. She and John had earned theirs. Yet, because she'd been stupid enough to let their attitudes rub off on her, she wasn't going to run to them now and make them feel guilty. The fault was hers.

All right, then. Skip going to friends for advice as long as she could. What were the other alternatives?

Selling something. Wasn't that what people did at times like this?

There was Grandmother Matthews's diamond brooch. But a small town of barely four thousand people has no pawn shop, and the idea of driving into the city to find one frightened Evelyn. Suddenly she remembered that Mary Lou DeKalb had always admired the brooch. The thought was like a beam of sunshine until she pictured herself saying brightly, "Mary Lou, I'm a bit short this month. Would you like to buy my brooch?"

She could almost see the look on Mary Lou's cosmetically-glazed face, her enormous baby blue eyes widening as obvious conclusions burst inside that self-centered but shrewd head. Despite her eternal search for youth, Mary Lou was no fool.

A last resort, perhaps.

What next? The bank. After all, it was a mutual problem. But the bank meant telling Liz Swan's husband, Ben. Yet — Ben would be in his professional capacity. That would be different. Wouldn't it?

She glanced at the clock. It was five of ten. Five minutes before good old easy-going Ben sat down behind that vast shining desk of his, winked at his pretty secretary, and started sifting through the morning's business. Did they tell Ben about overdrafts — or were vice presidents above such mundane things?

Making a wry face over the last gulp of cold and comfortless coffee, Evelyn picked up the empty cup and walked numbly into her newly-decorated kitchen. She put the cup in the dishwasher, started it, stood at the sink, and stared out the window at the familiar scene. Yet she was not consciously seeing the scarlet, pink, and jade coleus plants edging the terrace. Some of them are blooming; they need to be pinched, she

11

thought with a part of her mind, but it was like a tape, unheard but filed away for later. The fat-cheeked pewter jugs on the shelves flanking either side of the window reflected her image, distorted but curiously true, like a caricature: the round, solemn face beneath the short flow of thick, gray hair; the wide-set brown eyes under heavy dark brows; and the bright blue shirt over square shoulders a tad too broad for grace and a tad too busty to be youthful.

The blue was for John. She always ran out to the nursing home about eleven, and although he hadn't recognized her for months he still liked gay colors.

She wasn't thinking of John, just then. She really wasn't even functioning. She forced herself to turn and head for the stairs.

Halfway up, where the steps bent and the sun was pouring in on the graceful green sweep of a Boston fern, she paused and made herself come back down again.

The soft slish-slosh of the dishwasher had caught her ear.

Perhaps she'd better not run it just yet — it was only half-full.

Or — if she had to save money — perhaps she'd best not run it at all. It wouldn't hurt her to go back to doing dishes in the sink. Or would that take more water than the washer?

"Oh, damn!" said Evelyn out loud and grimaced. She didn't know. In fact, she didn't know an appalling number of obviously crucial things.

Why hadn't she realized how protected she was? When had she turned into such a pampered poop?

The first years of their marriage had been hard. John had struggled with the ghost of his first wife Pat's suicide, while she had struggled with Pat's rebellious three-year-old daughter. Before Jack there came a stillborn which grieved them both. But making the postwar hardware business go had pulled them together, had molded the marriage of the young, naive college drop-out and the emotionally-torn army veteran into something solid. Even when what had initially passed for love had been long gone, loyalty had remained. And friendship. And the firm attachment of dear and interlaced companions.

Evelyn retraced her steps, ascending the curve of the old oak stairs with one cold hand on the familiar rail. Her turgid brain was finally giving a few fitful jerks of primitive intelligence. She could get a job, it said, but not what kind. Book-keeping? Early in their marriage she had kept John's books. But now everything was computerized. She didn't know an input from an output.

A receptionist? But for whom? Everyone she knew wanted a cute young tootsie, not a gray-haired myopic with hot flashes — and who could fault them for that?

Check-out. She could check-out at the market.

She saw a lot of older women doing it. And run one of those automated registers that talks to people? And how long would it take to get over the agony, the humiliation of checking out people one knew? She could imagine their surprise, their quick cover-up, their inward speculation: Why is she here? You can't mean the Casses are broke! Mabel, did you see who I saw at the grocery yesterday . . .

She was at the top of the stairs. She said aloud, grimly, to the row of family portraits, "So I'm thin-skinned! I admit it. I can get over it! It appears," she added, "that I'll have to."

Grandfather and Grandmother Matthews stared straight ahead. A healthy, hefty John smiled at his "Salesman of the Year" award from Riley's Ratchets. Brenda, with long, lanky hair and daisies in her hands, stood by her blue-jeaned bridegroom, quite obviously pregnant with Poo, and having one of her few happy moments. Jack beamed at his bride, Michelle, all slipper satin, tulle, and calla lilies. Baby Poo — patently caught in the middle of a squirm — looked with the amazement of a confirmed doll-hater at the Cabbage Patch doll some well-meaning photographer had put in his rompered lap. John's mother, Jessie, gazed calmly outward with the school-teacher composure of one who has learned to accept limitation with good grace and disaster with stoic calm.

She loved them all. But they couldn't help.

Quite simply, it was up to her.

Her bedroom was warm with sun, bright with the deep patina of well-rubbed walnut and creamy drapes against blue, stenciled walls. For the first time it dawned on her how little of John was left after six months, how her own possessions had spread, taking over his drawers, his closet space. There was nothing left, not even his picture. Brenda had removed it for herself with covert defiance and Evelyn hadn't stopped her.

Yet, perhaps it was guilt — guilt from coping with loneliness by removing the traces — that inspired the sudden burst in her head: She could sell the house! Sell it and get a smaller one. Or an apartment.

Stunned by the idea, she stopped dead in her tracks. Sell her lovely, rambling old home, the place she and John had bought from his mother and expected to keep forever?

She couldn't. The idea brought tears to her eyes and she squeezed them shut, hurriedly rounding up defenses against such a dreadful idea. Wasn't she jumping the gun?

Be sensible, she told herself. Find out first how stupid you've really been. Perhaps it wasn't too bad. Perhaps there was something left. She really didn't know. Surely she could put off decisions of that magnitude until Ben Swan threw some light on her finances.

In the meantime she should find out if there was any other cash around. One thing she did know was that she had to round up one hundred and thirteen dollars.

It was a dim hope at best, and fast grew dimmer as she feverishly turned out pockets and emptied purses onto the cream-colored counterpane. She was staring in dismay at the small pile of bills and change when the telephone rang.

"Cass residence."

"Evie, have you a cold? You sound funny."

Mary Lou DeKalb. Exactly what she needed this morning. One of her three closest friends, Mary Lou could smell disaster with her nose plugged.

Hastily Evelyn said, "No. No, I'm fine. I guess I just haven't talked to anyone yet today."

"Okay. Good. I certainly don't need another cold since I dragged home that lulu from the new car show."

What Mary Lou and Porter also had dragged home had been hangovers almost historical in their scope, but Evelyn was willing to help preserve illusions. She said again, "No. I'm okay."

"Dandy. I just wanted to jog your memory about Janey's birthday lunch. I think I'll pick you up first, and Liz, then we'll go and get Jane. You know how slow she is, but between the three of us we can probably move her. I've made reservations on the club terrace for one-thirty. I thought that would give us all time to do the cake bit and play a few cards and have a drink or two. Okay? Porter's parents are coming to dinner at six, God help

16

me. Are you wearing that new white cotton dress you bought at Maples'? Because if you are, I'll wear mine. I'd like to have it on at least once before it gets too late although they do say you can wear white all winter. What Nan at the Princess Dress Shoppe is going to say when she sees me in a Maples' dress Lord only knows, but it was such a good buy, didn't you think so? Hey—what did you get for Jane? I picked up another bottle of that silly scent she likes so I hope to God you didn't. I never thought to ask. Evie? Evie? Are you still there?"

From a total, frozen panic Evelyn tried to make her mouth respond to her brain.

You bet she'd bought Jane a gift—that, plus the white cotton dress, rang up a healthy part of her overdraft. And in her distress she'd forgotten Jane Nixon's birthday party at Mary Lou's club where the total tab was bound to be over a hundred dollars. Even split among three hostesses, it was still thirty dollars she didn't possess!

Besides, she might have to return the gift *and* the dress!

She tried to answer calmly—as calmly as any woman could whose world was dropping apart. "I may have to cancel. Something—something has come up."

"Cancel!" Mary Lou's voice was almost a screech. "You can't cancel! We've done this for ten years. She expects it, and good God, don't leave me alone with Jane and Liz; they'll talk me to

17

death, I'll die of grandchilditis or cutesy-boo-boo or something. What's come up? What do you mean? Oh—" Then the voice dropped. "Oh, Evie, not John!"

"No, no, not John."

"Jack, then. The freighter has sunk. Michelle has run off with a Thai fisherman."

"No, of course not. They're fine."

"Oh. Oh, poor girl. Brenda. Evie, why don't you just give up and let them haul her off to some clinic where they'll dry her out—I mean, after all, enough is enough!"

"I'll call you back. Later," said Evelyn and hung up. Let her think it was Brenda. Brenda may as well be good for something.

It was after ten. Ben should be at his desk by now. Taking a deep breath and crossing her fingers mentally, she dialed the bank and identified herself. The receptionist had a velvety voice and skin to match—a fact observed at the club pool by Porter DeKalb and not well received by Mary Lou, who routinely spent a fortune on her own skin without the same results.

"Oh, Mrs. Cass! Hold on. I'll put you right through to Mr. Swan. He'll be delighted."

Evelyn took a deep breath to steady the heart that had begun thumping again.

Ben's voice was warm and friendly. "Well, well, Evie. What a nice surprise. What can I do for you?"

Evelyn sat down on the counterpane with a

18

surge of relief that left her knees weak. Of course. Ben would help her! They were old friends. He and John had gone to school together, served on church committees, gone to Rotary every Wednesday night. Ben had even helped with the storm windows last evening.

Almost croaking in her despair, she said, "Ben, I'm overdrawn! I've never been overdrawn before. I don't know what to do!"

"Oh, poor kid. No problem. No problem at all. Let's see, now. Okay. Why don't you drop by today and we'll convert a bond or two. Then when Jack's home we'll have him—"

She tried to interrupt: "Ben—"

"—come in and we'll just get his old mom into shape again. How are they doing, by the way. I've always wanted to go lollygagging off on a tramp freighter, but you know Liz: if there are no shopping malls on board she slides right into withdrawal—"

"Ben!"

Something in the urgency of her voice finally stopped him. Into the startled silence she said, swallowing hard, "I don't think there are any."

"Aren't any what?"

"Bonds. I . . . I think they've all been converted. Already."

"Oh." There was a small silence with the barest sense of discreet whispering in the background. "Okay. How about an IRA? You might lose some interest, but—"

"Those, too. At least, I think so."

"Gone?"

"Yes."

This time there was no mistake about the whispering. He said, "I see. I didn't know. My secretary is checking." Another pause. "What's the size of your overdraft?"

"One hundred and thirteen."

"One hundred and forty-five. A check came in from the carpet cleaners."

Through her anguish she realized he now had her sins spread before him on his desk.

"Okay," he said again, and there was a subtle change in his voice, a caution that chilled her. "It looks as if we need to talk about this, Evelyn."

"Yes."

"Tell you what." She could almost envision the wheels turning behind that high, balding forehead with the hairs tenderly gathered on one side and secured with Liz's mousse. "I'm pretty booked for this afternoon so come in tomorrow. About one. In the interim I think we can float a small loan. How many more checks do you have out?"

"I'm not sure. Not many. Truly." She could hear the humility in her voice and she hated it.

"Five hundred dollars cover them?"

"Yes. Yes, easily."

"Fine. We'll make it for five, then there's no need for collateral. You can sign the papers tomorrow. All right, Evie?"

"All right." It came out as a croak. "Thank you, Ben."

"Sure. Say hello to old John."

He hung up. Quickly, she thought. Too quickly for an old friend. It had started, hadn't it? With Ben's voice. That subtle change. Even if he was helping—which he was!

Something else John had always said: Don't try to mix money and friends. And he'd been right.

Her throat ached, but she couldn't take refuge in tears. Crying had almost been schooled out of her by her father. "Daddy's girl" was the only boy he'd ever had, and *boys* didn't cry. Edward Matthews had died twenty-five years ago, and his daughter still could not show her pain easily as other women did. Few people had ever seen Evie Cass break down—not at her parents' funeral, not when they'd showed her her beautiful stillborn child, not when John had experienced his terrible seizure. Tears would come—but rarely could she allow them to flow. Sometimes she wished she could. With strict discipline and crushing disapproval her father had left her the awful burden of false strength—and consequently other people's idea that Evie Cass could take anything. Even John had believed it. "Look at Evie," he'd say proudly. "I wish I was strong like that. Things just knock me for a loop—but not her."

The fact that she was bleeding inside had rarely been perceived, and never by her children. Her father had taught her too well.

In lieu of tears, her stomach hurt, and it was hurting now. She'd better take an ulcer tablet. She still had to visit John; unhappy faces upset him, even faces he didn't remember.

Wearily, Evelyn got to her feet. She went into the bathroom with its thick maroon towels that were never left in wet heaps on the tile floor anymore. Ignoring the water spots on the faucet, she swallowed her horse-sized tablet, made a face, and glanced in the mirror. She was shocked. The woman looking back was so colorless it dismayed her.

She picked up a lipstick and applied it. Too dark. She cleaned that off and applied a softer shade. That was better. Not much, but better.

She brushed her haystack of thick gray hair and then in a conditioned response, reached out to put down the toilet seat before remembering it was never left up any more.

She plodded downstairs, got her keys, climbed into the massive, shining Lincoln and drove to visit John. Not that he cared. Not that he remembered from one hour to the next who she was or why she came to see him.

And he never would again.

Two

She was amazed to find it still a lovely October day, crisp and brisk. Under a blue satin sky the fields on the edge of town were yellow with fall daisies, their fences thick with plumes of goldenrod. Each window of the long, low nursing home looked out on scarlet asters, and from an unseen patio crystal windchimes tinkled like fairy bells.

The patio, on such lovely days, was the place to find John. Thinking of him, erect and aloof in his wheelchair, Evelyn climbed from the car and sighed. She was trying to shake off the enormous depression that descended upon her every day at this time. Weeks ago she'd learned there was no virtue, only heartache, in dwelling on unfairness, on fate, on the cruel blow dealt a sixty-year-old man in his early retirement.

Forcing her feet briskly toward the massive entrance, she was unaware of anyone following until a long shadow fell before her and a pleasant voice said, "Allow me."

The gentleman pushing the heavy door was almost as long as his shadow, his arrow-straight military bearing hardly disguised by the uniform of the retired — slacks and a gray cardigan sweater. He had a lean, blunt-nosed profile above a white Bristol moustache and there were still traces of laugh lines about steady eyes the color of steel. They were sad eyes, although he was smiling down at her and she knew why they were sad. She'd seen him before, wheeling the crumpled shell of a once-classically-beautiful lady down the hall to the solarium. She said, "Thank you. Mr. Marsh, isn't it?"

"Bob." He stepped ahead and opened the second door. "Mrs. Cass?"

"Evelyn." Then she knew where else she'd glimpsed him: at the public library in the childrens' room. "You're Karen's father!"

"And Rob's 'Ganpa'," he added cheerily.

"Of course."

"And you're Poo's Grammy."

They both laughed. She said, "Isn't that absurd? He does have a real name — Paul — but when he was very small he named himself and it just stuck."

The light, airy central lounge was bustling as the personnel set up for coffee and bingo. John wasn't there, of course, nor could she see Bob

24

Marsh's wife. Smiling a little tightly in farewell they went in opposite directions down two brightly papered, gaily decorated hallways.

John was where she thought he would be—wheeled out into the clear, crisp air on the flagstone terrace where Ed and Charley, two of the other residents, sat at a wrought-iron table and terrorized each other with a domino game. Ed said cheerfully, "Hi, Mrs. Cass! Hey, John, your sweetie's here!"

John turned a thin, blank face to her. He smiled, for John was always a gentleman. "No orange juice today, please," he said in that carefully articulated voice that tried so hard to cover a lisp. "What a pretty blouse. My wife wears blue well, also. Perhaps you know my wife, Pat? We have a little girl, Brenda. But she's too small to come here, of course."

Pat Cass had been dead for thirty-six years, and *small* was hardly Brenda's excuse for not coming to the nursing home. But Evelyn had gotten accustomed to both. One could, she'd discovered, get accustomed to a lot of unpleasant things when there was no longer a choice.

She'd better keep that in mind, she thought grimly. She bent, kissed his cool forehead, smoothing back the thinning, gray-streaked hair. "How are you, dear? Porter sends his regards and says to tell you he actually parred the back nine on the golf course yesterday. And do you remember Mrs. Walters, who used to live across the alley from us? I met her downtown, and she says to tell you . . ."

It was pure drivel, endless drivel, all the time hoping and looking for one spark of recognition in those empty eyes. Not today, not yesterday, and probably never.

The plump little aide appeared with a tray of juice. Charley pinched her fanny as she passed; she jumped, giggled, slapped his hand. All three men took their glasses although John put his politely aside. Evelyn made her escape—because escape was what it had become—through the gate the girl had left unhooked, going around the end of the service drive, glancing at her watch and realizing that very soon she had to face up to calling Mary Lou.

She almost fell over Bob Marsh. He was slumped on an upended garbage can, his long legs sprawled, his white head clutched in his hands. She had the sudden, horrible realization that he was crying softly, the agonizing tears of a man in pain.

She probably should have excused herself swiftly and gone on. But her maternal instincts took over and she said, "Oh, I'm sorry—I didn't see you. Mr. Marsh, may I help?"

He wiped awkwardly at his brimming eyes, gritting his teeth. After a moment he answered her savagely, "Can you help my wife—my beautiful Sue-Ann? Christ, it's so unfair! It's so unfair. She's only fifty-five, and do you know how I found her today? Sitting there with her panties on outside her slacks, playing with a crayola! When she saw me she thought it was the bogeyman and screamed until I left! Oh God," he finished hoarsely, and choked. "It's horrible. Horrible. I think I've gotten calloused to it, then I'm not. I'm sorry. I apologize. I guess I'm just too new at the game to handle it well. She's only been ill since January."

He was pawing blindly at his pocket. Evelyn took a tissue from her bag, silently handing it to him. He used it sonorously and said, "Thanks, Mommy," with the ghost of a smile.

She asked, "It's Alzheimer's, isn't it?"

He nodded. "Yes. Early senility. It came on so fast. So fast. There wasn't time to—to do anything. Not that there's anything that could be done. But all the things we planned when I retired . . . Oh, well." He took a deep breath. "As they say—*c'est la vie*. I know you haven't had it any easier. Thanks for listening to me wallow in misery."

Soberly she replied, "It's a large club—The Wallow Society."

He gave her another smile that didn't·reach his eyes. "Please—don't tell Karen that her father belongs to it. She thinks I'm cast iron. I try not to disillusion her; she's cried enough for both of us."

Instinctively Evelyn realized that this was a proud man. He was embarrassed and probably wished she'd just go on and leave him alone.

She nodded, and decided against patting his wide shoulder. Nor did she utter easy words of false cheer. He probably heard plenty of those from do-gooders with healthy mates, just as she did.

What she could offer was her own departure.

She said, "Goodbye," and left. She had enough on her own plate for the day without playing Mrs. Sunshine to a stranger.

Her last glimpse of Bob Marsh as she shut the service gate was of his long legs stretched out from the garbage can, and she noticed he wore expensive jogging shoes. I hope, she thought wryly, that he can afford them. And that he *knows* he can.

In the meantime, there was Mary Lou—and the lunch for Jane Nixon. Since she'd garnered two dollars and twenty cents from her fevered search upstairs, that made her total wealth a magnificent fourteen dollars and eighty-four cents—hardly enough to cover her share of festivities at a very expensive club.

So face it, sweetie, she told herself grimly— you simply cannot go. So what are you going to tell Mary Lou? You know very well how fast news travels in this town. Furthermore, you've been as guilty as the rest. Remember when the Axelsons' furniture store failed? Your crowd knew about it almost before the Axelsons did. And none of those lovely folks are going to be any more discreet about you!

Blindly Evelyn rounded the corner of the nursing home and almost collided with two elderly ladies pushing walkers in the warm sun. She apologized, asking, "No bingo for you today?"

Mrs. Martin, whose high collar was reminiscent of Alice Roosevelt, gave an audible snort. "My dear, if I'd win one more pair of tatty ear bobs I could open a junk store!"

Her shorter, gentler companion protested, "Now, Emma—you know they do the best they can. Every prize is donated."

"It's still junk. Why don't they donate something useful like tokens for the soda machine."

"You can't have soda."

"My grandson can. And it would be nice to have something to give him when he comes. Or give us fruit. That's what they do where my sister is. Apples, or bananas. Or—" Suddenly she grinned impishly, "—or a good old dirty paperback novel. If I have to read one more romance I may get diabetes. Why in the world do people think sex drive goes when your teeth do?"

She was looking at Evelyn with bright, twinkling eyes. Evelyn laughed in spite of her troubles. She replied, "Emma, you want a sexy book, I'll bring you a sexy book! Regular print or large, and name your author."

The answer came promptly. "Large, if you can. If not, I'll use my magnifying glass on the good stuff. And some writer who has published since the printers stopped using those damned dashes instead of cuss words. You're a good girl, Evelyn. Now I remember why I liked your mother."

"My mother read sexy books?"

"No. But when she used to visit you, she'd bring me the old *True Confessions* from her beauty shop. That was about as sexy as they were allowed to get in those days. I missed her when she died."

"I missed her, too," said Evelyn and got into her car thinking how little one knew about one's own parents sometimes. As she pulled onto the highway, the gas gauge reminded her she'd better get fuel. John had taught her always to fill the tank when it was down to a quarter full. "Then," he'd said, "you'll never get in trouble because you're out of gas."

How much of a bill did she owe already to her service station, she wondered.

Guiltily, and for the first time in her life, Evelyn pulled into the big, noisy discount complex on the edge of town.

It must be easy to pump your own gas. She'd watched Liz Swan do it all the time, and besides being a notorious penny-pincher, Liz had the mechanical aptitude of a koala bear.

Finding the island that said "Self Serve • No Lead" was easy.

Okay, kiddo, she said to herself, sliding out onto the greasy concrete. Five dollars. That's all.

A young man in jeans and a pigtail was just sticking the gas nozzle back into the side of the "No Lead" pump. He smiled at her with the benign smile young people reserved for ladies the age of their mothers and pulled out his wallet. Evelyn lifted the gas flap on the Lincoln and tried to turn the cap. It was tight, and it made the arthritis in her left hand hurt. She said, "Oh!" audibly, both in pain and exasperation, and switched hands. The last person to use it must have had the grip of a gorilla, because it still wouldn't turn. Suddenly a young, tanned hand reached over and gave the recalcitrant part a masterful twist. The youngster said, "There you go, lady."

Evelyn said appreciatively, "Oh, thank you. I'm afraid I'm not very good at this."

Before he went to pay his bill he laid the cap carefully on her trunk lid. She turned and hoisted out the awkward nozzle on its length of dirty black hose, poked it into the hole and pressed the trigger. Nothing happened.

31

She pressed again.

Still nothing.

In dismay she called, "Young man—please—what am I doing wrong?"

Politely he wheeled, came back and flipped up the lever in the nozzle-rest on the pump. "Now try," he said politely just as she finally read the metal sign that said plainly LIFT LEVER FOR GAS.

Flushed with embarrassment, she said, "I'm sorry I'm so dumb. Thank you again."

"No problem. Now press the trigger."

She did. Magically she heard the gush of gas going into her tank. Lighted digits began to click in the pump face.

The young man was still lingering. "My mom has trouble, too. Would you like me to do it for you?"

"No, thank you. I've got it now."

She was watching the red digits mount on the price line as the gas went in when on the other side of the pump an old red pick-up slid into view with a large, solemn black labrador in the bed. His owner, a greasy tractor cap shoved to the back of his head, whistled cheerfully as he started his own pump. Then he leaned against the truck, absently rumpling a pair of black velvet ears.

Evelyn said, "He's very handsome. What's his name?"

"Thank you. It's Bumper, and he thinks so, too, don't you, old boy. Thank the lady, Bump."

Bumper extended a very large paw and Evelyn shook it. She said, "We owned a Lab once. I'm afraid all I have now is a very fat cat."

"Oh, we have cats—barn cats. Mousers. They and Bump have a sort of armed truce. That's a nice car. Is it a gas hog?"

"Oh, dear. I'm afraid I really don't know. I just put it in."

"And let the old man worry, hey? You wives are all alike. Aren't you Jack Cass's mom? Jack and I played varsity football together. Neither one of us much good, but we tried."

A discussion of Jack's virtues was interrupted when gas suddenly gushed from the car tank and all over Evelyn's skirt and shoes. She cried, "Oh! Oh!" and yanked the nozzle out, spilling fuel onto the concrete. Jack's friend reached and flipped up the lever.

"I'd say it was full," he said, grinning.

"I'd say so, too," she answered. Her dismay about her smelly clothes was nothing compared to her reaction when she noticed she'd rung up ten dollars worth.

She muttered a very bad word that would have shocked her husband—and slammed the gas flap shut. Ten dollars! Ten dollars she could ill afford! What a klutz she was!

As a matter of accuracy, it was ten dollars and

thirty-two cents. She hadn't noticed the cents, but the fat little lady chewing gum behind the cash register had it on her screen.

"Nice day," she said, taking Evelyn's ten dollars and thirty-two cents away forever.

Humbled, Evelyn got back in her car and drove off. The smell died as the fuel dried but she was still furious with herself. Now there was no doubt — she had to call Mary Lou and cancel. With her ineptitude she'd be likely to sign the wrong line at the club and end up paying the entire tab.

Her blocky old white house at the bend of Sycamore Street beckoned like a haven. Grateful to be back, she parked the Lincoln in the drive by the kitchen door, went inside, tossed her bag and keys on the breakfast bar and scowled at the telephone.

What was wrong with her? She didn't have to explain to Mary Lou!

But Evelyn knew in her soul, even as she dialed, that they'd been friends too long, and that beneath Mary Lou's expert probing she'd chicken out and mumble something inept, revealing, or both.

However, for the first time that day, the gods were with her. Mary Lou's cleaning lady answered. Mary Lou was in the shower. Remarkably strengthened, Evelyn left a cancellation and regrets. When — predictably — the phone rang barely two minutes later, she ignored its querulous sound, merely getting her coffee cup back out of the dishwasher. She needed support, and a good shot of old-fashioned caffeine might fill the bill.

The ringing stopped at the moment the microwave buzzed. In the blessed silence Evelyn took her re-heated coffee to the breakfast bar, sat down, and sipped. From the refrigerator door, Poo's small round face smiled at her and for the first time she failed to smile back.

"Poo," she said to the picture sadly, "you wouldn't believe what a mess your Grammy is in."

She knew in her soul that the income from the money management plan John had developed so proudly was severely crippled, that most of the CDs and IRAs were gone, and what was left would have to apply to John's expenses, not hers. Her parental inheritance of bonds and a small income property had been incorporated into John's plan. Please, God, she thought, let it take care of him.

So what were her options?

As she'd said earlier, two things: get a job; and sell something.

The latter first. What had she to sell?

Unhappily she recognized the one obvious thing: the house. She could put the house on the market. Tomorrow she'd ask Ben about it.

She could also probably sell the car. Yet, if she did get a job, a car was a necessity. Public transportation in this town had disappeared with high button shoes.

A smaller car, then. Trade for a more economical vehicle and make some cash besides.

That idea was almost agreeable. She really wasn't emotionally attached to the Lincoln. And she'd rather admired Liz Swan, zipping around in that little diesel whatsit of hers.

How does one go about selling a used car?

You ask a used-car dealer, and your friend Mary Lou happens to be married to the best one in town!

Porter DeKalb! And *if* Porter were agreeable, and *if* he just happened to have something suitable on his lot today, you could walk into Ben's bank tomorrow with your overdraft covered and some cash left over.

Exhilarated, she downed the rest of the coffee and reached for the telephone. It rang at that moment and she very nearly dropped it. Mary Lou again!

Stop being chicken, she admonished herself, and answered.

A nasal voice inquired, "This the lady who just bought gas at the Ayerco station? Ten dollars and thirty-two cents?"

For a moment her heart stopped. Then she

36

realized that checks bounce, cash does not. She said, "Yes."

"You didn't put your gas cap back on. The guy in the truck found it. You want to pick it up, I got it here on the counter."

Again — and not silently — Evelyn said the word that would have surprised her husband.

Then in a humbler voice she thanked the woman from the gas station and assured her she'd do just that.

She reheated more coffee and dialed Porter's business number.

When he answered, she could hear his wife's voice in the background.

Almost whispering, she said, "Port, don't tell Mary Lou. This is Evelyn."

He was undoubtedly surprised, but he covered it nicely. "Oh. Sure. What can I do for you, madam?"

Porter's voice was like rich, soothing syrup; she had the same thought she'd had for years — that he'd missed his calling and should have been a radio evangelist. On the radio no one would know about his solid paunch and his baldness. She said quickly, "I need to see you. Today, if you can."

If he was surprised, he didn't show it. "Of course. I thought you'd finally get around to me."

Now what did he mean by that?

She shrugged it off as a Porterism. "In about an hour."

Did she detect a slight hesitation? She guessed not, as he went on smoothly, "That will be fine."

"At your office?"

"At . . ." She had the same sense of hesitation, but again he went on, "Sure. Whatever you say."

"About two, then. Thanks, Port," she said, and hung up with a feeling of relief at having done something positive about her situation. Not only positive, but practical. She didn't need a car as large as the Lincoln. Best of all, it would be a business deal — nothing to embarrass Port.

Although she hated to open an old can of worms, she had to admit she was glad it was Porter she was meeting. Last month at the church supper, Jane Nixon's husband had cornered her stacking dishes in the pantry and actually made a pretty determined pass. It was the first time Evelyn had ever encountered the sort of male mentality that thought every divorced or widowed woman was hot to trot with any stud that happened by. It had both astonished and outraged her. She had settled his hash decisively without, thank God, letting Jane know — but she had no desire to repeat the experience.

Porter DeKalb, on the other hand, was as solid as Plymouth Rock. Married to Mary Lou, he had to be solid. The son of poor immigrants, he'd wed not only plenty of money, but a pretty girl who enjoyed spending it. Only a shrewd head and long, long hours on the job had kept him even with the expenses, if not augmenting the income. In the past few years, Evelyn and John had noticed that Mary Lou had stopped complaining about her husband's absences as long as he didn't curtail her spending. "My God!" he'd said many times at the Cass's kitchen table, confiding his troubles to a sympathetic John, "How that woman can shell it out!" Designer clothing, face lifts, and health spas did not come cheaply and Mary Lou had certainly hit them all in her almost frantic drive to stay young.

I hope I've grown old gracefully, Evelyn said to herself gazing in the cheval bedroom mirror, because I've certainly grown old.

The face wasn't too lined, although she had to be careful not to lose weight too fast; the fat left there first and she wrinkled like a prune.

She turned sideways, the gas-stained skirt in a heap at her feet, and sucked in her stomach as far as it would go. Even at that, a sylph she wasn't. Her clothes closet hadn't seen a size twelve in years, fourteens only when she starved for a week.

The age of the Elastic Waistband, she thought in resignation. That's what I'm in. Mom used to call it something else: Stylish Stout.

Ending that bit of musing with a mental razzberry, Evelyn pulled on a denim skirt and a white linen sport shirt that zipped up the front. She also changed her high heels for sandals and gave a brief brush to her softly-shaped gray hair. It was getting a bit long, but fortunately she had a standing appointment at the hairdresser's for Friday.

Whoa.

Fifteen dollars plus tip.

The cold, hollow feeling hit her stomach once more.

"Damn," she said softly, as the full weight of catastrophe descended again. Unless Ben was able to come up with a miracle she'd better cancel that, too. There were, now, three dollars in her wallet, and she didn't think that bankers specialized in miracles.

Also, even if she could deal a trade with Porter, any extra cash would have to go for mundane things like bills and insurance, not fancy haircuts.

Back down in the kitchen, she went to the door and called softly, "Romeo! Romeo! Here, kitty, kitty, kitty."

But no fat cat ambled from the syringa bushes. He was still out making his daily rounds, which were quite extensive. Romance was where one found it. The same food, the same pillow, the same manner of stroking his fur—in fact, Evelyn realized in dismay, we're very much alike: creatures of habit in a rut.

As she opened a new can of Kitty-Yum, she hoped he appreciated his rut. She had certainly been jarred out of hers!

While bending to fill his bowl with liver delight she remembered why she hadn't worn that particular shirt lately. The zipper would not lock and was inclined under pressure to zip silently downward, giving a splendid view of mammary amplitude.

It was a bit late to go back up and change—she'd already lollygagged too long.

Promising herself to watch it, she ran down the back steps and got into the car. But just fastening the seatbelt made the aggravating thing unzip! Exasperated, she rummaged in the car caddy and did a quick fix with a headless corsage pin, thinking she would tell Jane and she would fix it. Jane was a magic seamstress. For years they'd had a reciprocal agreement: Evelyn made Jane's jams and jellies; Jane altered Evelyn's clothes. It had worked out fine.

However, the corsage pin held while she ran in and picked up her gas cap. It held while she put the cap back on properly, closed the flap, and got into the car again. After that, she forgot it for more important matters.

As she drove toward Porter's used car lot, she realized that by now Mary Lou, Liz, and Jane were probably on the club verandah, toasting each other's recent success. Porter had finally bought Mary Lou the sapphire ring she'd wanted; Liz and Ben had taken a long-debated option on a house on Country Club Hill; and chubby Jane had lost four pounds.

Yet, she thought morosely, those are the wrong things, girls. That's not what's important. I'm learning the hard way and I know. Important things are your husband's good health, happy kids, and financial peace of mind. You've got those. I haven't. And when I did, I never realized how marvelous they were! Now I envy you all, which is awful, too, but I can't help it!

She turned off beneath the tall sign that said, "DeKalb's A-1 Used Cars." Porter was the bulky, balding man leaning against the open door of the glass-fronted showroom. As she slowed and waved, he stomped out a cigarette with his foot and said, "Park out back; it's shadier."

It was also out of sight of the street and pass-ersby, but she didn't think of that. At least, not just then.

Three

The rear door to Porter's showroom was open. As she walked inside, she saw him across the tops of the display cars. He was locking the glass doors. He waved at his office. "Go on in, kid."

Evelyn glanced into the parts room, ready to say hello to young Ed Wright who'd been in John's scout troop, but he didn't seem to be there. Shrugging, she entered Porter's private environs, where the decor plainly reflected Mary Lou's concept of a top businessman's office. From the tailored drapes and the potted palm, its soil unfortunately littered with cigarette butts, to the bulky leather chairs, Tiffany lamps, and half an acre of desk the place smacked of *success*. The one thing out of character was the Glen Fiddich scotch bottle and two glasses on a side table. Scotch was her drink. Porter was a bourbon man.

She made a remark about it as he came in. He answered lightly, "I'm flexible." Shutting the door and pulling its short curtain closed, he sat down in his immense leather chair, gesturing toward the other. He wore golf slacks and shirt—against their bright yellow he was very tanned, his teeth very white. Unfortunately, to Evelyn he just resembled a corpulent Tweetie Bird. Knitting his fingers together, he said, "You're looking good, kiddo."

"You, too."

"I feel like a kid in a candy store."

Well, she thought, *whatever turns you on, Port.*

Later, she was to remember that he hadn't inquired after John as he always did. She was suddenly and vaguely uneasy about the silence, the total lack of chatter and car noises, and strangely aware of the closed door. "It's so quiet. Is everyone gone?"

"Everyone. Trust me."

The "trust me" part missed her completely as all of a sudden she recognized the reason for the golf pants. How could she have forgotten that Thursday was men's day at the country club? She said penitently, "Oh, drat! You close at noon today!"

"Of course." But he was frowning a little. She went on hurriedly,

"Port—if I'm keeping you from your foursome—"

He cut in, "I can't think of anyone I'd rather see. Relax. It's okay. I called and got a later tee-off time. Ben didn't mind; he's never there on the button anyway."

"Still, I'm sorry! I just didn't realize—"

The small frown came back. "Then I'm the one who's sorry. I thought you did."

Agitated at her thoughtlessness, she shook her head ruefully. "I just knew I—I wanted to see you."

"And I wanted to see you." The answer came so quickly, so fervently—it touched her. "Always," he added, his knitted fingers almost white. He gestured with his balding head toward the sidetable. "Drink? I bought it for you."

"Port, how nice." Particularly since he must be in a real quandary as to why she was here—and messing up his golf game. "But, no, thank you. Let me explain why—"

"Not yet. Not yet." He'd lit a cigarette and was leaning back, eyes half-closed. "Evie—how long have we known each other?"

Surprised, she answered, "I've never thought about it much. Twenty years?"

"Twenty-four," he said. His voice seemed to flow from far away, its tone a rich caramel. She found herself thinking about radio evangelists again. "Twenty-four years," he repeated, and the accuracy suddenly seemed so purposeful it startled her. "I'd been married just long enough to realize some pretty harsh facts—then John came back to town with you. God, girl, you were lovely. Of course, you still are. At least, to me."

"Thank you kindly, sir." She tried to sound casual. She wasn't certain she was comfortable with his conversation. "It's nice someone remembers."

"I remember," Porter said. "It's an awful thing, Evie—awful to realize you've made a major mistake—then have to live with it for the next twenty-four years."

Evelyn began to wonder if he'd been at the scotch bottle already. Everyone knew Porter got maudlin when he'd been drinking. She could remember a night he'd shown up on her doorstep weeping, and she'd thanked her lucky stars John had made it back from his buying trip early! Uneasily, she said, "Offer me a cigarette, Port."

"I thought you quit a year ago."

"I did. But, still—sometimes—"

"You're nervous."

"What?"

"Don't be nervous. God, you'll make me nervous and I don't want to be. I want to relax and enjoy. I've waited so long."

Exasperated, she said, "Port—I'm not nervous. I want to explain—"

"And don't explain! Let the pieces fall naturally. Spin it out. Twenty-four years is a long time—too damned long to get in a hurry when it's finally time, it's finally right . . ."

He hoisted himself to his feet and stood over her, offering his cigarette pack, flicking his lighter. She noticed with alarm that there was a patina of light sweat on his forehead and his respiration seemed fast.

Oh, God, she thought, I've already been through one seizure! I don't need another!

"Porter, are you all right?"

He laughed. "All right? Honey, right now I'm aces high!"

"Okay," she said, putting the cigarette in her mouth and lifting her chin to the lighter.

At that point the corsage pin failed, sending the zipper silently slithering down.

For one moment Porter froze. Then, murmuring raggedly, "Oh, my dearest love," he plucked the cigarette away, dropped it on the floor, and bent to cover her open and astonished lips with his. At the same time he slid searching fingers inside her shirt and bra to caress the warm opulence.

Evelyn had not hit a man in years, but she open-handed Porter with a smack that must have been heard in the next block.

He reeled back, crashing into his desk, holding his reddening jaw, his eyes bulging. "Christ, woman! What do you think you're doing?"

Furiously she yelled back, "What do you think *you're* doing? Porter, this is Evelyn! Evelyn!"

"Damn right it's Evelyn! The girl who called my wife and cancelled an engagement of ten year's standing, who called me and said don't tell Mary Lou, who asked to meet me in my office when she knew no one else would be here. Now what the hell was I supposed to think — that you just wanted to play a little two-handed bridge? Christ, Evelyn! Christ! How much can a man stand?"

She was gibbering with shock. "You thought I wanted to — you thought I was coming because —"

He was rubbing his jaw. "Yes, dammit! I *hoped* you were coming *because!* Twenty-four years I've wanted you — and that's a long time to wait!"

She held her hands tightly against her face, trying to shut out everything. Almost whispering, she said, "Oh Port, I'm sorry, I'm so sorry — I can see now how you misunderstood, but Porter, believe me, I didn't mean it — I didn't mean any of that — none of it — and Port, I didn't know that you — that you felt . . ." How awful this was! ". . . that you felt — anything! Not about me!" About *John*'s wife. *John*'s! That's what she was saying.

"Wait a minute." Suddenly his angry voice was gentle. "Don't be sorry. Be honest. Maybe this was subconscious. Maybe you did know — inside, somewhere. Evie, John's been out of it for months. You haven't been getting any — and

God knows, I don't get much myself. For whatever reason you imagined you were coming, today—maybe deep in your heart you just knew you needed me! Evie, for God's sake, face it— you *are* one hell of a woman!"

If he'd tried for a year he couldn't have said anything to outrage her more. All shame, all remorse fled. Her nostrils pinched white, she said between clenched teeth, "And *you* are a poor excuse for a man!"

He stiffened. His eyes narrowed and his voice hardened. "You want me to show you what a man I am?"

She was too angry to recognize a threat when she heard it. Furiously she went on, "And don't talk to me about hearts! You've got a dick in place of yours, and that's not much of a recommendation!"

"Then why are you sitting there with your breasts hanging out?"

"God damn it!" she gritted and zipped the zipper, holding it with one hand. "You don't understand! You'd never understand! And I wish to hell I had understood you a long time ago, but I didn't. I didn't! But I sure do now. Unlock the door, Port. Unlock it!"

"Evie . . ."

Suddenly all anger seemed to go out of him. He slumped and put out one hand, a supplicating hand, palm up. He whispered, "Evie, please . . ." Then the dam seemed to break inside him. Words poured out, words of pain, words about Mary Lou and himself that she desperately did not want to hear, that she clapped her hands over her ears to keep from hearing. To her horror he went on his knees at her side, holding her, burying his face against her soft breasts, begging—the begging was the worst of all.

She couldn't bear it any longer. On top of everything else it was too much. Too much!

She struggled away, out of the chair, from his clutching hands, and almost screamed, "Open the door! Open the door, Port! This minute—or so help me, God, I'll find something and I'll kill you! I'll kill you dead!"

His twisted, bleary face went dark red. He stared up at her for a moment that seemed set in stone, a moment that was so still she could almost hear his heart beat, had her own not been a muffled drum in her ears.

Then he got to his feet, almost regally, dusting off the knees of his yellow pants. He went past her to the door and unlocked it.

He didn't try to touch her as she went swiftly by him, but his calm, melodious voice caught her in the hall. "Let me tell you something, Evie."

She didn't pause, but she heard him. He said, "You'll be back. That's a promise. You'll be back. And you'll beg. As I did. And I'll wait for it. Remember: twenty-four years. I'm very good at waiting."

And it will be a cold day in hell, she thought, but she didn't say it aloud. She didn't take time to say it. Enough had already been said.

She got into her car and drove away, bouncing off the curb into the street, narrowly missing a trash can, steering with one hand as she held up the zipper with the other.

She was realizing one clear, painful fact: with the good friends she had, who the hell needed enemies?

She turned in at the park drive and drove up the hill to her favorite outlook above the river. Today it was glassy gray-blue, with a tinker-toy bridge and tiny cars. On the far shore beyond green firs blended into the fall fire of scarlet maples and in the sandy curve of cove and beach, rows of bright marina pleasurecraft bobbed gently at anchor. It was a view that usually sent her spirit soaring with the beauty of autumn. Today the colors blurred before her aching eyes.

Twenty-four years! And in those years not once, never, had she consciously thought of giving Porter DeKalb one gesture, one look that had been more than simple friendliness!

Of course, she'd picked up over the years what the guys said—that Mary Lou disliked sex. "It disarranges her hair," John had once added wryly. But the wives did not talk about their husbands except in a domestic way. It had been almost an unwritten agreement, and Evelyn had really never given a thought to where Porter went to "get his," as he'd put it so crudely. She'd never cared. Porter was a friend—and Mary Lou's husband.

But oh, dear God, the dreadful intimate things she'd heard today, spilling out of the man on his knees, trying to hold her, almost gibbering his longings. And not talking lust—talking *love*—a love strong enough to risk jeopardizing his marriage to Mary Lou's money pots and to seriously endanger his status as a fine, upstanding city father.

And what really frightened her, as she lifted her hot face to the breeze that smelled faintly of fish and wet foliage, was the change in him at the last—the iron sound of his voice as he declared his intentions to pursue her until she capitulated.

The fact that it would be, as she'd stated, a cold day in hell, didn't seem to change the situation—if he'd even heard her.

This was deep shit, and she was in it to her eyebrows. Where had it started? Why hadn't she known? Where was the built-in antenna women were supposed to have about these things? When Mary Lou went out of town, Porter had loafed at her house like a—a brother. Mary Lou had said, "Thank goodness you look after him, Evie. If you didn't, he'd probably eat nothing but pizza and beer."

He had eaten a lot of pizza. Port liked pizza. But he'd bring it over to share. She liked pizza, too. John hadn't cared for it much.

On happy occasions, they'd hugged. All four couples hugged indiscriminately. They'd danced. Porter always held her too tightly, but he did that with the other three girls; they said so. There had been a few times like Christmas, and Jack's wedding, when Port had had more than a few drinks and maybe came on a little strong— but she'd dismissed it, thinking that special occasions bring out a streak of sentimentality in the most reasonable people.

Perhaps she shouldn't have dismissed it. Perhaps she should have taken the sudden, ardent kiss more seriously . . .

But Porter! Paunchy, balding Porter! To her, he had been as romantically appealing as a billiard ball!

Yet the warning signal inside her head pointed out one important fact: billiard ball or not, Porter had enormous self-pride. He had literally bared his soul to her and she had rejected him.

Porter would not suffer humiliation lightly.

She got out of the car and went to the rail, leaning on it, looking down at the river below.

This couldn't be happening, especially not to Evelyn Cass, fifty-five years old, almost fifty-six, gray-haired, a grandmother, good wife, good citizen . . .

In fact, a paragon.

A smug paragon. A self-satisfied paragon.

Perhaps she'd had this coming. Perhaps it was what she deserved.

It was an astonishing idea. She didn't much like it. Perhaps, subconsciously she *had* been applauding herself for handling all her troubles with such virtue.

Well, Evelyn. Now get on with it. Besides one of your best friend's husband just making a serious pass, you are still overdrawn, still owe bills, still need to trade your car — and said best friend's husband is obviously not going to be of much help there except on terms you would find unacceptable.

Where exactly do you go from here?

Suddenly, from behind, she heard another car climbing the high hill. Self-consciously, she zipped the zipper again but she didn't turn, avoiding any sort of confrontation, until a familiar voice said, "So this is where you are!"

Karen Marsh Evans expertly twisted the wheel of her little Ford Escort and slid it in beside the Lincoln. Two heads bobbed in the front seat, one of which crowed, "Grammy Cass!", popped out of the car, and threw two sticky, enthusiastic arms about Evelyn's knees.

"Well, hi, Poo!" said Evelyn. She bent, scooped her tow-headed grandson into her arms, and kissed his round, rosy cheek. "Where did you come from?" The question was directed to Karen, who was getting out of her side of the car, her small son in hand.

"Oh, Poo came to my story hour at the library and I told Brenda I'd deliver him to your house." Karen told her story with studied casualness, but Evelyn wasn't deceived. Brenda had more likely unloaded her occasionally inconvenient child at the public library, knowing full well Karen would see to him. Her arm unconsciously tightened around the solid, wiggly, three-year-old.

Karen continued, "We had ice cream and were just driving to your house when Poo saw the car up the hill. The Lincoln," she added, grinning, "is hard to miss." When Karen grinned she was a tomboy version of her father. "Oh! Look, boys — see — in the west above the trees, coming this way!"

"Airp'ane," said Poo.

"Ganpa," said Karen's child, Robby. He began to jump up and down. "Ganpa! Ganpa!"

Evelyn followed his grubby, pointing finger, and saw the venerable blue biplane thrumming steadily toward them over the river channel. She glanced at Karen. She was leaning against her car hood, polishing her sunglasses.

"It's Dad, all right," she said to Evelyn. "I thought he might be flying this afternoon. He came by the library feeling pretty down, and he always says it's good therapy for him. He's been retired two years now, and the Stearman's his toy."

As Evelyn watched, the graceful airplane moving peacefully through the untroubled air caught at her sense of earth and space. It seemed a visitor from another era, a glitch from a simpler time. Perhaps that's what it was to Bob Marsh, too.

Robby Evans was chanting, "Uppidy, Ganpa, uppidy!"

Almost as if the pilot had heard, the plane began to nose higher and higher. The roar of the powerful engine reached them as it bit the air, chewing until it was a mere dot in the sky. Then it soared downward again, then up once more, and over in a carefree parabola.

Evelyn caught her breath. Karen laughed.

"Dad's good," she said. "He can wring out that old Stearman and put it to dry if he wants to. Mom never cared for the old planes, even Daddy's. She had her license, but she liked to fly level and fast in her Piper Arrow and get places."

"How about you?"

"An air force brat, and you ask? I loved

everything from trainers to F-16s. I ride with Dad in the Stearman sometimes, and he'll let me fly, but I'm not strong enough to horse her around like he does. I got her over once and couldn't get her back. There we flew, upside down with Dad laughing his head off. It taught me to listen to him. Okay, Robby, back into the car. Grandpa's done; see, he's heading for the airport, and we need to get home before your father does. Say goodbye to Paul."

" 'Bye, Poo, see you 'morrow," said Rob agreeably, and climbed into the Escort.

His mother hesitated. Shoving at the smooth brown hair falling against her cheek, she said, "Evie, why don't you and Poo come out to dinner with us? Tim's taking us to that new barbecue place for the ribs—and they have hotdogs, too. The boys will love it. Besides, I owe you for that huge lunch in Springfield last month. Do come."

"Dogs," said Poo, who had caught the operative word. "Go."

Well. Why not? Evelyn pondered briefly. After all, what was there at home besides feeding and bathing Poo—and after the little boy went to sleep, all she'd do then was listen for Brenda's car hoping she came in sober, hoping she came at all, hoping it would not be the police instead—and thinking long, unhapppy thoughts about what tomorrow might bring. At least having dinner with the Evanses would put the blues off for a while.

"Okay," she said, accompanied by a happy bounce from Poo. "I'll run home and set out some food for Romeo. I haven't seen him all day; he's probably catting around again."

"With that Siamese in the next block?" Karen asked with a grin. "Tell him it's a lost cause. The lady brought her into Tim's clinic and had her fixed last week. Give us about an hour and we'll pick you up. No sense in taking two cars. Oh—and by the way . . ." She was leaning out the window of her Escort, still grinning. "Please do something about that zipper. My husband's a boob person and I don't want him drooling into the barbecue sauce; it's so unbecoming for a married man."

"Oh dear," said Evelyn. Turning a little pink, she zipped again. "I will. I promise. Thanks for the invitation."

Poo rode to his Grammy's house very happily and submitted to a bath with astonishing grace although he usually regarded it as a total waste of time better spent watching television.

She established him, in clean shorts with shining rosy cheeks, on the front step to wait for the Evans family while she tidied the bathroom. Then she shrugged herself into a safer shirt with flowers on it in pink and rose. It was fairly new, one her husband had never seen. John had never cared for pink on her, and she'd surprised herself when she'd bought it, rationalizing that it was, after all, on sale.

Somewhere there was a rose-colored lipstick. She rummaged for it successfully and was pleased with the result. Pink tones hadn't been right for her with brown hair, but with gray it wasn't too bad.

The tinge of righteousness left with the glance at the three thin dollars in her wallet. She probably wouldn't need money; yet, on the other hand . . .

She slipped her checkbook into her bag with her wallet. Ben had said he'd lend her five hundred and she certainly didn't have *that* much outstanding! One small check surely wouldn't hurt if she needed it. She'd so hate to be embarrassed . . .

Lady, she told herself grimly, *I suspect you don't even know yet what it is to be embarrassed!*

She put the checkbook back on the desk and went out to join Poo.

Romeo, a black and white cat the size of a Sumo wrestler, had already joined Poo. He was nestled inside one small arm, purring like a furnace bellows.

"O-mo back." Poo announced the obvious.

"I see he is." His grandmother sat down with him on the step, not too thrilled at the plethora of white hairs on his dark blue shorts. "Let him go, Poo. His supper is on the kitchen porch."

Romeo, as good as Poo at catching the operative word, released himself at the sound of "supper" and trotted off around the syringa bushes. Fat, Evelyn thought, watching him go. Really fat. Was it her imagination, or could she actually feel the ground shake beneath his paws?

John had never liked cats although she'd always loved them dearly. Romeo, a stray, had spent his kittenhood at the neighbor's, only moving in on her when John was gone. Strange, how cats knew . . .

The Escort pulled to the curb, cheerful, curly-headed Tim Evans at the wheel. Evelyn got into the back with the boys, and the trip to the barbecue place was a noisy one. Tim was recounting his typical veterinarian's day inoculating a dairy herd whose communal opinion had not been asked, and the two boys punctuated the tale with loud and enthusiastic mooing.

They found a booth with ample elbow room in the back of the crowded restaurant. Shortly the waitress delivered an enormous stack of blackened, reeking ribs, served with a necklace of hotdogs and a mountain of slaw. Everyone was hungry, even—to her surprise—Evelyn. After all, she told herself, condemned men do eat hearty meals.

Just at the point where she knew barbecue sauce had splashed even on her eyebrows, Karen laughed and said suddenly, "Hey!—there's Daddy! Hi! Dad! Over here!"

Bob Marsh's tall, lanky form, in a different colored cardigan sweater, made his way through the crowd toward them.

"Hi, old buddy," he said, rumpling his grandson's curly top. "Hi, guys. Got room?"

Tim said, "Sure," and everyone scooted around. Evelyn found the newcomer next to her as, in surprise, he said, "Well, hello again," and Karen murmured through a mouthful, "Evie Cass, my father, Bob Marsh."

"We've met," said Bob a little briefly, but his eyes were smiling at Evelyn, and she found them clear gray and direct beneath those bars of white. "A double order of whatever they're having, please," he said to the hovering waitress, "and beers all around with soda for the young gentlemen."

His young-gentleman grandson said, "We seed you. In the Stear."

"Your loop was sloppy," said his daughter.

"The updraft between the bluffs got me."

"Yeah. Tell it to Sweeney," jeered Karen. "It was just sloppy. Here. Don't wait for your order. Start in on ours. Wasn't it sloppy, Evelyn? We both said so."

"It looked fine to me," said Evelyn, unwilling to be part of an argument even in jest. "I was impressed."

61

Karen laughed. "She impresses easy. Hey—I talked to Aunt Sue today. She may come down for the weekend."

"And I may go to St. Louis," said her father. Catching a startled look in the brown eyes next to him, he said to Evelyn a bit sheepishly, "My sister-in-law and I are not precisely—" and he was obviously searching for words, "—on the same wave length," he finished.

His daughter chortled. "My father the diplomat."

A little stiffly he rejoined, "But that's not the only reason, you upstart. There's a fly-in down there. Pete wants me to bring the Stearman."

"And do your sloppy loops?"

"Why didn't I drown you at birth?"

"Because you were in Asia flying F-4s. When you came home Mom had gotten attached to me. Watch it; here's your order."

Karen beckoned to Evelyn and led the way to the restroom. Mopping barbecue sauce from her face, she said a little ruefully, "I'm glad Dad will be gone. Aunt Sue is my mother's twin—Sue-Ellen and Sue-Ann; aren't those terrible names? Anyway, Aunt Sue has always had the hots for Dad, and now with Mom out of the picture, she's really giving him a shot. Shows a lot of sensitivity, doesn't it? I have trouble dealing with her calmly when she goes out and weeps over my mother then comes on to my father like gangbusters. It's so unfair, damn it! Oh, well." She took a deep breath. "I'm stuffed. Tim ordered dessert. Sherbet, I think. Can you handle it?"

"Sure. It's called the Elastic Waistband Capability," Evelyn answered. But she was disturbed, and as she reapplied the rose lipstick and fluffed her hair she watched Karen's face in the mirror. She was looking again for the expression she thought she'd seen back in the restaurant when Bob Marsh had appeared. His "appearance" was not an accident. She'd bet on that. She'd been set up, with or without his approval. And she was resolved firmly not to be a backfire against Karen's Aunt Sue—no matter how high the compliment, and she recognized how high it was. Karen obviously adored her dad.

But Karen said nothing more. Evelyn followed her quick, slim figure back through the crowd, wrestling with a quandary.

The two men and the boys were confronting nothing but a stack of stripped bones. Bob Marsh slid closer to his son-in-law which made room for Evelyn on the end of the bench. His eyes were approving enough to make her almost wish she hadn't restored the lipstick.

But all he said was, "Sherbet, madam? The young fry decided on pink, but I tend toward green myself."

"Pink will be fine," Evelyn answered.

Her grandson knit downy brows. "Grammy, you don't wike pink!"

"Then you may eat it," Evelyn said swiftly, and turned slightly pink herself at the amused look in her neighbor's gray eyes.

She was relieved when, all sherbet consumed, they rose to go. The two boys were allowed to walk ahead—walk, not *run*—they were admonished by their experienced elders. Karen lingered with her husband as he paid the check. Evelyn found herself waiting by the door with Bob Marsh. That was when it opened, and the DeKalbs came in.

Mary Lou's azure-shadowed eyes whipped from Evelyn to Bob Marsh and back again like a tracking hound on the scent. Then they turned so shrewd and so terribly comprehending that Evelyn in desperation almost cried out loud, "No, Mary Lou, no! This is not why I cancelled our date for lunch!"

But she didn't. She just stood there looking foolish—until she caught the look on Porter's face. It was fleeting, but it had been there, and it was pure, baffled fury.

"Well, well, Evie," he said. His hand was on her shoulder and the fingers bit. Yet his rich, caramel voice was as casual and cool as usual. "Look who's here! Mother, Dad, you remember Evelyn Cass? John's wife. My old friend, John."

In the ensuing smother of civilities, Evelyn's

heart quieted down. But she didn't forget Porter's eyes. She couldn't.

Three good friends zapped in a single day!

It might even be some sort of record, she thought wearily, and followed the assorted Evanses and one quiet Marsh to the parking lot.

Four

In the orange-lighted parking lot, Karen said brightly, "Dad, you go Evie's way. Why don't you drop her off?"

It was a remark of dubious innocence. To Evelyn it turned mere speculation into concrete reality. Helplessly aware of being maneuvered, yet seeing no other recourse but to accept, she found herself in Bob Marsh's old Datsun with Poo on her lap. The Evanses waved goodbye. As they drove past the bright restaurant windows, she plainly saw Mary Lou and Porter watching their departure, and Mary Lou's mouth was moving like a typewriter. It took little effort to imagine what she said. Evelyn was so bothered that she almost didn't hear Bob Marsh:

"Sorry about that."

She turned, glancing at him uncomprehendingly. He was looking straight ahead but there was a wry set to his jaw. He went on, "I hope

you didn't mind too much. I'm afraid my darling daughter is something of a meddler—at
least where her old man is concerned."

So he'd recognized it, too! He added ruefully,
"She does mean well."

"Of course she does. Don't give it a thought. I
live at the bend of Sycamore—the square, white
place."

"Thank you."

She knew his gratitude was for more than her
directions.

He said nothing more. The silence was suddenly comfortable. Poo broke it by yawning cav-
ernously. "S'eepy," he announced and closed his
eyes.

Bob said, "Hang in there, old man, we're almost home." He made the turn into Sycamore,
pulling to the curb before her house. Unfolding
his long legs, he came around to open her door.
"So this is your place."

"Yes. We bought it ten years ago. And we're
obviously going to have to paint this spring."

He put out his hand. His voice was unexpectedly harsh. "How long before we both stop saying 'we'?"

Caught, she stayed very still, Poo snoring
faintly on her lap. Her own voice honest, she
answered, "I don't know. Must we stop?"

"Do you still feel you're a 'we'?"

Then he answered himself, smacking one fist

67

lightly on the car roof. "Sorry. Don't even try to answer such a self-serving question. This just has not been one of my better days. Come along, old buddy, let Bob carry you. You're quite a load for your grandmother."

Inside, while Evelyn snapped on the lamps, he deposited Poo on the couch and glanced around briefly. "Nice," he said. "Good night. I've enjoyed it," and went back to the door.

Enormously relieved that he plainly didn't expect to stay, she followed, echoed his farewell, and locked the door behind him.

Then she felt a brief moment of guilt, but it was mercifully transient. She needed no more thrills for the day.

Still, as he pulled away, she did wonder fleetingly where he was going. Home to watch TV? To a bar? A club somewhere? Where did a sixty-year-old man go in the evenings when his wife had Alzheimer's?

It's not your affair where he goes, she told herself severely. Nor your problem, thank God.

She turned around and looked at the tousled heap that was Poo on the sofa. He was sound asleep, his snubby nose smashed against the cross-stitch pillows. Gently she turned his head and pulled the afghan over him.

Heaven only knew where his mother was. In a bar. With a man. Or both.

If only I wasn't so damned reliable, Evelyn

thought wearily. She knows Poo will be looked after. My schedule doesn't count. And poor little fellow, it's not his fault.

She patted the small fanny tenderly, sighed, and went to the phone. Nancy, next door, would probably step over and watch him while she made her night run to the nursing home.

Leaving her neighbor comfortably ensconced with a drink in front of the television, Evelyn drove to the edge of town, saw her husband safely into his pajamas, made sure he'd taken his medication, kissed him, and turned out the light.

She was back in the car heading home almost before she knew it. The entire process was totally automated. How many times had she repeated the performance, and how many times would she repeat it yet?

Despite herself, Bob Marsh's poignant words rang in her ears: "Do you still feel you're a 'we'?"

It was a habit. A habit of thirty years. One doesn't too often think about habits. One just — does them.

Yet — how did she feel?

I don't want to know, she told herself in sudden near-hysteria. With frantic fingers she snapped on the radio and dialed for something, anything to drown out her doubts. Still, the remorseless words echoed inside her head: When is it over? When do you resign yourself to being one, not two?

And who the hell was Bob Marsh, who was he to make her ask such things of herself? What right had he?

A cacophony of sound behind her made her realize she was sitting immobile at a green light.

She urged the Lincoln forward and almost missed her street. As she drove around the familiar bend she could see a car parked in front of her house. Her throat tightened. She wasn't expecting anyone. Furthermore, she didn't want anyone!

But as she approached, the car drove away. Left behind was a slight figure in jeans, long hair blowing in the breeze.

Brenda.

And probably crocked. Lovely. At least she didn't do the heavy drugs. Having been totally unable to help the girl cope with alcohol, Evelyn knew she wouldn't get to square one if Brenda abused those. After all the years of heartache, trying to replace Brenda's real mother, trying to give love and being repulsed, Evelyn was very tired of Brenda's problems.

As she got out of her car and her stepdaughter approached, the kitchen light fell on both their faces. Evelyn could see that Brenda's eyes—John's eyes, faintly slanted and hazel—were clear, and her face a little placating.

"I'm sober," Brenda said. "Honest, Mom. Where's Poo?"

"Inside, asleep. Nancy's watching him."

"Thanks. I couldn't find you and I had things I had to do. I was sure Karen wouldn't mind."

Evelyn ignored her words. "Sit down," she said, pulling out a kitchen chair, and went to tell Nancy she was free to go.

When she returned, Brenda was taking a coffee cup from the microwave. She'd smoothed her long, straight hair away from the pale scrubbed face that was getting a bit old for the "flower child" style. Her shirt was neatly tucked into the faded jeans with the tattered peace sign embroidered on a pocket. She sat, sliding bare feet from thong sandals, and asked, "How was Daddy?"

"The same."

"I don't see how you take it. Time after time. I'd go insane."

Evelyn had heard that speech so often she ignored it as she sat down at the table across from her stepdaughter.

Brenda asked, "Coffee? I didn't pour it all."

"No."

Evelyn dropped her eyes with an effort as she thought for the thousandth time: This is the darling, motherless child I thought I could handle!

I couldn't. I never had a chance. John never let me.

Brenda was fiddling with her cup. She opened her shoulder bag, took out a long, misshapen cigarette, looked at Evelyn, and put it back.

Grimly, her stepmother said, "Thank you," but she knew now, knew for certain: something was coming. She sighed and went on, "All right, Bren. Let's get it over. What's wrong?"

"Does there have to be something wrong?"

"You're here. Isn't there usually?"

"I used to live here, damn it!" Resentment sprang into the pale face. But as Evelyn watched, unmoved by it, the color faded. Brenda said tonelessly, "Yes. I guess there usually is. Oh, Mom, if Jimmy hadn't been killed . . ."

Evelyn had heard that, too. She'd heard it all. "You were drinking when Jimmy was killed, and so was he. Don't lay that on me, Bren. I'm too tired tonight. Just come out with it."

"I've lost my job."

Well, that was indeed coming out with it. "Lovely. Why this time?" But she already knew. Just pick one: mouthy, undependable, drunk.

Brenda sighed. "What does it matter?" she said limply. "They didn't like me. The girls talked behind my back, they told lies. And I got canned."

Impatiently her stepmother said, "Oh, Bren,

stop that nonsense! I've heard it all before and I'm tired of it!"

Two large crystal tears gathered at the corners of Brenda's eyes and rolled slowly down, plopping into her coffee cup. Evelyn thought, That should move me. But it doesn't. It just doesn't even bother me anymore.

Yet, her voice was kinder as she said, "Have you eaten? There's ham salad in the fridge."

Brenda didn't move. Evie got up wearily, made a sandwich, and placed it beneath her stepdaughter's nose. "Eat, eat. Listen to your good Jewish mother."

It was an old joke they'd shared for years. Brenda half-smiled, lifted the sandwich, and took a bite. She said soberly, "Mom, I need help."

Evelyn sat down again, crossing her arms on the table.

Brenda absently tore the crusts from her bread and made a square on the calico place mat. Beyond them, in the living room, the old clock boomed sonorously. A sudden splat of light rain dashed against the windows, surprising them both.

With a nervous scoop of her hand, Brenda collected the crusts, twisted them together and threw them down again. A little defiantly she said, "I want to check myself into the hospital. I want to dry out."

If she was expecting applause, she didn't get it. Evelyn had been stung before and was too wary. Instead, she nodded and answered, "Good. I'm very glad to hear it."

"Can you take Poo? Just part of the time. Jim's mom will, mostly. She's being very — cooperative."

"I don't know. Probably. We can arrange something. Where have you decided to go?"

"The clinic in Springfield. Don't give me that look, Mom. It's legitimate this time. I've already talked to them. I can sign myself in but I can't sign myself out."

"All right. I believe you."

"Then you want me to do it?"

"Brenda, of course! Of course I do."

"Fine. Because I'm broke. And for two weeks plus the rehabilitation classes it will take fifteen hundred dollars."

There. The bomb just dropped.

More of a bomb, Evelyn realized with a very tired feeling, than her stepdaughter knew.

Steadily she returned the girl's gaze.

"Not from me, Bren."

"But you said — "

"I said I wanted you to go for it. I do. I think it's possibly your only option."

"Then — "

"Let me finish. Bren — I haven't got fifteen hundred dollars."

Brenda's thin face flushed in surly disbelief. "Bull!"

"I haven't."

"Mom! Mom, please! Please! I'm really serious this time!"

"So am I!"

Both their voices had risen to high, thin rasps. Suddenly Brenda lunged to her feet, toppling the chair behind her. She turned, gripped the edge of the kitchen sink with white-knuckled hands. Over her shoulder she hissed, "My daddy wouldn't do this to me!"

Evelyn threw her hands in the air. "Oh, for heaven's sake, don't be maudlin! Neither would I if I had the money! But I haven't! Do you know how much it has taken to see your daddy through his illness, and to keep him in the nursing home? Brenda, I'm wiped out. I may have to sell the house."

Brenda whirled around. "Sell the—You can't! You can't sell Daddy's house! What do you expect him to come home to?"

Evelyn's mouth tightened. With an immense effort, she brought her own voice down, made it quiet, steady. "Brenda, your daddy is not coming home. Never."

"Of course he isn't! Of course he isn't, because he's married to a selfish, grasping bitch who won't take care of him!"

"Listen to me. I have to go to work." Even as

she said it she knew it was so. "Do you hear? Even then, I may have to sell the house—and whatever else I can lay my hands on. And while I work, while I'm away, who's going to look after your daddy at home—dress him, feed him, take him to the bathroom—you, Bren? You?"

Brenda's fist had gone into her mouth. Silent now, her wide eyes terrified, she stared at Evelyn. She began to whimper.

"Oh, no—not me—I couldn't—not Daddy . . ."

"Well, then," said her stepmother, who felt centuries old. "Who then? What do you suggest? I'll certainly listen."

"There's—there's no more money?"

"There's no more money."

"Jack—"

"Try Jack for a loan when he returns in December. But don't count on it. I know he's invested every cent he could get together in the business."

"He can go on a cruise!"

"The cruise is his business. And if no one likes it, he stands to lose everything. You know that. Brenda, I'm sorry. Sit back down. Maybe we can work something out."

"Oh, sure," said Brenda, her mouth in an ugly twist. "Don't bother Jack—Jack the fair-haired angel! But no one cares about old Bren. Let her sink. Oh, God! Daddy, I need you so much— *you'd* help me . . ."

She turned again, and the sobs came loudly, wracking shudders accompanied by one fist beating impotently on the counter top. Evelyn rose, put her arm about the girl, and was shoved away. So she merely stood quietly until the storm subsided. She felt sapped. She'd tried so hard for so many years to be a mother, to show Brenda they needn't compete for John's love. Finally she'd accepted the simple bitter truth: it was hopeless. John's first wife would always be there between them, and Pat's daughter would never stop competing.

The tears became hiccups. Brenda turned again, her thin face blotched and swollen. She picked up her shoulder bag, flung it on her arm.

"I'm going now," she said hoarsely. "I'll get Poo tomorrow. Some time. Right now, I'm going, and you'll be sorry!"

"Bren—"

"You'll be sorry!" the distraught girl cried. She shoved past Evelyn and slammed out into the night.

Evelyn let her go.

When the sound of running feet died away in the patter of rain, she picked up the worn sandals and set them neatly by the door. Then she went back into the living room. She sat on the sofa next to Poo's warm little body, and at her touch he sleepily cuddled up into her arm.

A pleasant "Maiow" announced Romeo, tail

erect, strolling in behind her from the kitchen. An unseen flash, he'd entered as Brenda had slammed out.

He hopped up on Evelyn's other side, and insinuated his fat, silky self beneath her left arm. He was purring richly. Poo snored a baby snore.

And so she sat, flanked by child and cat, staring at a world that seemed to be slipping further and further away.

Five

She had no idea how long she sat there. It must have been quite a while. With a sudden shock, she realized she was staring at an animated television screen as intently as though her life depended on it — and she had no recollection of having even turned the set on.

How many other single women all over the country tuned in at ten o'clock to see the news and weather? How many of them still gave a damn — or had ever given a damn — about the chance of showers? But Charlie had, or Will, or Ted, and for a hundred and ten years they'd sat in matching chairs and raptly watched the news, the forecast, and the ball scores!

And they were still doing it! Why? Because it offered the comforting fantasy of a routine that was normal, that it held, for a few brief moments, the soothing idea that nothing had really changed.

Evelyn made herself do two things. First, she took a deep breath; second, she turned off the television.

Things had changed. Even if she protectively ignored Bob Marsh's harsh questions about "we," blindly trying to pursue a daily routine crippled beyond repair by John's going, it was at best a poor existence. And she couldn't do it. She wouldn't do it any more.

Putting a chairback against the couch so Poo wouldn't fall on the floor and plumping a sleepy cat into his rug-lined grocery box, she went upstairs to bed. All that thinking had worn her out.

She rarely glanced in the pier mirror as she undressed. At fifty-five the female form does not bear close inspection unless, of course, one was in the business of preserving the female form—which Evelyn, unlike Mary Lou, was not. After fifty she'd tended toward letting the chocolate chip cookie have its way with her. She'd been aided, of course, by John's indulgent attitude—he thought bones belonged on a turkey.

However, something odd in the mirrored image must have caught her peripheral vision. Having donned her rather limp nylon nightie, she suddenly found herself hauling it off again, wheeling around and looking.

Aloud, she said softly, "Oh damn."

Quite distinctly on her left shoulder were the four black and blue imprints of Porter DeKalb's angry fingers.

Her first reaction was to thank God that John wasn't here to see; her second was dismay. Her third was less easily definable.

Slowly she put the nightgown back on, pulled the bed covers down, sat on the edge of the mattress, and stared at her bare feet.

She realized poignantly that things were never going to be the same between herself and the De-Kalbs. Porter had felt humiliated, and in that humiliation and anger he'd said too many intimate things. Although she passionately wished she didn't remember them, she did—and so would he. She'd stung his pride, that strange male essential. She hadn't meant to do it, but she had and there was no retreating now.

John had said once that offending Porter was like throwing a rock in a pond. Besides stirring up mud, the circles got wider and wider. Of course, John had been talking about the car business. Yet, Evelyn knew in her soul that this was no different. There would still be the spreading circles—and the mud.

The only real option was getting out of the pond. That would be a little hard to do in a small town.

She said a brisk short word of agricultural derivation and swung her feet up beneath the sheet. Arms linked beneath her head, she found the ceiling no source of inspiration either. Seeing her with Bob Marsh had obviously started new trains of thought in both DeKalbs. Just dandy — especially since both were angry with her, although for different reasons. Mary Lou thought she'd welshed on the birthday party because of a man, and Porter thought he'd been rejected.

And of the two, Evelyn thought soberly, she was far more able to deal with Mary Lou.

Damn.

Fifty-five years old, and Evelyn Matthews Cass was suddenly an Object of Desire! If it wasn't so serious it would be funny.

And also — suddenly — she wanted John, she wanted John to lie there beside her in the half-dark with the moonlight streaming in through the dry leaves of the old oak beyond her window, John to put his substantial arms around her and hold her as he'd done for so many tender years until a faint snore told her he'd gone to sleep. Dear and understanding John . . .

She was the standard product of her generation. There had been, of course, the usual giggling tussles in the back of various nondescript automobiles, and wrestling matches on her family's front porch swing in the dark of the lilac bushes. But she'd never gone to bed with a man before she married. Even through four years of college, she and her friends — "nice girls" — had been contemptuous of those poor dopes who "you know — did it — all the way!" Then in her senior year she'd met John. He'd been taking a refresher course in Business Ad while his mother looked after his little girl, and besides being ineffably and romantically saddened by his first wife's suicide, he'd been that enticing article, the "older man."

She dropped out her senior year to marry him. After all, who needed a degree in education when one's Mission in Life was to be a wife and mother to a ready-made child?

She almost laughed, even as she stared at the ceiling. They'd all spoken in capital letters in those green years. How Much they'd thought they Knew! How Little they'd Really Known!

Absently fingering the worn lace on her limp gown, she smiled, remembering her wedding nightie, all chiffon and fluff. She remembered how she'd blushed, and how John had admired it before he'd gently effected its removal. John had been gentle. John was a kind man, but his gentleness went beyond that. His wife, Pat, with her unstable and deranged voraciousness, had offended, had destroyed something deep in his sexual appetite. His need was minimal and brief, and he was of the wrong generation to consider hers. By the time Brenda was nine and Jack was four their relationship had almost diminished totally into simple, close affection — comfortable, undemanding, and reliable.

One never missed what one never had. Evelyn's mother had always said that, and with sex she'd apparently been right.

Yet, as she stayed quiet and supine in the silvered dark, Evelyn wondered what Mary Lou and Porter had had—or not had—that caused Mary Lou's frantic search for elusive youth and Porter's agonized reaching out to other women.

It *was* agonized. She'd heard it in his voice.

"I must remember Emma's sexy novels tomorrow," she said out loud, then suddenly found herself hot and blushing between the cool sheets. What *was* she thinking? Had she missed something? She read those novels, too, and had wondered, even feeling a little superior amusement at her own lack of response to those panting and ecstatic damsels.

Yet there had been heat in Porter's fingers hungrily caressing her breasts, and truth in his cry, "Evelyn, you're one hell of a woman!"

Good God. Was she?

She hadn't meant to be—ever! She didn't need it! She had enough coping to do without battling the sex urge, too! Why did the upsets in her life have to come in bunches?

She never knew when she drifted into sleep. But when she wakened to gray morning light with the drowsy cheeping of the birds in the oak tree making music in her ears, it was with an elusive memory of being young again. Young, and dancing slowly, tightly, in close rhythm with someone tall whose lean body moved in perfect tune with hers . . .

Taller than John. That impression stayed as she blinked herself awake. John hadn't cared for dancing; he'd always said dancing was for the kids, and did it only under duress. Well, considering what her day was likely to be, she hardly had time to entertain fantasies.

Shrugging off the warm feeling with the covers, she shoved her feet into lambswool slippers and padded into the bathroom. One look at herself certainly banished the Cinderella stuff.

Evelyn filled a water glass and swallowed her two ulcer tablets. Then she took a cold shower — she needed all the alertness she could get.

As she went downstairs she smelled coffee and was not particularly edified at the sight of her step-daughter, in shabby jeans and sweatshirt, sitting at the breakfast bar. Brenda shoved a mug over to her and said a little stiffly, "I heard the shower. Sorry about last night."

Sorry for the nine thousandth time, Evelyn thought, but didn't say so. She merely nodded and tasted the coffee. It was very good — so good, in fact, that she knew Brenda had sniffed out the expensive custom blend hidden in the cupboard for special occasions.

Well, perhaps this was one, employing the term "special" loosely. They both could probably use a bit of pleasure.

Brenda said, "I brought Poo clean clothes. If you don't mind, I'll bathe him here and drop him off at pre-school."

"Of course I don't mind, Bren. If you'll do it. I have to get out to see Daddy shortly."

Brenda's tan, thin fingers curled around her mug, savoring the heat. Her long hair swung forward; nervously pushing it back, she asked, "So — there really isn't any money?"

"No. No, hon, there really isn't."

"How about Jessie?"

"No. No to that, too. Bren, your grandmother is existing nicely on a very tight budget. Anything jars it, the existence won't be 'nicely' any more."

"But Gram said —"

Then Brenda stopped, but Evelyn, deep in her own thoughts of her brisk and elderly mother-in-law, failed to notice. She was certain that John's mother should be kept out of the present situation at all costs. Living in another town helped. Jessie Cass was a darling, but at eighty-five, church socials and going out to dinner with the other retired schoolteachers was about all she could manage. Evelyn went on, "We'll do something, somehow. Don't bother Gram."

Brenda shifted on her stool uneasily. "You're still going to work?"

"Yes."

"Doing what?"

Evelyn shrugged, and laughed ruefully. "I don't know. Can you suggest something?"

Brenda shrugged. "You went four years to college. What was it for?"

"Teaching. But I never finished, so I'm not certified."

"What would it take?"

"Just now it would take too much and too long."

"You like kids. How about babysitting?"

"Where? Here?"

"Oh, no—not in Daddy's—not in this house! At the kids' homes."

Evelyn added dryly, "And a little cooking and cleaning on the side?"

"If that's what it takes."

Evelyn felt hot burgeoning resentment at Brenda's calm acceptance and made herself look at the paradox: in her own head she was simply too damned good to do drudgery; yet in Brenda's young and strangely practical mind, it would be all right if the means justified the end. Brenda wasn't putting her down; she was being realistic. *She* was the one with the mental block.

"When the bough breaks
The cradle will fall.
And down will come baby
Cradle and all . . ."

"What?" Brenda was looking at her sharply, and Evelyn realized she'd been thinking out loud. She made a rude face.

"The old nursery rhyme," she said, and let it go at that. No point in telling Brenda that yesterday with the overdraft her "bough" had broken. Brenda was not given to flights of fancy any more. She went on, "I'm to see Ben Swan at one. Then I'll know a little more about what I have to do."

"Will you sell the house?"

"Not unless I have to. Brenda, I won't do anything unless I must! But I will have to pay attention to Ben's advice. I can't jeopardize your father's situation; that's priority. Then if I can do anything for you, I will."

"Forget it."

"Forget it?"

"That's what I said. I'll work something out."

The girl slid off the stool, came around the end of the bar and awkwardly kissed Evelyn's cheek. "Don't worry. Things will get better. You may not like the way they do, but if they do, that's the bottom line, isn't it? Run on out to Daddy. I'll wake Poo."

Evelyn was in the Lincoln and driving away before she realized one small fact: not once had Brenda looked her in the eye. What had she done?

Six

Evelyn stopped by the library and checked out two of the raciest current novels she could find in large print, plus Harold Bell Wright's *Shepherd of the Hills*. At the nursing home, she tracked down Emma, muffled in a large apron, helping to make funnel cakes. Wiping her hands, the elderly lady accepted the romantic novels with glee, frowned at the Wright.

She said, "I've read that."

"Take it. You may overdose on the first two."

"That good?"

"That good," Evelyn nodded, adding, " 'Good' being, in this case, somewhat ambiguous. Hi, Charlie. You've powdered sugar on your moustache."

Charlie wiped it away. "Push me out on the patio, will you, Mrs. Cass? I've already eaten enough of those damn things to founder a bull calf. Tasty, though."

Evelyn put her bag on his overalled lap and wheeled him across the tiled floor toward the glass doors. "Isn't this a different chair? I thought you had a motor on yours."

"It's up for repairs."

Laughter came from one of the young aides, clearing a table of crumpled napkins and cake crumbs. "Sure it is," she said. "He burned out his engine chasing that new blond R.N. in the west wing, didn't you, Charlie?"

The old man laughed. "Actually," he went on as they trundled through the door, "I got me a new gadget. You know that Marsh fellow — wife's got Alzheimer's?"

"We've met."

"Ex-air force. Bird colonel, I think. No matter. He knew I used to work for McDonnell Douglas. When the throttle on my chair gave out he brought me one off an F-4 fighter plane. Ain't that neat? My son says he can adapt the sucker so it'll work just fine."

Bracing the open door with her toe, Evelyn maneuvered him through, and she was laughing. "Wow," she said. "How about a tape of machine gun fire for your cassette player? Then you can really terrorize the halls. Good morning, Ed."

She parked Charlie at the patio table, and

turned toward her husband, sitting quiescently in the bright sunshine. He was clean-shaven and tidy, the neck of his shirt carefully buttoned. She kissed him, pulled a chair across the cement to sit near him, and gestured at the crisp funnel cake, untouched on the napkin at his elbow.

"Those are so good, John. Wouldn't you like a bite?"

Obediently he took the piece she tore off, chewed, swallowed, and said, "That's enough. They're sweet, aren't they? I'm afraid I'm not used to eating sweets any more. My wife Pat is diabetic."

That, from a man whose standard breakfast for thirty years was sugared coffee and three frosted doughnuts, unsettled her. Or perhaps it was the persistent mention of his first wife. She didn't take time to analyze, she just spoke. "John, that's not true. You love sweets. Don't you remember my German chocolate cake? We always had it for your birthday. And the cinnamon rolls — you could eat your weight in cinnamon rolls!"

He smiled pleasantly. "I'm afraid you have the wrong person. Perhaps that fellow over there — "

He gestured at Ed. A little wildly Evelyn

took the gesturing hand and held it. "No," she protested. "No! You! Remember—Brenda makes chocolate chip cookies—it's the only thing she really cooks well—and you can eat a dozen at a sitting! Remember, John! Try!"

Gently he removed his hand from hers, and with that movement all the frustrated exasperation left her in an instant. She felt foolish, vulnerable. And helpless. Helpless, most of all, an emotion she found familiar, and thought she'd learned to handle. But she hadn't. Would she ever?

Quietly now, she answered, "All right. Isn't it nice in the sun this morning? The coleus around our patio is blazing scarlet and green—the prettiest we've ever had, I think, although I do need to pinch it back . . ."

He simply sat, regarding her with polite attention, nodding his head as though he were listening to a stranger on a bus.

Why did she even try?

Dominoes clattered at the table as Charlie tipped them from the box. "Want to play, John?"

"No, thank you. I'll just sit here and wait for my wife."

I *am* your wife!

I've been your wife for thirty years, John.

"Her name's Pat. Patricia, really."

And she's dead. She became mentally unbalanced, as had her mother before her, and she took her own life. She's dead, John.

But there was no use in saying it. Nothing was any use. Not here. She might as well go.

She went, and was painfully aware that her husband didn't even turn his head to watch her depart. In his way, John was gone also, and somehow she *had* to learn to accept the fact.

When she reached home everyone was gone there, too, even Romeo. Besides leaving behind an empty dish the cat had also left a neatly scratched-up spot in the lovely soft loam of her new tulip bed, disinterring three expensive Holland bulbs in the process. Gnashing her teeth, Evelyn restored the bulbs, sprinkled the rest of the area with moth flakes and hoped for the best. She had other affairs to pursue.

Thumbing through her collection of secondhand wrapping paper, she found a large enough piece to wrap Jane Nixon's birthday sweater, got back in the Lincoln, and drove around to Jane's house. She was half-hoping Jane wouldn't be home, but the Chevy was in the drive and Jane was clipping hedge.

"It's time I quit," Jane said, pulling off her bandana headband and wiping sweat with it. "Come around back and we'll have an iced tea."

Was there constraint in her voice? Evelyn, following the stocky figure in lavender walking-shorts around the barberry bushes to the old-fashioned back porch, felt that there was. She *knew* there was, after Jane re-emerged from her kitchen with two tall amber glasses and sat down in the porch swing beside her.

"We missed you yesterday," she said, and added nothing more.

"I'm sorry," Evelyn answered, and held out the package.

Jane parked her tea, undid the paper and said, "Oh, lovely," holding the violet knit against her ratty pullover. Jane wore a lot of shades of purple. It matched, she said, her hair, which through a long string of home experimentation had run the gamut from silver to orchid. "I do like it," she went on. "Thank you."

And again Evelyn felt the constraint. She hated it. Of all the four good friends, Jane was her favorite. She sighed, knowing the reason in her very bones, and said, "Okay. What did Mary Lou tell you?"

"That you couldn't make it."

"No, no. After that. Last night—or this morning. Come on, Janey, I know Mary Lou and I know what she was thinking. She was wrong, but I know what she thought."

"All right." Jane's rather nasal voice was quiet. "So what did she say—that was wrong, I mean."

"She—" Evelyn took the plunge. "She said I stood you girls up for a man."

"Bingo."

"Damn. I knew it."

The wrapping paper crackled as Jane creased it with one grass-stained finger. Not looking up, she said, "All right. Evelyn for the defense. I admit it didn't seem like you. What do you say? And stop that!"

"What?"

"Stop making circles with your foot. I can't swing in circles; it makes me dizzy. That's better. Go ahead."

Evelyn told her about Karen and the barbecue place and Karen's father showing up. Then she explained about his taking her home. And, since it was Jane to whom she was talking, that she suspected she'd been set up.

"Ah," said Jane, and with one torn sneaker

96

pushed the swing a little harder. "So. What are you going to do?"

"About what?"

"About this Bob Marsh."

"He didn't set me up. Karen did."

"That's what you think."

"That's what I know. He apologized."

"Oh, okay. Back to square one. Square two, really. What are you going to do?"

"About Bob? Nothing—because there is nothing. He was as embarrassed as I was. And worst of all, it had absolutely nothing to do with my missing the party!"

"You mean you weren't frolicking in bed with this character all afternoon while we snarfed cake and drank cheap champagne?"

That idea was a little close, considering Porter DeKalb. A bit grimly, Evelyn said, "Is that where Mary Lou had us?"

"Only by implication. Mary Lou always wants to be the first to know as soon as there's something to know. Implication is her insurance. Mostly, I think she was just torqued because she didn't understand and you didn't confide. Then, when she saw you in the company of what'shisname, that was the icing on the cookie."

Evelyn gritted her teeth and shook her head.

"Thank you, Mary Lou."

Jane sipped her tea. "So?"

"So what?"

"So square one: where were you?"

Three thoughts went through Evelyn's gray-capped head in rapid succession. One was that Jane was a genuine friend, another was that eventually the crowd would know about her money problems whether she liked it or not, and the last was that Jane would get it straight in the telling. She knitted her fingers together, looked at them as though they belonged to somebody else, and blurted part of the truth: "I'm broke. Really broke, Jane. I got an overdraft. I was out trying to stir up some money."

Jane answered softly, "Oh, Evie—poor kid. I'm so sorry. What can I do? I've a little squirreled away of my own, and you're welcome to it if it'll help."

Evelyn could take adversity better than genuine kindness. She put out a hand and found Jane's.

"You're a doll," she said, and her voice quavered just a little.

"I mean it."

"I know you mean it. Thank you. It's the nicest thing anyone has said to me in days. But—no. I'll manage."

"For sure?" Jane's hazel eyes were steady. "No one need know about it—not even Charles. Of course, he doesn't even know I have it anyway, or it would have been gone long ago." She laughed a bit at that, and for the first time Evelyn looked beyond the daily, familiar sight of a round, kind face and saw unfamiliar territory. With something of a shock she realized that Jane was far more cognizant of the eddies and swirls about her than anybody probably gave her credit for.

Even Charles.

"For sure," she answered, squeezed the warm hand, and gave it back.

Jane blinked rapidly, then bent, pushed off her sneakers, and stuck both feet out straight in front of her. They were surprisingly large for her chunky stature, bony, and with rather ugly twisted toes. "Look at that," she said. "Awful, aren't they? See why I never wear sandals like the rest of you? My mother thought no lady ever wore size nine shoes so she crammed me into sevens. I was ashamed to wear a proper fit until I married. Of course, by then it was too late."

The digression had let her gain control of her emotions again. Her voice was back to its normal, almost gravelly tone with the strange

99

tightness gone. She asked, "What can I do?"

Evelyn told her about Ben and their scheduled meeting.

Jane nodded. "Got your bills together?"

"Oh. I guess that would be a good idea."

"Yes, it would, dummy. All your household expenses, plus insurance payments and whatever else costs you money. You may as well know the worst."

"I'm still not going to have anything left."

"Probably." Jane had always been a believer in calling a spade a spade. Her hands smoothed the new sweater. "So what are your options?"

Evelyn shrugged. "A job, for one thing."

"What do you have in mind?"

"That's the catch. I don't."

Jane bit her lower lip thoughtfully. "How about the Princess Dress Shoppe? God knows, we've all spent fortunes in that place; perhaps it's time one of us started getting some of it back. Since it went under new management I hear there are going to be some changes anyway."

"I didn't know it was in new hands. What happened?"

"Well, old Mattie Barswell owned controlling interest — you knew that."

"Yes. And Mattie died."

"Right. Just recently. And her family doesn't live here anymore, so they put her share in the hands of some brokerage outfit and somebody local bought it as an investment. Charles doesn't know who. Yet, that is. Anyway, you might give that place a shot. We'd certainly all recommend you."

Evelyn nodded. On the surface it seemed a fairly cheerful idea—certainly a little more in her line than cleaning other people's toilets. Best of all, it wouldn't have to be dealt with until after she'd talked to Ben Swan. At the moment she felt capable of doing only one thing at a time.

As she got back into the Lincoln and started up the long hill from Jane's house, something light, something teasing touched the perimeter of her mind about the Princess Dress Shoppe. What was it? Something she'd heard somewhere. Whatever, she had the vague recollection of finding it, at that time, amusing—but now the elusive little shadows in her head were making small warning flickers.

What had she heard, and how in the world could it affect her?

I have quite enough to worry about, thank you, she told the shadows sternly, and turned

101

to other things. The Lincoln was making pinging noises as it pulled the grade to the main street. "Cheap gas," John would say.

Learn to live with it, she thought grimly, and pointed the long, elegant hood toward home.

Seven

When she got home the mail was there. It had probably arrived before she left for Jane's, but in view of yesterday's surprise she had developed an understandable reluctance to look at it.

However, this morning's collection was relatively tame. Intermingled with three of John's sport magazines was a Pepto Bismol-pink envelope which, on perusal, turned out to be an early birthday greeting from Mother Cass. Jessie was big on cards. Evelyn, however, had a decided aversion to them, stemming from two art major-roommates in college who made their spending money writing verses for a card company and betting beers on how sickeningly maudlin they could get. Still, she could imagine how many samples Jessie had pored over before selecting this one, so she made herself read the verse which, of course, was very nice. Nicer yet was the check for twenty dollars which fell out on the floor. Not quite so nice was the unsettling realization that she did indeed have a birthday next week. Her only hope—and a vain one—was that all those cute little red date books the girls owned would fall down a collective and mysterious hole. This year she wasn't quite up to the demands of a birthday gala.

Neither was she particularly hungry, but it was past noon, and going in to see Ben Swan with her stomach growling probably wouldn't be too smart.

She heated up the morning coffee, and while she was cutting off a hunk of yellow cheese Romeo strolled by, exuding an unfamiliar odor identified later as attar of mothflakes. He deposited himself like a bean bag in his cardboard box for a snooze and she said, "Hey. You. Fat boy. We need a word or two."

His yellow eyes said plainly "Later, perhaps," just before he closed them. She shrugged, acknowledging that she was easy, and turned back to her cheese. It was good strong Wisconsin. John wouldn't have cared for it at all. His favorite had been plain old rat cheese or Velveeta, sliced thin. Cheddar was one more thing in which she'd begun to indulge herself since he'd been gone. If I made a list, she thought guiltily, I'd probably be shocked at how many items would go on it.

How in the world had she and John lived together for thirty years with such dissimilar tastes?

But it didn't matter. Not any more. Besides, she had only half an hour to gather material for Ben, not analyze what had been a happy marriage.

Holding that thought and leaving a trail of cracker crumbs, she extracted a battered envelope of last month's bill receipts from beneath two flower catalogs and a half-finished letter to a cousin she disliked. She looked at the bills in dismay, realized that she was going to come off badly enough in Ben's eyes without further evidence of her incompetence, muttered a prayer that her checkbook stubs would be enough, and went upstairs to change. Somehow shorts and a shirt that was faded beneath the arms didn't seem quite fitting. If Ben *had* prepared a tumbril, she was going to roll to her execution in style!

In a distinct act of defiance, she struggled into the new white dress from Maples' Department store. She wasn't thin enough for her neck to go crepey; nonetheless she tied a soft blue scarf loosely around her throat and added blue earrings. As for shoes, unlike Jane she still had rather nice feet. She put on white sandals and dabbed pink polish on one chipped toenail.

As she locked the car in the bank parking lot and went across the concrete to the door she told herself desperately that she was not afraid, that her heart was not thumping in her chest. She stood still in the cool foyer for a moment, vainly trying to pull everything together, but was even foiled in this by Ben's secretary cooing, "Oh, Mrs. Cass! There you are!"

She could hear the tumbril.

"If you'd just step in here and have a seat," breathed the young woman. "How nice you look."

Her soothing tone had already reduced Evelyn's confidence to the despairing level. This was suddenly compounded by her realization that the room to which she had been conducted was not Ben Swan's office.

She said "But—" in a voice that sounded croaky, even to her, and was swiftly interrupted.

"I'm supposed to tell you how sorry, how *very* sorry Mr. Swan is to have been called away. But our Mr. Martin will be in shortly and he'll take good care of you. Would you like a cup of coffee?"

106

How about warm milk, Evelyn thought disagreeably, but had the sense not to say it aloud. She was alarmed and beset by a feeling of betrayal. It wouldn't be Ben. It was going to be someone she didn't even know.

She sat down in the puffy leather chair and answered politely, "No, thank you," not even hearing herself.

"All righty; Mr. Martin will be with you in a sec," said the girl and disappeared.

She had the feeling of impending disaster, which did not impend very long. It entered in the brisk shape of a young man in a three-piece suit and owl glasses who sat down behind the desk, shuffled papers rapidly, and muttered, "Oh, yes," to himself, then said to her, "Mrs. Cass. I'm afraid I have very bad news."

He was, at the very least, succinct. Fifteen minutes later, Evelyn paused in the same cool foyer outward bound and leaned against the plastic wall to assimilate what she'd heard. Basically the income from the trust John had set up on retirement was only sufficient to maintain his needs. There was little left for her, and what there was would amount to not quite three hundred dollars a month.

Drearily she was thinking that the property taxes were due next month when the inimitable

Mr. Martin's voice caught her ear. It was obviously coming from some unseen office behind one of the myriad closed doors on her left. "Well, I told her. She seems a nice old girl. It's a shame, really."

Another voice said, "She is a nice old girl." Evelyn knew the voice—it was Ben's. As she stiffened in disbelief and dismay, Mr. Martin continued cheerfully, "All right, you promised me lunch if I did your dirty work. Let's go."

Evelyn scuttled. There was no other word for it. She panicked and she scuttled—out the door, and into her car, like a frightened little cricket. She also drove away very quickly and got back up to the park above the river again before she started to shake.

"If these are friends," she said aloud through clenched teeth, "I'll take bananas!"

A sort of rude reason finally began to assert itself. Ben had only been trying to save himself embarrassment. And her. She'd wanted the truth. On the other hand, Ben Swan had proved himself to be peculiarly gutless, and that was that!

Three hundred dollars a month! She ordinarily spent that much on groceries for herself! She obviously wouldn't spend it anymore. With what was left of the borrowed five hundred, three dollars in her wallet, and Mother Cass's check for twenty, she had the magnificent sum of one hundred and seventy-four dollars to last about two weeks. And in that length of time if she didn't find a job, trade her car, or put her house on the market she was going to be in a king-sized fix. She just hoped that there was suddenly a hell of a demand for "nice old girls!"

Well, you nice old girl, you. You're downtown. You're dressed fairly decently. Maybe now is the time to give the Princess Dress Shoppe a whirl.

But it was far easier said than done. She parked and sat in the Lincoln a full half-hour, trying to psych herself up and waiting until the shop was, at least, cleared of acquaintances.

At last, with the deep breathing at which she was becoming so proficient, she got out of the car, smoothed her dress, and—as nervous as she'd ever been in her life—walked across the cracked sidewalk and into the store.

Two clerks glanced around and smiled. They should—they'd sold her enough over a period of twenty years. Beth had a customer, promenading before the triple mirror in a flowing gown that from the rear made her look like the Shah of Iran. Isabel advanced and said, "Hi, Mrs.

Cass. What can we do for you today?"

"Hi, Isabel. I need to talk to Nan." Nan was the manager, a classy lady with fashionable bones, both hip and cheek, and eternally blond hair.

"Oh, okay. She's in the office on the phone right now. I'll tell her. Are you sure I can't help? I've got the new fall colors in pantyhose just your size."

"I'll wait. I really need to see her."

"Fine." Puzzled but willing, Isabel stuck her head in Nan's small cubicle, said, "Mrs. Cass outside, when you're through," and disappeared into the back.

Nan took five minutes, five interminable minutes during which Evelyn leaned against the jewelry counter staring raptly at an awful imitation sapphire ring, trying to frame a speech.

She came up with all sorts of pretty words, yet when Nan at last appeared all she could blurt was, "Nan, I'm in a jam. Have you any sort of job opening?"

Nan blinked and paused. Then she said, "Come on into the office." She preceded Evelyn and sat back on the tiny wire chair behind the littered desk. A cigarette burned in the ashtray atop a swatch of green satin. She picked it up, blew a trail of wispy blue toward the open win-

110

dow and said, "Sit down, Evie. I'm glad to hear someone else has problems, too. Smoke?"

"No. I quit. I think."

"Good for you. I wish I could. Okay. I don't mean to be nosey, but I'll make an assumption: Mr. Cass's illness is breaking you."

Evelyn nodded and sighed. "You're right. An educated guess?"

"No. Not really. My mom's in a nursing home. She's been there six years. Even splitting the tab among four kids the bill is enormous. So. You need a job and you think you'd like to work here."

"Do you think I could?"

"Handle the work? Of course you could. Not only that, but I think you'd also be an asset." She grinned, and leaned forward to squash out her cigarette stub, her gold earrings flashing. "You have a lot of well-heeled friends, and it's a fair certainty they'd buy from you. Although, one never does really know. Friends are funny."

A little grimly Evelyn said, "I'm beginning to find that out."

She watched the light from the window shine on the matte of the other woman's make-up, turning it almost golden, but not hiding the fine lines around her eyes and mouth. How old was Nan? Forty? Forty-five? It seemed she'd been in this shop forever.

She was turning a sharpened pencil end over end on the desk top, flicking her lips pensively with a pink tongue. Suddenly she glanced back over at Evelyn and smiled. "There's no opening," she said, adding quickly as Evelyn caught her breath in disappointment, "but I think I can make one. With permission, of course. We have a new major stockholder and everything has to go through him."

"I see."

"He wants—frankly, he wants to seek a younger clientele. Beth is retiring the first of the month, and Isabel will stay on. She's young enough." She said the latter ruefully. "However, I've been maintaining that without our older customers we'll go broke before we get started with new ones. That's where I think you could come in—holding the older ladies. We need 'em," she added, suddenly. "God knows, we need 'em. But I can't guarantee this new boss's approval. That's number one. Number two is that I can't guarantee how long the job will last if you get it. But the pay is good, we usually jockey hours around to suit everyone, and if you last thirty days you'll go on full group insurance and other benefits. Okay? Do you want a shot at it?"

Evelyn drew a shaky breath. "Talk about being in the right place at the right time!"

"As to that, I don't know. I could be fired tomorrow, and both you and Isabel with me. But I'll ask his Nibs, and call you as soon as I clear it with him. Okay?"

"Okay."

"Assuming I get a go-ahead, could you start Monday?"

Evelyn swallowed. "Sure. I don't know why not."

"Great. We'll leave it at that. Just one thing—"

"What?"

"Don't wear that dress from Maples'."

Evelyn glanced down and suddenly felt herself blushing. "Oh, I'm sorry! I didn't even think!"

"No problem."

Nan was standing up, holding out a long, slender hand. She added, "Welcome aboard, and all that. We always got along. I'm sure we'll continue."

"Oh, I hope so!" Evelyn said fervently.

She went back to her car walking on air, feeling the weight of centuries rolling from her shoulders. The world was bright and tinted shiny new. The horrors of the past two days were washed away in the silver stream of pure relief. She drove by the package store and blew most of her twenty-dollar check on a bottle of Asti Spumante champagne. She went home and drank it by herself while watching a VCR tape of Katharine Hepburn in *Little Women*. At ten o'clock, thoroughly and happily slushed, she treated Romeo to the last dregs, made a precarious but successful job of climbing the stairs, and fell into bed in her Maples' dress.

Muzzily, she had noticed a curious thing as she opened the door for the cat. Across the street in the dark between the pole lights had been the black shape of a car and the silhouette of a man in it, just sitting. It had looked strangely like Porter DeKalb.

But then, that idea was ridiculous. Why should Porter DeKalb be sitting across the street from her house? What would he expect to see?

She had sense enough to lock the doors.

Eight

The next morning, by some inexplicable metamorphosis, the sweet cheeps of the tiny birds outside Evelyn's window had changed to raucous "Bracks!" from the throat of ravening vultures. Also, her very skull seemed pierced by legions of needles. When she put her fingers to it even her hair hurt.

The cause had probably been well worth the celebration, but that decision had to be reached at a later date. The best she could do at seven o'clock was moan her way to the bathroom, at which point she became quite disgustingly ill.

Champagne affects different people different ways. Evelyn had no prior knowledge as she'd never been drunk on champagne before. She had not, as a matter of record, ever been drunk at all before. She decided it was a situation she didn't choose to repeat.

Later in the morning she tottered down the stairs on watery knees, removing the pantyhose from the Boston fern on the way. The VCR was still on. She turned it off. The jeweled light cast by the cheerful sun through leaded glass was blinding. Eyes narrowed to painful slits, she plodded into the kitchen, filled the icebag to the deafening roar of ice cubes, went back to the couch, and flopped with the bag on her head. Oblivion descended once more.

At a quarter of twelve she cautiously opened her eyes and found the world relatively acceptable. Of course, the icebag had leaked onto the couch, but her relief at no longer having fire demons in her head was so enormous she was disinclined to quibble.

Coffee might — possibly — stay down.

It did.

Definitely on the mend, she toasted the Princess Dress Shoppe with another cup of expensive coffee. After all, her money problems were solved, thanks to lovely, lovely Nan whatever-her-name-was. The past two days seemed like bad dreams, outrageous fantasies. She could make it on less than three hundred a month now. No problem!

The dark blue housecoat in which she had chosen to creep down the stairs to die had long skirts and full sleeves. Now that survival was once more a possible option, she slid her ample fanny up on the bar stool, curled bare toes around the rungs, rolled the sleeves above the elbow, and sipped her coffee cautiously. The white mug said in red letters "Hogs Are Beautiful." She'd used that mug many times when defiantly eating four sugar doughnuts in a row, but today it had a different meaning.

Today was Wednesday, five days before she became — what was that phrase — a working girl. "Working girl!" she said aloud and giggled. In the meantime the operative word was HOG, which was what she'd be living like if she didn't get a move on while she had time. The kitchen needed cleaning, the living room carpet could stand the sweeper, and she could see plainly through the window that the coleus still needed attention.

That she could do while she drank her coffee.

"I'm going to pinch the coleus, the coleus, the coleus!" she sang cheerfully, unchaining the kitchen door. "I'm going to pinch the coleus wherever it may be!"

When had she felt so well? The sun was shining, warming the tiles beneath her bare feet, the crimson geraniums were burgeoning in their bright green pots atop the retaining wall along the drive. Even Romeo was an ornamen-

117

tal arrangement, a study in black and white as
he lay in plush opulence absolutely still between
the geraniums, his eyes focused on something
unseen far down the street.

Fate took its first reprisal on this blissful
scene as the bent to the carmine and jade of
the coleus plants.

"Oh!" she said in pain, and straightened up
very quickly.

The fire demons went away again, but good
sense would seem to dictate leaving the coleus
until tomorrow.

At that point another painful jab arrived,
and the sun definitely dimmed its golden hue;
last night, for the first time, she had forgotten
to go out to see John.

"Oh!" she said again, not in pain but in
guilt. How could she? How could she have forgotten? What if no one got him into his pajamas? What if he sat in his chair all night
waiting?

Now that was patently ridiculous and she
knew it! It was much too well-run an establishment to allow things of that sort. But it didn't
absolve her. Not at all.

Reason told her it was too late to go dashing
out there now, right in the middle of their
lunch hour. And if anything had happened to

118

John, of course, they would have called.

But still . . .

"Damn," she said softly, her eyes shut. She hated it. She felt awful.

Just how awful was never to be determined. At that moment all hell broke loose in the driveway beyond her retaining wall. Barks and yelps and yells and the keening snarl of Romeo's war cry intermingled for about thirty seconds. Then an ominous silence descended.

Bewildered and frightened, Evelyn tore at the wooden gate latch, flung it open, ran in her bare feet around the end of the Lincoln, and came to a skittering stop on the grassy verge, her jaw ajar.

A very large, calm Labrador retriever stood quietly on four substantial paws in her drive. His cream-colored back was in some disarray. Appending from his jaws was a softly sputtering black and white tomcat whose fury was necessarily diminished by the constriction about his plush neck. The Labrador's eyes were deep brown, steady, and serene.

Also steady and deep was an inquiring voice: "Yours?"

Evelyn turned and saw a short, wide man in running gear, attached to the Labrador by a leather leash.

"Oh my," she said, uncertain whether to laugh or cry. "If you mean the cat, I guess so. What—what happened?"

"I'm not really sure." To the dog the man said, "Drop, Baron."

Romeo landed with a heavy thunk, gave them all a sweeping, incredulous look and huffed away into the syringas.

Evelyn said, "I'm so sorry." She wasn't sure for *what,* but it seemed an obligatory thing to say. "Is he hurt?"

"The cat? I don't think so."

"No, no. Your dog."

"Oh." The man swept thick fingers along the broad, creamy back, smoothing the fur into place. The dog wagged his tail. "No. No, Baron's pretty tough."

She asked again, "What happened?"

He shrugged. "We were just jogging when right out of the blue came this aerial attack. No one even blew a siren." Suddenly he grinned at her, and in that broad, Slav-like face it was rather a nice grin. "I was looking for a new place to run, but I'm not sure we find your street hospitable."

She'd already been redundant enough to say she was sorry again. She was also suddenly aware of her bare feet, her somewhat faded

120

navy blue *déshabillé* and the fact she had only finger-combed her hair. As though sensing her discomfort, the man's grin faded. His voice short, he said, "Well—good morning. Come, Baron," and started on down the street. Then he stopped again, looking back.

"Isn't this the old Cass place?"

"Yes."

"John's not around?"

"No. Not—not at the moment."

"Tell him Vic Bonnelli said hello."

"Vic—Bonnelli?"

"Right. Vic the Invincible. He'll know."

For some reason the deep voice turned dry. Hard. With a last wave he went on.

Man and dog both ran easily for all their size. She watched until they rounded the bend of Sycamore Street and jogged out of sight, then chewing a lower lip thoughtfully she went back up the drive. Bonnelli. Bonnelli. It rang no bells with her, but she wasn't local. He was obviously John's age—she'd ask Porter about him . . .

Whoa. Not Porter. She wasn't asking Porter anything!

Her head was aching again. She pulled the metal chair out of the sun and slouched into it. Frowning against the pain and the sunshine,

121

she was trying to remember when she'd last taken aspirin and how many when another unsettling fact dawned. It wasn't just the sun warming her. She was in the shade of the two old apple trees where the October morning chill still lingered.

She was having a hot flash. Damn. Of all inconvenient nuisances . . .

Sweat popped out on her forehead and ran in trickles down from her hairline, dampening the collar of her housecoat, as waves of heat warmed the concrete beneath her bare toes. She opened the top of the cotton coat, pushed up the sleeves, hitched the skirt above her knees and waited for it to subside. Five years' experience had taught her that there wasn't much else to do.

So she'd have to go get another shot. She hated those shots—she always had the horrid fear she'd awaken some morning with a moustache. Yet, on the other hand, she certainly couldn't do a very good job at the dress shop if she went about looking like a water spaniel—and there was absolutely no way of predicting when one would occur. Sometimes there'd be none for days, then she'd have them every hour on the hour.

At least now she knew she could afford the

thirty bucks for the shot.

Five minutes later the enormous wave of body heat was over. She felt clammy and uncomfortably cool, and her headache was definitely worse.

She arose carefully, pulling the wet cotton away from her backbone. Romeo was crouched at the back door, and as she approached he gave a yowl.

"You!" she said crisply, "You are going to get us both in trouble!"

Resigned, she let him in, filled his bowl, and went for the mail.

The white-painted-board floor of the old, two-column portico was lace-patterned from the shadows of the waving green ivy. Its clinging tendrils had even crept across the leaded glass fanlight above the door, and Evelyn absently tore those away as she reached for the post with the other hand. John always said a jungle knife wouldn't hurt that stuff, but she rather liked it.

The contents of the box were sparse. A large, colorful mailer depicting a lop-eared rabbit moving at full speed alerted the neighborhood that a new Bunny Burger would be opening soon downtown. "Bunny-Burgers, Quick as a Bunny!" proclaimed the ad. "Fast food can be quality food! Wait until you try our famous Quiche-to-go!" Added on was a small slip which said, "Now hiring."

Evelyn's attention was on a scribbled postcard from her son, Jack. She shifted the Bunny Burger stuff under one arm and squinted, trying to decipher the familiar scrawl. "Dear Mom," it read. "When they say casual on Aruba, they mean *casual!* All beaches nude. XXXX Love to Dad. See you in December."

In Jack's code four X's meant that everything was fine. Pleased, she turned the card over and glanced at the two amply endowed Caribbean ladies wearing only smiles. Casual, indeed! Bemused at the idea of some of Jack's paunchy male customers clad only in Havana cigars, she padded back into the cool foyer. She was just dropping the Bunny Burger mailer into the wastepaper basket when the telephone rang on John's desk.

Collapsing into his old oak swivel chair and shutting her eyes against the incipient ache, she picked it up.

Mary Lou DeKalb's solicitous voice said, "Hi, Evie, dear, how are you?" and Evelyn realized immediately Mary Lou had talked to Jane.

"I'm fine," she answered, knowing full well whatever reply Mary Lou wanted she'd make up for herself.

"Really? I'm a friend, now; don't try to snow me."

"Really. Things are working out."

"I'm so glad." She probably was. "I just never — you know — imagined —"

"Neither," said Evelyn a bit wryly, "did I."

She was encountering a strange reluctance to tell Mary Lou she was going to work and where. She rather disliked the feeling in herself, but did nothing to correct it. She had never confided in Mary Lou as she had in Jane. Nobody did, really. "I'm sorry about Janey's birthday."

"Oh, that's okay. We all understand. Now, I mean. Well. Why I called this morning was to say we talked it over — we girls, I mean — and thought that this year we'd do something different. Okay?"

"Different for what?"

"*Your* birthday, you idiot! Don't tell me you've forgotten you have one coming up next week! The big old five-six, sweetie; we've all had ours and now it's your turn. What we decided we'd do this time was get together in the evening with the guys for a change at my house, or Jane's or Liz's. Okay?"

"That's not necessary!" she protested. "It's just a birthday!"

"Never mind, we've all decided, and my dear, you haven't a prayer! You need a lift, and a bang-up party will do the trick. I'll let you in on details later. Right now I just need to know one thing: do you want to bring anyone?"

"What?"

"Darling, don't be coy. We're all adults! Just yes or no so I can count steaks."

Evelyn was having difficulty keeping the sudden surging anger from her voice. "No," she said, and her voice sounded thick in her own ears. "No, because I really don't think I'm up to a party. Please, Mary Lou. Thank you anyway. Maybe later in the fall, but—not now. Just—not now. There's someone at the door. I'll talk to you later."

Having uttered a barefaced lie, she hung up on Mary Lou's sputtering, and lay back in the chair suddenly exhausted. Her head hurt, her stomach was quivering, and her legs felt weak.

Bring someone indeed! Bob Marsh! That's who Mary Lou had meant! She never gave up, did she? What sort of person did Mary Lou think she was? Hadn't all those years of running around together taught her anything about the Casses? Or—

Or was Porter at the bottom of this? If Mary Lou had *ever* had an original idea she would have stifled it at birth; she never played anything but sure things, things already tried and true.

Her hands gripped the smooth ends of the chair arms. Shutting her eyes, she remembered Porter and John laughing like two school boys at the breakfast table, sitting during long evenings in the kitchen playing pitch and kidding about their encroaching bellies. She remembered them spading up the bed for the new roses, coming in hot and dirty, making bets on whose plantings bloomed first. She remembered waiting in the car at the bend of the road beyond Scout camp, so they could sneak out and enjoy a quiet drink while their charges slept. All those years—and Porter said he'd been in love with her! It seemed so incredible. Women are supposed to sense when men loved them. Why hadn't she?

Suddenly she knew part of the answer: she'd been so secure with John. So content. So—whole. Many times John had said, "Poor Port, he's a saint. Mary Lou would drive me right up the wall." And she'd only said like an echo, "Poor Port," giving lip service, not really listening because to her it was John and Evelyn, Jane and Charles, Liz and Ben, Mary Lou and Porter; neat, tidy bundles, one inseparable from the other like Siamese twins. She had never even bothered to think differently, assuming that they all were set in cement like *John and Evelyn*.

Well, they weren't. Nothing was. And Porter DeKalb was no longer her friend. Porter wanted to go to bed with her. Porter wanted to make love to her. Mary Lou's Porter. The fruit basket was upset, the checkers on the board were scrambled. She didn't know the rules anymore.

Nine

She spent the first part of the afternoon stoked to the eyeballs on aspirin, putting in some laundry, taking out the trash, and running the sweeper. Between fishing in the vacuum bag for an inadvertently-collected quarter and cleaning the lint filter on the dryer, she had a second hot flash which spurred her to make a doctor's appointment for Friday after she got her hair done. Thank God she could afford both again!

The only real upset came at four when she changed into the good gray slacks she'd bought last fall. She did get them up over her knees, but for one rather demeaning minute she thought she was going to fall in two neat halves, one per leg.

Admitting grimly to too many summer double chocolate sundaes with nuts and whipped cream, she hauled them off again. Now what?

Looking at the matronly figure in the pier mirror, she allowed herself to be distracted by the worn lace on her bra matched by the stretched elastic on her panties.

"Evelyn LaVern," she said aloud to the image. "You are positively ragged. What if you get hit by a truck and are taken to the hospital with a safety pin in your drawers?"

The old gray doubleknit pants would do very well, especially if she wore the paisley-print shirt with the long tails that would hide the pink Kool-Aid stain right on the area of her navel.

She went back downstairs. Romeo's bowl, as usual, was empty. Wondering when his black and white pelt was also going to get too tight in the crotch, she opened the refrigerator door for the last half of the Kitty-Yum tin. Jessie Cass's birthday card caught her eye. She'd stuck it on the top panel with the rest of the family *graffiti*, but this was the first time she'd noticed the writing in the corner below the "Love, Jessie." Bending, she read the three additional words: "See you soon."

Now what did that mean?

Jessie didn't live that far away. The retirement village where she happily whiled away her hours making cute Kleenex boxes out of bleach bottles was only forty-five minutes on the Interstate. She frequently popped in between visits to her doctor and other old friends, and sometimes when, as she said, the Past Worthy Matrons were having "a geriatric orgy" she stayed all night. She rarely mentioned going to see John, but Evelyn knew she did it faithfully. It was a very painful thing for Jessie to find herself so well and her son so disabled. Yet in all her goings and comings she'd never found it necessary to make a formal announcement.

So what was with this "see you soon"?

She mulled it while scraping fishy cat food into the empty bowl and gave up while washing her hands. John's birthday was in the spring, their anniversary in early summer. Perhaps she meant *Thanksgiving*. A few weeks' distance probably qualified as "soon," she decided. She locked the door, got into the Lincoln and drove away.

Her first destination was Wal-Mart, the large shopping enclave on the edge of town. Therein, she bought sixty-five dollars worth of bras and panties and — in a fit of self-indulgence — a really nice zippered housecoat in rose with satin binding. She knew she was left with only $88.33 cash money, but she reasoned blithely that the things *were* on sale, after all. Total loyalty to the Princess Dress Shoppe couldn't be

131

expected to begin until Monday, and surely she could get by for two weeks until her first paycheck.

It occurred to her for the first time that she'd never asked precisely what that paycheck would be.

However, in the sublime conviction that everything was turning up roses even yet, she loaded her bundles quite cheerfully into the Lincoln. A polite engine sound alerted her to the battered Datsun with a large cream Labrador sitting upright in the front seat. The license plate said California, yet it was, nonetheless, Baron.

She said, "Well, hi, how are you?" and he wagged his tail pleasantly. Baron was apparently of the forget-and-forgive persuasion. He watched with large, interested brown eyes as she backed away and headed out the exit. The last she saw was his attention swivelling back to the store entrance, waiting patiently, she guessed, for the reappearance of Vic Bonnelli.

Driving to the opposite side of town and the nursing home took her past the site of the new Bunny Burger. A crew of men was busy erecting some sort of statue-like edifice beyond bright "Drive-In" signs. Whatever it was, it had lop ears. Another crew was scattering woodchips around hopeful sprigs of spreading juniper, and still another was slapping white paint on the pink-roofed establishment itself. Also notable was a silent line of people before a door with a large scrawled "Hiring here" taped on its upper window.

"There but for the grace of God," thought Evelyn gratefully to herself, and drove right on by. But the line stayed with her. It had been a combination of shabby elders and dispirited teen-agers, laced with a few Brendas wearing jeans, long hair from the sixties, and carrying restless children.

Had she looked, Brenda might even have been there. She hadn't seen her for a couple of days, so she didn't know. Since dropping out of high school and marrying Jim, then becoming a widow, Brenda hadn't missed many job lines like that.

By five-thirty, dinner hour at the nursing home was over, although the smell of coffee remained along with the vague whisper of frying oil. In the main lobby there was a Disney film on the VCR and Evelyn heard the sound of laughter as she whisked by and on down the western hallway. The clatter of dishes from the steamy kitchen followed her clicking heels, receding as she went. Unconsciously she softened her own tread until there was no noise at all, only indistinct whispers from behind closed doors. Of necessity, life in West Hall ended with suppertime.

An enormous bundle of soiled sheets with legs said, "Hi, Mrs. Cass. Thanks for bringing Emma those books. We've hardly heard a word out of her all day."

Evelyn looked behind the sheets, found a round, tired face, and answered, "Oh, hi, Alice. You're welcome. Is that good? Not hearing from Emma, I mean."

"It's great. She's our number one rabble-rouser—and it's just because she's bored. All the girls on afternoon shift may line up to kiss you. We got more chores done in that section today than we have since she came."

"I'll certainly bring her more."

"Good. She's such a nice old lady."

The sheets proceeded on toward the laundry, leaving Evelyn a bit jarred.

Yesterday *she* had been the "nice old lady."

It was obviously relevant to where one was at the time. To Moses, only in his hundredth year, Methuselah at nine hundred had probably been a "nice old man." And at the tender age of seven she, herself, had angrily told a forty-year-old aunt, "Who cares about you? You'll

134

soon be dead!"

As a matter of fact, Aunt Edith, a spry ninety now, had reminded her niece of that very remark just a few weeks ago.

And at the rate I'm going, Evelyn told herself ruefully, she may outlive me!

She turned the knob on John's door and walked into a crowd. Porter DeKalb was stretched out in John's lounge chair, Charles Nixon was perched awkwardly on the foot of the bed, John was in the bed, his roommate Ed was in the other bed, and Ben Swan snapped to his feet from somewhere. At the same time he quickly threw Ed's sheet over something on the narrow table across Ed's chest.

The communal guilt was so thick it could have been sliced. Evelyn had to laugh.

"All right," she said, giggling. "This is a raid. You know this place has no license to gamble. Either turn in your chips or split with me."

Ed snorted. Ben said, "Funny lady," and turned back the sheet, revealing a pile of pennies and a heap of cards. "All right, McCarthy, hit me. Don't worry about her; she's on the take."

Ed fished his own cards from beneath his pillow and fanned them expertly. "Raise you one," he said.

Evelyn shook her head and turned to the other bed. "You guys," she said of the two-handed poker game that went on secretly every other Wednesday. "You're going to get both John and me thrown out. I forgot this was Rotary night. Hi, honey, how are you?" This was to her husband, supine beneath a light blanket, hands clasped quietly across his shirt front.

"He's just aces," said Charley Nixon in that super-hearty voice that so many use to cover distress. "We were just telling him about the Rams and the Cowboys and what a hell of a good quarterback the Rams have this year, weren't we, John?"

John smiled politely and moved his neat head just enough to keep Charley from blocking his view of the television.

From behind Evelyn she heard Porter say, "Here, Evie," and got up from the chair.

"No, no, Port, that's all right," she said quickly and perched by John's shoulder, her left arm draped across the pillow above his head. It was a false note. She'd never sat like that before, and she knew it and Porter knew it. The chair was her place; she always wanted to be where she could watch John's face. Her sudden pose made a statement hard to miss. Porter didn't miss it. For one brief moment his mouth was a thin line and high color surged to his angular cheekbones.

But all he did was glance at his wristwatch. "We'd better go, guys. We still have to roll out the piano. Are you coming to hear us sing, Evie?"

From the other bed Ed cried out triumphantly, "Gotcha!", threw down his hand and raked the pennies toward him. Ben moaned, "You old turkey!" and held up his own hand for his friends to see. While they looked and laughed, Porter bent over John and patted his shoulder.

He said, "Hang in there, buddy." His other hand, light as a butterfly, traced Evelyn's cheek. "You, too, kid."

To the others—if they even noticed—the gesture was merely that of an old, affectionate friend, attempting to show sympathy. None of them caught the last two words: "I'll wait."

Leaving her stiff with outrage, he walked on into the hall, a big, balding man with his belt buckle bent floorward by the surge of the paunch inside the tan knit shirt. An easy-going man with a reputation for kindness. A man Evelyn and John had known for over twenty years and, she remembered bitterly, called a friend.

Charles Nixon joined him; they looked at each other and shook their heads. She could almost read their lips: "Damn. Poor old John. What a shame."

Ben Swan was lingering at the door. His eyes looked anxious, almost apologetic. Like a collie pup, she thought.

He said, "Sorry I had to miss you yesterday, Evie. Did Martin take care of everything all right?"

Feeling very tired, Evelyn got out the proper words. "Yes. Yes, fine." What else was there to say anymore besides the proper words — unless she really wanted to reach down underneath — and she was already learning that sometimes there were worms underneath.

Let Ben get off free. He might be a coward, but at least he hadn't made a pass at her as had the pair in the hallway. Don't embarrass him. Don't embarrass anybody. Just don't lose sight of the bottom line again — the bottom line that said "You're on your own."

He nodded, flapped his pudgy hand in a vague farewell, and followed his buddies. The door closed softly.

"Nice fellas."

Evelyn jumped. "What?"

Ed repeated. "Nice fellas."

"Oh. Yes. Yes, they are."

"Come in here every week. The three of 'em. That Ben, he ain't no poker player, but he thinks he is. I don't mind givin' his money a little exercise."

Ed was sitting up, pulling his walker toward him. "Got to go to the pot," he said briskly. "Then I allow I'll go down and listen to the singin'."

He clomp-shuffled his way into the bathroom. Evelyn slid from her awkward perch on John's bed and sat in the chair. He turned his eyes from the TV and asked mildly, "Is it time for bed?"

"If you like."

The procedure was routine: hand him his pajamas, turn down the bed, adjust the television. Something suddenly came to her as she found the old "Green Acres" re-run. "John, do you remember a Victor Bonnelli?"

"Turn it up, please. Who?"

"In a moment. Victor Bonnelli."

"Oh. Vic. Sure. Golden Gloves. Joined the marines. Was Fleet Champion in the Pacific if I remember right. Good football player, too. Please turn it louder. I can't hear."

The revelation was not exciting, just interesting. John's memory of the forties was excellent.

It was the fifties when he'd married her that he couldn't remember.

She said, "He wanted to be mentioned to you," and turned up the TV.

John nodded, but his eyes were on the screen. "Thank you. That's all. You may go now."

So she went.

Earlier in his illness she'd sat there until late at night, trying to talk, coaxing, cajoling. Not any more. As the doctor said, when brain cells were dead, they were dead.

It wasn't John's fault. There was no blame. That's just the way it was. And neither was it John's fault that things were not so simple for her.

She kissed him, said "Good night," and went out, closing the door. She was aware as she left that he wiped the kiss off his cheek with the resigned repugnance of a small child suffering unwanted affection politely.

Far down the hall she could hear the sound of community singing, rising raggedly above the determined tinkle of a very poorly-tuned piano. As she drew nearer, she caught Porter's rich voice saying, "That was fine, that was mighty fine!" through the spate of applause generated determinedly by staff. "Now let us

140

sing one. What'll it be?"

Evelyn couldn't catch the suggestions they called out. But as she entered the periphery of the crowded central lounge twelve Rotarians, their heads together, launched into a very harmonious rendition of "Five Foot Two" while others passed out bowls of popcorn, and applause accompanied an old gentleman doing an impromptu buck-and-wing in the corner.

Alice, off the soiled-sheet detail, scooted over to make room on a table top, and Evelyn hoisted herself up beside her. Why not? She wasn't going anywhere. She didn't turn into a pumpkin until twelve.

She shook her head at the proffered popcorn. It got, to be perfectly frank, up under her partial plate and it hurt so much it wasn't worth it.

The last "kootchy-koos" died down to be replaced by a number of ribald suggestions accompanied by laughter. Emma rose from her chair and with enormous authority banged on the table. "Enough! Listen! Porter, you sing."

Porter was wiping sweat from his forehead. "Let me get my breath back," he said to the tall old lady. "What would you like, Emma?"

"How about 'Minnie the Mermaid'?"

Everybody laughed. Porter laughed. He said,

"Come on, be nice! I know. Sit tight, darlin'. This one's especially for you."

Gratified, the old lady sat down again. Porter bent to the pianist, whispered, then walked over and knelt by her chair. At the end of a crescendo of rippled notes his rich, melodious voice began to flow, " 'Let me call you sweetheart . . . I'm in love with you . . .' "

He picked up the gnarled hand, kissed it, and Emma bridled. " 'Let me hear you whisper . . . that you love me, too . . .' "

He got to his feet, smiling down at the old lady who was suddenly misty-eyed. " 'Keep the love light glowing . . . in your eyes so blue . . .' "

He looked around, and to Evelyn's dismay for one, brief but unmistakably poignant moment he sang directly to her, " 'Let me call you sweetheart . . . I'm in love with you . . .' "

"Oh boy," said Alice, beside her. "He can make the wiggles down your spine, can't he?"

"Yes," Evelyn said grimly, "he can." But with an enormous surge of relief she realized it was a general statement. No one was taking Porter personally. He was moving among the clusters of elderly ladies, singing to them, reprising the song, and at the end he said to the Rotarian

142

chorus, "Come on, guys, all of us," and they joined him.

A quiet voice said in Evelyn's ear, "He's damned good. Who is it?"

She turned her head and saw Bob Marsh standing behind her. His gray eyes were calm, interested, and he'd obviously seen nothing untoward in Porter's singing.

"Porter DeKalb," she whispered back, and added, "The used car dealer."

"Oh. Sure."

Porter finished the number to rousing applause, and they started a lively round of "I've Been Working on the Railroad."

Evelyn slipped off the table to make her escape. At the door, with the music fading behind her, she reached for the handle and found the door already being opened by a sweatered arm.

"Me, too," said Bob Marsh.

She said, "Thank you," noting that this time the sweater was maroon. Together, they walked out into the last golden glow of the setting sun. "How was Mrs. Marsh?"

"The same. And—yours?"

"The same."

"And on that happy note," he muttered and turned to walk away. Suddenly he wheeled around. "Hey. I've got the willies. Would you let me buy you a cup of coffee? Or a beer? Something?"

As she obviously hesitated, he flushed and grimaced. "Please. I need some normal conversation without crises, politics, or family feelings. It would be appreciated."

Suddenly feeling reckless and totally irresponsible, Evelyn said, "Okay. I think I probably need the same thing. Where to?"

"Where won't we attract attention?"

Then he flushed again, like an awkward boy. "I put that nicely, didn't I? Shit. I'm sorry. It's not you, it's me. My sister-in-law is in town and I'd rather spend the evening catching measles."

Recalling what Karen had said, Evelyn suspected she understood more than he realized.

She could suggest her place, but she didn't think she was quite ready for that.

She said, "The marina restaurant on the river. It's usually so full of transients no one notices the locals."

"Bingo. If they'll let me in the place with Kool-Aid on my pants. I spent the afternoon with my grandson."

Evelyn found herself laughing. She pulled up her paisley shirt tails and pointed. "Strawberry."

144

"Grape," he said. "I feel better already. My car okay?"

The old brown Datsun smelled of tobacco and some kind of petroleum. The passenger seat was full of aerial maps and something called a flight plotter. He swept it all up and tossed it in the back.

"My housekeeping has gotten a bit lax," he said, shutting the door for her. Sliding in on his side, he clicked his belt into place, saw her searching for hers and said, "Oh damn. It's there, somewhere. Feel between the cushions."

"Got it," she said triumphantly, started to fasten it, then said "Ooof!" The belt required letting out about eight inches. "What happened to the last midget that sat here?"

It was meant to be humorous. It wasn't. She would have given a lot to take it back.

Ten

She could only say humbly, "I'm sorry. That was thoughtless." She was a victim of her own awkwardness, knowing full well that his grandson would ride in a safety seat in the back, that his daughter was not that petite, and the only one she knew who *was* lay in the nursing home behind them.

But he merely shrugged. "Actually, I think the last person to sit there was you the other evening. After what my Karen laid on us we were both too bemused to belt."

The Datsun had a stick shift on the console between them. He moved the gears smoothly and pointed the car down the highway. "Will your whale be okay if you leave it?"

She glanced back at the Lincoln. Since the large afternoon crew had left in their cars it was sitting in rather isolated splendor in the parking lot. "I think it will. If they're not crowded, they don't mind. And it's a very nice whale."

"But do you really need that much car?"

Then it was his turn to look abashed. "Sorry. None of my business. Your husband was a Ford man, probably. I expect he had a very high regard for Lincolns."

"Yes. He did," she said, and let it go at that. They were hardly at the point to be sharing problems yet.

They were just driving by the new Bunny Burger. He asked, "Ever eat at one of those?"

"No, I never have. Are they good?"

"Not too bad, really. They had them all around the last place we were based. In Florida. The kids are pretty cute in those bunny ears. It was always my luck to get waited on by some broad-butted gal who looked more like a moose."

"They wear ears?"

"Plush ones. With pink lining. Like Bugs."

"Oh, my. Shades of Hugh Hefner."

"No, no. No powderpuff tails. No opera hose. Just ears. And their burgers are pretty fair. I expect when it opens that one will see a lot of me. I'm turning into a fast food freak."

"You don't like to cook?"

"I don't like to open my refrigerator door. It's

147

scary. Things reach out and grab me."

"Mystery meat."

"What?"

"Mystery meat. It's been there so long no one remembers what it is. I have some, too. I call it the 'Living Alone Syndrome'."

He grinned. When he did, his white-moustached face in profile lost its sharpness and showed a nice lean curve of jawline.

The road to the marina turned away from the flat land on the western edge of town and wound along the feet of the bluffs. The gunmetal sheen of the river was on their left but, with the setting sun, the towering hills made a shadowy wall of tangled sumac and soaring scrub oak, darkening the right side of the car. From its protective gloom Evelyn found herself looking at Bob with sudden but genuine dismay. What was she doing? Was she out of her mind? This was a strange man; she didn't even have the rationale of his being an old friend — yet here she was, in his car, going with him for a social drink!

Something of her feeling must have communicated itself to him. Perhaps she stiffened, or withdrew. It might even have been a thought flashing between them, so keen was her abrupt discomfort. She saw his back straighten, his hands clamp on the wheel, and his jutting profile lock on the road ahead. She suspected that the man in control of his F-16 with bogies on the screen had looked a great deal like the man sitting next to her now.

"Feel strange, don't you?"

She jumped, then nodded. "Yes." She tried to explain. "It's not you. I mean—I'm just so used to having John—"

"Sitting here where I am."

"Yes."

His eyes never wavered from the road. "When do you suppose we'll both get used to it?"

"When we must."

"Good God, Evelyn—smell the coffee!"

Stubbornly she said, "When I want to smell it! And I'm not sure I'm ready!"

"Bull shit. Don't start that nonsense again! How long has it been? Six months? A year? You're a bright girl, Evelyn, you know the truth when you see it. Sue-Ann is never going to be there where you are, and John's not going to be here in my seat again. Not ever."

Then he loosed one hand, hit the steering wheel with it lightly. "Sorry. Heavy conversation. I said I had the willies. Hey. Are you okay?"

149

She was fine. She was just having another hot flash. Sometimes emotion set them off and this was one of the times.

Embarrassed, she explained. "If you don't mind turning on your air full blast and directing the vents straight at me it will be over quicker."

"Sure. But you'll freeze your patoot! This air conditioner puts out!"

"So," she said grimly, "do I," and laid her hand on his. "Feel."

In amazement he said, "My God!" and did as she asked. "It's too bad you can't store that up; you'd knock a slab off your winter heating bills. Here." Fishing beneath his seat, he proffered Kleenex.

"Thanks. I'm scheduled for a shot tomorrow."

"That will stop them?"

"For a while. I keep hoping they'll go away permanently. I hate looking like an aging mermaid."

He laughed. "Listen," he said. "You're a classy lady, and classy ladies can look however they damn well please. Where do we park at this place?"

"To the left, then along the sea wall."

By the time he'd nosed the Datsun against the crumbling stonework and turned off his engine she was pretty well dried. It had been mercifully short.

He swung his long legs out, then came around and bent to her window. "Okay?"

"Okay. There's nothing to it, really, except nuisance."

"The things I learn," he said and opened the door. "I thought menopause was mysterious, that women were supposed to nibble doilies and whimper a lot."

She stood up, and the damp air from the river blew her soft short hair against his chest. Incredulously she echoed, "Nibble doilies?"

"Well—do strange things."

"That's strange, all right," she said, and giggled. It was a rather endearing noise. "I promise—I'm not even attracted to place mats, so we can go inside safely."

"Thanks."

It was a floating restaurant. A waitress in a sailor hat seated them by a window overlooking the broad, calm river, took their orders for one beer, draft, and one coffee, black.

As she left, Bob pointed to the plastic place mats and whispered, "One tiny bite and I'll promise I won't even look."

"You're an idiot!"

"I try hard."

She picked up the large menu board. From behind it she covertly surveyed the crowded dining room, was relieved to find no one she knew, laid the menu down, and found he had been doing the same thing. They both grimaced.

"Evelyn Cass, we have to lick this guilt thing before it licks us! Are we doing something wrong?"

"N-no."

"Love your confidence. Have I imperiled your virtue? Have you imperiled mine? Will there be some controlled substance in my beer, and do you intend to lure me into your web and attack my body?"

"Bob, honestly—"

"That's it. That's the operative word. Honest. And as long as we stay that way with each other, the world can damn well go hang. Now before someone stands up and sings 'My Buddy' with tremolos, pick something off the menu. I'll give you one more reprieve from the Mystery Meat."

His voice was light, but his gray eyes were very steady. He meant every word, and she knew he did.

She blinked a little and said softly, "Thank you. Thank you for asking me to come. I get the willies, too."

She chose a tenderloin and fries. He picked the Reuben. When the sauerkraut-oozing sandwich arrived, he picked up one half, took a healthy bite, and froze. His heavy white brows went up his tanned forehead like leaping fish.

"What is it?"

"Mmmgph!" he said, which shortly translated into "Good God!" as he laid the half back down on his plate and explored its contents. "I thought so! Thousand Island Dressing! That's sacrilege!"

"That's local. They always put Thousand Island Dressing on Reubens around here."

"I'm among barbarians!"

"I'm sorry. I could have said something. I thought you knew."

"It's like putting catsup on beef bourguignon."

"They do that, too."

He was busily scraping off the offending goo and readjusting the Swiss cheese. His brows had returned to normal and he looked at her from beneath them. "I don't want to hear about it. You must not be, either."

"Either what?"

"Local."

"Oh." The tenderloin was very good and she'd discovered she was hungry. Munching, she said,

"No—not originally. Before he was killed in a car wreck my dad was an English prof at the university. In those days the faculty was a pretty cosmopolitan outfit. John and I were married in '56 and moved here. I made beef bourguignon for my first company dinner. I looked all over town for scallions, had to settle for green onions—and canned mushrooms. But it was good and I was so proud."

She laughed ruefully. Glancing at her, he said in a gentle voice, "But your guests didn't like it."

"They didn't know what it was. Oh they tried to be nice, but most of the sauce got scraped off, and Charley Nixon dipped his meat in catsup like he was eating French fries. The next time we grilled steak like everyone else."

"Coward."

"No. Not really. When in Rome, you know. And there's nothing wrong with a good charcoaled sirloin."

"True. My Sue-Ann wasn't so good with the bourguignon but she made a superior stroganoff. God. One night here I had a stroganoff attack and thought I'd die if I didn't get some. The only stuff I could find was in a can. Terrible."

"You can buy it frozen."

"Damn. Now you tell me."

"So could Karen. You probably never asked."

He shrugged. "Change that to being too bull-headed to ask. At first I made such a big deal of getting along just dandy by myself that I got as prickly as a hedgehog. I'm beginning to see things a little differently now."

"That's good." She wasn't quite prepared to explore any more in that vein. "How in the world did you happen to retire here, anyway? Karen?"

"I didn't retire here. We own a condo on the coast of Florida and I retired there. Then, after just a few weeks, Sue-Ann began to — go." His calm voice had suddenly gotten just a little deeper. "We fought it. Both of us. She's — she was — such a sweetheart. But you can't fight Alzheimer's. And Sue didn't want her friends to see her like — like she is now. She couldn't bear the idea. She was always so — beautiful, so charming, so — so on top of things."

He stopped abruptly, turned, and stared out the window where the last rays of the sun misted the broad river in pale gold. She could see the cords in his throat working.

She put out one hand, touched his. "Bob. I know. I understand."

He didn't look at her, but his hand turned,

his long, hard fingers laced hers in a grip that was almost painful.

"Yeah," he said. "You really do. I know it. God damn, Evelyn, what could hell possibly have to offer that we've not been through already?"

"I don't know. I just keep hoping I've made some brownie points somewhere."

"You've made some now."

He turned back to her smiling a little, and released her hand, giving it a quick pat as he did so. "End of wail. I promise. More coffee? I'll join you. I only cry in beer."

When it came, he slouched back against the padded booth, one long leg cocked up, and held the cup with both hands savoring the rich steam. And he talked—about his condo and wanting to get back down there, about his air force tours of duty, tossing off words like "Laos" and "Japan" and "Iwo" as though they were as common as bread and cheese. She listened with half her mind, nodding, not actually hearing. It was more like putting it on tape for listening later. The other half of her brain thought about herself and John, about the fact that in thirty years of marriage they'd taken two vacations— one to Canada in a fold-out camper with both the kids and Jessie, and the other by themselves to Phoenix to see if they'd want to retire there with the other snowbirds. They hadn't. John had a thing about sleeping comfortably only in his own bed. She'd been dismayed by seeing so few young people, and had also taken an instant dislike to the small cacti-edged squares of pink- and orange-colored rock that passed for lawns.

The waitress snapped her reverie, hovering with the coffee pot. She shook her head, covering her cup with her hand. She usually drank decaf at night, and this definitely wasn't. Climbing the walls at three A.M. was not her favorite indoor sport, but she might be doing it later anyway—and definitely would if she didn't quit now.

A chunky boater in creased dungarees and a peaked cap reading "I Am the Captain" fed change into a modern version of a jukebox. His frizzy-haired companion, in a tee-shirt that labeled each breast appropriately "Port" and "Starboard," took his arm and they went out on a miniscule dance floor, moving slowly together.

Bob Marsh looked at Evelyn and his eyebrows peaked.

"Les Brown and his Band of Renown," he said in amazement. "This is my kind of joint. Would you like a whirl?"

157

Evelyn shook her head. She'd had a sudden poignant recollection of that recent dream, of her circling a dance floor held tightly against someone's lean, warm body. She put down the coffee cup in a jerky movement that splashed dark brown on the place mat. Trying to make her voice commonplace, she said, "We'd probably better go."

"You mean—don't push our luck."

He sounded whimsical. Without looking at him, she crumpled her napkin on the plate, running quick fingers through the gray hair sliding over one cheek. He went to pay the check, and she waited for him by the swaying gangplank, savoring the cool night air, the smell of wet, the sound of water slapping at mossy pilings. Familiar things, sane things—they knew their place.

He came toward her, striding tall across the deck, casting a long black shadow beneath the yellow dock light.

"Not too bad," he said, putting the wallet back into his hip pocket. "I can still eat tomorrow. Thank you for waiting. I thought you'd run."

"I wouldn't run!" She sounded as indignant as she felt. "I—I just don't like being pushed into things."

158

"Pushed! Good God. I wasn't pushing. Music starts, people are dancing, a guy asks the girl he's with. It's a standard response, for Pete's sake. Come off it."

They got into his car and she huddled against the damp cushion as the Datsun nosed back up onto the bluff road.

She said. "It was a mistake. Probably this whole thing is a mistake."

Almost angrily he said, "It's not a mistake. For God's sake, Evelyn. I've enjoyed your company. I wouldn't have enjoyed it more or less had Sue and John been along. I'm not on the make, you dumb broad, I'm lonesome! And so are you, if you'd admit it. What's wrong with that?"

The "dumb broad" part had not come out with anger, but with humor. The anger had died. He reached over, hugged her stiff shoulders briefly, and put his hand back on the wheel again.

"Nothing," she admitted slowly. "Nothing at all. Except—except that it's so long since I've been anything but a mom and a wife that I just—don't know how to act. Besides poopy."

"Poopy?"

"That's a Poo word. It means *dumb*. As in *broad*."

159

He chuckled. "I see. It wouldn't have been my choice, but both Poo and Robby seem to fly rather well on their own beams."

Poo and Robby were safe subjects, but neither Evelyn nor her companion appeared inclined to pursue them.

I have been, Evelyn admitted to herself, about as much fun as a mortuary visitation. Thank God we don't have far to go.

He'll never ask me again. How do I feel about that?

She'd just decided that she'd feel badly for the simple fact that no one likes to be a failure when he spoke out of the darkness, proving her quite wrong.

"Listen. I've had a thought. Sunday morning why don't you fly down to St. Louis with me and watch my air show?"

She caught her breath and quite audibly gulped. "M-m-me?"

"Y-y-you. You're not scared of my airplane, are you?"

She had a sudden mental vision of the great, solid, four-winged bird soaring above the river. "No. At least I don't think I am."

"Good enough. Are you emotionally attached to some rigid Sunday regimen?"

Her mind was darting in all directions like a

trapped bird. There seemed to be no truthful way out. "No. Not really. But—"

"All right, then. I'll be down there all Friday and Saturday. Sunday early I'll zip back up here. You meet me at the field at seven sharp, allowing for morning fog. Wear slacks. There's no way of getting out of a biplane cockpit in skirts that won't give a male ground crew heart failure."

Weakly she said, "I usually babysit Poo for Brenda on Sunday evenings."

"No sweat. We'll be back by eight at the latest. Seven-thirty is more likely. Just don't tell anyone."

"Oh. Of course not." She said it a bit wryly. "Just two brass bands and the town crier. Unless you have a buddy who will tow a banner over the Wal-mart parking lot."

"Now look," he said evenly. "Didn't we just go through that? No more guilt. Right? Damn it—I'm talking about my sister-in-law. I admit that with her I'm chicken. If she isn't sure I'll be in Sunday evening she'll go back where she belongs about noon."

His voice was slightly hang-dog, but unrepentant. "Okay? Come on. Think of it—a whole day completely away from our troubles?"

A whole day away from it all. Evelyn shut

her eyes, grimaced, and decided. "Okay."

"Good girl."

The nursing home was a long, dark mass, lying quietly against tall trees. Its row of small globe lamps shone like a string of beads, making yellow, blurry dots on the side of her dew-covered Lincoln.

They got out of his Datsun rather silently. He handed her in and waited for the engine to start. She rolled down the power window and said, "Thank you for a nice time."

"I'll bet when you were a little girl in pink ankle socks you made a nice curtsey."

She couldn't see but she knew he was grinning. "I was also taught to tell the truth. It was nice, Bob. I appreciate your time."

He reached in a long finger and lightly ticked her nose. "Sunday at seven sharp," he said. "Give me an hour's leeway in case the visibility is poor. You never know around St. Louis. But I'll be there. And you had better be there, too, or I'll come and get you. Good night, Evelyn Cass."

"Good night."

He was already getting back in his car. With a sense of pure unreality she put the Lincoln in gear and drove away.

She had no way of knowing that after she'd

gone, he sat motionless in his Datsun a long, long time. And that then, abruptly, he got out and went into the quiet nursing home.

Nor could she know, of course, that her telephone had been ringing intermittently all evening, just stopping for the last time as she unlocked her kitchen door.

The house seemed silent, cold. Empty, she acknowledged sadly. But with the kitchen light familiar things sprang into proper focus: the fat-cheeked pewter jugs above the sink, her HOGS coffee cup upended on the drainboard, Poo's charming round-cheeked face beaming from the refrigerator. Hearing Romeo's plaintive cry, she let him in. He gave his half-empty dish a cursory look and requested to be let out again. She let him out. When in only a few more minutes he asked for readmittance she said, "Tough cookies, buster," turned off the light, and went through the living room toward the stairs.

It had been a long day and her head was aching again. For a lot of reasons. Too many, in fact. Coping on one's own seemed to have a lot of side effects. She devoutly hoped she could sleep and not think.

At least, she thought wearily, I have a job — and she went to bed.

Eleven

The birds in the oak tree were back to their normal chattering next morning. Evelyn lay still for a few moments, listening, remembering through the years how many times she'd done just that with the children beginning to stir in their rooms and John beside her, saying sleepily, "Morning, hon, I love you."

She loved him. She missed him—not the polite stranger in the nursing home, but the stocky figure with mussed hair, leaving a shower of bristle over the sink as he cleaned his razor, forgetting to put the seat down on the stool, whistling as he descended the stairs, pinching her fanny as he breezed by to check the weather, shovel the walks, start the car, inspect the tomatoes, or whatever else he'd set aside to do before he went to work.

He'd been a good man.

He was gone.

At the hospital, while the news of his brain

damage had sunk in, one of the girls had cried, "Oh, Evie—it could be worse! He could be dead!"

Then, she'd believed it. Now, she wasn't so sure. She wasn't sure at all. He was comfortable. He was not unhappy. He was insulated. But he wasn't—John. He was nobody.

She sighed, kicking back the covers, got up and found the room cold.

One of these days, she thought as she extracted her old woolly bathrobe from the closet, I'll have to turn the furnace on; then watch the utility bills soar.

Padding downstairs with the wry taste of her ulcer medication in her mouth, she made coffee—the ordinary brand—poked in two pieces of whole-wheat toast and sat hunched on a stool, trying to get warm. The heat from the toaster felt pretty good. Where were the hot flashes when she needed them?

An agitated yowl announced the presence of Romeo. When she opened the door he slunk inside dejectedly and made for his box. One ear was bleeding.

"Siamese or Labrador?" Evelyn inquired acidly, none too thrilled to notice muddy cat tracks over the top of the Lincoln and down the hood. "It's a good thing John isn't around, fat boy," she said, dumping Liver Delight in his

165

bowl. "You'd have been a nice throw rug weeks ago."

The telephone rang as her toast popped up. She answered with one hand, buttering with the other. "Cass's."

"It's me." *Me* was Brenda. "How's Daddy?"

"The same. How's Poo?"

"Fine. He has a new word, but you don't want to hear it. If he remembers the taste of deodorant soap I won't have to hear it, either. I just wanted to tell you — the clinic in Springfield can take me the first of November."

"Good. I'm glad, hon. Except — who's paying for it, and what are you going to do with Poo?"

"I told you, Mom. Don't worry. I'm working things out."

That's what worries me, Evelyn thought, but she didn't say it aloud.

Brenda went on, "What I called about — can you look after Poo Sunday night? There's a Disney matinee at five and I thought if you — "

"Bren, I won't be home until about eight. I've — made plans. I had no idea you'd need me sooner." She was so absorbed in actually saying the words, acknowledging to herself that she was going with Bob Marsh to St. Louis, that she didn't notice the subtle shift in Brenda's voice.

"Oh. You won't be home?"

"Not until seven-thirty or eight. I'm sorry."

"That's all right. Really. No problem. If you won't be home —"

"No. I won't be home."

"— Then I'll bring him over about eight. Don't plan dinner. I'll feed him."

Dinner at eight for a three-year-old would be a little much, anyway, for heaven's sake. Brenda was sounding even flakier than usual. "Have you found a job?"

"Sort of. I think I'm on at Bunny Burger. How about you?"

For some reason Evelyn was reluctant to tell her stepdaughter about the Princess Dress Shoppe. "I'm not sure. I've been looking."

"You might join me at Bunny Burger. We could be the first mother-daughter team in town."

"I thought you said you entered the clinic in November."

"That's a month, Mom. Two pay checks."

"Did you tell them?"

"No, I didn't. I need the job."

The ethics of the young weren't Evelyn's problem. It was a different world, all right.

Her toast was getting cold. She said, "Okay, honey, happy ears to you."

Brenda giggled. "I have mine. They're kind of cute. Well, Poo's calling. I'd better run. See you."

"See you," Evelyn echoed absently and hung up.

167

Unfortunately, the toast had all the taste of high-grade cardboard. She broke it into a napkin for the birds to eat, put in two more slices, and started scrambling some eggs.

The telephone rang again.

Grimacing, she picked it up, one eye on the thickening eggs. "Cass's." Single-handed, she dumped eggs into a dish and buttered the toast.

"Evie? Nan. At the dress shop."

"Oh. Good morning, Nan." Salt. Pepper.

"Not really," said Nan's low voice, and on cue Evelyn's heart dropped to her lambswool slippers. "I tried to call you last night—"

"I'm sorry—I didn't come in until about ten."

"Evie—I have to say no to you. I—I can't understand why he changed his mind from yesterday afternoon—but he did. And he's the boss now. I'm so sorry. I was really sure we had things worked out. I just—hate this."

In a croaky voice she said, "Don't feel so badly, Nan. You didn't say no. Your boss did. Thanks for calling."

Hanging up, she stared at the toast as though it wasn't even there. In her stunned mind it wasn't. In her mind she was seeing herself.

She'd been too fat. She was not *chic* enough.

It was kind of Nan not to say so, but that was it.

She was sloppy, old, and matronly. Her stomach stuck out and her boobs hung.

If she'd been Mary Lou with her bright hair and skinny waist and aerobics-firmed thighs she'd probably have the job.

But she wasn't, and she didn't.

Suddenly she said aloud, "Oh God!" She'd remembered the $88.33. After her insane splurge yesterday that was all she had in the world to last her for two and a half weeks when the bank would pay the minus three hundred into her account. And that was already eaten up by bills.

The eggs were cold. She didn't care. She dumped them.

With the usual final "glug!" the coffeemaker quit. She grabbed her up-ended HOG cup from the drainboard and filled it. She found the motif singularly appropriate.

Back to square one, lady—broke.

John had always said to take the sure thing first, then work from there—which was probably where his daughter got her philosophy.

Thinking of Brenda, Evelyn thought of Bunny Burger.

That was probably the sure thing: Bunny Burger. And it served her right for letting herself get sloppy, old, and matronly, with a pooched stomach and hanging boobs.

Then in a sort of crystal-clear horror she remembered Bob Marsh's words: "I always got

169

waited on by some broad-butted gal who looked like a moose."

Bingo.

She covered her eyes with her cold hands. Oh God. She might die, she might just drop dead there on the floor amid the hamburgers when he came in, when he recognized her — and with her luck that was what would happen.

Suddenly catching herself up short, she realized she was being a fool. Pride could not stand up to bills. If her stupid alter ego had any other solution, she'd listen. But in the meantime she'd better remove her tail from between her legs and get it downtown. Walking.

In the first place, the gas in the car was to take her to the nursing home, which was a bit far to walk.

In the second place, getting out of a big Lincoln to ask for a job at a hamburger joint didn't seem right.

In the third place, it would probably help the stomach, the boobs, and the thighs — which was very, very secondary at the moment, but couldn't hurt.

As she went up the stairs she had a hot flash which felt pretty good in the chilly house until she remembered that her appointment for a shot would cost thirty bucks which she no longer had. Nor could she afford the haircut.

On the way to the shower she called and cancelled both. It gave her no glow of virtue whatsoever—and the hot flash quit before the shower water warmed and she nearly froze.

Standing on the tile with her face raised to the needles of water, she let its heat beat on her hair, her eyelids, run down her naked fanny, gurgle into the drain. The wheels were churning inside her wet head. If not Bunny Burger, where else? Stuffing envelopes at home? How many times had she read that ad and heard John say what a come-on it was, how little money those hard-pressed women really made. Babysitting. The paper was full of pleas for sitting jobs and she knew it. A small town only has so many young children—and young mothers out working the jobs for which businesses will not hire grandmothers, she acknowledged grimly. Reaching for a towel, she forthrightly refused to look in the pier mirror. Then, grabbing her nail clippers, she snipped the sale tags from a new bra and panties. They couldn't be returned. None of the stuff she'd bought could be returned. She may as well apply for the job with snappy boobs and pants that wouldn't fall down around her knees. At least she owed her self-esteem that much.

As she opened the laundry hamper, last night's slacks and paisley shirt caught her eye. She totally panicked. Oh God! Oh good, righteous, ever-loving God! Sunday! Sunday, and Bob Marsh!

She couldn't go. She absolutely, unequivocally couldn't go. She was chicken. Whatever tall, courtly Bob Marsh needed with his friendly grin and his clear gray eyes, it was not "a broad-butted gal who looked like a moose" in — sweet Jesus — pink plush rabbit ears!

Blindly she sat down on the disheveled bed. In an action totally disengaged from her brain she reached back, let the new bra out another notch.

Nine o'clock. He was long gone. And he wouldn't be back until seven Sunday morning. For her.

Dandy. Evie, when you do it you do it good!

Tomorrow. She'd think about it tomorrow.

In the meantime, Scarlett, what does one wear on a brisk fall day while applying for a job slinging hash?

Wearily she put on brown slacks and a tan shirt, aware that nowadays brown and tan made her look like mud, and not particularly caring. After blow-drying, she found her hair too long to brush into shape and doggedly got out the curling iron. Standing before the bathroom mirror, patiently waiting the required ten seconds per curl, she remembered why indulging herself in professional hair appointments had become such a pleasure. Holding her arm up in the air that

172

long made the shoulder joint ache fiercely.

Done at last, she flexed the hurting arm a few times and swallowed a hefty dose of aspirin. Putting on lipstick, she noted that despite the brown and tan her face seemed hardly muddy—then realized the flush probably meant her blood pressure was up again. At least getting that checked was free, and on the way home she'd better do it. She missed lying beside John in bed, but she hardly wanted to join him in the one he was using now.

The shuffle at the mailbox told her the postman had arrived. Stepping off the bottom stair, she went across the sunny living room and opened the door. "Good morning, Harold."

Stopping halfway down the walk, he came back, dodging ivy. "Good morning, Mrs. Cass. I've been meaning to ask. How's John?"

"All right. About as well as he'll be."

"Damn. That's sure a shame. I'm sorry, Mrs. Cass. Tell him we miss him at lodge. I got a state office, now; tell him that, too." He pushed his cap back, scratched at salted black hair, grinned. "Had to buy me a tux. At my time of life."

"I'll bet you look handsome."

"My wife says so. Oh, well. It's fun. Have a good day."

"Have a good day," she echoed, and riffled through the mail in her hand. Another birthday card. From Kansas. Probably that cousin she disliked. A notice of insurance due on the car. And a long, windowed envelope from the county treasurer. Great. Property taxes.

She really didn't need to face up to either of them just now. Enough was enough.

Laying the whole pile on John's increasingly cluttered desk top, she picked up her shoulder bag from the counter and went out the kitchen door. Romeo accompanied her as far as the retaining wall where he hopped up and composed himself.

"Stay out of trouble!" she admonished him severely, and went around the Lincoln with its muddy paw marks toward the sidewalk.

Tumbril time again.

Twelve

If her destination hadn't been so scary, Evelyn would have enjoyed the walk. Each block was filled with memories. So many times she'd pushed little Jackie in his stroller down these same sidewalks, going, "Bumpity-bumpity bump!" as they went over the brick ones, Jackie echoing, "Bumpy-bumpy!" Brenda would have been lingering behind, befriending each dog, each kitten, each vagrant pet, running up, holding some furry wretch against her checkered and chubby stomach, begging, "Please, Mommy, please!"

Even in those days Bren had identified with the downtrodden. Jack, on the other hand, had always gone with the winners—as he had, even in choosing the clients for his cruise. He'd known each and every patron's financial statement by heart before he'd ever welcomed them on board. His mother had no doubt of his success—at least financially. And Michelle was charming enough to make it a social triumph.

Ruefully, she wondered—in view of her recent disasters—if he'd even let his mother on board—then chided herself for an unworthy thought. Jack was patently not selfish. Jack was practical.

And he got that, she acknowledged silently, from his father. Certainly not from her!

The maples above her head were blazing scarlet and gold, with a light breeze scuffling little windrows of leaves across the walk before her, making dry whispers and whirling small eddies through the translucent shafts of sunshine. She found herself loitering, exchanging small talk across the hedge with old Mrs. Lucas who, with her sparse gray hair in an uncompromising knob, was ruthlessly shearing dead dahlia heads. And crotchety Bill Cagan as he swept twigs and dust from his hard-surfaced driveway, and Everett Morris as he leaned on his cane, contemplating the blistered paint on the tall tower of his Italianate, one-hundred-year-old family home.

"It ain't no use," he complained as she turned to go on. "You can't get up in there. It's just for show. I've half a mind to take it off."

He wouldn't. He knew it, and as Evelyn went on down the walk, she knew it. The tower would outlast Everett.

Lord, she thought with sudden insight, it will outlast us all! We're all *old* on Sycamore Street!

Why hadn't she ever noticed that before?

"Hi! Evie!"

It was Liz Swan, pulling alongside of her in her small Toyota. Her nicely-tinted brown hair was a well-cut fluff in the morning sun, her eyes smiling behind the huge dark glasses, and her double chin comfortably buried in a turtle-neck. Liz had been Evelyn's companion for quite a few of those sundaes.

Now she gestured toward her small grand-daughter, who was waving from the child's seat in the back. "We're on our way to the Y for Judy's swimming lesson, but we're early. Need a ride somewhere?"

Evelyn waved at Judy. "No, thanks, Liz. I need the walk."

"Woman, wash your mouth! If you're going to do a Mary-Lou and leave me, I may kill myself!"

"On double cheeseburgers?"

"With bacon and mayo," Liz added and laughed. "Anyway. How are you, doll? Ben says you've been having some tough times."

"I'm okay."

"Truly? I can't help?"

"Truly. But thanks, Liz."

"Now look here, Evie Cass—if something happens you can't handle, call me—or Jane. I mean it. We've been good friends too long."

Evelyn reached out, squeezed the tanned hand on the window edge. She said, "I promise."

"Scout's honor?"

"Scout's honor."

After a long moment, Liz dropped her eyes from Evelyn's, saying, "I'll believe it when I hear it, but hope springs eternal. See you."

"See you," Evelyn echoed. As the Toyota drove out of sight, she went back to the sidewalk and turned right at the intersection. Halfway down the next block she could see the new pink of Bunny Burger, shining in the sun like strawberry flavored Maalox.

Good God, she thought. Even my metaphors betray me!

Sucking in her stomach, she made the last half block as briskly as she could, ignoring the fact her legs ached.

The small juniper bushes were neatly surrounded by wood chips, all the painting was done, and the lop-eared edifice stood alone, now revealed to be a grinning bunny with gaping mouth and a menu board on its stomach.

The busy crews had disappeared, and so—it suddenly dawned on Evelyn—had the lines of applicants.

Her heart beating with sudden rapidity, she approached the battered sign on the door and found it crossed out in big, marking-pencil slashes. However, at the bottom was the cryptic message, "Try there," and an arrow.

There was another door.

Evelyn crossed her fingers like a small child avoiding a hex and knocked.

There was a short hiatus. Then a weary voice said, "All right. Come in."

Inside was a small room, half-painted, piled high with packing boxes. It contained one straight chair, a littered desk, a chair behind the desk, and on the chair a young woman with light hair carelessly twigged up in back, wearing over-large glasses, and shuffling through an enormous stack of papers. She took off the glasses and looked at Evelyn with tired blue eyes. "May I help you?"

"I'm looking for a job," Evelyn said, sensing strongly that what she said was precisely what the young woman had hoped not to hear.

"Want mine?" The woman asked, rubbed her eyes, shook her head and half-laughed. "Sorry. Not even funny."

179

She put the glasses on the paper stack and clasped her hands on the desk before her. Evelyn was conscious of being quite impersonally looked over. "There's not much left. Almost nothing, really. But—if you like, sit there. We'll see."

Evelyn sat on the designated chair. Her bag strap fell down on her arm. Feeling awkward, she put the whole thing on the floor. The woman said,

"It's pretty dirty down there."

Evelyn looked, saw that it was. There were muddy tracks everywhere. "Oh. That's all right. It washes."

The woman shrugged. "Margaret Daniels. Ms."

"Evelyn Cass." Evelyn skipped the rest. She'd never been able to say it properly anyway. She always sounded like a honey bee.

Ms. Daniels pulled a form block toward her, shoved the other papers aside, and uncapped a ball-point pen. "Married?"

"Yes."

"Widowed?"

"No."

"Husband unemployed?"

"Nursing home."

"Ouch," said Ms. Daniels, and for a moment

sounded less like a machine and more like a human being. But it was brief. "Reason for wanting employment?"

"I'm broke," said Evelyn frankly.

The human being came back. "At least you're honest," the woman said and put down her pen. "Here," she went on, leaning forward and handing Evelyn the sheet of paper torn from the block. "Fill it in yourself. It's a refreshing change to find someone who can probably spell." She leaned back and stretched long, muscled arms from orange-colored sweater sleeves. "It's privileged information — still, fill in only what you choose. We can't quibble. Excuse me a moment."

She got up, revealing a long length of athletic body in slate-colored slacks, and went out a connecting door. As Evelyn was thumbing through her wallet trying to find her Social Security number she came back, carrying two paper cups of steaming coffee. The cups were pink with a smiling bunny on them. "Here," she said for the second time, and handed one over. "If I do say so, our stuff is pretty good."

Evelyn said, "Thank you." She found her number, scribbled it in, and handed the form back. And the woman was right about the coffee.

She put the glasses back on, ran through the information, and looked at Evelyn over the top of them. "Cass. Cass. Someone I interviewed gave that name as a reference."

"My — daughter, probably." The hesitation was because she almost said "step," then realized that irritation was no excuse for pettiness.

The interviewer didn't seem to notice. She said, "Thin girl, with long hair and slanted eyes."

"Yes. Brenda. Brenda Moore."

"That's it. She'd worked fast food before. Have you?"

"No."

"We hired her, I think."

"She thought so."

"Right. Please realize — that if we also hired you, we couldn't put her on your shift. That's company policy."

"It wouldn't matter. Brenda and I don't live together."

Ms. Daniels was tapping her teeth with her pen. "Mmm," she said. "Well."

Then she leaned forward again. "We try to put young mothers on days. What I need — what I'm looking for — are responsible people to work night shift. Five to eleven, close and clean. Nights are hard. You're not only busy, you tend to get the freaks and flakes. Are you interested?"

"At this point," Evelyn answered flatly, "I would be interested in climbing the St. Louis arch. Hand over hand. If it paid."

The other woman laughed. "We pay. But only minimum wages—at least, at first. And it's just a six-hour shift, but believe me, lady, you'll work your tail off."

Her eyes had gone back to the form, scanning it in a cursory manner. Then suddenly the scan became less cursory. She went back, reread some lines, then looked at Evelyn again—a very level look and Evelyn's heart sank.

But her words were not negative.

"It says here," she said, "that you have three and a half years of college."

"Yes." How long ago that seemed!

"You never finished."

"I got married."

"What was your major?"

"Education. With a minor in business."

"Good God."

"I beg your pardon?"

This woman's air of self-sufficiency—and her *age*—were beginning to irritate Evelyn—an irritation she knew, sensibly, she could not afford. But did she look *that* doddering?

Ms. Daniels, however, was smiling. "I'm sorry. I didn't mean to sound rude. It's just that I've interviewed so many drop-outs and illiterates in the last few days— Never mind. I'm almost scared to ask the next question, but I will. Have you possibly had any experience with computers?"

Evelyn thought wryly of the one John had lugged home and installed in his den after he'd updated the system at the hardware store. He'd insisted she sit down and tinker with it, and she had—enough to get the rudiments. But later, after his father was in the nursing home, her son had hauled it away to his house, saying, "You don't need this, Mom," and she'd been glad. The shelf was an ideal spot for Poo's picture books.

To Ms. Daniels she said uncertainly, "A little. We had one. My husband used it for business. I mostly played with it."

"I see." Margaret Daniels was tapping her teeth again. She gestured around her with her free hand. "This will be our computer set-up. It should be in tomorrow. I hope."

She paused. Evelyn wondered if she should say something inane like "That's nice," but settled for nodding.

The woman took a deep breath. "There's just

184

been no one else," she said almost inaudibly. Her tired blue eyes swept Evelyn's application form again, then Evelyn herself. "I need someone willing to train for manager."

Evelyn's jaw dropped. Manager! Visions of a desk, a nice business suit, a secretary zipped through her head. Incredulously she said, "But you're the manager!"

"Only until I train a local. I move from place to place."

Then, looking straight into Evelyn's wide eyes and accurately guessing at the heart suddenly triphammering beneath the tan shirt, she said gently, "It's not a sugarplum job. Not only must you deal with personnel and supplies and things of that sort, but company policy dictates that *first* you go on the floor and train with the whole crew. Managers have to know how to do everything from drive-up to shake machine and do it whenever there's a need. You'll notice the day we open that no one is allowed to stand on protocol. The district supervisor may be sacking fries and the home office man running the shake machine. That's the way it is. Everyone together. A team."

She took a deep breath and leaned back. "Also, you must be willing to greet the customers, find seats for them, fill their coffee

185

cups—take their schlock. With a smile. Always a smile. Even when you long to paste them a good one."

Evelyn said wryly, "You make it sound like a real treat."

"Anyone who works with the public knows the great American mass *is* no treat. But—there are some very fine people in that mass."

Evelyn thought of Porter. And Bob Marsh. "Yes," she said.

"What I'm saying is don't underrate the demands of the job. You'll go limping home many a night thinking you're going to die, and even then I'll have you coming in the next morning doing extra hours on the computer. You'll wear a uniform and ears. But—there will be more pay if you prove up. And it's a damned good company."

Evelyn took a deep breath and mentally scratched the business suit. And the secretary. *Beggars can't be choosers* came to mind, but she didn't say that. What she did say was, "How long will I train—before I know—or you know—I can handle it?"

Ms. Daniels shrugged. "A month. Two. That will tell me. But you will get paid more from the start, and it goes up again when I hand over the store." She quoted a dollar over minimum wage and then the manager's salary — not royal — in fact, just about what Mary Lou spent on her jaunts to the beauty spas, but enough to make a sizeable dent in Evelyn's debts. If she could do it. She swallowed and said, "I'll try. Thank you for the opportunity."

And Margaret Daniels smiled — a real smile. "Welcome," she said. "You're now a Bunny Person."

She came around the desk, looked Evelyn up and down. "Let's see. Size sixteen? Or eighteen? The pants are tight. Try eighteen. You can always take them in, and comfort rates before glamour around here. A sixteen in shirts? No, an eighteen there, too. You're pretty chesty, and the inspectors don't like gaping buttons when they come looking." She had turned to rummage through the stack of boxes. Dropping tissue paper on the floor, she laid a pair of double-knit gray slacks across Evelyn's arm, added a gray shirt with pink piping, and held out a plastic bag. At Evelyn's blank look, she said, "Your ears. Sorry. Regulation. Here — let me show you how to put them on."

Evelyn sat still, not because she was obedient, but because she didn't believe quite yet that this was really happening to her.

A gray plastic hairband held a stretch-knit

187

cap to confine the hair. From each side sprang a nine-inch, gray plush rabbit ear. Pink-lined. Lopped.

Margaret Daniels adjusted the concoction to her satisfaction, then leaned back against the desk, arms crossed.

"Not too bad," she said critically. "You look rather like a Mommy Bunny."

"Would you like to know," asked Evelyn rashly, "what I feel like?"

"A perfect idiot," Margaret answered, and nodded. "I know. I've worn one. But keep this in mind: out there on the floor there will be twelve of you, all alike, all wearing ears, and most of the time you'll be so damned busy you wouldn't know if you had Minnie Mouse on your head. That helps. It really does."

She went back around the desk and sat down, draining her coffee cup. "This is Friday. Right? Night-shift training sessions start Monday at eight in the morning. The side door will be unlocked—the one on the east. They last all day and you eat the trial runs. Pay starts Monday, too. No uniforms worn until we open. That's a week from Monday. Let's see—have I covered everything? Oh—wear comfortable shoes. I mean it. No one at Bunny Burger sits down except on break."

Then she took off her glasses again and smiled. "End of tape recording. Questions?"

Evelyn was taking off the ears. She looked at them, shook her head, and put them back in the plastic bag. She was thinking that Poo would love them. "No," she answered and couldn't seem to keep the wryness from her voice. "I don't think so."

"Evelyn."

The tone caught Evelyn's ear, even before she glanced up. She found Margaret Daniels looking at her very levelly.

"Don't put us down, Evelyn. We fill a public need, and we try to do a good job. No one needs to feel demeaned working for Bunny Burger. If they do—then they'd better get on at the Ritz."

It was a verbal slap. And Evelyn had it coming.

She knew it, and she felt the red mount to her face. Seeing the flush, the other woman went on more kindly, "I'm sorry if I was rude. I'm really glad you applied. I think we can work together. And—honestly—it's a good company, Evelyn. They reward competence. I'll see you Monday."

Evelyn made herself speak. "Thank you for giving me this chance. I really appreciate it."

Margaret Daniels smiled. The door closed. Evelyn was back on the street, uniforms over her arm and plastic bag in hand. As she started in a daze back up to her own neighborhood a hot flash hit her in waves and the sweat began to pour. Muttering, "Damn!" she faced into the cool fall breeze, grateful that it was blowing toward her down Sycamore.

She had not come off well in that interview, and she had gotten far better than she deserved—by chance. Only by chance. That made prospects precarious no matter how she rationalized. The managerial position was no plum until she had it—and obviously it must be earned. Earned! By a fifty-six-year-old matron who hadn't worked for pay since the late forties when she'd shelved books in the library for a quarter an hour!

Crackling in her bag were the insurance and benefit papers Ms. Daniels had given her—policies which wouldn't kick in until training was over. That was all right; she didn't plan on breaking a leg or anything. And after all, she was eventually going to be more than a hash slinger. A far better thing than she'd anticipated. If she could keep up. Well, she'd have to keep up. It was called "survival."

Also, something told her she'd best not mention the managerial part to Brenda—at least not until she had to. Brenda had a way of turning things to her own benefit regardless of the welfare of others. She'd experienced that before.

In fact, she'd best not mention it to anyone. Not yet. It was a cowardly form of self-protection. If she failed . . .

On that uncertain note the noon whistle blew.

The factory had been packed up and gone for years, but the fellows down at city hall still punched the twelve o'clock button. If they didn't, they said, some folks would never even eat lunch.

All her neighbors along Sycamore had gone inside, probably to do just that, and Evelyn was grateful for it. She didn't want anyone to see her looking six inches tall.

Would things ever, ever be normal again?

No, Evelyn. Not what *had* been normal.

John was gone. The house was going.

Change. That's what she was in for—and there was no use kicking and screaming about it anymore.

"With your shield or on it," her father used to say. Evelyn sighed and entered her house.

Thirteen

Back home, Evelyn rather humbly climbed the stairs to try on her uniform. The jacket was fine. The pants were a little large around the waist, but even a total klutz like she was could take in a band of elastic—if the pants didn't shrink. If they shrunk, she'd be in trouble.

She did not look in the pier mirror, nor did she try on the bunny ears.

Gathering up the rest of her laundry, she threw both top and bottom in the wash with it. Wearing the brown and tan again, and munching warmed-over toast, she went out on the patio to regroup her forces.

The coleus still needed pinching. A few plants had even thrust out spiky blue blossoms—not a desirable thing. She turned her back on them, pulled the chair around to catch the sun, and slouched in it dispiritedly.

Then she remembered she'd forgotten to have

her blood pressure checked. Drat. Tomorrow. Surely she'd had her quota of disasters for today.

What was her next magical trick, she asked herself and thought of Bob Marsh.

At least he couldn't accuse her of growing moss!

She found herself twisting her wedding band around and around her finger, watching the deep-set double row of diamonds flash in the afternoon sun. It was her second ring. John had surprised her with it on their thirtieth anniversary; since then he'd laughingly named it her "worry stone." He could always tell when she was upset, he'd said, because she'd spin the circle around and around.

As she was doing then.

So, Evelyn Matthews Cass. What now?

The answer was patently all about her. She'd better list the house.

At least I don't have any friends in the real estate business, she thought wryly as she went into the kitchen for the telephone. She chewed on the second piece of toast as she dialed the first of ten choices. Small towns may not have much else to offer but there was always property to sell.

The lady-like voice that answered said, "Why,

yes, indeed. We would be interested. As a matter of fact, I think we have an agent in your vicinity at the moment, looking at store buildings. If I can get him on our radio, would it be convenient if he called right now?"

Why not? Bite the bullet, Evelyn.

"I'd be very happy to talk to him," she said, and hung up, realizing grimly she *had* been happier by a considerable degree. Nonetheless, putting it off wouldn't advance any cause, especially hers.

Her sole sop to hospitality was wiping off the toast crumbs and mending her lipstick. Real estate agents wouldn't expect to be entertained.

Hardly ten minutes had passed before she heard the authoritative "clunk" of a car door. She took a deep breath, plumped a divan pillow as she passed, and opened the front door.

Coming up the walk *sans* Labrador but with the same swaggering gait she'd seen the other day was Victor Bonnelli.

He saw her standing there, and said, "Hi. No cats?"

"Not—at the moment. You don't like cats?"

"I like civilized animals. A cat is never civilized, whatever you may think."

He'd gained the porch and stepped up on it, turning to look back down beneath the fringe

194

of ivy to the tree-lined street stretching quietly in stately red and gold splendor. He said over his thick shoulder, "You really want to sell this place, Mrs. Cass?"

"I have to sell this place, Mr. Bonnelli."

"Yeah. I heard about John. Sorry."

He turned around. He was just her height and four times as wide. His eyes were very black in the broad, olive face. His brows were black, too, and the heavy, springing crest of curly, gray-streaked hair made him look curiously like a cherub grown older. "I used to stay all night with John," he said, "when my old man was on a drunk. Which happened often when he was out of work—which was also often. We made our own wine so he had an unlimited supply. May I come in?"

"Oh. Of course. I'm new at this. What do you need to do?"

"As far as you're concerned, not much. Poke around a little, if you don't mind."

"No. No, not at all. Can I help?"

"Later. Say, in about ten minutes. I know this place pretty well."

He'd taken out a notebook and was moving around the living room, jotting as he went. He pushed aside a drape on the large windows, put a finger on the leak stain, glanced back at her and said, "Ooops." Then he started for the stairs.

Suddenly she didn't want to watch. It was like undressing a friend. She said, "I'll be out back."

On the way she considered making coffee and decided Mr. Bonnelli might prefer a beer.

She was right. He reappeared a little later and said, "Yes, thank you." When she came back with it, he shook his head at the Pilsener glass, popped the tab on the can, and drank deeply. Then he put the can on the metal table and sighed. "Good stuff."

He plopped into one of the chairs, one leg stretched out straight in front of him. From this position he turned and looked at her closely.

"You're not Pat."

"No. Pat died. I'm Evelyn."

"That's right. Shit!" he said, slapping his forehead. "Mama wrote me about that. I just forgot. It's been a long time. Sorry."

"That's all right. It was thirty-some years ago."

"Wow," he said, and blew out his cheeks. "Yeah. I guess. I was still in Golden Gloves when I saw John last. I've had this thing thirty-nine." He slapped his knee, saw her puzzlement, and explained, "A wooden leg, lady. Prosthesis, in polite terms. You didn't notice?"

"No. Not at all." But that explained the odd gait. It wasn't swagger, it was necessity.

On the other hand, she thought, with this man it possibly might be swagger.

He was saying, "Funny. After all this time I still think everybody notices."

With a strong sense of asking because he wanted her to, she said, "What happened?"

"Bad carrier landing. Blew off my leg and half my private parts." He grinned. "I've still got the yen, just not the means."

The words were outrageous, but Evelyn found herself thinking that was probably what he said when he first met any woman. He wants us to know. He doesn't want any misunderstandings. She answered, "You were probably lucky to keep your life."

He drank again. "There was a time when I didn't think so. It took me out of the fight ring. It lost me my girl. When you're twenty-one you have different priorities."

"Tell me about it," she said a bit grimly.

He glanced over at her, and suddenly laughed. "I have," he said. "Jesus. It's been a longer day than I thought. Anyway. As far as I can see, the place is in pretty good shape.

197

A few leaks. A plumbing problem. A good roof—"

She interrupted: "Plumbing? What's wrong with the plumbing?"

"The drains are going. It's that old pipe. They use all plastic stuff now. It looks like you've insulated—"

"Two years ago."

"Good. It needed it. In that north bedroom of John's I used to freeze my dick off. When I had it. Oh—and central air. That's always a plus. I need some figures—monthly water, heat, that sort."

She knew them and he wrote them down, leaning on the table, writing with an enormous fist, curls falling in his eyes. He asked about other things—like the taxes—and said, "Wow. These grand old places—they'll eat you up! By the way, how's Jessie?"

"She's fine. She'll be over for Thanksgiving. You must drop by."

"Ring me. If you don't, I'll forget—and I'd like to see her. She's a doll. Okay, lady. Let's try—say—forty-five-five. Then we can drop it if someone squawks on the basement. They won't notice the plumbing."

She caught her breath—$45,500! It sounded like a fortune. "Do you think I'll get it?"

"You need it?"

"Yes. I'm afraid I do."

"I'll get it for you. For a friend. For John. It just might take a while. Can you scrape up the taxes?"

"I don't know. I don't see how."

"On the bottom rung?"

"Pretty close."

"Maybe we can make some sort of deal. I'll talk to the boss. I've only been back from California a while but my track record's pretty good. He knows it."

"Whatever you can do. I'll really be grateful."

"Ask me to dinner some night. I'm getting damned tired of canned rigatoni." He was gathering up his papers. Squashing the beer can in one massive hand, he laid it on the table. Evelyn didn't think he was showing off. It was something he probably always did, had done for years.

He was shoving back the curls, looking at her soberly. "If I went to see John—would it do any good?"

"He only remembers the '40s. He might think you were your father."

"You're kidding." Then he went on swiftly, "I'm sorry. Of course you're not. You wouldn't kid about a thing like that. I just didn't realize

. . . Shit," he ended lamely and held out his hand. "Hang in there. John deserved the best. It looks like he finally got it. But if he doesn't know he's got it, think about yourself. I learned that little gem thirty-nine years ago."

She took the hand, and found it warm, friendly.

"Thank you for coming."

"Sure. Do you want a sign in your yard or not?"

She grimaced. "Must I?"

"No. I don't need it. Thanks for the beer. When I have a customer, I'll call in advance. Okay?"

"Oh, yes. I'd appreciate it."

"No sweat. Say hi to John again. For what it's worth. See you around, kid."

After he left, the patio seemed twenty percent larger. He was a big man. Not urbane, like Bob Marsh. Not exactly hail-fellow like Porter and the others. Forthright. That was it. Very forthright.

She liked him, she decided, as she picked up the scrunched beer can and took it into the house.

Fourteen

Saturday, between trips to the nursing home, Evelyn roamed about her house distractedly. Dreading the ring of the telephone and the sound of Vic Bonnelli's voice, which it never was, she was also looking around her with the stark realization that she might suddenly have to move — and how does one deal quickly with the accumulation of four people over thirty years? Also, having made the deal without considering the consequences, where would she go?

She finally took refuge in a large pan of walnut brownies, and since Brenda's number didn't answer, she sat down with coffee and munched by herself.

This brought on another fit of self-pity. Not only did she have to meet Bob Marsh in the morning, but she was fatter than she'd been the day before!

By the time she made her last call at the nursing home she was wrapped in the calm cloak of simple despair. There was no way out of anything. If she could simply live through Sunday, the next day would mark the era of a New Evelyn. Working a job, budgeting, squeezing pennies, cutting corners — in short, Wonder Woman!

Old Evelyn said the barnyard word that was fast becoming her favorite. John, halfway into his pajamas, looked at her sharply. For one brief moment, she was glad he didn't know who she was.

"Sorry," she mumbled, and helped him into bed, tucking the covers around his knees. "Green Acres" was already on the television screen. Followed by "Beverly Hillbillies," an hour's worth of the old "Gunsmoke" series would see him through the evening and into sleep. Thank God his roommate liked them also. If Ed had been a night soap opera fan there would have been real trouble.

She had kissed him and started out of the room when his mild voice caught her: "You need a haircut."

Her heart surged. Shivering, she swung around with her very breath stopped in her chest. "John? JOHN!"

He frowned. "Don't yell," he said. "I didn't mean to be rude. My wife, Pat, wears her hair long and kind of fluffy. You couldn't do that. Your neck's too short. You just need a good shaping job, that's all."

Exultation drained from her. Lifelessly she answered, "Probably. Good night, John."

"Good night," he said, but his eyes were already on the screen. He didn't even watch as she left. He never watched.

In the silent hallway she leaned against the shadowed wall, feeling the strength flow back into her knees. At the desk, beneath a round pool of yellow light, the young male nurse asked anxiously, "Mrs. Cass—are you okay?"

She took a deep breath. "I'm fine. I just thought—for one minute there I thought he recognized me."

The young man shook his head. "He won't," he said kindly. "Don't kid yourself, Mrs. Cass, because he won't. Not ever. The capacity is gone. Would you like a cup of coffee?"

"No," she said, and forced a smile. "I need to get going."

"Oh—I almost forgot. Emma said if I saw you to hand over these." He held out two books. "She'd like more."

Evelyn took the books. "Monday. Tell her I promise." She glanced at what she had, saw one of the glitzes and the Harold Bell Wright. "Is she still reading the third one?"

He said vaguely, "I—I suppose so," and she had the sudden brilliant flash that what he'd been doing with his feet propped up had hardly been sorting room charts. Oh, well. Nights were probably pretty long at the nursing home.

"I'll bring more next time," she promised, and went out to the car.

The Lincoln didn't seem to want to start. Then when it did the engine had a strange burring sound for a moment before settling into its usual powerful hum.

It had done that the other day at the grocery store. She remembered, now. But—it seemed okay. Cheap gas, she thought, and dismissed the subject. Another was pressing hard on her mind.

If that had been recognition in her husband's voice she would be having the happiest moment of her entire life right at this time, in John's arms again, needing only to wait for him to get well.

It had not been recognition.

Moreover, the keen disappointment was having a reverse effect. There were no longer waves of anger or resentment. She seemed to have fought her way through them to something else: admission that there was no hope—and with admission was the bare, beginning edge of acceptance.

Perhaps Bob Marsh was right. Was it a dangerous thought, or was it her only salvation, her personal ticket to a dignified survival?

Many women nowadays lived to be ninety. That was twenty or thirty years without the one they loved knowing a single day of it!

Suddenly Evelyn was beset with the enormous sense of needing to make some vital decisions—without the slightest presence or thread or influence or memory of what had been so for three decades.

She drove up the long grade to the park at the top of the bluff, nosed the Lincoln against the retaining wall, turned it off, and sat very still.

John had never come up here. John hadn't cared for boats and water made him seasick. His long voyages on troop transports during the war had been miserable weeks of pure hell.

She was the one who loved the river. This evening it was a broad band of steel, running between tall humps of darkening hills. The dying sun gave each ripple a rose colored edge. The burnished red and gold of the far shore had turned to maroon and black with the advancing autumn, the bare bones of the trees beginning to show through tattered leaves. There was no movement, not even tiny cars on the miniscule bridge—only a seagull, wearily flapping home.

She thought of Bob Marsh. He was not like that gull, far away from the salt flats and coastlines, totally content in narrow inland waterways. The gull had probably been born inland, had never known anything other than the rocky points and cluttered wingdoms of the Mississippi. He'd die happy, never aware he'd missed the open sea, the untrammeled sky above it.

Bob knew.

Pondering the poignant difference between man and bird, Evelyn got out of the car and wandered slowly over to an empty picnic table. She sat down where she could see the long barges with their huffy little towboats cleaving the waters upstream through the swing bridge, the bobbing buoys marking the deep channel, the ragged line of eagles hunched in broken trees at the waterline where they watched with fierce yellow eyes for anything edible to break the moving surface.

A tiny bargeman tossed something over the side—a sandwich crust, a fragment of cookie, a piece of cheese. It never touched the water.

Evelyn applauded. The eagle soared to an empty tree, landed, and tore at his booty. The others never even glanced away from their intense stares.

The tug tooted and the bridge began to swing majestically. The sun dropped to a red rim behind a western bluff. All alone, Evelyn put her chin in her hands and shut her eyes. She tried to banish all thoughts of Bob—and John—and Jack and Brenda—from her head. All outside influences. She had to do this by herself. For herself.

There were many other women precisely in

her position. She nodded to them every day; they never seemed to want to talk. They crept in and out of the nursing home, sat endless hours at a bedside, holding a flaccid hand, bringing goodies that stayed uneaten, messages that were unheard. They walked a certain path week after week like patient cows, treading deeper and deeper, narrower and narrower until they were in a canyon of their own creation, out of sight and sound, moving in the circle of their day's routine.

She'd not done that. Yet.

In old India, when a man died, his wife was burned with him on his funeral pyre. It was called *suttee*.

What she'd been doing was trying to commit emotional *suttee*. It certainly wasn't good for Brenda, nor Poo, nor Jack, nor Jessie—and it very likely would bury her, too.

Was that what they wanted—that hopeless sisterhood of women who found themselves, as she had, a pair but not a pair?

A lucid corner of her mind protested, and she listened. It told her that was the wrong question. The right one was what would their husbands have wanted for them?

And she wasn't thinking of poor marriages. That was a different situation. She was thinking of good marriages, such as she had had with John. In that case, was she not only doing herself an injustice, but was she being unjust to him?

Was she? Wouldn't a good man like John want her to be happy? Or was she selfishly deluding herself?

She moved uneasily in the long shadowy fingers of dusk creeping across the rough grass beneath her feet. It sounded so crass: John is dead. Long live Evelyn.

What if it were: Evelyn is dead. Long live John?

Please God, she said softly, her eyes shut tight against the pain. I think I'd mean it. I think I'd feel that one good relationship deserves another.

No. She didn't mean that. Not purely that. There were inflections there about relationships she wasn't yet prepared to consider. What she did mean was simple, dignified human living with her family and with friends. John would never want to be a millstone. She mustn't allow him to be what he'd never want.

It seemed a clear, fair resolution. Her mind moved to Bob Marsh, and now—at least at this moment—there was at last no real sense of betrayal.

"I enjoy your company," he'd said last evening. "I wouldn't enjoy it more or less if Sue or John were sitting here. I'm not on the make. I'm lonesome. And if you'd admit it, so are you."

He'd also called her a "dumb broad"—and

probably justly.

Getting up and walking slowly back to her car she stooped, picked up a small, round pebble, and threw it high in the air arching toward the water.

An eagle soared, wheeled, caught it. With an indignant squawk he also dropped it. She could almost feel his yellow-eyed glare. She shrugged and laughed.

"Sorry," she said, "but we can't win them all, you know."

One or two would be nice, she added silently. She started the car, waited through the burring noise, and drove down the hill toward home. She felt almost as if she'd had a shower and washed her hair.

What she had done, rightly or wrongly, was reason herself out from beneath a sense of betrayal. She hoped it was right. She hoped fervently it was right and that she could continue to think so.

Bob Marsh had been sound in saying that guilt could defeat both of them.

At this point she could go with Bob tomorrow without an emotional burden on her shoulders. Other burdens were more mundane and had nothing to do with him. Also, she decided, she could tell Bob about Bunny Burger. He'd be the first to know—her trial balloon. Then as the news gradually seeped around to the girls—and especially Mary Lou—she would have learned to handle it gracefully.

The idea was great. She hoped it worked. Mary Lou had not one mean bone in her firmly disciplined body. It was just that unfortunately her tongue operated on her impulses and her impulses many times came too quickly. They'd all seen her turn on Porter, making him feel like a perfect idiot, then be immediately sorry and try to make amends, optimistically disregarding the sting that had to remain.

Yet the idea of anything happening to Porter, of losing her husband, frightened Mary Lou beyond words. Even the simple problem of his catching a cold had her hovering like a mother hen. He was her rock, her stone foundation.

With cracks, Evelyn reminded herself wryly. Don't I know! I found a nasty one yesterday and I'm still in shock!

John had always said Port was a *lonely* man. When Mary Lou had been out of town, he'd always wanted Porter to come to their house for a beer, a meal, a casual night of television. On a few occasions he'd even gone off to bed, leaving his friend and his wife to finish the crossword together, to watch the news and weather, to see the last of the movie. He certainly wouldn't have done that if he'd had any idea Port had a yen for

Evelyn. John was kind, but not that kind!

She felt uncomfortable now, remembering those evenings, yet she couldn't recall one instance in which Port had even tried to hold her hand! Were yesterday's conclusions right? Had the signs been there anyway, and she had been too secure, too disinterested to notice?

As she got out of the car, she saw a pitiful bundle crouched on her kitchen step.

"Move!" she said, using her foot. Romeo was a mere streak shooting into the kitchen before she even got the light on. While she fumbled for it the "slup-slup" in the dark proved that after a few hours' lapse Kitty Yum had become palatable again.

As for herself, there was still the tuna fish.

Unfortunately, on inspection, it had all the appeal of the Mystery Meat.

Recklessly she scooped up the last four brownies and went on into the living room. What the hell? Wonder Woman didn't start until Monday.

Fifteen

Sunday morning dawned crisp and hazy. The ragged tops of the bluffs poked through tattered patches of misty fog. At a quarter of seven, Evelyn parked at the fence of the airport. Rows of bright aircraft shone with dew and the resident dog poking his nose through the chain-link by her car had enormous and muddy paws.

The sky was silent, obscure.

As she waited, she must have napped a little for when she opened her eyes again, bright shafts of sun had dried the quiet wings. The dog was stretched on the warming office doorstep cleaning himself languorously. There was the thrum of a distant engine coming from the south.

Immediately she panicked. All yesterday's calm rationale deserted her and logic dissolved into uncertainty. She was wearing the only pair of good blue jeans she owned and a blue cotton shirt: were they the right things? She'd curled her hair carefully so that at least temporarily it flowed in a smooth silver line that moved with her head, she'd taken care with her eye make-up and her lipstick—the only things that wouldn't run when she got hot—she'd put on penny loafers and shined them, and loaded her junk and a wad of Kleenex into a denim bag. She was, in short, as good as she could get with what she had for basics.

How was that to stack up against "beautiful, charming" Sue-Ann?

It probably wouldn't. In despair she said the agricultural word she'd noticed Vic Bonnelli seemed to favor, too. Yet the situation was already out of hand—it was too late to back off. He'd said he'd come and get her at home if she wasn't here, and she knew in her bones that he would.

Well—damn it, he'd asked her. He surely knew what he was getting!

She reached into her bag, got an antacid tablet, and crunched it to combat the breakfast toast that seemed to be making lumps in the pit of her stomach. The dog's ears had pricked. He got up, stretched, and ambled over to the fence. She locked her car and stood beside him, saying, "Jump on me and you're a dead puppy!" She leaned on the fence to support her knees. They both waited.

She was expecting the morning-black silhouette of an old biplane to burst through the haze at the end of the runway, land smoothly, and taxi up to her. A dapper form in whipcord jodhpurs, leather jacket and helmet, white scarf blowing, would then swing from the cockpit, circa 1934 and C. B. DeMille.

Instead, the old Stearman came from behind her, roaring in over the roof of the office building. Its big balloon tires settled firmly into the drying grass beside the surfaced runway, tossing up bits of leaves and dandelion heads. With a faintly weaving grace it rolled on down toward the south, slowed, again roared as the tail swung around, bobbled up on to the asphalt, and grumbled its way back to the fence. The sudden cut of the old Wright engine left a vacuum, an emptiness filled only by the last few lops of the enormous propeller.

A cheerful voice said, "Good morning!"

A long leg in faded jeans thrust a sneakered foot out and down on the lower wing, followed by another. The rest of Bob Marsh appeared, sliding lightly to the ground. As he came around the back side of the big wings toward

Evelyn, she saw he also wore a red pullover shirt and had goggle-marks around his gray eyes. His lean face was grinning.

"Good girl!" he said, opening the gate for her. "I knew you'd be here. Hooray for our side. Here, Snarf, I brought you a goody."

He took a plastic-wrapped steak bone from his hip pocket, stripped the wrapping, and handed it to the dog who accepted it calmly and trotted back to the step. "His name's Snarf," he added, "for evident reasons. Hey, you look great! Golly, I'm glad to see you. This is going to be a good day. C'mon."

She followed him around the towering wings. Her heart was bumping inside her shirt. The airplane was big. Not big—it was huge; its nose soared high above her head.

"Step up on the bottom wing," he said, taking her hand and boosting. "Stay to the rubber strip or I'll bat you one. Nobody steps off on the fabric without being mortally wounded by the pilot. Remember that. Upsadaisy. Now, go on—you're riding in the front hole. I fly from the back."

She felt the wings tip a little as he followed her, and heard him chuckle.

"Remember, I said there isn't any graceful way to get in and out of a cockpit? Swing one

215

leg over, put it on the seat, get the other one in and sit down. There we go. Good show."

Graceful she hadn't been but at least she was *in*.

She found herself on a padded seat, straddling a stick, with the cockpit about chin level on both sides and absolutely nothing to see up front but round, black engine. Now she understood why in old World War II movies the pilot was always weaving from side to side.

Bob was saying, "Here," and handing her a leather helmet. "Put it on and we'll adjust the goggles."

She obeyed. He tightened the chin strap, snugged the goggles, pushed them back up on top, and suddenly became aware that the brown eyes looking at him were a little anxious. He said, "Hey. Not scared?"

"N-no. I don't think so."

"Don't be. This old gal is as sturdy as a Mack truck."

"No — no parachutes?"

"You want to jump out of a perfectly good airplane?"

He looked so indignant she laughed. She had to laugh.

"No. I guess not."

"Okay then. See the doobies on the floor?

Those are rudder pedals and control cables. Keep offa d' feet. I'm flying this one and I don't want help. Now, fasten your seat belt and fasten it tight. Good. Ignore the stick. When it waggles I'm waggling mine in back. Here's our program. I'll start the engine—I put in a starter a few years ago; I got tired of either bumming a prop or tying her tail to the fence—and we'll sit a minute while I check her out. And don't worry about sitting; it doesn't mean there's anything wrong. I'll turn her around, and we'll take off from here. It will be about a twenty-minute ride. We'll circle the St. Louis field, and unless the wind has changed we'll land from the north there, too, taxi up, and tie down. Okay? Because once that Wright J 6-7 starts, kiddo, there's no talking."

"Oh."

His eyes crinkled. Suddenly he was kneeling beside her, scooping up both cold hands in his warm ones, and his face was very close. "Look," he said gently, "I'm not going to let you back out. I decided that coming up here—because I want you to go, I want you to fly with me. If I'm being selfish, what the hell. But—there is one thing you do need to know, Evelyn Cass. You're breaking new ground. My wife never flew with me in this aircraft. There are no ghosts sitting with you. It's a different ballgame. Okay?"

"Okay."

He looked at her a moment longer. And with her heart beating rapidly she returned the gaze. "Okay," she said, and she *thought* she meant it. She *knew* she wanted to please this man beyond mere courtesy, but the reason was not yet looming with any particular importance other than sheer ego.

He nodded, satisfied, squeezed her hands and put them back in her lap. "Attagirl. Oh—it may get a little bumpy as we cross the river; it often does. No sweat. Ready?"

She nodded.

He disappeared. She felt the aircraft shake as he climbed into the rear cockpit and did unseen things back there—things that buzzed and gurgled and clacked. Between her knees the stick wiggled from side to side and the rudder pedals went in and out. He called, "Ready to go?"

She nodded and closed her eyes. Ahead of her, the big radial engine coughed, sputtered, hesitated. The propeller swung erratically, then the Wright burst into an ear-shattering roar as the prop became a blur. True to what he said, it snarled, slowed, snarled again. The entire aircraft bucked, trying to fly, but held back by enormous forces.

Then everything settled into a steady thrum. The tail moved around. They rumbled forward majestically, bumping over into the grass, the bumping intensified and smoothed as the air began to rush by her ears. Then the nose went gently upward, the flying wires began to sing — and when she opened her eyes they were in the air.

Nevertheless, it took her a good five minutes to unclench her fingers from the sides of the cockpit, relax the shoulder muscles whose rigidity was beginning to hurt, pull down the goggles, and timidly sit erect enough to look over the side.

It was a toy world below, a world of tiny houses and barns, of miniature cars on threadlike highways, and even more miniscule cows and horses calmly breakfasting on pasture grass. To her amazement she noted that farm ponds were not round but neatly halved ovals, and that the blazing gold of the Spanish-needle daisy that rioted along the roadways also spread like a flowing yellow river across the rolling farmlands, and that the abandoned stone quarries held waters of jeweled and iridescent blue.

In a field below two leggy colts gamboled happily while their mothers munched. Evelyn laughed, turned back to the helmeted, goggled head in the rear, and pointed over the side. He looked, nodded, and suddenly put the two left wings down, turning in a gentle circle. After her stomach settled, they watched the two babies frolic for a moment, then the Stearman regally righted itself and flew on.

By the time they reached the majestic bend of the Missouri River into the Mississippi, Evelyn had genuinely begun to enjoy herself and could happily have flown on and on. Yet, just at the other side were the lines of tied-down aircraft looking like bright strings of crosses on brown-green grass, the mushroom tent tops of stalls and refreshment pavilions clustered about hangar buildings with unintelligible hieroglyphics on their roofs, and the milling colonies of people.

They began to circle. When Evelyn felt the big nose go down and the flying wires start singing a different song, she closed her eyes, gripped the cockpit sides again, and braced herself. The wind seemed to roar by her ears forever. So I'm chicken, she told herself, but he won't know and I'm too old to handle more than one thing at a time. I just wish we were down —

Then she realized they were, and had been for some time.

A little sheepishly she glanced around and caught his eyes, below the raised goggles. They were crinkled again, and she knew he was being too polite to laugh.

The old Stearman was chugging its way to an empty gap in the parked rows. Once there it roared and swung its tail around, then chuckled into silence. Whang, whang, whang went the slowing propeller.

The aircraft shook as Bob climbed out and made the one long stride up the wing to her side. His helmet was in his hand. As she pulled off hers, he asked the word she was becoming quite accustomed to hearing from him. "Okay?" he said.

"Okay," she said, and she meant it. He knew she did. He suddenly reached out one brown hand and gently fluffed up her smooth silver hair. It was almost a tender gesture — and he cured it swiftly by grabbing a soft handful, tilting her head back and smacking her exuberantly on both cheeks. "Welcome aboard!" he said, and inside she could almost hear a chorus of "My Buddy." "Now. Getting out is the reverse of getting in. There isn't any good way. Stand on the seat, hold on to this strut, and ally-oop!"

It was awkward, but she managed. He took her hand, squeezed it in warm approval and helped her down, catching her as she jumped from the lower wing.

A cheerful voice from the next aircraft said, "Nice flight?"

Bob echoed, "Nice flight. A few patches of fog earlier, but it burned off. The air's like glass. Even better, there doesn't seem to be any weather coming in. Oh—Evelyn, this is Herb Green. Waco jockey. Herb, Evelyn Cass."

Herb Green proved to be a gangly young man in patched levis, coming around the wing end of his aircraft carrying a hair dryer. He gestured with it. "M' wife's," he said. "Mags were wet this morning. Waco," he added, pointing at his red plane. "Hi, Evelyn. Coffee in the tent yonder."

"Not yet," Bob said severely. He reached into his cockpit and threw a rumpled ball of cloth at Evelyn. "No free rides. You're a working crew. Wipe while I tie down."

"Wipe?"

He rubbed a clean streak through the oil smirching the shining sides of the Stearman fuselage and tossed the cloth back. "She sprays oil like it was on sale. Earn your coffee, lady."

She earned. When they were both through, he took back the cloth, tucked it into some unseen pocket, and glanced at her sharply. "Hey. I didn't work you that hard!"

"Hot," she answered grimly. "You know."

"I thought you were going to get a shot for that."

"I didn't."

"Hell. I don't care if you don't care. Here." He handed her his handkerchief, neatly folded. She unfolded it and mopped, leaving the wad of tissue in her bag. The linen smelled faintly of clove.

"The breeze is blowing from here," he said, and led her around the plane to the other side. "Better?"

"Better," she mumbled, feeling the cool wind dry her face. "I'm sorry."

"For what? If I pop a tooth off my partial plate you help me find it, okay? Us old folks have to help each other. Come on, let's get that coffee."

It was a pleasant day. They wandered the rows of aircraft, looking, talking, and—in Evelyn's case—learning. Everyone seemed to know Bob—in fact, everyone seemed to know each other, but it was a superficial acquaintance based on a common denominator—flying. Only one young man named Dave called Bob "Colonel" and refrained from saluting with almost superhuman effort. Bob laughed softly as he and Evelyn sauntered away.

"You may have guessed," he said. "I had him in my command. Good boy. Solid pilot. He's flying commercial now—United, I think. Look—it's almost time to close the field for the airshow. My share of thrilling the masses is about half an hour away. Let's walk over to the Stearman. I'll do my check-out; then you can sit in the shade of Herb's Waco while I go gas and get in position."

Herb's curly-headed young wife had spread a blanket on the grass and she invited Evelyn to join her. "Herb, honey, get that camp stool out."

Evelyn demurred. "No, no, don't trouble. I can sit on the ground."

"Really? My mom can't. Of course she's heavier than you, but when she's down it takes Daddy and two other guys to get her up again."

"I'll be fine," Evelyn assured her, adding to herself, if it kills me. It was the first time that day she'd felt—elderly. However, from then on it went fairly well. The girl confided that she was newly pregnant and Evelyn made the appropriate response and things rather took care of themselves.

Evelyn was brought back to the present by Bob's voice. "I guess I'm set. See you in about thirty minutes," he called, climbing into the rear cockpit and pulling on his helmet.

"Want a prop?" asked Herb.

"Not unless she doesn't start."

She did. With a roar, the Stearman sprang to life and trundled slowly down the taxiway. The air blast from the tail sent everything flying. Herb rescued napkins, programs, and a vagrant fast-food sack. Evelyn noticed a lop-eared rabbit on the sack and wished she hadn't. Stuffing it all in a garbage bag, he said, "I watched him yesterday. He's damned good. Clean. Sharp. No sloppy stuff. Ex-air force, somebody said."

He was looking at her. Evelyn nodded.

"You fly with him?"

"Down here."

"I mean doing his routine."

"No. Oh, no."

"Me neither," said his wife. She turned up the cuffs of her shorts to expose a new patch of white to the sun. "I tell Herb—I'll come with you, honey—but no funny stuff. Straight and level, that's me. I'd still rather have one foot on

225

the ground."

"But you're doing fine, doll," Herb said, stooping and kissing her. They fondled each other briefly, and Evelyn found herself looking away. She was definitely a different generation.

The girl giggled and said, "Herb, stop it. Mrs. Cass is blushing."

"Probably sheer envy."

"With a guy like Bob? Hardly. Now stop it, I said. Go get us both a soda. Diet, Mrs. Cass, or caffeine free?"

"Either," said Mrs. Cass, who was still reeling from the first part of her remark. Herb departed, grinning. His wife said suddenly, "Oh, darn!", displaying the upper end of a broken bra strap, and departed for the rest rooms. Evelyn was left alone on the rumpled blanket with a sort of dismayed emotion.

Damn people! Damn their careless assumptions! Why did they have to get ahead of her when she was trying to deal with one thing at a time?

Why did she mind?

That was the point. Why did she? Was it a simple social annoyance, or was it the old guilt trap again?

You are making a federal case, she told herself, out of nothing. Now stop it. Those kids don't care, and besides, you'll never see them again, never have to deal with what they think! You probably ought to feel complimented.

As a matter of fact — she did, and was suddenly wise enough not to explore the reasons why.

Sixteen

Herb came ambling back, handed Evelyn a soda, put one on the cooler top for his wife, and popped the tab on his own. As he stretched out on the blanket, arms beneath his head, the public address system suddenly sprang to life. After the usual "testing-testing," the man on the mike rattled off a number of service announcements, declared the airport officially closed to incoming or departing traffic, and launched into a list of the day's performers with their accompanying credentials and aircraft. Evelyn only caught Bob Marsh's name among the multitude, but Herb said suddenly, "Hey, there he is!" just as the corroborating announcer went on, "And if you will look far north, ladies and gentlemen, you will see Colonel Bob Marsh in his beautiful blue Stearman gaining altitude, gaining altitude until—there we go, down and around in a fine loop—pulling up—up, up, up—staying inverted—now a forty-five degree down slope, rolling out halfway down—"

"A Cuban Eight, you dummy," said Herb. "Watch him! He'll roll out, hit bottom, pull the nose back and kick 'er into a snap roll—look at that; isn't that fine, clean as a whistle—now he'll pop it out level, climb, do an Immelman on top—see? The nose is coming up, up, kick the rudder, Bob—there we go—fall off into a three-turn spin—easy, easy—next a slow roll on points—isn't that pretty as a picture! God! I wish it was me! I wish I was with him!"

Evelyn was staring upward amazed, almost aghast, trying to relate the solid, humming big old airplane in which she'd ridden with the soaring, free bird wheeling about the endless sky.

Suddenly, at the top of the slow roll as the Stearman lay on its back in the air the old Wright engine sputtered and stopped. Into the horrible silence Evelyn gave a choked gasp of sheer terror. Herb laughed.

"Me, too," he said. "I know it cuts out inverted. I know it. I always say, God, what if it doesn't start again! But it does. Listen—there she goes, solid as a rock!"

As the plane silently completed its roll, righting itself, the big engine caught, the steady thrum resumed, and the nose thrust upward sharply, gaining altitude.

"There he goes," Herb was saying happily, "holding her steady, bleeding off the air speed — and a hammerhead — beautiful, beautiful, look at him kick that baby around — oh Jesus, Bob, don't quit now!"

But the airplane had leveled off and was waggling its wings. A few moments later it landed to a spatter of applause as the audience turned their attention to three new aerobats wing to wing in the northern sky.

"Neato," murmured Herb, and closed his eyes briefly, content. "Really neato."

Evelyn mopped sweat, and held the cold soda can to her throat, savoring its cool. I have led, she thought grimly, a very sheltered life. The only dangerous thing I ever did for *fun* was try to skate on one foot like Sonja Henie — and then I got a sprained ankle out of it!

Yet Bob Marsh had been hundreds of feet in the air, doing twirlies in a forty-year-old airplane, hanging in his seatbelt upside-down with a dead engine — and that's what he called fun. And this young idiot on the blanket — he called it fun also.

Yet — what skill it took! And what a challenge it must be every time — to do a little better, a little different, a little higher, a little faster . . .

When the old Stearman tailed around and cut its engine and Bob climbed out, she knew she was right about the challenge. He looked as if all his cares had fallen away.

Herb hopped up, and the two men pushed the airplane into her slot. As Bob reached for the tie-down rope at Evelyn's feet he glanced at her. In his eyes she saw a small boy awaiting praise.

She shook her head, smiling. "I don't know what to say," he said. "I've never watched you do that before. I have no measure. But I think you must be very, very good."

"What you really did," said Herb, popping out from under the nose, "was scare her spitless when the engine quit."

"It always quits," said Bob directly to Evelyn, "and it always starts again. I promise."

So he thought she'd be around to watch him again. Or he wanted to think that. And would she be around?

Suddenly Evelyn was scared—a different sort of fear.

He'd smiled at her answer and turned away. He and Herb were talking about his routine, Bob dissatisfied with his snap rolls and Herb indicating that from the ground they'd looked fine. Overhead the three small Christen Eagles zoomed toward each other then peeled upward in feathered plumes of smoke. Evelyn looked but didn't really see.

He was so sure with her, so comfortable. Why

wasn't she?

It was past three. Usually at this time on Sundays she was at the nursing home, trying to interest John in the papers, trying to get him to laugh at "Garfield," bringing him ice cream as a special treat. She'd told them she wouldn't be there today, and the supervisor had said, "No problem."

And no problem with John either, she told herself. He was not missing her, nor wondering where she was, nor worrying. Yesterday she'd accepted that fact, dealt with it. Where were her brains today?

"Catch!"

The wiping cloth came sailing at her.

She caught it, asking, "Again?"

"Every time she flies. Get cracking. I'm beginning to develop hunger pangs for a chili dog."

He took another cloth and ducked under the nose to the opposite side. Herb mumbled, "See you," and wandered away to find his wife. Evelyn found herself mopping grease as though her life depended on it, taking her anxiety out on the paint.

Suddenly she heard Bob mutter, "Hell!"

Over it came—a happy, shrill young girl's voice and the sound of running feet. "Colonel Bob! Colonel Bob! Dave said you were here but I just couldn't believe it—"

Stooping, Evelyn glimpsed brown legs in sandals disappear, and Bob's legs stagger back off balance. Whoever she was, she must have thrown herself into his arms. Evelyn straightened and went on wiping, half amused. Snatches of the girl's ecstatic voice carried clearly: "I had to see you—we've missed you both so much—you look just great—" Then with a little squeal, "Is that Sue-Ann on the other side? Super!"

Ducking around the nose came a young whirlwind with blond hair flying, arms outstretched. "Sue-Ann, it's me, it's really me, it's Patsy—"

Then the voice lamely died away. "Oh. I'm sorry. I thought you were—someone else."

Bob Marsh came around the old plane, wiping cloth in hand. His face looked set as though struggling with some indefinable emotion. He said, "Patsy, this is Mrs. Cass. She's a friend. Evelyn, Patsy Messner. Dave's wife. The young man we met."

Evelyn said, "How do you do?"

Patsy's wide blue eyes were going from the broad diamond wedding band on Evelyn's hand to the greasy cloth clutched in it. She said again, "Oh, I see. Where's Sue-Ann?"

"Not here. She's very ill."

"Ill! with what?"

"Alzheimer's."

"Alzheimer's! That's the—oh, God! God! How

233

far has it gone?"

"It's quite advanced."

Bob's voice was calm. Too calm. His lean face seemed calm also, but his eyes were wary.

Patsy Messner's pretty face twisted as though she were going to cry. Her words tumbled out like an explosion: "Then why are you here? Enjoying yourself? Why aren't you with her, helping her? I don't believe this! I don't believe my eyes!"

She swung around to Evelyn. "And why are *you* here? Here with him? Because you are, aren't you? How could you? I—I've heard of piranhas, but I've never met one before!"

Bob interrupted harshly, "Patsy, that's enough!" Evelyn said quietly, "It's all right, Bob. She just doesn't understand."

"Oh, I understand, all right! I understand that my lovely, precious Sue-Ann is dying and you're here having fun! That's what I understand!" Her piercing voice skirled skyward, then suddenly choked off in an eruption of tears. She wiped at them childishly with both fists. Bob's face softened. He said, "Patsy, please listen—"

But it was no use. She shoved his hand away and shrilled through hiccups, "You're awful! Both of you! Monsters! You should be ashamed!" and turned, stumbling, to run away from them across the crowded aircraft lines with people staring at the distraught girl then back at the old

234

blue Stearman.

Bob said, "Christ!" deep in his chest. He looked at Evelyn with such misery in his pale face that her heart turned inside her.

She said gently, "She's just a baby herself, Bob. She doesn't understand."

"I never meant for this to happen. Ever. I didn't think it would. Certainly not here. But when I saw Dave I should have known. She—she was a friend of Karen's on base and had a school girl crush on both of us—she was always a twit."

But he was asking for reassurance. She knew it, she saw it in his desperate face, his gray eyes darkened with pain.

The positions are reversed, she thought. Now he needs *me* to reassure *him*, to say that our being together is all right, that there's no tangible hurt or loss to anyone.

It was her turn to put out her hand, close it on his, to say quietly, "Now you're losing perspective, Bob, Don't. Don't let an unthinking child do that to you."

For a long moment he stared at the hand as though it were a foreign object. Then he took a deep, slow, painful breath, threw his shoulders back, held them rigid, and let them fall again. He swallowed hard.

"Okay," he said to the hand on his. "Okay. You're right."

He turned his fingers, clasped hers, and met her eyes. His were still clouded, unhappy, but his mouth smiled a little.

"Help me finish my side," he said. "Then we'll go get that chili dog."

"Bob—"

"What?"

"If you want to leave, it's all right. It doesn't matter to me."

"No!" He said the word almost harshly. "No! I won't run! If you can take it, I can. My God! I'm sixty-two years old! No twenty-year-old twit is going to see my tail!"

He stalked around the airplane and they finished the cleaning. His swipes were done with a heavy, angry hand for now he was simply that—angry.

It's better, she thought, than hurt. Anger she understood. Anger she could deal with.

An embarrassed throat-clearing turned them both around.

Dave Messner stood at the rear of the airplane, his thin young face wry with the awkwardness of his mission. He was almost standing at attention. He spoke stiffly.

"Shall I spank her, sir? I'm awfully sorry. She was—she was totally out of line."

Bob's shoulders relaxed. "No," he answered quietly. "No, of course not. I should have realized what a shock it would be. Sue — Sue didn't want anyone to know, particularly you kids."

Dave relaxed but his face stayed wry. "She does this to me all the time," he said. "If I didn't love her so I'd drown her. About Mrs. Marsh — is there anything I can do?"

"No. Nothing." Then, to soften the short reply, Bob went on easily, "How are things going, Dave?"

The tension lessened. They talked fairly comfortably, then shook hands when they parted. Evelyn was touched at the hero worship in Dave's eyes. God, she thought, what a commander Bob must have been!

Afterwards, they went to the chili dog stand — by way of China, she thought wryly as her legs were beginning to ache from the unaccustomed walking. But Bob chatted his way up and down the lines of parked aircraft, even stopping to scribble an address on a scrap of paper held firmly against her sun-warmed back. He handed it to a distracted young pilot with knobby knees, assuring him that if those folks didn't have a curious thing called an air box they'd know where he could get it.

He was very much himself again. Evelyn, who still felt awkward, admired his personal discipline, his total command. He was courtly with the people commending him on his aerobatic routine, patient with the various small fry who saw in him a grandfatherly figure and wrapped sticky arms around his leg with instant devotion. When at last they got their napkin-swathed concoctions, they settled down on the crushed and powdery grass with their backs against a redwood fence and stretched out with a concerted sigh of relief—and looked at each other. And laughed.

He said, "You're getting sun-burned."

"So are you. Your nose is red."

"It's my most prominent part. I never have a sunburned moustache."

"But you do have chili on it."

"That's all right. I always wanted to be a redhead." He took a large bite, squirting sauce; he wiped at it with the napkin and looked sideways at her. Quietly he said, "I still feel as if I should apologize to you. I wanted this to be a nice, relaxing day."

"It has been. Truly."

"You're a good girl. I guess whatever we do, we take the consequences."

"My dad used to say, 'With your shield or on it.'"

He had balled up the napkin from one chili dog and was now opening another. He glanced at her sharply, white brows drawn over gray eyes. "I like that. It sounds familiar."

"College literature class, probably. It's what my dad taught. But he meant it, too. He'd say, 'Are you right? Then if you're right, get back out there!' And back I'd go. At age seven or eight things are very black and white."

"It's later they get complicated." He picked a stray chili bean from his shirt and ate it meditatively. "I'll bet you were a cute little girl."

She laughed. "I was fat."

"Come on."

"I was fat. I hated it. When they chose up sides I was the last—unless the kids were playing Dog Pile."

"Dog Pile?"

She made a face. "No, no—not *dog*—it was when everybody piled on top and the one on the bottom lost. Then they chose me first. It was a signal honor, believe me. But I was so pleased to be wanted I didn't care."

"We never do quite get over that."

"No. But our priorities change."

He grinned. "So you don't play Dog Pile any more? Nuts. There goes the evening."

There was a pungent smell of fennel as he scooted his fanny lower in the grass, put his arms behind his head, and gazed skyward. He obviously attached absolutely no significance to his last remark—nor should she!

Wryly she realized she'd gotten sensitive since

239

Charles Nixon and Porter DeKalb had made their grubby little passes. The long, lean man next to her with his lanky knees drawn up and his blunt, sunburned nose turned to the white thread of a jet contrail in the cornflower air had the guileless ease of someone relaxing with a friend. "Hey," he said. "Here comes that pretty T-6."

With a roar an old World War II fighter shot across their vision a scant hundred feet above the runway, peeled upward, waggled its wings, and continued south.

"That's his gun run," Bob went on. "The field's open again and he's going home. Hear them starting up?"

All up and down the lines came the sputter and pop, the backfire and "ka-chunk" of engines springing to life. Evelyn nodded. He went on, "If you don't mind, let's let them go. Some of the guys have a pretty good number of miles ahead of them and we're fairly close. Besides, I'm too comfortable to move. You got me up early this morning, lady."

"I got you up!"

He was grinning. "Well—the term 'up' being relevant to when one went down, I must confess that wasn't too early either. Let's just say the local saloons did good business last night, and I contributed my share."

240

"Poor baby."

"Poorer, anyway. I fell in with a guy who flew Grummans and thought he'd won the war and I knew damn well *I'd* won it, then the guy in the T-6 showed up and said he'd won it in his Mustang. After that, things kind of went to hell."

"Who did win?"

"We split it three ways."

"Good thinking."

"Yeah. I thought so."

One by one the airplanes were bobbling and trundling along the taxiway, wheeling in circles and roaring their engines. The ones ahead, in polite rotation, thundered down the strip and lifted themselves gracefully into the air. It was an organized pavanne of flight.

"Good-looking Travelair," Bob was muttering, and Evelyn caught a trace of envy in his voice. He shrugged. "I had one once. In my green years. I traded it for Karen."

At her startled glance, he explained, grinning, "When it comes to a choice between feeding babies and feeding airplanes and your wife has become attached to the baby, there really isn't much choice. Although I must admit, I've never regretted it. She's a dandy, my Karen. Hey—did I tell you—I met your daughter the other afternoon. She stopped to pick up Poo."

She must have been sober, Evelyn thought

241

painfully. Let her have been sober . . . She must have been because he went on quite cheerfully.

"She tells me she's going to work at Bunny Burger."

Zap. There it is, Evelyn. The opening. There was no time to think, to frame graceful words. She swallowed, and said with painful clarity, "So am I."

There was a silence. It was there between them. It was real. He leaned forward, clasped brown arms on his knees, and finally after an eternity turned and looked directly at her.

"I'm fighting," he said, "the enormous impulse to pry into what is obviously none of my business. None whatsoever. Based on that premise, I have to make the assumption it's something you must do. Right?"

"Yes."

"I pay Sue-Ann's bills. I know how monstrous they are."

"John is all right."

"But you aren't."

"No. I'm not."

"I say this cautiously: is there something I can do to help?"

She swallowed again. "No. Thank you. Learning to cope is an area I need to improve. I hope it builds my character."

There was another small silence while she

made herself meet those searching eyes. Then he grinned.

"I congratulate you," he said. "You're a hell of a lady. Of course, I knew that already. And your character's just fine with me."

As inexplicable relief washed over her as palpable as a cool wind he went on, "Now I know where I'm eating lunch. Roast beef rare, hold the mayo, and what are you doing after hours? Oh — one more thing: can I try on the ears?"

He was laughing. She tried to laugh, too, but there was a rueful quaver in the sound. She said, "I'm not sure how I'm going to handle the ears."

"You'll handle them fine."

He was getting to his feet awkwardly, brushing dead grass off his seat. He held out one hand to her. "Up you come!"

When she came up, he didn't let go of the hand. They were standing very close and she was suddenly, poignantly aware of the closeness, of his gray eyes looking down and the half grin turning one corner of his mouth. "Good for you, Evelinda," he was saying softly to her. Just to her. "Good for you."

He squeezed her hand, dropped it, and went on casually, "Don't forget your bag by the fence. Let's go untie. The crowd's about cleared out and I want to miss the groundfog gathering in the hollows."

She walked with him almost blindly, trying to deal with the inexplicable glow of happiness inside her. Good God, had she become so emotionally impoverished that simple commendation from a casual friend put her on top of the world?

She glanced sideways at him. He was striding along over the crumpled grass tufts and oil stains with his hands thrust deep in his pockets like an elderly boy on holiday. He was saying to her, "Untie your side. Coil up the tie-down ropes. Neatly. You may as well learn now to do things right. Hand them to me and I'll stow. Then if you need to go potty, run and do it. I'll meet you at the gas pumps."

Discretion being, in her case, the better part of valor by far, she did as she was told.

The tiny restroom waste barrel was overflowing onto the tracked-up floor, and someone had left a cigarette burning on the side of the sink, but Evelyn ignored all that. Washing her hands beneath the tepid flow of water, she made herself meet her own eyes in the mirror.

She hadn't changed. She was still a round-cheeked matron without a trace of lipstick, and gray hair a little too long on her neck. Her stomach still pooched and there was a dab of chili dog on her chin.

Well. It was better than lettuce on the teeth.

She mended the lipstick, fluffed the hair. It was an improvement but certainly no miracle.

Goofy, she thought to herself and earnestly tried to dismiss the things that were just teasing the edges of her consciousness. She had an invalid husband, a daughter almost a drunk, and eighty-eight dollars in the bank — plus a house for sale and nowhere to go if it sold. Those were the realities.

Anything else was — was cotton candy.

On that resolute and practical note she turned on her heel and came face to face with Patsy Messner.

The girl's features were still tear-stained. She put out a hand — then drew it back quickly as though afraid of a rebuff. Her voice quavered. "Colonel Bob — he said you were here."

Evelyn waited. She said nothing. There was nothing yet to say.

Patsy's hands were twisting each other. Her rosy lip quivered. Suddenly she burst out, "Karen says I owe you an apology!"

"Karen!" Evelyn replied, despite her firm intention to let the girl get herself off the hook.

Patsy nodded and gulped. "I called her. On the phone. I wanted her to know what her father was — oh, well. I was wrong. She said I was wrong. She told me about — your husband and how he is, and she said you both needed awfully to just get away if only for a little while — and she was pretty mad at me. So — I'm sorry. I apologize."

That was Evelyn's cue. But she wasn't feeling too gracious, not even yet. The memory of Bob's anguish was still with her. She said a bit coldly, "Colonel Marsh deserves your apology more than I. You really hurt him."

"I know. I have. He sent me in here."

Then the tears spurted again, and Patsy Messner turned her wet face to the wall. Her voice wavered in pitiful jerks. "I still can't believe it — she was such a beautiful lady and Colonel Bob loved her so — we adored them both, they were very special people — but Sue was — was perfect — tall and slender with a fabulous figure and those gorgeous violet eyes and masses of dark hair —"

Well, Evelyn said to herself, one out of five isn't a total loss. She'd had masses of dark hair, too. When she was thirteen.

Sensing strongly that she'd better accept Patsy's apology before it became pointlessly obscured again, she murmured, "Yes. Of course. If you'll excuse me," and left.

Still she was rather sober as she took her short and matronly figure, her garden-variety brown eyes, and uneven gray hair back across the trampled field.

What the hell was she doing here anyway?

The answer was simple and it came to her clarion clear: Bob Marsh had asked her to come. He'd asked her and he liked her company.

Reassured, she went on through the diminishing ranks of aircraft toward him.

Seventeen

The sun was now a rosy ball, softened by a filmy sweep of western cloud and hovering just above the treeline. A cool briskness swept across the empty rows where so many bright moths had spent the day. A few were even yet winging off, growing smaller in the copper light.

Bob was just shrugging into an old leather jacket with some ancient insignia half-peeled and obscure on the back and sleeves. He tossed her the crumpled bundle of a dark blue windbreaker. It smelled of tobacco, fuel, and old apple cores, and she accepted it gratefully. He also raised his brows. She nodded. So much for Patsy Messner.

As she rolled up the sleeves that hung over her hands the young lineboy said, "Okay, colonel, she's gassed. Oil all right?"

"Oil's fine."

"How much does this old baby use?"

248

Bob was peeling bills from his wallet. "A quart an hour whether she's flying or not."

The boy said, "Aw!", glanced at the money in his hand, and added, "Thank you, sir. Thank you very much."

Turning to Evelyn, Bob asked, "Ready to mount up?"

"Ready."

This time it was easier, if not more graceful. She picked the helmet off the seat before she flopped into it, snapped the seat belt, and turned. He was still kneeling on the wing beside her. "Are you in a hurry?"

"No. Why?"

"We're ahead of schedule. Let's get across the river and a little closer to home. Then I know of an airport restaurant where they don't put salad dressing on the Reubens. Okay?"

"Okay."

"Good girl."

He patted her shoulder lightly. The aircraft bobbed as he made his way down the wing, climbed inside his own cockpit, and fastened his helmet.

The lineboy called, "You want a prop, sir?"

Bob laughed. "Son," he said, "I've watched you today. You've propped so many airplanes you can hardly get your leg up off the ground. "No, thank you. She'll start. Clear!"

"Clear," said the boy gratefully. He stepped back and gave them the "thumbs up" sign. Ahead of Evelyn the big engine made a sucking sound. She coughed, then chuckled. The silver propeller lopped a few times, then caught with a roar.

They moved majestically down the taxiway. The few remaining people waved. Evelyn found herself waving back. This time, when they took off, she didn't close her eyes.

The river, as they crossed it, was a snake of molten lead, and the timber beyond seemed blanketed in rubies and emeralds and gold. It was strange to see the eastern horizon smothered in dark and the western sky ablaze with sunlight. Below in a clearing three tiny figures grazed, and only when they took off in graceful, bounding flight did Evelyn realize they were deer. She caught her breath at their simple beauty and found herself murmuring, "Godspeed, Godspeed . . ."

A scant ten-minute flight found the Stearman on descent again. The chilly rush of air took them briefly through billowing films of cottony white, and Evelyn had only time to murmur, "We're flying through clouds!" when they broke into old-gold sunlight just above a runway. This time she did close her eyes. The trees and buildings were coming up a bit too fast for her taste.

Skeek! Skeek! went the old tires on concrete.

While they rolled to a bumping halt she looked again.

There was a row of what she had just learned that day were hangars with wide, gaping doors, gas pumps, the usual fence, and beyond it an office and a building proclaiming EAT! As Bob lifted her down, she said excitedly, "I've never flown through clouds before!" and he forbore telling her that it had just been fog blowing over Salt River.

A blocky young man standing by his Lear jet was watching them with wide eyes. As they walked past, he said to them, "God damn!" and his voice was shaking. "Do you guys know how you looked? Do you? I'm standing here, minding my own business, and suddenly without a sound out of the fog comes this antique biplane. It rolls up and shuts down and these two gray-headed people in old flying gear climb out. Christ! It's like a — a glitch in time! You are real, aren't you? You haven't been caught up there for forty years, just flying around?"

Bob stopped. With the utmost sobriety he asked, "What year is it?"

The young man froze. Then he relaxed. "Damn!" he said. "You almost had me again. Come on. I'll buy coffee."

Despite its corner-diner look, the small café had excellent food. They ordered, drank the young man's coffee, and watched through the window as he took off in his sleek white Lear.

Evelyn, enjoying excellent onion rings, looked up and saw her companion watching her.

"A glitch," he said quietly. "A glitch in time. Your life suspended. It doesn't sound too bad."

Evelyn shut her eyes, considered the idea, then shook her head.

"No," she said. "Not unless nothing else changes, either. I want to see Poo grow up. I want to see Brenda solve her problems. I want to see my Peace rose finally bloom. I want to—" She hesitated, swallowed, then said it anyway: "I want to prove that I can make it on my own. I know that doesn't sound like much—not against other people's high aspirations—but when you have 1940 skills in a 1990 world as I do—that's an awful lot."

"Yes. It is."

"You're not like that. Not like me."

"Oh but I am. Sixty-two and technologically outdated. Out to pasture in fields that they told me would be Elysian. Crap. That guy in the Lear was closer than he thought—because I probably am a glitch."

He was jabbing at his fries angrily, his voice bitter.

"Then—up with glitches!"

"What?"

"Glitches of the world, unite!"

"You're crazy!"

"I know," she said, and suddenly both of them laughed, and the heavy moment was over. He said, after a moment, in a sober voice, "Well — I'll tell you something, Evelinda — glitch or not, you're good for me. I sure as hell hope I'm good for you."

"You're probably not."

Because he looked startled, she went on, "You see, I'm going to ask you to let me have a banana split with nuts and whipped cream — which may mean that I might not fit into my Bunny Burger uniform. Which also," she continued, pursuing the thought, "will make the gal who hired me very nasty about it. What do you suppose she'd do?"

"Dock an ear?"

"Oh golly," she said. "Perhaps I'd better not."

"Nonsense. You might become the rage. Buy from the bunny with the cock-eyed ear!"

"Now who's crazy?"

"Better than glitchy?"

"Much."

"Good. Waitress, two banana splits."

They ate them with relish, Evelyn once more giving silent thanks for elastic waistbands. She did covertly let her seat belt out a notch as he walked around his airplane, waggling things.

When he heaved himself in, he groaned.

"Oh, God! My belt is now set on 'waddle.' We may not get off the ground."

"Try."

"You may have to throw out your purse."

"You're threatening me because it was my idea."

"You're right."

They did, however, get into the air handsomely. The old Stearman almost glided through the silken sky, so still and quiet had the world become at sundown. As the big wheels touched down on the home field, Evelyn's watch said exactly seven o'clock.

She helped him tail his aircraft into the open hangar doors and watched as he attached a hook and cable to the small rear wheel and winched it slowly inside. The building was as spare and neat as the man himself. Flying equipment, parts, oil cans, and cleaning material were all shelved and stacked on one side wall with his Datsun parked next to them. Calendars chosen, she suspected, more for their art than their current value, dotted the back. On the other side was an army cot, neatly made, flanked by a Coleman lantern on an upended box.

He backed his car out, pushed shut the rattledy-bang sliding sections of hangar doors, and came around to where she stood in the last section that swung on hinges.

She asked idly, "Do you sleep here?"

"Sometimes. When they predict a strong wind or a storm."

"Is that equivalent to a captain going down with his ship?"

"In a way. Also, I happen to like storms."

She shivered, and he asked, "Don't you?"

"Not by myself."

"Other times," he went on, "I just—like it out here. I came the other evening and stayed. When Sue-Ellen got to town, blast her. I didn't want to listen to her braying, so I just left. She doesn't know about this place, and Karen wouldn't tell."

"Poor Bob."

"It's a minor nuisance. Really. Anyway—see the pond down there?" He moved closer, and pointed. At the end of a gentle slope a small body of water gleamed in the silver dusk. "I'm sitting here in the doorway, having a beer and watching the fish flop and the little frogs go plip-plip. A big old bazoom bull tunes up in the cat-tails. And all of a sudden this young doe steps out of the trees into the moonlight—and she's got a fawn with her. God—it was so damned pretty I almost went in my pants. Sorry. But you don't see things like that very often."

"Bob—"

"What?"

"She's there, now. Look."

Delicately the slender deer stepped into view, ears up and flickering. For a moment she didn't move. Behind them in the locust trees sleepy birds chirped drowsily, and far away on the highway a truck changed gears. They were both holding their breath.

Bob said in her ear, "Stay still. Maybe she'll bring her little fellow out. I'll bet he's there in the thicket."

The seconds passed silently. Overhead a nightjar wheeled and squawked. Then from the brush came a miniature on gawky sticks. While the doe watched, the youngster went to the marshy brink, spread his knobby-kneed legs, and slupped. Small circles spread across the calm water from his velvet nose.

Sated, he stepped back, his tiny scut twitching. Before their eyes the two melted back into the dark of the trees.

Sometime during the last few minutes Bob's arm had gone about her shoulders and was still there, warm and comforting. Evelyn put both her hands up to his. Blinking, she said, "I'm sorry. I haven't cried in years."

"Idiot. I don't care. Go ahead."

"It's been such a lovely day. Lovelier than I've had for—for a long time. I'm so glad I came."

His fingers had turned, clasped hers. "Will you

256

come again?"

"I — I don't know." She moved her head, found that it was against the hollow of his shoulder. A small, inexplicable pulse began to throb in her throat.

Above her, from a distance, as if he were staring out into space, she heard his voice and it was careful, precise:

"Will you come again — if I tell you what I'm *not* going to do?"

She tried to answer, but couldn't. He said in the same soft, tight, curiously controlled tone, "I'm not going to kiss you. I'm not going to ask you to play Dog Pile with me on that cot behind you. I'm not." She felt his throat against the back of her head, felt him swallow. "But God knows," he said, "I want to."

If he expected rigidity, or outrage, or even surrender, he got none of them. He only heard a small sigh. She said in a small voice, "Cotton candy."

"What?"

She repeated: "Cotton candy. Sweet and frail. Melting and gone. And leaving a mess." Her voice caught. "That's what mustn't happen here. With us. We mustn't make a mess. Of anything. I couldn't bear it if we did."

Now his breath was like a sigh — long and shuddering.

"Oh, Evelinda," he said. "Oh, Evelinda." And he was turning her, tilting up her chin, looking her directly in the eyes. "We won't make a mess," he said gently. "I'll promise. If you'll promise. It's a two-way street, love."

"I promise."

"Good enough. So do I. Now let's get the hell out of here."

He was turning away, shutting the door and locking it quickly as though against an adversary. "Hop in the Datsun. I'll run you over to the parking lot."

It was a brief trip during which neither spoke, but a surprisingly comfortable one — like the calm, Evelyn thought, after a storm. And that, as a matter of fact, was what it was.

Her Lincoln was dew-covered. The seats were clammy. It wouldn't start.

There wasn't even the usual funny burr.

She told Bob about the burr. He said succinctly, "Oh, shit," slid in beside her and tried it. He got under the hood and fiddled, then tried it again. Then he said, "Jumper cables," got a set from his car, attached them to hers, and between the two of them the Lincoln groaned, sputtered, and started.

He yelled, "Don't shut it off!"

After stowing the cables back in his Datsun and slamming down the Lincoln's hood, he came

258

to her window.

"Listen," he said. "I'm going to follow you home because it may die on you."

"What's wrong?"

He shook his head. "It's hard to tell. Starter—regulator or alternator. I'd guess alternator."

Her heart went into her shoes. Dandy. She'd paid for alternators before—when she had more than eighty-eight dollars.

"Anyway," he said, "Scoot for home. I'll be right behind."

It was not a pleasant trip. She was cold, but when she turned on the heater the lights dimmed; and naturally they caught all the traffic lights on red.

She pulled into her drive gratefully, shut the car down, got the keys, and went around to the front where he was sitting in his Datsun. There were no lights in the house so Brenda must not have brought Poo yet.

"Come on in and wash," she said. "You're all greasy. The least I can do is make some coffee."

He followed her up the walk. She said, "Mind the ivy," and fitted her key into the door.

On cue her living room blazed with light. She was dazzled with bright, floating balloons, deafened with braying party horns, and equally assaulted by an assortment of voices, all of them crying,

"Happy Birthday!"

To say that she was not too pleased might be the understatement of the year.

Eighteen

She said, "Oh my goodness!"—which was vastly more socially acceptable than the "Oh shit!" she distinctly heard in her ear. She smiled, knowing full well she was showing at least a hundred and twenty teeth, all of them bared. And she added, "How nice." Which, correctly interpreted, meant, "Mary Lou, I'll kill you!"

Now they had all caught a glimpse of Bob Marsh. The momentum of the party wavered just a little. Six pairs of startled eyes swung from him to Evelyn again. The braying horns stopped. She knew with terrible clarity that there would be a small silence, unbearable in its significance, before everyone started talking at once to fill the void.

She plunged. "What a surprise! I never expected—Mary Lou, I'll get you for this—"

She was gabbling. She knew it. But didn't everyone gabble when they found their living room full of balloons and idiots? She turned to the man behind her and said, "Come on in, Bob. They're harmless. Guys, this is Bob Marsh. My car died. He got it started for me then followed me home to be sure it didn't die again." It was an explanation with a capital E because they expected one. They had been friends for twenty years and they were entitled to that — and to the truth. Which it was, as far as it went. She went on, "I promised him a drink. Ben, would you get him something? Please?"

Behind her, Bob said swiftly, "Oh, no, that's all right. I'd better mosey on down the road."

Mary Lou cried, "Oh, stay! Stay!"

She wore skinny-legged slacks and high heels. They clicked on the foyer tile as she grabbed Bob's arm and Evelyn's and a waft of perfume almost sent them both backwards. Her pert, thin face looked from one to the other entreatingly. "There are plenty of steaks and we'd love to have you! What does he drink, Evie?"

Evelyn answered, "I've no idea. But do stay, Bob."

She looked him right in the eyes, desperately trying to communicate one important thought: she was not running, and no one was going to see her tail either!

He took his cue. She saw him relax and grin and shrug. Seeing him through suddenly-detached vision, she realized for the first time what a courtly, charming grin it was and how wide and straight his shoulders were.

He said, "Okay. A beer would be fine. Is there somewhere I can wash up?"

He held out greasy hands. Everyone's antenna went down with an almost audible click. If this guy didn't even know where Evie's bathrooms were—the rest of the conclusion was so patently obvious that Evelyn suddenly, irrationally loved them all. But she had one more brownie point to make. Innocently she said, "Port, would you show him where? Bob, have you met Porter De-Kalb? He's John's oldest friend."

She didn't even wait to see them shake hands. Turning and ducking three red balloons, she said, "Girls, I have to clean up, too. You all look so nice you're disgusting."

She ran upstairs, hauled off the chili dog shirt, washed the grease from her hands, looked at herself in the mirror, and grimaced. At this rate, Daddy, she thought grimly, I'm going to wear out the damned "shield." One way or the other, on it or with it, and right now I'm not sure which!

The blue marks of Porter's fingers were fading, but seeing them didn't make her feel any more friendly toward him.

Shivering, she banged down the bedroom window, rummaged hastily through a drawer, and yanked on a gray varsity sweater of Jack's. Wryly she wondered what the reaction would have been had she not left Bob's old windbreaker back in the Stearman. That really would have looked cozy!

Suddenly she remembered Bob Marsh's shadowed hangar, the warmth of his shoulder against her head, the quiet intensity of the words he'd said. The memory was alien in this intimate room, yet it pervaded and was strong—stronger than other memories which were fading.

For so long John had been her warmth, her strength, her companion, her friend . . .

Twisting the diamond band around her finger, she shut her eyes and brought her feelings under control. The priority, just now, was this birthday nonsense downstairs, and keeping her well-intentioned friends—at least most of them—from making asses of themselves after they'd had a few drinks.

She suspected Bob would leave as soon as he gracefully could. She found she wanted him to do just that. Having quite enough on her plate at the moment to ask herself *why* she wanted him to do that, she pulled the sweater back into place and went downstairs.

Jane Nixon was waiting at the bottom.

She was wearing her new violet sweater and her hair almost matched. Her eyes were amused.

She said, "I thought you'd died up there." The nasal voice dropped. "This wasn't my doing, kid. I tried to warn you all day but you weren't home."

"No, I wasn't. But thanks, anyway."

"Have you got the rest of your story together?"

Startled, Evelyn stopped pulling dead leaves from the Boston fern and turned. She glanced past Jane at Mary Lou, happily laying out paper plates and napkins on her dining room table, and at Liz in the kitchen forking baked potatoes in the microwave. Each was doing what they did best, and had done so many times it was rote. Jane usually tossed the salad with her special homemade dressing that no one had ever been able to duplicate. But this time she was standing at the steps and asking that question which she explained quickly. "If not, don't stand next to your swain in full light. It won't take them long to notice you two have his-and-hers sunburns."

"Oh, Lord," said Evelyn and rolled her eyes upward briefly. "I suppose. This is such idiocy. We haven't done anything wrong. It would be almost easier to deal with if we had. I probably shouldn't have asked him to stay."

"No—you did the right thing there. What you need to do now is get rid of him before Mary Lou can fasten her hooks."

"The poor man is beginning to sound like a

side of meat!"

"The 'poor man' makes Porter look like pot roast! My Charles doesn't come off too well, either."

In amazement, Evelyn said, "Jane, you're serious!"

Jane nodded. "Deadly," she answered. "You have some tough days coming up. You may need all the help we can give—including help from the prima donnas in this crowd. If I were you—and if I could—I'd put Mr. Marsh on the back burner."

"Well—I can. Of course."

"Can you?"

"Jane, really—"

"Honey, listen to me. You walked in that door tonight looking ten years younger. I'm green with envy. But I also don't want to see you hurt any more. "I'm tired," Jane added suddenly in a desperate voice, "of hurting. Okay, can it, here comes Mary Lou. Where are the champagne glasses? I refuse to drink good champagne from paper cups."

"Me, too," said Mary Lou, clicking over on her tiny heels. "The guys went out to look at your car, Evie. Except Ben, of course, and he's doing the steaks. How does Bob want his? He looks like a 'rare' man."

"I have no idea," Evelyn answered truthfully.

266

"Go ask him. Come on, Janey, help me. The glasses are on the top shelf and I need to stand on a chair."

As she carefully handed down the thin glasses, saying ruefully, "I hope they're clean. They haven't been used since New Year's," the back door opened. The three men trooped in on a waft of barbecue smoke, preceded by a large cat who looked around incredulously at the number of legs in his kitchen and disappeared into the pantry.

Now all three men were greasy. Charles Nixon, holding his dirty hands before him as if bearing precious gifts, glanced from the black and white streak to Evelyn and said, "You want the cat in? If not, I'll boot him out."

Evelyn handed down the last glass. "He's all right. He's gone to ground behind the freezer. He probably won't come out until you're gone."

"Hate cats," Charles added and shivered. To Bob he said in a reproving voice Evelyn was supposed to hear, "So did old John. He'd have a fit."

Bob nodded noncommittally. As Evelyn started to jump down from her chair, Porter said, "Hey, Evie, let me help!" and put both hands on her hips, lifting her. Mary Lou screamed, "Porter, think what you're doing!"

It was, of course, too late. There was a pair of greasy handprints, rather well defined, on

Evelyn's jeans.

Porter said, "Oops."

Mary Lou said in indulgent despair, "Oh, Port, really! See what you've done!"

Evelyn said, "Oh, it's all right." Which it wasn't. Not at all. She was chilled with an anger she struggled hard to conceal. Porter had soiled her deliberately. She refused to glance at him, knowing what she'd see — a complacent bull, marking his cows.

His official "cow" was reaching up, shaking his porky shoulders with her two long-nailed hands, saying in her baby voice, "Oh, honestly! When are you going to grow up? If the steaks weren't so nearly done, I'd send you home, you bad boy! What about Evie's car? Did you fix it?"

Porter's answer was to put his dirty hands on his wife's white cotton butt — which made her scream and say, "Oh, Porter DeKalb, stop it!" To Evelyn he said in that guileless caramel rumble, "I'm afraid Marsh may be right. Nothing we tried worked. Tell you what, Evie. I'll send one of my guys up tomorrow with a loaner car and haul the Lincoln in to our shop. We'll fix the sucker. Don't worry about it."

Porter DeKalb, now playing the lead in *My Best Friend's Wife*, and playing it beautifully with approving murmurs from the audience around him.

As to the wife in question, Evelyn thought numbly, she is in deep trouble. Not only would she owe him money she didn't have, she'd also be driving one of his cars because she had to have transportation—and he knew it.

Bob Marsh penetrated her dismay, saying, "Hey, everybody—thank you for the hospitality but I really can't stay. I usually watch my grandson at nine while my kids go out for a while. Glad to have met you all."

"I'll see you to the door," Evelyn said.

"No, no, you needn't," he answered, and his tone was one she'd heard before—the sound of command. "Have a happy birthday. Good night, everyone. Thanks for the beer."

And he was gone, the door shutting gently behind him.

Porter shrugged and went to clean his hands. Liz Swan said with a little laugh, "Well—good. Now it's just us again. I like it better. I guess I'm too old to change."

"He's—really very nice. I rather wish he'd stayed." The remark, from Mary Lou, had Liz shrugging her heavy shoulders. She opened the refrigerator and hauled out a bowl of greens. "Here, Janey, do the salad. Yes, he's nice—I didn't mean that."

"I think it's nice to have pairs again," Mary Lou said ingenuously. "I mean—it's awfully hard

269

to play games with singles."

Not the games your husband plays, Evelyn thought darkly. Mary Lou caught the look and fortunately misinterpreted it, flushing right up to her blue eyelids. "Oh, Evie, I'm sorry! I didn't intend—I wasn't thinking—"

Feeling apologetic herself, Evelyn reached out to hug the thin shoulders, giving them a shake at the same time.

"Hush! I know what you mean! It's all right."

From the patio someone bellowed, "Will somebody please bring a platter?" At this plaintive roar all four women sprang into the routine they'd followed together for years, well-mapped, well-coordinated, and unimpaired by there being three husbands, not four.

I could do it blind, Evelyn thought dismally. In fact, I guess I have been doing it blind. For some time.

She was unreasonably haunted by the memory of Bob Marsh going out the door, closing it behind him with such precision. Would she ever see him again? Would he even call?

"Evie. EVIE!"

Evelyn jumped. She realized guiltily she'd been standing stock still, staring at the refrigerator.

"Oh. Sorry," she said, and got out the butter.

It was a good meal. They toasted her with

270

champagne, then rather quickly went back to beer, which was fine with Evelyn. Her gifts were nice. She received a dozen more Holland tulip bulbs and a carved ivory bracelet she'd admired at the Princess Dress Shoppe but had also found vastly overpriced.

Sensing her dismay, Mary Lou murmured, "Don't worry, kid. I get a discount now."

But the remark hardly dented Evelyn's consciousness. She slipped on the bracelet and said, "Thank you all. Thank you so much," and wished desperately that they'd go home.

They did, of course, after the news and weather and a heated male discussion of the local hog market while their wives yawned at the kitchen table.

The silence of the empty house was almost a benison. Romeo came grumpily out from behind the freezer and condescended to a little of Liz's baked beans but ignored the potato. Evelyn put the party horns in a bag to save for Poo, but gathered the balloons in a garbage sack. The men, of course, had left the TV on. She turned it off with the lights in the kitchen and dining room and adjusted the floor lamp by the stairs to low.

Then she stood by the front window, looking out.

The street lamp sent a muted glow through

271

the leaded panes above her head, casting those familiar iridescent jewels of emerald, ruby, and sapphire on the carpet behind her. Fingers of ivy, blowing in a light wind, tapped against the porch columns in graceful waves. A silent flurry of dry leaves whirled across the walk. The old clock ticking at the bend of the stairs was like the heartbeat of the house, and for one sudden, awful moment, she desperately wished it would stop.

Then the telephone rang.

Brenda's alcohol-glazed voice said, "Hi, Mom, was it a good party? Were you s'prised?"

"Yes. Yes, I was. Bren, where's Poo?"

"S'kay. We're both home. He's sleepin'. Don' worry. See you tomorrow. Happy birthday. I love you."

Slowly Evelyn hung the receiver up, turned, and plodded stairward. She was astonished to find genuine tears running down her face, wetting her collar, and tasting salty in the corners of her mouth. Twice in one day — when she hadn't been able to weep in years and years!

The phone rang again. She couldn't ignore it. It might be about John. She wearily kicked off her shoes and slogged back, mopping at the strange wet that bleared her eyes. "Hello."

"Evelinda?"

Bob. It was Bob.

She answered, "Yes," screwing up her face against the pain. She knew he'd called to say goodbye.

But he was saying harshly, "I had to leave. If I'd stayed any longer I was going to kill that idiot, DeKalb."

She sat down on the desk chair because her legs wouldn't hold her up. Incredulously she whispered, "You knew?"

"No problem. He told me. Well—not in so many words, but I got the message. He warned me off, then he did that little number with his dirty hands and I realized that if I didn't clear out pronto I was going to break him in two. What do you want done about that piece of crud?"

Something poured over her that was part relief, part laughter, and part joy. Unsteadily, but chuckling like a fool, she said, "Nothing. I can handle him."

"Are you sure?"

"Now I am. But—oh, Bob Marsh—thank you! Thank you!"

"Any time. Special knight-on-a-white-horse department, dedicated to the rescue of Evelindas everywhere."

"Bob—"

"What?"

"Who—who is she?"

"She who?"

"Evelinda." She said it tentatively, almost shyly. No one had ever called her that before.

Through the telephone she heard his quiet laughter. "And you the daughter of a literature prof!"

She protested. "He was my dad, not my instructor!"

"Small excuse. He named you. He must have had someone in mind."

She forebore saying she was named after a heavily-freckled aunt in Milwaukee. "Don't tease. Tell me."

"You don't mind? I'm not secure enough to be pushy."

He was secure enough, and he probably knew it, but at the moment that was unimportant.

"Of course I don't mind. I think it's pretty."

"Okay, I'll tell you." There was a small pause. Then his steady voice came to her in the archaic cant of medieval times:

" 'This is my gracious lady, Evelinda.
Silver, her hair,
As slender reeds in the wind, her fingers
When she smoothes it,
Shining silken against her falling sleeves.
Warm, her smile.
Warm as summer sun, as autumn fire

As she welcomes me home,
Takes to her gentle breast her tired and
  weary knight.
My gracious lady,
Evelinda.' "

It was her turn to do the small pause. Then unsteadily she said, "That's lovely. Thank you. Who wrote it?"

"It's from *Lays of a Saxon Bard,* circa the twelfth century."

"And you've remembered it all this time?"

"From the twelfth century? Thanks, kid, you're a real pal."

"No, you idiot! From college."

"Oh. No, not really. I read a lot of strange stuff at night, medieval poetry being one of them. I happened on that piece just the other day and thought it was—nice."

Nice enough to memorize. Nice enough to repeat without any hesitation.

He caught the small sound she made. He asked sternly, "What are you doing?"

Then the snuffle was plain. "C-crying."

"It sounds rusty."

"I don't do it very often."

He whistled softly, just to himself, but it was plain and she heard it. He said, "Enough. Call it a day, Evelinda. Good luck tomorrow."

"Thank you for that, too. I'll need it."

"I didn't know about your birthday."

"I didn't tell you."

"Well—we'll make it up sometime. Good night," he said.

The line clicked.

Into the velvet dark she said softly, "You already have."

She didn't sleep for a long time as she had some complex thoughts to sift through. After a while she got up and padded through the gloom to the bathroom. Gulping down some Maalox for the baked potato on top of the steak on top of the banana split still hovering over remnants of the chili dog, she also said out loud to the shadowy image in the mirror, "Happy birthday—Evelinda."

Cupping her hands against her warm breast as though holding something precious, she went back to bed.

When the clock struck one, she didn't hear.

Neither, fortunately for her peace of mind, could she hear the old drainpipe in the basement quietly breaking away from the soft rust above it and settling askew against the wall.

Nineteen

Unfortunately she woke at five, and the gentle euphoria of the previous day was quickly numbed by real exigencies. Sheer terror gripped her stomach; she tried to soften it by putting her mind on ordinary, mundane things.

The room was stuffy. She opened the window and leaned on the dusty sill, breathing fresh air and looking down through tattered tree leaves at the patio where a thin trail of smoke spiraled upward from the stone barbecue.

John and Jack had built that barbecue from creekbed limestone, just three years ago. They'd christened it by having the whole crowd over — for the standard steak and baked potato, of course. Jack's wife, Michelle, had brought a casserole. The girls had eaten it with delight. The guys said it looked as though someone already had.

They had never been, she thought idly as she

twiddled with the blind tassel, a particularly innovative crowd. Why? Security? A sense of well-being only in the old things? Liz had said that last night, glad that Bob was going.

But Mary Lou hadn't. Mary Lou had been more comfortable when they'd been paired again.

And Evelyn suddenly recognized a home truth: any single woman represented a threat to Mary Lou. Even her, and she doubted that Mary Lou had ever caught a whiff of Porter's endeavors in her direction.

Anyway, she hoped to God she hadn't. Things were already bad enough!

The room was still dark, barely light-streaked from the window. She snapped on the bed lamp, hauled off the limp nightie, glanced at herself in the pier mirror, and was not gratified. Her legs were brown to about three inches below her fanny. To that she had added, yesterday, circular bands on her arms where the shirt had ended, and a sharp, Indian colored vee between her breasts — plus the red dabs on cheekbones, nose, and chin.

She looked as if she were wearing cream-colored rompers with pink buttons on the pockets. It was not a gratifying sight — particularly since she was now, officially, fifty-six years old. And more particularly, since the rompers bagged.

I really should do some waistbends, she told herself.

She didn't. She padded into the bathroom, brushed her teeth while the water heated, then stepped into the shower.

Unfortunately for the condition of the drainpipe in the basement, it was a long shower. She had a lot to think about. One item was about writing checks to pay the bills — and not exceeding the three hundred and some Mr. Martin had assured her would be paid into her account today. The second item was deciding what bill would not be paid just yet — but would have to wait for her first Bunny Burger paycheck.

The third item was the bill for the Lincoln — whatever it was, it was going to be paid by check, in the mail, even if it wiped her out. She knew Porter would suggest some sort of arrangement. She thought she had a pretty good idea of the nature of Porter's "arrangements." Under the guise of friendship he was trying to hook her into a game she absolutely refused to play!

She lifted her face to the warm, pelting needles of the shower and grimaced. How the holy hell did a fifty-six-year-old broad get into things like that? She didn't think she was a fanny waggler. She'd never worn plunging necklines or halter tops. Even her swimsuit had a skirt! The nearest she'd ever come to exposing either fanny or boobs had been in a hospital gown when she'd had Jack, and John hadn't even been there then!

It made no sense but it was real and she was stuck with a giant-sized nuisance!

I really need it, too, she thought grimly, stepping out on the plush mat and grabbing a towel for her wet head.

In the bedroom the alarm clock was burring.

Wrapping another towel about her middle, she padded back, smacked down the clock button, and flopped on the bed again, staring at the ceiling.

Bunny Burger time.

So — what does one properly wear when going to work for the first time?

Washable slacks. A plain shirt. Sensible shoes.

Rising, she laid them out, went back into the bathroom, plugged in the curling iron, and started drying her hair.

John was right about that, too, she realized grimly. That strange lady who put him to bed and turned on his TV every night was a little short-necked to wear hair on her collar.

She got out the scissors and committed the first disaster of the day.

Thank God for curling irons.

Sucking up the silver trimmings with a hand vacuum, she told herself bravely it really wasn't much shorter on one side than the other and it curled around her face rather pleasantly.

Jessie's adage about "spilt milk" ringing in her ears, she went downstairs, made coffee, let Romeo out, and refused to look in the mirror any more, even when she put on a dab of lipstick.

Where she did look was in the freezer. Once packed with neatly-wrapped stacks of meat and vegetables, it now yawned like Mammoth Cave—if Mammoth Cave ever harbored two TV dinners of a brand no one had liked, a carton of tomato sauce, a fistful of hamburger and a single, foil-covered pork chop.

She sighed again, took out the chop and laid it on the drainboard, thinking that if she survived the day she might possibly need solid food.

Vaguely she remembered also thinking that she'd better phone some day soon and cancel John's yearly order of a side of beef and a whole hog from the meat processor's—but the old clock in the stairwell booming seven-thirty

281

sounded like a death knell, and she promptly forgot even her name in simple fear.

Out the door. Lock it. Put key in bag. Walk.

It took ten minutes of brisk walking to get to the Bunny Burger parking lot. I must remember that, Evelyn told herself, and was going around the baby junipers to the east side when a young woman jumped from a bright yellow sports car and joined her.

"Hi," she said. She had deep acne scars, bad teeth, and a pleasant smile. "Are you hired? Me, too. I'm Eileen. My boyfriend took off and left me with a kid and a Trans-Am that wasn't paid for. I swore I'd never work in one of these joints again, but here I am." She pulled open the heavy metal door and motioned for Evelyn to follow. The sudden change from bright sun to the dim interior made them both blink. Eileen chattered on cheerfully, "Good morning, Ms. Daniels!"

Ms. Daniels answered calmly, "Good morning, Eileen—and Evelyn. I'm glad to see you came early. That's a good start." She was standing by a table in the narrow hall. From it she handed them white labels with their names already printed neatly on the front and indicated an open doorway. "Go on in. There's three more left to come."

Eileen slapped the sticky side of her label on her yellow tee shirt with an expert hand, preceded Evelyn into a small, lounge-type room, and cried out, "Kooky! You, too?" and deserted her for a tiny girl with an enormous red frizz of hair.

The room had twelve chairs in a semi-circle, a projector and a movie screen, a water fountain, and a coffee-maker with a stack of cups. Nine of the chairs were occupied. Evelyn slipped into the nearest vacant one and took a deep breath. A soft drawl next to her said, "Why—Mrs. Cass!" and she turned a startled face to the woman on her right.

"Betty!" she said.

The woman nodded, pushing back a wisp of gray hair that had escaped from an old-fashioned bun. "I thought that was you. It's been a few years—but you don't change."

"Aren't you cleaning anymore?"

Betty shrugged. "I broke my arm so the elbow don't work right. But it doesn't keep me from cookin'. I heard you been on hard times. I guess I heard rightly. How's your man?"

Amazed at the calmly accurate appraisal of her situation, yet also rather reassured by it, Evelyn thought wryly that bad news must travel through the atmosphere. She hadn't seen Betty

283

since she cleaned for Liz when Judy was small. To the woman's question she answered, "Not good."

"Pity. A nice fellow. Mine's out there, too. Suckin' on an air tank and paying for all those damn cigarettes he smoked for fifty years. He's Public Aid, of course—but every time I see the hunk gone out of my check I figure I'm doing my share. How's Brenda? She straighten up yet?"

Evelyn was rescued from this testimony to the total social awareness of a small town by a tall, gaunt woman in a tight jump suit and shoulder-length blond-green hair. She took the end chair next to Evelyn's and said, "Hi," in a husky voice. "Am I late? God, that would really tear it!"

Evelyn said, "I don't think so."

"Good. Then there's time to get coffee? Want some?"

Without waiting for an answer, she went over, poured two, and brought them back. Evelyn thought to herself that *there* was a fanny wiggle, accepted the coffee, and sipped it. Good—as good as the other day's cup.

"Marva," said the second woman, glancing at Evelyn's label. "Evelyn. Okay."

"Betty."

"Hi, Betty. Now what do we do? I've never worked fast food before."

"We watch training films until you feel you've won sergeant's stripes. Then we get the hand-washing, no make-up, no fingernails talk. Last, they show us how to run the equipment and write the tabs. Where'd you work before?"

Marva said she was a *chanteuse*, pronouncing it chan-toosey. "At least," she said, "until the manager split with the take over the weekend, the rat. What do you mean — no fingernails?"

"You'll see," Betty answered enigmatically. "Shh. Here comes El Bosso."

Margaret Daniels closed the door behind an older man in a crewcut and a tie and two boys in their late teens wearing camouflage pants. She smiled the same practiced smile Evelyn had seen before and said, "Okay, guys, we're all here. This is Mr. Jennings. He will be Opening Manager."

"Tom," said Mr. Jennings. "There are no last names here, only first ones. Everyone have coffee if they want it? We'll start up the soda machine a little later. Right now we want you to watch these little films."

The first "little film" portrayed the origin of Bunny Burger, was somewhat scratchy, and had the soundtrack quality of poor elevator music.

285

The next one was narrated by a cartoon bug with eight legs, pertained to sanitation habits, and generated in Evelyn a terrible desire to giggle. The last one had two self-consciously cute girls in Bunny uniform mouthing the phrase vocabulary with which to entice the innocent public into ordering more than they had intended to.

When the lights went on again, Evelyn felt vaguely as if she had earned a merit badge. She also had the suspicion that Betty had been sound asleep. Marva was bright and interested.

"Wasn't that little bugger cute?" she whispered. "I could watch him again!"

"You will," Betty whispered back. "Tomorrow."

Margaret Daniels said from the rear, "Potty break. Five minutes. No smoking out front or in the building. Just here."

It must have been the standard five minutes, but Evelyn—foregoing the potty break—got Marva's life history instead. Not that it wasn't interesting—just interminable, and periodically dotted with male rats to which she dedicated her life and got—in Marva's phrase—dumped on.

When they reconvened, the next item was the edict on personal appearance: covered hair, light make-up, no perfume, little jewelry, and

286

short nails. Marva moaned audibly, looking at her bright scarlet talons, and Ms. Daniels said, "I know. Sorry. That's the rule. Buy some stick-ons for after-hours. They work fine and everyone will be happy."

From the front row Eileen raised her hand and pointed to her enormous dangling circle earrings. "Last place I worked, they let me keep these."

Margaret shook her head. "The last place you worked obviously was not Bunny Burger. They have to go, Eileen. Right down to the posts. No accidents, no regrets, the Corp says. Sorry. Any other questions? Okay, then. Tom will give you the tour."

Bunched like sheep, they viewed the cooler, freezer, store room and, finally, dining area and kitchen.

The décor was oak and calico — what Evelyn called silently "Early Aunt Martha." They gave their orders and sat at the shiny new tables while Tom and Margaret cooked lunch. It had somewhat less than the carefree atmosphere of a Sunday School picnic, but the food was good. Evelyn, having breakfasted on coffee, ate with relish.

Afterwards they viewed three more films, received a lecture on uniform care, group insurance, and profit-sharing, were given their time cards, and dismissed. For tomorrow they were promised a go at the food machines, and on the next day, a full schedule of cleaning procedures.

"Thrillsville," said Marva, blinking in the glare from the new paving in the parking lot. "Anyone want a drink of good stuff? My throat feels like the inside of a goat's stomach."

Eileen and two of the young men accepted. Betty murmured something about "groceries" and took off in an old Chevy. Evelyn also declined, and on pausing around the corner to tie her shoelace, caught the cheerful opinion from Marva that she "seemed like a good old skate. Betty, too. Reminds me of my mom."

Going much more slowly back up the slope to Sycamore Street, Evelyn wondered which of the two of them Marva had meant. She also entertained herself building a mental image of Marva's mom.

Suddenly she realized that the Lincoln had disappeared, and there was no loaner in its place. This did not give her great comfort, presaging as it did a visit from Porter DeKalb.

She was sitting at John's desk about seven o'clock writing checks and grimly totting the amounts up on her pocket calculator. The property tax bill was shoved out of sight in a pigeonhole because it intimidated her, and the car insurance had been chosen to wait the absolute limit of its grace days. She knew now the amount of her Bunny Burger check and when it would appear, but the modest sum had hardly sent her spirits soaring. There were groceries to buy, and the damned car repair bill to pay, and nowhere could she find enough extra for a hot-flash shot—or a hair cut.

Romeo had sniffed at the cut-down portion of cat food and disappeared in the syringa bushes, presumably to scare up something more adequate. The house was totally quiet except for the plip-plip of her calculator in counterpoint to the more refined tick-tock of the tall case clock.

When the front doorbell chimed, it had the sound of impending doom.

She knew who was there.

Porter was on the step in a dark suit and tie, vest buttoned neatly across his paunch by the artistic genius of a good tailor. He held a set of car keys out to her. He said in that mellifluous voice, "Mary Lou's in the Caddie. We're going out to dinner."

Mary Lou was, indeed. She responded to Evelyn's wave with a flash of white fingers.

"You weren't home this afternoon."

"No."

"Because you thought I'd come?"

"No. I never really thought about it at all."

"Good. Because it wouldn't have stopped a thing."

"Porter, for God's sake—"

"Keep your voice down, Evie. This has nothing to do with my wife."

"It has everything to do with your wife!"

"You don't understand. She's my showpiece. My prestige. Did you ever see a life-sized cardboard cut-out in a window? That's Mary Lou. I have to have that. I also need something else."

She swallowed hard. Desperately she said, "Not from me, Port. Go buy it, for heaven's sake."

"Crude. And a nice try. Of course I can buy almost any whore I want. But you're not a whore, Evie, you're a soft, warm, loving woman, and that's what I need in my arms. That's what I dream about—I'm looking at you now and I'm feeling the velvet of your breasts against my mouth, your silky thighs beneath my hands—"

He was making love to her with his voice! Outraged, she shut the door on him—not slamming it because of Mary Lou, but closing it firmly, and leaning against the inside, her heart thudding indignantly.

She heard him laugh. She heard the clatter of keys being dropped inside the storm door. She heard him say softly, "Almost got you, didn't I? I'll wait, Evie. I'll wait."

It was long after the Cadillac door slammed with the dull "thunk" of expensive parts, and long after she heard it purr down the street that she opened her door again, stooped, and picked up the keys.

A small Ford sat in the Lincoln's place. Mustang, she thought. It didn't matter. She just wished desperately that she didn't even have to touch it.

But she did. She knew she did. She couldn't possibly walk to the nursing home in the dark every night.

Rubbing the back of her neck wearily, she sat down again, pulled her reading glasses off the top of her head, adjusted them, and started where she'd left off—signing "Evelyn Matthews Cass" to the last of the money in her account.

The telephone rang at her elbow, and she answered it absently. Karen Evans's voice said, "Evie?"

"Oh. Yes. Hi."

"How'd you do today?"

Good God, did everyone know? Was it emblazoned on the courthouse?

Then, thoroughly ashamed of herself, she answered cheerfully, "Fine. I guess. It's a new experience."

"There. I told Daddy you'd be all right. He was worried, the old fussbudget. Anyway. I have a message. Okay?"

"Okay." And as she said it, she thought of Karen's father and smiled, hearing him in his daughter's unconscious mimicry.

"They had to take my mother to Springfield for a few days. I don't know why. Tests, or something. Of course Daddy went, too. He says to hang in there. He'll call when he gets back."

"Oh. That's very nice of him, Karen."

"He's a very nice man. Please notice."

"I have." Evelyn kept her voice determinedly casual. "We had a lovely day Sunday."

"I'm glad. Aunt Sue was not so thrilled. In fact, she left in a huff—but at least she left. There's Tim coming in. I have to run. Take care."

"Take care," Evelyn echoed, and hung up. Suddenly in the quiet house she felt lonely. A few days. How many days made a few?

Not really liking herself very much, she went

into the kitchen, shoved the pork chop back into the freezer, and drove out to the nursing home.

The Mustang was full of gas and it ran fine.

He just doesn't want anything to damage my velvet boobs and my silky thighs, she thought furiously and almost hit a Chinese elm in the driveway.

Twenty

The next few days were, as Evelyn had said in her college years, real dillies.

She found herself going in two hours ahead of everyone else to be closeted with Margaret, trying to absorb such things as oversupply, need anticipations, and disciplinary practices. Then she joined the rest of the crew for the routine nitty-gritty and found it all intense. The actual cooking process in the stainless steel and porcelain kitchen area was a revelation. Everything was pre-cut, pre-measured, pre-weighed, and governed entirely by small flashing lights that told one when to do, as Marva said inelegantly, "everything but pee." The quiche was especially delicious until Evelyn had eaten it for three days, after which her enthusiasm ebbed.

However, she not only mastered the menu fairly well, but passed the voice test which entitled her to run the drive-up window as well as the "front line"—corporation argot for the order-taking area.

The cleaning process, however, was ferocious.

After explaining the various mops, brushes, squirt bottles, and towels, Margaret Daniels said distinctly, "You have exactly one hour from closing time to mop the floors, do the windows, tables, and doors, the cash registers and the bins. The soda and shake machines are disassembled, the parts put in a sterile solution, the grills polished, and the trash cans hosed. You know your jobs. Get cracking."

To Evelyn's weary dismay, managerial trainees were far from exempt. As Margaret has said, the "Corp" expected everyone's all.

"My gawd," Marva moaned as they walked out together Saturday in the early dusk. "And we do this every night? To think I thought that damned bug was cute!"

Betty, with her purse clenched beneath her arm, was opening her pay envelope. She shrugged. "Not too bad. At least it won't bounce."

"Jeez, I hope not!" Marva was tearing hers open, too. "Boy, the government sure doesn't just sit there and smile, does it? I've made more than this on a one-night-stand. Singing," she added, and grinned. "Who's this 'Corp' our

Maggie keeps talking about?"

"God."

"What?"

"God," repeated Eileen. She tossed her shoulder bag on the front seat of her Trans-Am and stretched. "The corporation. The brass. They'll come in on Monday when we open and stay all week."

"Doing what?"

"Telling us what we're doing wrong, nit-picking if they're assholes, and helping us out if they're not. Hey, guys. We got a day off tomorrow. Let's all go find an open drive-in bank, cash these dudes, and have a drink somewhere! Come on, Evelyn, come on, Betty! You've earned it!"

Betty smiled, but she said, "No, I can't. Thanks."

"Me neither," said Evelyn wearily. "My legs ache, my shoulders ache, and I could peel off my smile like tape. In fact, I may, and save it for Monday. You gals run along. I'm going home to die."

"Sure?"

"Sure."

Betty opened the door of her Chevy. "Give you a lift."

Evelyn said, "I'll take it," and climbed in,

moving a stuffed rabbit to make room. "I could wish," she added, as the elderly car nosed out of the parking lot behind the flashy Trans Am, "that your grandson had a different taste in toys."

"He's always been bunny happy," Betty said, tooting her car horn in answer to the Trans-Am, which had just played the first bars of "Dixie." "His daddy raises Belgians. Pretty things. Are you still on Sycamore?"

"Yes."

"When did you buy that house from Jessie?"

"About ten years ago."

"I figured it would get too much for her."

"It's too much for me."

"Pretty easy stairs, though. Not like some."

She pulled to the curb.

Evelyn climbed out stiffly. "See you Monday."

"If the good Lord's willing and the creeks don't rise," Betty answered cheerfully, "and the place don't burn down. I hear there's some folks not happy about non-union hirin'."

"I really needed to hear that," said Evelyn and waved as the car drove off.

Then she turned and glimpsed the Lincoln in the drive.

Her heart sank. She glanced around and saw no one. The Mustang was gone, though.

Gritting her teeth, she approached her car with all the enthusiasm of nearing a time bomb.

The keys were stuck up on the visor.

There was no bill in sight.

Somehow that was worse than finding she'd been grossly overcharged. A bill would have at least been a known quantity. No bill was—limbo.

Limbo, she said to herself again. Keeping me up in the air. Porter is really a dancing master. Damn him. What am I to do?

There was not a bill stuck in either door, nor the mail box. There was, simply, not a bill.

She said the succinct word that John didn't care for, entered the kitchen, threw the pork chop back into the freezer for the second time, went painfully upstairs, and ran a hot tub. She was there when the phone rang.

Damn. It could be Porter.

Well, if it was, she'd just have to face him. This was getting to be worse than a nuisance—it was harassment. She was in a particularly unenviable position in terms of combating it. She knew that. But enough was, after all, enough!

She got out, dripping, mopped the worst with a towel, and padded in bare feet into the bedroom. The telephone was still ringing persistently as she picked it up.

"Cass residence."

"Evelinda?"

She sat down suddenly in such enormous relief that the satin counterpane slid beneath her and landed them both on the floor with a thud.

In the receiver she could hear Bob's voice saying, "Evelyn? Evelyn? What happened? Are you all right?"

She giggled. "I'm fine. I just fell off the bed."

"You what?"

"Never mind. It's too silly. Or I'm so tired I'm silly. Or something. How are you?"

"I'm fine. You do sound tired. How'd your week go?"

"Let's say it's been an experience." She wiggled her damp fanny into a more comfortable position on the wadded quilt. "Did you know, for example, that after ten minutes all the food in the holding bins is counted, garbage-bagged, and trashed? Everything!"

"It sounds like a waste."

"It is a waste! Think of all the poor dogs in the pounds that would love those burgers!"

He sounded amused. "Are you going to start a smuggling racket on the side? Contraband Bunny Burgers?"

"You're laughing. But I'd love to do something!"

"Oh, Evelinda—we're just of the 'clean your plate' generation, you and I! How's my boy Poo?"

"He's dandy. He's learned to spit on the sidewalk."

He laughed again. "I found new ball caps for him and Robby."

"They'll love them. Bob—" She hesitated. "I know things aren't easy for you. Is anything—better?"

"No. No better. Only worse. It's horrible and unfair and I wish it was over. Does that shock you?"

"No. No, it doesn't. Is there an end?"

"Foreseeable? I don't know. If it was in my hands, God knows there would be! God knows!" She could envision his teeth clenched. "But it's not. And we agreed—when this thing began—that if her trauma could possibly help someone else, we would do it. That's what we're doing now. That's why we're here. That's the only reason." She heard him expel a long, shaky breath. "Okay. Tell me about the Lincoln."

"I just got it back. Today."

"How much?"

300

"I don't know. There wasn't a bill."

"There wasn't a— Have you talked to him?"

"No."

"That bastard. You know what he's doing."

"Putting the arm on me. I know. I know that's what he thinks he's doing. But he won't."

"Attagirl, Evelinda. Hang in there."

"Glitches of the world, unite!"

He laughed, and it was genuine, again. "I have to go. See you soon."

"See you," she echoed, and hung up.

When she got back to the tub the water was cold. Leaving it gurgling in the drain, she threw the hamburger-smelling clothes in the hamper, put on clean slacks and shirt, and suddenly noticed at least one pleasant thing in her day: the elastic waistband was loose.

The Lincoln started promptly and was also full of gas. She mulled this on the way to the nursing home, while she tucked John in, delivered four sexy books to Emma, and deposited her check at the drive-through bank just before the bar went down. The more she mulled, the less she liked the situation. The last thing she wanted, certainly, was a public confrontation, but it was also patently obvious that Porter would avoid that at all costs. They both could lose a certain credibility, although, she realized wryly, as the female in the case and for all useful purposes single, she was the one who might take the brunt. Porter, the solid businessman and happy husband, could well come out unscathed. She would be the predator.

At any rate, it would destroy their group. Somehow Evelyn sensed that Porter didn't want that, either . . . although just how he figured *any* combination of them could be sleeping around without affecting the others was beyond her.

Would it do any good to talk to him on the phone?

Probably not.

If this was just another facet in his war of nerves, she had to admit it was working.

Being Porter, he let it work until Sunday noon as she was taking the two TV dinner rejects from the oven for herself and Poo.

"Hi there, gorgeous," he said. "How's the Lincoln running?"

"It's running fine. I want a bill, Porter."

"I have a proposition."

"I don't want your proposition, I want a bill."

"I have to go to Springfield for a weekend dealer meeting. Mary Lou hates dealer meetings. Why don't you meet me there? We can cancel all debts."

"Porter, I wouldn't meet you at a dog fight."

"Think about it. The second weekend in November."

And he hung up!

Well, she thought, hanging up also. He's made his move. That should be relief of a sort.

"Grammy," said Poo, who had been exploring his dinner, "nasty."

Evelyn looked at hers. "You're right," she said.

She put both dinners into Romeo's bowl and made waffles.

He wandered off while the iron was heating. When she called, he reappeared promptly, closing the basement door behind him.

"Boat," he said. "Play boats."

"You don't have any of your boats here, dear. Only tractors. After lunch, we'll go out in the garden and you can help Grammy plant tulip bulbs, okay?"

Life with Brenda had made him very flexible. He climbed up in his chair again and ate the waffle with relish, saying no more about boats.

Romeo requested entrance, strolled to his bowl, gave it one incredulous sniff, sent an indignant glance Evelyn's way, and requested to go out again. Not really blaming him, she opened the door. She noticed that peculiar odor once more but didn't identify it until she and her grandson approached the tulip bed. Thirteen bulbs lay in disarray among the mothflakes and other detritus peculiar to catdom.

Cursing Romeo with every breath, she replaced the bulbs tenderly, added the ones from her birthday, and hosed down the area with a gentle spray, wondering morosely what to try next. Maybe the remains of the TV dinners.

"Get him a litterbox," said Brenda when she appeared to collect her son. "Mom, admit it— you're stuck with him. Make it official. How did Poo get his tennies so wet?"

"Oh—I guess in the hose," said her mother absently. "Are you set for Monday?"

"Bunny ears and all. I can't wait to see yours. The whole day crew is going to come by at night to cheer you on. Want a piece of advice?"

"Sure."

"Smile," said Brenda, "if it kills you. Hot or cold, happy or hung—smile. Come along, son. Mommy has TV dinners in the oven."

Evelyn chose to pretend she didn't hear Poo's reply. But she did see him spit on the sidewalk.

Twenty-one

Monday morning, because her stomach was doing flip-flops, Evelyn dusted the windowsills and ran the vacuum upstairs. Brenda having taken her furniture when she finally married — thus ending relationships with a string of men with whom she'd lived in pursuit of her elusive ideal — her room had been Poo's for some time, his small crib looking lonely in the vast space that once accommodated his mother's waterbed. Jack's domain was virtually unchanged. Fading posters of flamboyant rock groups, long since disintegrated, joined team photographs on the walls; skeet shoot trophies and sports gear still filled the corners and a "Star Trek" quilt covered both narrow bunks.

It always gratified Jack to walk in and see things just as he'd left them. He seemed to find a sort of security in his own time capsule. Evelyn had wondered on occasion if he needed the reassurance that he'd really given his father pleasure in doing the things John wanted. He'd worked so hard to please him. John had never fully understood how hard—natural athletic ability had flowed from John, and the fact that it wasn't so easy for his son was something he'd refused to believe.

Jack and I both bear those scars, Evelyn remembered sadly. She finished up the impersonal dusting of the impersonal guest room and closed its door. The room lived only when her mother-in-law was there with her books and sweaters and necklaces flung all over the place, her glasses on the bureau with ten family photographs around them, and uncounted pairs of shoes toeing the wall. Jessie was a shoe nut.

Well, the place was tidy now if Jessie did come for Thanksgiving, or sooner.

Just not, please God, for a couple of weeks, Evelyn thought. Not until I'm adjusted to Bunny Burger and have paid a few bills. Not until I'm brave enough to tell her I've listed the house . . .

She looked at the vacuum bag, decided emptying could wait one more time, and shoved it in the closet.

Downstairs the tall case clock struck a sonorous ten.

She went to work at four — if her stomach held out.

She showered, dressed, picked up Emma's returned library books, and went out to the Lincoln.

As she got in, she noticed a peculiar smell again, but with a swift glance she saw that the tulip bulbs were intact. Besides, it was more like a sewer odor — not impossible, as old as the system was on Sycamore, she thought as she drove off to the library.

It was then she became aware that the entire town had gone bunny crazy. Bobbing balloons with pink ears floating above myriad small fists and countless car antennas. They soared in the freedom of escape in the blue sky. One even leaped in the breeze from her own postman's mail cart bar. Someone had tethered two to the handle of the drop-box outside the library steps — for later retrieval, she supposed, and went inside.

If she'd hoped for a respite from bunny mania there, she was disappointed. Karen was just letting an orderly file of her story-hour patrons out the side door. Each wore his own cardboard bunny ears, and as she closed the exit on the last one she smiled at Evelyn.

"You just missed it."

"Missed what?" Evelyn asked.

"Mr. Bunny Burger himself. All six feet of him in a plush suit with a powderpuff tail the size of a toilet lid. The kids loved it."

"I'll bet they did."

"Cup of coffee?"

"Have you time?"

"I'll take time," Karen said with a wink. She slapped a "Be Right Back" sign on her desk, poured two, led the way to the furnace room, flopped on a folding chair, and lit a cigarette. "How are you doing?"

"Fine. I guess." Evelyn unfolded another chair, sat in it and shook her head at the cigarette, sipping cautiously at the coffee.

"Heard from Daddy?"

"Yes." Then, more severely, "Karen, I love you—but don't push."

"Never."

"Bull."

The girl laughed, running slender fingers through her shiny brown hair in a gesture very like her father's, and dropped ash in a trash bucket. "Okay," she said, which was very like her father, also. "Anyway, I'm glad you came by. I was going to call you. I'm snowed. Would you like another temporary part-time job? Only a few hours in the morning—but I've *got* to get

308

my inventory done and you're the only one I know who could help me without screwing up the system. How about it?"

Evelyn hesitated. "I could try. When do you have to know?"

"Oh — on the weekend would be fine. You're not keeping Poo?"

"No. At least, Brenda hasn't asked me. He's usually at his other grandmother's."

"She's a nice lady. Oops," she said, and mashed out the stub of her smoke as the call bell on her desk chimed. "I have to get back. Think about it."

Evelyn left the books on the desk upstairs and went home. She had thought she'd stop at Bunny Burger as a customer, just to get the feel of the day, but the enormous lines of people and cars extending across the lot and into the street put her off. The idea of dealing personally with such organized pandemonium sent her straight to the Maalox bottle.

Just as she arrived home, the telephone rang.

"Cass residence."

"Evelyn? It is Evelyn?"

"Yes. Sorry."

"I'm not sorry, I'm ecstatic," said the voice and with a definite sinking feeling Evelyn recognized Margaret Daniels. "I thought I wasn't going to get you. Can you come in an hour instead of at four? Tom has two more school appearances in the damned bunny suit, I've got Corp working drive-through because the girl there lost her voice, I've had to send another girl to Springfield for more balloons, one girl quit in the middle of a quiche, and this place is a madhouse."

Evelyn swallowed in pure panic. When she answered, her voice quavered; nonetheless she said, "Yes. I'll be there as fast as I can."

"Bless you. Walk or be dropped off. Anything but bringing another car on the lot. Don't forget the ears. I've already loaned the extras."

At least she'd already showered.

Fifteen minutes got her to Bunny Burger, where a constant litany of "Excuse me," got her across the customer line that curved around the employee entrance. Margaret Daniels literally snatched her inside, hissed, "Drive-up window!" and gave her a shove.

There was certainly no time to feel self-conscious.

Jamming the ears on her head, she was tucking in her hair as she trotted. The chubby man in the shirt and tie croaked, "You're beautiful!" and slid out of the small order nook so fast she wasn't really sure he'd been there. Drinks first, she said to herself, shakes and sundaes last unless they ask, money before food. She put her finger on the speaker key and said, "Welcome to Bunny Burger; may I help you?"

The answer was growled back, "Damn right you can—I thought you'd died in there. Gimme a small fry, a Diet Coke, and two orders of qwish with ham, hold the mushrooms."

Qwish?

Somehow that small streak of human frailty righted her world. She almost giggled, suppressed it, repeated the order, rang up the tab, and was on her way. She was also careful to repeat the word *qwish* also. "Never embarrass the customer," Margaret Daniels had said, and now she understood why.

Vaguely she noticed when Marva came in to back her up, and on her precious break when she simply leaned against the hall wall and breathed, she saw Betty at the grill and Eileen on the run from the storeroom with a stack of buns. After five Brenda came through the drive-up with Poo. She looked exhausted, but Poo was bouncing beside her wearing his pink cardboard ears and saying, "Burger, Grammy, burger!"

Brenda asked, "Mom, you okay?"

"I'm numb. That will be two-ninety-four, please."

"Me, too. Sit down, Poo; Grammy's hurrying. See you."

"See you. Bye, honey. Welcome to Bunny Burger; may I help you?"

The next voice was in shock: "Evie?"

Just what she needed! Clenching her teeth, she said, "Yes. May I take your order please?"

Mary Lou was with him. Thank God for small favors. As they drove up, she was trilling excitedly, "I told him! I told him! He didn't believe me! How you doing—you look so cute! Isn't this simply wild?"

Evelyn had no time—nor inclination—to divine *what* precisely was wild, although she had the feeling that Mary Lou, out of touch with reality as usual, probably thought she was just slumming. She took Porter's money, avoiding his fingers, and handed out their Bunny Burger bag, saying briskly, "The fries are on top. Have a balloon."

Mary Lou giggled and said, "This is such fun! Isn't it fun, Port?"

Porter said, "I may eat here every day," and winked at her.

"Port, don't flirt with the help! Mmm. It smells divine. Bye-bye."

312

"Bye-bye" said Evelyn thankfully. "Welcome to Bunny Burger; may I help you?"

She said it the last time at eight, when Margaret took her off drive-up and put her on grill until ten-thirty when at last the lights went off outside and they closed down.

"I'm sorry," said Margaret to her dazed crew. "But there's always tomorrow. Let's clean."

They cleaned.

At eleven thirty-five, looking a bit strange in his headless plush bunny suit, Tom Jennings said, "You're a good bunch. I'd doff my tail to you if I wasn't so tired. See you tomorrow."

The parking lot was empty beneath the arc lights and the air was cool. Evelyn, coatless, shivered and Eileen glanced at her. "Okay," she said to all four of them shuffling out the side door, "No excuses this time! I'm buyin'! You're goin'!"

Kooky, her frizz gone limp, said hoarsely, "I'm takin'. Where's your car?"

Betty demurred. "Uniforms."

"What?"

"Uniforms. We're all wearing Bunny Burger. You can't go into a joint in this rig; it's against company policy and I sure don't want to get fired."

In disgust, Eileen said, "Put your damned

coat on, then. Here, Evelyn—" and she tossed her the jacket on her arm. It was bright red and smelled of smoke. "I've got another in the Trans Am. And the place we're going has a booth in back where you could be naked and nobody'd notice. Besides, it's my treat—my old man came through with a support payment."

So tired that sitting down anywhere had enormous appeal, Evelyn found herself in a scarlet windbreaker that said BUDWEISER on the back jamming into a crowded rear seat with two other women and driving away in the roar of twin carburetors.

Wearily, she did say, "You could drop me off."

"Drop hell!" Eileen shouted happily. "We're a team! We're a team, gals, and we made it through the whole fuckin' day, and we're gonna drink to that! Off to Buffalo Bill's!"

Eileen punctuated her declaration by turning onto a sidestreet that led to the edge of town, jolting up a rutted lane, rounding a tall mass of cedar thicket, and stopping in a parking lot crowded with pickup trucks.

"All out!" she said loudly against a background of Waylon Jennings singing "Luckenbach Texas" from a speaker on a pole above their heads. "And in the side door; I got con-

314

nections. Bill's an old boyfriend."

The noisy confusion, the smoke, and the smell of warm beer hit them like a wall, but Eileen was right about the back booth. Evelyn slid in on the outside, next to Betty. The gangling waiter got a hug and a smack from Eileen, wiped the table top with the remains of a plaid shirt, emptied the tin ashtray on the sawdust floor, and said, "Okay, ladies, what'll it be?"

"Beer," said Eileen, as she dragged her gold hoops from her shoulder bag and affixed them expertly back onto her ears. "Whatever you want, gals, go ahead. My tab, Ernie."

"Mrs. Rich Bitch," grinned the waiter, moistening his pencil with his tongue.

"Beer and a shot on the side," said Betty.

Somehow sensing this was not the place to order a gin and tonic, Evelyn said, "Busch Light." Leaning back against the high booth cushions, she looked down the row toward the open area ahead. On one side was a big oak bar with every stool occupied and a varied collection of boots on the brass rail. In the middle was a pool table, equally busy. From the shouts and rattles, there were obviously video games and a dance floor, as she caught an occasional fleeting glimpse of people in jeans gyrating to a

315

rhythm of their own. The noise had quieted somewhat — or she had simply adjusted to it. The overall sense was comfortable *country,* very — as Porter would probably say with a sneer — "good ol' boy." But as two girls from the bar leaned back waving their beers and saying, "Hi, Leeny!" and their own order came on a tin tray, she took her Busch Light, sipped, and almost felt relaxed.

"Shoot!" said Marva, leaning across Betty. By the simple expedient of turning her Bunny Burger collar in, unbuttoning the two top buttons, and swinging her long, relatively blond hair up into a rubber-banded tail on one side of her head, she had transported her garb from uniform to seductive. "Shoot! Will you look at that guy at the pool table! The square one with the curly black hair and the cute butt — if he's as sexy from the front as he is from the back, I got dibs, girls!"

Evelyn looked, and almost laughed. Before she thought, she said, "That's Vic Bonnelli."

"You know him? No kidding? Yours?"

"Not hardly."

"Geronimo! Vic! Vic!"

Marva didn't have the vocal power of a "chantoosey" for nothing. Half-chagrined, half-laughing, Evelyn saw "Vic the Invincible" stop, turn, put down his pool cue, and come toward them.

" 'Evening, ladies," he said to them and pointed a finger the size of a bratwurst at Evelyn. "You! Why don't you stay home?"

A little embarrassed, Evelyn found herself the focal point of all the eyes in the booth.

Marva said, "Yeah—why don't you? I sure as hell would!"

Vic ignored her—at least for the moment. "I've been calling for three days," he said. "Three damned days! Thursday. Can you be there Thursday? About ten o'clock?"

Sometimes the best thing to do is simply let it ride. Evelyn laughed, nodded her head, and said, "Sure. Ten o'clock." Why explain? Nobody cared, anyway—at least, not in this crowd.

"All right," said Vic. "That's better. Now—introduce me to your pals."

"Betty. Marva. Eileen. Kooky."

They all said hi. He frowned and peered a little closer through the dim light. "A club? Y'all play poker together or something?" Then it hit him. "My God! I know! You're Burger Bunnies! You got me some sour cream for my fries—"

Kooky nodded.

"—And you brought me my second salad

317

with extra cherry tomatoes."

Eileen nodded.

The finger swung back to Evelyn. "And you, too. You're a bunny?"

Eileen answered for her: "She sure as hell ain't our den mother," she said. "We're a team, buster. The best damned team in town. And we're drinkin' to it!"

"I'll buy," said Vic. "Scoot over, Blondie."

Marva scooted.

"A little more," said Vic and slapped her thigh. "There are two halves to my butt, honey, and when one of them is still hanging over, my center of gravity gets a bit displaced. That's better. Okay, Ernie, whatever the ladies are drinking, keep it comin'. And tell Tony to shoot my turn for a while; I'm tied up. How come I haven't seen you girls out here before?"

"We haven't had any money before. This is payday."

Marva murmured, "And Evelyn never told us about you."

Vic sat directly across from Evelyn. Under the tangled, curly mop of salted hair, his black eyes sparkled at her. "Well—what Evelyn and I have going is a little different. Open-ended, you might say."

"What does that mean?"

"It means, Blondie, that I can ask you to dance and she won't have a hissy fit. So come on."

They moved out of sight, past the pool table. Eileen was grinning. "Talk about the long and the short of it!" she said. "He comes about up to Marva's boobs — which I guess from his point of view ain't too bad."

"If they stretched out his width he'd be eighteen feet tall," said Kooky, finishing her Miller Light and expertly popping the tab on the second.

Betty took her shot of whiskey neat without a blink, and followed with a long draft from the Pilsener. "I remember the Bonnellis," she said. "His grandpa was my grandpa's bootlegger. My dad always said on Sundays that we had the best communion wine in town." She sent a glance sideways at Evelyn. "I heard tell this one was back. Real estate, ain't he?"

Evelyn nodded. She knew in her soul Betty had already figured out the connection between herself and Vic — and could probably even come close to the house's asking price. Someone — Liz Swan, she thought — had once said, "Never think you can keep secrets from your cleaning woman." Mary Lou had answered flippantly, "They're just nosey," and Liz had challenged

her: "No. But cleaning for a living doesn't
mean they're not bright — and they see so
much. Who empties your wastepaper basket?
What did you throw in it? What's shoved in the
back of a drawer that you forgot about when
you asked her to straighten it? Who was scrub-
bing the bathroom floor when your husband
came in and started yelling at you?" Mary Lou
had been appalled, but Evelyn — recalling the
conversation now — suddenly felt the enormous
gap between her old friends in their insulated
existence and the women with whom she sat
this evening . . . and the widening crack between them and herself.

Kooky said, "Where's the john? My eyeballs
are floating."

Eileen stood up to let her pass, pointed out
the accommodations, and over Betty's head directed Evelyn's attention downward. Betty had
three empty shot glasses lined up and was
pouring down the fourth. The ratio of whiskey
to beer was a bit awry.

Catching the signal, Evelyn said, "Listen —
I'm bushed. Whenever you'd like to run me
home. Are you ready, Betty?"

Betty said, "Sure." She picked up the two un-
opened beers and shoved them in her bag.
"Mama taught me never to waste nothin'.

Where's Kook?"

"In the pot."

Betty flipped her hand at the closed door. "G'night, Kook!"

Evelyn lingered, hesitating. "Do you tip?"

Eileen was mothering Betty toward the door. "I'm coming back. But you can leave something if you want. Ernie'd appreciate it—he's trying to save for new boots."

Evelyn put down a crumpled dollar bill, hoping it was adequate. Her last glimpse, beyond the pool table, was that of Marva and Vic slow-dancing, Vic's nose buried in her ample frontage. When Betty yelled, " 'Bye, Marvel!" she raised her cheek from his curly hair and winked.

The noise followed them out, receding as the door shut. The parking lot was shot with moonlight trailing through the ragged branches of the cedar trees. Two fellows in jeans and boots were leaning against the pickup next to the Trans-Am. One of them asked cheerfully, "Folding early, aren't you, ladies? The arm wrestling starts in about ten minutes."

"Be still my heart," said Eileen, but she was laughing. "Who's on tonight?"

"Buffalo Billy and Vic the Invincible. It should be a doozy."

321

"See you later," Eileen caroled and started the Trans-Am. As she backed around, she asked Evelyn, "Is that Vic your buddy?"

Betty had dropped her head on Evelyn's shoulder and shut her eyes. Evelyn put an arm around her to keep her from sagging into Eileen as they rounded corners and was amazed at how frail the little lady felt. As for Vic, she shrugged and gave an honest answer, "I guess. He used to box. Now I imagine he arm wrestles." She felt it somewhat pointless to go into Vic's personal problems. "He went to school with my husband."

"He's cute. You're on Sycamore, aren't you?"

"Right at the bend. That's it. Thanks, Eileen. I enjoyed it. I think I can get to sleep now."

As the big sports car roared back down the street and she rounded the Lincoln with her doorkey in hand Romeo came strolling from the syringas. Together they went into the dark kitchen and by the time she had the light on he was already curled snugly in his box.

"Do they arm wrestle where you were?" she asked him wearily, "or paw wrestle as the case may be. Hi, John —" she said to his Salesman-of-the-Year picture on her fridge. "You would never in the world believe where I've been. So never mind."

He wouldn't believe it. He wouldn't be able even to imagine his matronly, conservative wife sitting in a country bar having a beer with Liz Swan's former cleaning lady, an out-of-work singer, a walking frizz, and an unwed mother wearing three-inch hoops in her pierced ears.

She wasn't certain she believed it herself. It was a properly unreal end to a totally unreal day.

Too tired to debate the fuzzy fringes of class-consciousness, she fell into bed with her nightgown on backwards and slept until noon.

Twenty-two

Monday, while working drive-up, Evelyn was offered twenty-five dollars for her bunny ears by two high school seniors on a scavenger hunt. She was tempted. Tuesday, while working a Bunny Burger Birthday Party, the birthday child was crowned with his own chocolate cake by his sister whose birthday was not until January. Wednesday, while working front line, the hose on the shake machine came loose in mid-operation, spraying Evelyn, Eileen, and Kooky with vanilla ice cream. Eileen said she'd had a lot of items in her bra before but ice cream had not been one of them—a remark that amused all of the customers but the small child who was waiting for his shake.

Wednesday closing time was delayed by the same surly man complaining his "qwish" was cold. Evelyn had difficulty being polite. They'd all had about enough of him. He always ordered the same quiche and it was never right. She went home, not looking forward to Thursday.

However, Thursday came, right on schedule. By eight-thirty she had persuaded herself to rise and cope. Sitting limply in her kitchen sipping warmed-over coffee, she suddenly remembered Vic Bonnelli and ten o'clock. This fact was greatly reinforced by Vic himself appearing on her step at nine o'clock.

Reluctantly she opened the door, aware of her tatty old blue housecoat and homebrew haircut.

He said breezily, "Hi, doll," with the disgusting enthusiasm of someone who has the world by the tail every morning, rain or shine. "How come you didn't stay for the arm wrestling the other night? I took that sucker two out of three. What smells?"

"Sewer," she answered briefly. "Sit down. Coffee?"

He slid two bar stools together, hoisted himself up and grinned across the bar at her. "No, thanks. I got a full tank already. I'm just checking to be sure you're ready for my clients. These folks are serious."

That familiar icy lump formed in the pit of her stomach again. "You think they might — buy?"

"Or lease — with an option to buy. Would you go for that?"

"I'd still have to move."

"Unless you'd want to live in the attic and shinny up and down the drainpipe — which can be done because John and I did it."

As usual, stress was bringing on a hot flash. She folded a paper napkin, blotting her forehead.

He said, "My God, you too? My sister still does that. Why don't you get a shot — scared of a moustache?"

"Scared of a bill."

"Oops. Sorry. Shall I open the door?"

"It will be gone in a minute."

He opened the door anyway, then came back and sat down again. She suddenly realized how light he was on his feet, moving that square bulk with the grace of a panther. It must have been the boxing.

He was loosening the tie about his massive neck, and she found herself wondering what shirt size went beyond seventeen — the limit of her experience. Whatever it was, it served very adequately; there was no unsightly button gap above his belt buckle.

His next words brought her back with a snap. He was sniffing, his blocky nose wrinkled. "What did you say that smell was?"

"Sewer. I suppose."

"I hope."

"Why?"

326

"Because it smells more like—"

He stopped and grimaced. "Christ. How long's it been since you went down in your basement?"

"A week. I don't know. My washer and dryer are up here; I don't very often—"

Then she remembered Poo. And his request for boats. She said, "Oh my goodness!" He read her face and beat her to the basement door, snapping on the light.

The smell was from there, all right. And just beyond the steps the black gleam of water lapped at the uneven floor. A pie tin full of mouse bait rode the surface like a small, round raft.

Vic dragged one big hand across his face, clenching his teeth. "Shit! Look at that! Look at that! Any time you ran water in the last few days, lady, this is where it went. Why didn't I know the damned pipe was ready to give? Now what do we do?"

He turned around, and at the sight of her frozen face he softened.

"All right, all right, don't look like I stepped on your puppy. It's not your fault. Let me think. None of these old houses have sump pumps, so Jessie didn't either. Right?"

He bent over, kicking off his shoes, peeling off his socks and rolling up his pants legs. His voice came up muffled: "Call my office." He gave her the number. Numbly she dialed and handed him the phone. She heard the word "sump pump" again and "On the double. Get cracking." Then he said to her, "Fans. You got fans? Go get 'em — all of 'em!"

As she ran awkwardly for the stairs in her lambswool shoes she heard his voice on the phone again, and this time in dulcet tones: "Mrs. Carlyle — good morning; how are you? That's fine. You know that nice home on Sycamore — yes, that's the one — we have a small hang-up in my schedule today. Do you suppose I could show it to you tomorrow?"

Two square window fans were stored in the closet at the head of the stairs. She grabbed them, pushing coats and skirts out of her face and tumbling a stack of shoe boxes. One was full of wooden beads that ran riot over the floor and bounced down the stairs ahead of her like a rain of tiny cannon balls. Dragging the fans, she followed.

Vic was standing in the doorway. He grinned and met her, taking the fans. "Good girl. Got any more?"

"In the garage — John's shop. I think."

"Okay — if we want them. These may do. It's not as bad as I thought. We'll get the water out, then dry off with the fans. But you do need a plumber. You got a favorite or shall I call one?"

"Go ahead."

She sat down again, out of the way, twisting her diamond band around and around. She felt sick. Money. Money. Plumbers were more expensive than mink; she'd heard John say that. And where was the money coming from for new pipe?

Hanging up the telephone again, Vic glanced over at her. Shoving the tangled curly mop from his forehead, he smiled. Padding around the bar in his curious gait, he reached out and tousled her head, tipped it back, and smacked her on one round cheek. It was a friendly, brotherly kiss.

"All right!" he said. "Be cool, doll. We're in control."

"Vic, you don't understand—"

"Bull. Yes I do. Don't worry; I'll put it on your tab."

Her first thought was that she seemed to be running a "tab" with Porter and she sure as hell didn't want another with this guy—but he clarified that immediately. "When we unload the place we'll settle all the bills. Not until. Now before my boy comes with the sump pump, why don't you trot back upstairs and get dressed?"

Suddenly aware that she'd torn one pocket with a fan, her housecoat was dusty, her hair a mess, and she wore no bra, Evelyn blushed.

Vic looked startled. Then he smiled. Not a

329

grin. A smile. "Nice," he said. "I didn't know girls did that anymore. You've made my day." Then he yelled after her, "And for God's sake, don't run the water! Go to the neighbor's!"

As she pulled on slacks and the first shirt that came to hand — a red one — she heard the sound of a truck and voices, feet on her basement steps, a curse or two, then the noise of rushing water. Looking out she saw a stream begin to jet from a hose thrust from a basement window to her driveway. It was sudsy. It also smelled. She murmured a silent apology to the neighborhood.

Retrieving the wooden balls was a real experience. Some could be seen. Others were felt as sharp pangs beneath her knees as she gathered. Some had gone into the heat registers. Some would never be seen again. She couldn't remember why she'd had them in the first place, but it had been a major mistake.

She had her fanny in the air and was scraping under the desk with a broom handle when she heard a polite throat-clearing. Glancing up, she saw a young man in a white apron and cap standing in the door to the kitchen.

"I knocked," he said apologetically. "I guess you couldn't hear me. How are you, Mrs. Cass? How's Mr. Cass?"

"Fine," she answered in polite vagueness. Her mind was racing. His face was rather familiar.

330

Who was he?

Then he answered the question himself. "I brought your meat order. Most of it's in the freezer as usual, but there's some left over. Would you like me to put the rest in the fridge?"

Stunned, Evelyn nodded.

Why hadn't she cancelled the meat processor? Why?

It was too late now. Everything was custom-cut to John's specifications.

Still on her knees, she heard him rattling around in the kitchen, heard the refrigerator door slam.

"Bill's on the table," he yelled. "See you!"

She thought dismally, probably behind bars. She knew what the bill would be—around two or three hundred dollars, depending on market value. And somehow she suspected Vic Bonnelli could not put a meat delivery on his realty tab.

Soberly, she stood up, put the bead box on John's desk, dialed Karen, and told her she'd take the library job.

The plumber came as she hung up. With a sense of ushering the pallbearers in to her own funeral, she showed him to the basement. Then, feeling a desperate need, she fished out the expensive brand and made another pot of coffee.

When it was done, she carried her cup out to the patio.

Romeo was crouched on the opposite side of the drive, his access to the house cut off by the moving stream. As she hopped the flood and sat down on the metal chair, he sprang into her lap, thrusting his furry head beneath her chin.

He crouched on her stomach, kneading his paws as she stroked his silky back. An airplane silently scored the blue sky, a tiny black arrow piercing cotton clouds. She thought of Bob Marsh, and was rather glad he wasn't here to see all this. His hands were full enough — Karen had said her mother wasn't good at all.

Karen looked like her father. Robby resembled his dad. What legacy was Sue-Ann Marsh leaving behind — besides the pain in her husband's voice?

Beauty. Joy. Laughter. Evelyn had heard of all those things when people spoke of Sue-Ann. Karen. Bob. The distraught young wife at the fly-in. Perhaps that wasn't too bad, wasn't too poor an estate.

What would John's children remember of him?

Sternness. Discipline. Practicality. Love.

Whatever happened, they'd never doubted the love.

Nor had she. Nor should she now. The kernel of anguish in John's mind she'd never been able to erase had blossomed into fantasy about his wife, Pat. But John was ill. If his fantasy was healing some sense of guilt in the heart of Pat's John, all right. Evelyn's John was no longer, and could intend no hurt.

Nor, thank God, was he trapped in that nursing home worrying about her problems here! His concern would be monumental. She would have to lie, to cover up—and be no further ahead than she was now. Sometimes things do make a rude sort of sense if one twists them right.

The sound of voices and scuffling feet in her kitchen brought her around, looking over her shoulder. Romeo stopped kneading, pricking his ears. Three men marched out carrying various impedimenta. The fourth was Vic Bonnelli. The first three got into their trucks and left with cheery farewells. Vic, carrying his shoes and socks, came across the damp driveway toward her as Romeo, launching himself like a missile, just squeaked into the kitchen before the door slammed shut.

Vic sat down in the opposite chair and stretched out his legs. "Which twin has the Toni?"

"What?"

Then she looked at his feet and understood. Trying to imitate his own matter-of-fact tone, she said, "Unless you have a fetish about shaving only one leg—the left one."

"Good girl. God, I'm tired, lady. I hopped a

lot down there. This prosthesis is expensive. But it's worth it. I can run, and I can dance, and at least do the preliminaries on some other fun things." He winked at her and she knew she was supposed to ask. However, having a pretty good idea of the subject, she chose not to. He only grinned.

"Of course," he said, "kneeling in church is still a little tough. Too bad I have to do so much of it. But like I tell Father McDermott, it's really God's fault for making sin so much fun. How about getting a disabled vet that cup of coffee now?"

"Sure. Black?"

"Never! Sugar. And cream. On occasion I've been known even to take Irish whiskey. But not today."

The basement door was open and the smell was still there, but it was fading. The sound of fans made a steady hum. Evelyn poured the coffee, got the sugar, slopped in a dollop of milk and emptied the rest of the carton into Romeo's bowl. It had been around quite a while. She was not a milk drinker. She also freshened two bagels in the microwave and got out the cream cheese. When she reemerged into the sunshine Vic had put his shoes back on and propped his feet on the opposite chair.

He grinned at the bagels and said, "Good girl.

You can start today, minimum wage, and we'll discuss increments at the proper time."

Then as she sat down again, he added, "You're thinner."

"I think it's called the Bunny Burger Trot."

"Just don't overdo. I don't like skinny broads. Going up and down the stairs in that housecoat, you were a real treat."

If she blushed again, he was paying no attention, wiping cheese from his chin with a napkin and burying his nose in his coffee. "I think we got it licked," he went on. "She'll be dry down there tomorrow and Pete did a good fix on the pipe. Now I want you to realize, doll, that these people looking at this house are serious. So you had better be."

"I am. Truly."

But he was suddenly gazing at his coffee. "Milk!" he said. "Damn. And here I thought I'd discovered perfection. Anyway—if I were you, I'd start apartment hunting. They're living in a motel and pretty tired of it."

Evelyn felt as though she were being buried beneath a load of rocks.

She said in horror, "Oh God! Moving! All my stuff—and I have to work! How can I manage?"

"You could offer a lease with contents. I think they'd do it. They've got a house in Michigan that's sitting there unsold, dead in the water, and

I don't think he's too sure about this job he's got here. We could try that angle. Just pull out enough for survival in an apartment and rent the rest. Or find a furnished apartment and leave everything but your undies."

Slowly, with relief, she said, "I could do that. If I could find an apartment."

"You never know until you try. Have you looked?"

"No."

"Then do it."

"How? The phone book?"

"And newspaper ads and asking other people if they know of one! Christ, woman! What did John Cass do for thirty years? Keep you in cotton wool?"

She suddenly realized how backward she must seem. She felt ashamed and disgusted.

"Yes," she said flatly. "And some of it lodged in my brain. Sure. I can do that. In fact, it would be the perfect solution."

"That's me: solutions on demand."

He drained the cup, brushed bagel crumbs from his handsome foulard tie, and shoved the tie up properly again, standing as he did it. "Okay. One o'clock tomorrow. And no more surprises, please. When do you go to work?"

She frowned, remembering. "Ten o'clock, first. Margaret is having me practice my 'greeting.'

336

That's part of the job, too—meeting customers, seating them. People like to have managers bring them coffee, I guess. I should be home by twelve-thirty. But I leave at three for the nursing home to see John. Then I'm back here and go again at four-ish. I go 'on' at Bunny about five."

"That's quite a night crew you work with."

"They've been awfully nice to me."

"It takes one to know one," he said cheerfully. "Say hi to old John. See you."

"See you," she echoed. She watched him pass the Lincoln and go out of sight around the syringa bushes. Then, gathering up the cups and the crumpled napkin, she took them into the kitchen, and in a small spurt of defiance, rummaged a T-bone steak from the freezer.

"The condemned woman ate a hearty meal," she murmured acidly and put it on the drainboard to defrost.

Twenty-three

Friday she was sitting at John's desk adding up her bills again when Vic called. It was or was not a propitious moment, depending on where one stood. On one hand she was already more than a thousand dollars in the hole with her taxes and the damned meat bill, her three hundred gone to pay utilities before she ever got acquainted with it. On the other, she would be making about two hundred per week clear with Bunny and the library which surely could be used to soak up the deficit thousand if . . . If. Damn. If she knew how much Porter's bill was. If she didn't get sick. If she didn't get fired . . .

She was thinking grimly that she was going to be eating a lot of Bunny Burgers when the telephone rang.

Vic said cheerfully, "I have good news and bad news. The good news is that they'll lease. The bad news is that she has to go back to Michigan for a while and they won't want possession until December."

He waited.

Nothing.

Then he heard a croaky, "Oh." Alarmed, he said, "Hey, doll — if he can still say okay after a pratfall on a wooden bead, you're surely not going to bug out because his wife said your decorating taste was Grand Rapids!"

"*Late* Grand Rapids," corrected Evelyn, who hadn't been supposed to hear the remark in the first place. Looking across at her dear, cozy oak-and-needlepoint living room with its neutral drapes and one hundred percent nylon wall-to-wall carpet, its Andrew Wyeth repros and ginger-jar lamps, she acknowledged the label but resented the woman. "No. I'm not bugging out. I can't afford it. What do they want?"

"Everything. Grand Rapids and all. She's going to try to lease her house on the same basis."

"I hope she gets someone who thinks her Jacomini furniture is tat."

"That's not nice."

"I know. Anyway — how much?"

"We're dickering. You understand this is with an option to buy."

"Yes. Does my signing the lease set the option in cement?"

"Ethically, yes. Evie, come on—you don't need that house! Not unless you're going to take in boarders."

"We're zoned against it or I might."

"Bull. You're not the landlady type. If you were, I could set you up in a place a few miles from here. They rent more by the hour than by the month but I'll bet you'd look gorgeous in marabou."

"Marabou what?"

"Nothing. Just marabou." He was rewarded by the sound of laughter. "Anyway, I just wanted you to know things are cooking. I'll be in touch. In the meantime, find a damn apartment. December is five weeks away."

"I will. Thanks, Vic. Oh—" She was hit with a sudden brainstorm. "Vic, you don't suppose they'd take a freezer full of meat?"

He didn't even gulp. "How new?"

"Delivered yesterday."

"Goofed up, didn't you?"

"Goofed up good."

"I'll ask. See you."

"See you," she echoed, and put down the receiver.

God, if the man would only buy it! She could scratch off almost half of that thousand-dollar deficit right then and there!

She leaned back in John's oak swivel chair and moved it gently from side to side with her lambswool toe, listening to the familiar squeak. She was tired. At this point she couldn't remember not being tired.

She wasn't sleeping well. Last night she'd dreamed of the kids being small again, of playing Farmer-in-the-Dell with them and their friends, of dancing around and around. The children's shrill voices had called off the wife, the child, the dog, the cat, the rat, and the mice—until the cheese stood alone. She had been the cheese. She'd stood there helplessly watching everything fade away—the kids, the voices, the sunlight, until it began to rain from the darkness, soaking her, stringing her hair, chilling her into shivers. She'd awakened shaking, John's pillow on the floor. Alone. Alone, alone, alone!

She'd realized with terrible clarity that this was why many women who were suddenly widowed, divorced, or abandoned rushed right out and either tried blindly to bury themselves in their unfortunate children's lives or took on the first man who happened by. Women had a backlog of centuries of dependence. They couldn't beat it in a day, some wouldn't try, and some couldn't beat it, trying.

Which was she?

She hadn't beaten it yet but she was trying. Wasn't she?

She flounced over in bed, retrieved John's pillow, and buried her face in its cold slip, then with a grimace she turned over again. Eyes screwed shut against the first glimmering gray bars of daylight, she tried to marshal her emotions and think about herself dispassionately. Blubbering in the dark wouldn't help.

Hadn't her experiences with Porter and Charles Nixon taught her a thing? Was Bob Marsh's shoulder just a place to cry on? Had she already leaned too much on Vic, halfway expecting him to find an apartment for her all wrapped up in a satin bow? If he didn't, wasn't she prepared to be a little resentful? And when she ran out of men — which she probably had done, then what?

The things she'd decided in the cold light of dawn in the comfort of her warm bed, the brave, sturdy things, came back to her as scary as a dive into cold water. But they were the right things.

The cheese must stand alone.

And the cheese sure as hell better find an apartment.

She was showered, dressed, had six possibles marked in the local ads, and her keys in her hand when Jane Nixon walked in the kitchen door.

Jane's hair had the normal gray color and the crisp, curled look of the beauty shop. She said, "Hi. I thought you didn't go to work until evening."

"I don't."

"Then have you got a minute?"

"Sure."

"Those damned dryers leave me stiff as a rock." Jane was getting a glass from the cupboard, filling it with ice, and pouring tea from the refrigerator pitcher. She downed the glass, filled it again, and turned around, the fridge door clunking softly behind her. Her brown eyes swept over Evelyn. "Well, you're obviously loaded for bear. Am I interrupting something?"

"I'm leasing this place as of the first of December. I have to find an apartment."

Evelyn was braced. But Jane merely heaved her ample fanny up on a kitchen bar stool and rummaged in her enormous shoulder bag. Taking out cigarettes, she lit one, blew smoke to the ceiling, and said, "Ah. I survived. My hair dresser is on a non-smoking kick."

Evelyn said a bit desperately, "Janey—did you hear me?"

"Of course I heard you. But you know my

343

brains run on nicotine. Wait until I have this one smoke and I'll catch up with you. If we can find a reasonable two-bedroom place, I'll pay half."

Evelyn had a sensation not unlike having a chair kicked from beneath her. "Good God. You're not leaving Charles!"

Jane flicked ash in the tray. "I've thought about it. Probably not — at least until I think about it some more. Right now I'd just like a place to go that's all mine." She suddenly looked at Evelyn directly. "Shocked?"

"No. I don't think I am."

"Seen it coming?"

"No. Not that, either." Honestly, she added, "I've wondered."

"You've probably had reason. Don't blush, Evie, and don't feel badly. I know my old goat. I knew him when he wasn't so old and he hasn't changed. And that's really not the problem — or, more plainly, if Charles is my problem, then so am I his. Evie, for God's sake, we've been married for almost forty years. I never dated anyone else. I was a fat, homely girl with nothing going for me but money and I knew it. Now I'm a fat, homely matron — with less money, but enough to keep him home. More or less. Now isn't that a nice, warm, rewarding situation for both of us? Surely there's something else in this world

344

before we both die!"

Evelyn sat down on the opposite stool and held out her hand. "Give me one of those."

"I thought you'd quit."

"I have. Just give me one and shut up. Maybe nicotine will help *my* brains. Because you're serious. Aren't you?"

"Absolutely. I've been watching you. And you're breaking loose—"

"Well—"

"Yes, you are. So I've said to myself, Fellow Ostriches of the World, arise! If Evie can do it, so can I."

"Fellow what?"

"Ostriches."

"Okay."

Jane repeated, "Ostriches. You heard me right. Listen—what do ostriches do?"

"Bury their heads in the sand?"

"Bingo. The ostrich syndrome: don't look and it won't get you. That's our generation, Evie. Our group. Mary Lou will never pull her head out because she's scared. Liz won't because she doesn't have to. But you did have to—and I think I want to. Make sense?"

The cigarette was acrid. Evelyn coughed and mashed it out. Slowly she answered, "I think so. But it's kind of scary."

"Haven't you been scared?"

"Oh Lord. Yes."

"Me, too. You want to know what started this? Not Charles, poor bugger. Emily's little girl — my youngest grand-kid. At school they were asked to describe their grandmothers. Carolyn wrote that I cooked nice, grew pretty flowers, and knitted things."

"That's bad?"

"Not until you see it as an epitaph. Is that all I'm going to get from my life? Isn't there anything else?"

"What do you want?"

"What do *you* want?"

Evelyn blew out her cheeks. "At the moment? Financial survival would be nice."

"And after that?"

"I guess to be — happy again. Whatever it takes."

"Okay. That's yours. It's mine, too. In a way. The happy part. To do it I need a place away from my house, from Charles, from everything. I need to get my perspective back. You probably need help on rent. Can we work it?"

"We can try."

"Then let's go," Jane said as she slid from the stool and mashed out her cigarette.

Outside, she said, "My car."

"I can drive."

"Honey, we don't look for a cheap apartment with a Lincoln."

Evelyn saw the wisdom in that. They got into Jane's utility Chevy. She read off addresses and Jane drove.

"I have seen," said Jane at noon as they drank chocolate shakes at the shopping center, "every specie of cockroach known to science — from the ones in tuxedos at that gold-rimmed duplex to the ones in jogging shorts trying to get away from the wolves in the dump by the river. Wasn't that a beauty, by the way?"

"Hot and cold running bugs," Evelyn agreed. She tasted her shake critically and thought, we make better at Bunny. This one's full of lumps. "I wonder what in the world had been roosting in that closet?"

"I don't know, but I think it died. Well. The one with the shower wasn't too bad, except I don't like living over the bank."

"How about the place behind the Methodist Church? I could walk to work from there."

"You could walk to work from that one on Mercy Street, too, and it had parking slots. What was the problem?"

Evelyn looked at her notes. "No private entrance and the second bedroom was large enough

347

for a midget if he had short arms."

They looked at each other. Jane said, "The lady was nice."

"Yes. She was."

"No bugs."

"At least only friendly ones. The bathroom needed a new screen on its window."

"She said she'd fix that."

They sipped. Jane said thoughtfully, "You know, Evie, we're looking at that place in terms of where we're living now. At least I am. And I'm wrong. I only want a bed, not a dance floor. Let's go see it again."

"It's three-fifty a month plus deposit."

"I'll pay the deposit."

The cheese stands alone. Evelyn said, "I'll pay my half—if you can wait until Friday."

"Sure."

They went. Jane took her shake. Evelyn abandoned hers. Lumps! Margaret Daniels would have a fit, she thought but was unaware that she was thinking it with pride.

They took the apartment. Unfortunately, with Evelyn the glow of the cheese standing alone lasted only until mid-evening at work when suddenly absolute terror set in. She sat in the empty little lounge on her break and stared at the coffee maker. She had coffee in her hand and didn't recall having poured it.

She had committed herself. She was moving.

There were going to be strangers in John's house.

How could she tell Jessie — and Brenda — and Jack, to whom the entire situation was going to be an undeclared disaster fraught with self-recrimination on Jack's part. She could already hear him: "Mom, why didn't you let me know, why didn't you tell me?"

Eileen and the girls noticed her distraction. At closing, Marva said, "Can we buy you a drink, hon? You look done in."

"No. No, thanks. Not tonight."

She purposely lingered in the lounge until they were gone, calling back the last "See you Monday." Margaret had the key in her hand. "Ready, Evelyn? You look bushed."

"I guess I am."

She went out ahead of the manager, leaving her to lock up. The parking lot was sharply, crisply cool, and already the few cars still parked were wet with dew beneath the lights.

She sighed. Running one hand through the loop of the bunny ears bag, she began buttoning her coat against the long shadowy walk up Sycamore.

"Evelinda."

349

Unbelieving, she turned. He was really standing there, the collar of that old army jacket upturned. The light made his white hair shine like a silver helmet and his cheeks looked gaunt. But he was smiling, and he said, "You look like you could use a hug. So could I."

Without a word she walked into his arms. For a long moment they held each other tightly, not speaking. Neither noticed the heavy car at the end of the lot suddenly putting on its lights and growling away.

Twenty-four

At last, to the top of her head, he said, "I had to come. I felt as if I was losing my marbles, as if there was nothing else in the world but tubes and needles and signing forms for horrible things I didn't understand and didn't want to see."

His heart was thudding against her breast. Not moving, she asked, "When do you have to be back?"

"Tomorrow. About noon."

"Then let's go home."

They walked to his car. He put her inside, then went around and slid in, fitting his long legs into their proper places. Not looking, he said, "I could buy you dinner. Or a drink."

His voice struggled with the words. He was trying very hard. Her own voice didn't actually seem to belong to her. "No. Don't be silly. Home, James."

He followed her through her kitchen door. The

outside light cast a long leggy shadow into the syringa bushes, disappearing as she turned it off and closed the door behind him.

The kitchen was a diffused pale yellow and black from the low wattage bulb of the range hood. He was just standing, his arms at his sides and his face in the dark. She said, "Come on," and knew as she went through the dining room toward the stairs that he was following, watching her snap on the lamps.

At the couch she stopped. Not really looking at him, she said, "I'm going to go change and get rid of the hamburger smell. Sit down. There's beer if you want it."

Almost savagely he said, "I don't mind the hamburger smell. It's real. It's normal."

"I mind. I don't want to smell like a hamburger."

Suddenly she felt his fingers, just touching the back of her head. He said, "What do you want to smell like?"

"Evelinda," she answered. Then abruptly frightened, uncertain of herself, of him, of everything, she turned and almost ran up the stairs.

His laughter followed her. But it sounded quiet, gentle, like the Bob she knew. Reassured, she went into her room, unbuttoning as she opened the closet door. The new rose-colored house coat was there and she put it on, not looking. She fluffed her hair, not looking. She couldn't bear to look. She might see a fat, matronly old lady with pooches and flops—and if she did, then the madness would be over before it ever began. And of all the things in the world she didn't want it to be over.

She saw from the shadows of the stairs, peeping timidly, that he'd folded his jacket on a chair and put a beer can neatly on a coaster close to the couch.

She didn't realize until she reached his side on silent bare feet that he was asleep.

Her heart caught and wavered perilously. It might be the first sleep he'd had for days. He was so thin. There were deep new lines around his eyes. Be sensible. Be kind.

Getting the afghan from the couch back, she started to unfold it. A hand came out and caught at hers. Bob said quietly, "I didn't drive almost a hundred miles to sleep."

His hand was pulling her down to her knees on the rug beside him. The afghan fell, draping its soft wool across his long length and sliding further to cover her white feet.

There was hardly room in her mouth for words because of her heart. Barely whispering, she said, "Why did you drive almost a hundred miles?"

"To be happy. For a few hours. To find someone who would be happy with me. To find — I think — to find Evelinda."

He let go of her hand, put his long, warm fingers up and stroked the soft curve of her throat, winding them in her hair. He said, "If you can — hold me. I need to be held. And loved."

She made one small noise — of pity, of despair, of longing — she really didn't know. She put her arms around him against the pillows, gathering him to her, his head, his broad shoulders against her breast, but not as a mother would gather a child and he knew it. He sighed and it was almost like crying. "No more pain, Evelinda, no more sorrow — not for these few hours?"

"No. No more."

Her cheek was on top of his head. It was silky soft. Below, against her throat his lips moved. "When I said I wasn't on the make for you, I wasn't lying then . . . but I'd be lying now. I am. I want to make love to you — it seems like the most desirable thing in the world. If you must, stop me now — while I can stop."

Perhaps her brain was disconnected from her body. She didn't know — she didn't care. She only knew that they were both disconnected from the world. From tomorrow.

She said in his ear, "I don't want to stop you. But — do this for me."

"What?"

"Go with me. Upstairs."

"Bless you."

He got to his feet, tall in the lamplight, and pulled her to him. Not letting go, walking side by side, they mounted the steps.

She opened the door of the guest room. Moonlight was filtering across the impersonal bed, the neat bureau. He knew. He said softly, "No ghosts?"

"No ghosts."

The stairs had not diminished his desire. He pulled her hard against him and she felt the surging lump of his erection pressed against her. He said fiercely in her ear, "Oh, God, I want you so badly—but I want to taste you, love you, feel you—help me . . ."

"Teach me. Teach me." Sex with John, dear John, had been pure mechanical intercourse. A wifely chore. She'd known that—always. With this man it could be different; she sensed the difference, and she wanted it. Standing quite still, she felt him step away, felt his fingers in the dark on the zipper of her robe. When it fell with a shimmering whisper, he turned her gently, to unfasten her bra. As it too fell away, he pushed the white panties down from her hips and she felt the light touch of his mouth on her neck, the curve of her warm back.

"Lovely," he whispered. Then his hands came

around her, cupping the softness of her breasts in his palms, stroking them with his fingertips. She had only time to think how different, how alien from Porter's forcible intrusion when the hands fell away and Bob picked her up in his arms and laid her on the bed in the moonlight. She could catch the glint of his eyes and he was smiling. "Now, me," he said and sat beside her, guiding her hands to the buttons of his shirt. "Slowly, love, slowly," he whispered, and as she obeyed he began stroking her breasts again, amazing her at the surging sense of joy his fingers brought.

She bared his broad chest with its thick silver mat and tugged at his shirt tails. He laughed suddenly and said, "Wait. I'll do it myself."

He stood, pulling off his shirt, unbuckling and dropping his pants, sliding out of the neat white brief that hugged his narrow flanks, and stripping off his shoes and socks.

"Now," he said, and lay beside her, propped on one arm. "I think kissing is nice." And he began touching his lips to her mouth, her breasts, her belly, and the soft mound of pubic hair. She caught her breath as one hand slipped between her thighs, stroking her and she arched her back as his mouth returned to her breasts, kissing their satin softness. She realized only one tumultuous thing—whether it was the long span of pedestrian sex or simply this one man—she desired him as she had never in her life desired anyone.

She said thickly, "Bob, please—"

Against the ball of her breast he murmured, "Wait—just a little longer, a little longer . . ." But the loving kiss of his caressing mouth, the stroke of his hand, the almost sudden and frantic arch of their backs toward each other put absolute ecstasy before pleasure. She never remembered opening for him but she did, receiving his hardness with joyous abandon, going with him to the heights, then, softly, to the gentle depths of fluid, fluttering languor.

Then a second miracle occurred. He continued to hold her, to stroke her back, to rub his mouth against her hair and caress her breasts as they touched his chest. And he said in her ear, "Oh, my Evelinda, we did it together. I knew we could. I knew we would. My Evelinda . . ."

Gone was the man who rolled away from her saying, "God, I'm tired," and lapsed within minutes into snoring sleep. Tomorrow she'd remember the comfortable things with that man, the friendship, the laughter, the loyalty that had made up for this kind of love.

This night she only remembered the man beside her and the discovery that there was another kind of love, a love that surpassed the joy in Emma's books. She knew that she could now understand that joy—and that she was capable of having that love—she, Evelyn Matthews Cass, age fifty-six.

Bob was saying languorously into her hair, "I want a promise."

"What?"

"If I go to sleep, wake me. This is too lovely to waste."

She suddenly giggled. It sounded throaty in his ears. "I promise. If you promise."

"Lady, you got it," he sighed. Running a tender hand down the length of her, he added, "Boy, have you got it."

Evelyn Matthews Cass, sex symbol, she thought before they both went to sleep.

She awakened at six. The sun was sending its first rays over the treetops, and the place beside her was empty.

Sick with betrayal, with disappointment, she struggled to her feet, pulling on the abandoned robe—then with exquisite relief she heard him in the shower.

He turned and saw her standing in the bathroom door. Sliding open the shower, he said, "Good morning, Evelinda! You're beautiful if a bit overly clad. Come in."

"What?"

"Come in. The water's fine."

Lost in unreality, she let the robe slip to the floor again and stepped beneath the warm needles into his arms against his wet body. They made love in the shower, giggling like children, then clinging to each other as if there were no one else in the world.

He toweled her off, lovingly drying each warm, secret place, and said, "Come back to bed."

"Bob—breakfast—"

"I can eat breakfast any time. I cannot make love to my Evelinda."

At ten he sat on the side of the bed and began to get dressed. She could see the burdens of his world settling back on his shoulders.

From against the rumpled pillows she said gently, "Breakfast, now?"

"No, love. I'd rather leave you here. Do you realize what a gift you've given me?" He reached out, took the bare arm from the covers, kissed the hand. "You took me from a rude wrestling match on the couch and brought me up here to heaven. Whatever happens, I'll never forget that."

The "whatever happens" chilled her, made her look at reality. Like a child, she asked, "Will you come back?"

"When I can. Will you bring me here?"

"If I can. I'm—I'm leasing the house."

"Then the word 'here' is not literal. It means 'wherever you are'. Wherever we can be together."

He finished tying his shoes and stood up. He

towered, looking down. "Where are you moving?"

"I think I have an apartment."

"If you don't, I do."

"Bob, I couldn't—"

"Why not? I won't be in it—and if I am, Karen would be delighted. Hell. I can't leave you like this. We haven't talked, and I like to talk to you, too. Get out of bed and make me some coffee."

"I guess I needn't shower."

He grinned. "I'll make the coffee," he said. "You're too distracting."

At the kitchen bar he questioned her about Vic and the lease, and about Porter. He said grimly, "He's trying to make you dependent on him."

"I know. He won't."

"I don't like it."

"Bob, he won't risk losing Mary Lou. Everything will be overt. I can handle that."

"I'd like to break his neck."

"You may get to help me."

Then she realized that lovely though it was to have someone else fighting her battles it was hardly the cheese standing alone. She added, "Don't fuss about it. I'll manage. He doesn't frighten me; he's too small a man inside. Outside, in those golf-pants Mary Lou buys him, he looks like a two-hundred-pound canary, which is hardly romantic."

He grinned and looked at his watch. "I have to run by Karen's. What shall I tell her?"

Evelyn said faintly, "Oh dear. Must you tell her anything?"

"No. She may guess. Do you mind?"

He was looking at her directly. There was no evasion, no escape from those gray eyes.

She sighed, and half-smiled. "I don't know," she said truthfully. "I just haven't got it together yet. Bob—you're looking at a middle-class, morally upright, conservative matron who's never done anything like this before—who has never even thought of doing anything like this before! Who is not sorry—but who also needs to adjust her sights a little."

He reached out and covered her hand with his. "It took two," he said. "Remember that. Okay? And something else—indiscriminate seduction has never been my bag. I'm not a tomcat. Selective love-making is something God pretty much left to human beings. I always figured there was a reason for it that exceeded simple procreation—like sharing laughter and joy. Heavy, Evelinda? Take it or leave it."

"I'll take it."

She clasped his fingers with hers. He lifted hers to his lips, touched them lightly and put the hand back on the kitchen bar. "I've got to run. I'll call you next weekend if I can't get away — and I don't know. I really don't know. I just go from day to day. But you've helped, love. You've really helped."

When he was gone, she gathered up the coffee cups, put them in the dishwasher, wandered into the bathroom, and looked at herself in the mirror.

It was the same familiar face that looked back — gray hair that needed curling, round cheeks, brown eyes that, today, seemed a little wistful.

I have made love, she said to the face, with a man who was not my husband — who, indeed, is someone else's. And I don't feel guilty.

Perhaps tomorrow it would crash in on her like original sin. Perhaps, but she doubted it. The person inhabiting John's body couldn't care less. Sue-Ann was beyond caring. What she and Bob Marsh had shared last night was something that had happened because John was beyond caring and so was Sue-Ann, and turned them to each other for solace.

If that's rationalizing, she told herself, so be it.

She went upstairs and opened the door of the guest room. It was filled with sunlight. The bed looked merely as though someone had slept there and gone away.

Yet Evelyn Matthews Cass had made love — more than that — had *joined* in making love in that bed for the first time in her life. For the first time she'd known that there could be a joy beyond obligation. For the first time she'd been a partner, not a loyal and obliging wife. It had been a discovery of magnitudinous proportions that she could do such a thing — ordinary, matronly, respectable Evelyn.

She touched the rumpled sheets, remembering. She blushed. She felt like a young girl. She'd like to make daisy chains and dance in clover.

And he said he'd be back. That he wanted to come.

Holding that dear thought, she stripped off the sheets and made up the bed with new ones, fresh from their package, all crisp and cool, taking tactile pleasure in plumping the pillows and folding down the counterpane.

It was a very good move though not precisely what she'd had in mind for the next use of the freshened bed.

At one o'clock that afternoon, Jessie Cass moved in — bag and baggage.

Twenty-five

Jessie Cass was tall, thin, erect, and rather distinguished. She had an old fashioned "school-marm" bearing and bright blue almond-shaped eyes, a characteristic inherited by both her grandchildren. It remained to be seen whether they would also get her calico hair where brown blended into blond and blond into gray, all swept back briskly into a no-nonsense fluff.

She had pulled her Dodge Dart in behind the Lincoln, and had already unloaded two large suitcases when Evelyn appeared in the driveway.

"Hi, hon," she said with a swift hug and kiss. "How are you? Get my train case, will you? It's on the front seat. Oh—and that bag of Snickers. I find myself waking up with a sweet attack these days. Your coleus needs pinching."

Evelyn said, "I know. I don't seem to find time."

She got the train case and the Snickers and

364

followed her mother-in-law into the house and up the stairs—not with a sense of dismay, but more of puzzlement. This was not like Jessie.

"Goodness," she was puffing, opening the door of the guest room with the end of a suitcase. "I'm not in the habit of stairs anymore. Just put those on the bed, Evie. I have a garment bag, too, but it can wait. Right now I just want a cup of coffee. I want a cigarette, also, but I won't. Did Brenda tell you I'd quit smoking?"

Evelyn's antenna had suddenly gone up like a balloon. Cautiously she said, "No."

But Jessie caught the caution. She swung around with an abrupt flip of a tailored skirt and looked at her daughter-in-law. "Didn't Brenda tell you I was coming today?"

"No. But—"

She cut her off. "Did Brenda tell you I was coming?"

"No."

"Oh merciful heavens! That girl! I'll wring her neck!"

"Jessie, you know you're welcome anytime."

Except last night. And Evelyn's heart shot into her throat about what might have happened if Jessie'd come last night. Fortunately, Jessie saw the expression and misinterpreted, reading exasperation for guilt and giving her daughter-in-law a chance to examine in private a reaction she didn't care for at all. Jessie said crisply,

"I know I am, hon, but this transcends being welcome. If Brenda didn't tell you I was coming, then she also didn't tell you why. Honestly! Come on—give me my coffee and *I'll* tell you why. Then you can shoot us both if you like."

There was enough coffee in the pot for two scant cups. Evelyn poured, giving the balance to Jessie, then sat down and waited uncomfortably. Her mother-in-law, who had lingered to go to the bathroom, snap a dead frond from the Boston fern, and look through the front door at the scarlet ivy, came in, pulled out one of the oak kitchen chairs and looked upward at Evelyn on the bar stool.

"Now I know," she said calmly, "that you're having a hard time. Don't frown, hon. It's not your fault—nor is it Bren's. Nor is it precisely Bren's fault that she always comes running to me because I started that, myself, long ago, when Pat was of no earthly use."

"But I asked her—"

"Not to. Of course you did. She told me."

Evelyn rolled her eyes upward expressively and sipped her coffee. Jessie sipped hers, said, "Wahoo!", got up and put water in it.

"Now," she said, sitting again. "You know Brenda needs money. Right?"

"Right. And I said I didn't have it but—"

"But that you'd try to work something out. But Bren, being Bren, couldn't wait."

"Obviously."

She should have known. She should have seen the signs—they'd all been there. How stupid to have deceived herself in thinking Brenda was displaying a little independence at last—when of course she'd just gone and got up on Grandma's lap again. Evelyn sighed, shrugged, pushed her cup aside. Carefully she said, "I don't know what she asked for. But Jessie, please don't put yourself in jeopardy. Please. For this month I can hardly help myself, let alone help you. And Brenda can make it—at least for a little longer until I *can* help her."

"But that's what I'm going to tell you. This month it is working out for *me*. Listen and stop frowning. You know the Parsons—Wendy and Jim—in the condo next door? They have their children visiting. They came just today. Now. I've rented my little place to them for their stay because Wendy's is too small. That gives me extra money which I, in turn, can give to Bren—if I may stay with you."

"Well, of course you may, but—"

"Then it's settled," said Jessie and dumped her cup in the sink. "Bleah. Terrible. May I make some more? Settled, I mean," she went on, rinsing out the pot, "if I still don't break Brenda's

367

neck. I feel awful about crashing in on you like this."

Evelyn shrugged. Shaking her head, she said, "Coffee in the canister on the right. She did it deliberately. I'd bet money on it. She knew if she laid back long enough we'd fix it up between us without hassle — and it's worked. That girl. Honestly."

"She's a lot like Pat, Evie. Pat never could face up to things either. Oh, well. How many measures?"

Evelyn glanced at the clock. "Make a full pot. We can go sit on the patio with it. I tend to loaf a lot on my day off."

"I did, too."

Catching Evelyn's startled glance, Jessie suddenly laughed.

"I've never told you, have I — about how it was when John's father died. I had nothing — and no way to make a living unless I got my teaching certificate renewed. I went to class by day, with my baby in a basket at my feet. And every night after I got him to sleep, I sewed on buttons by hand for the overall factory. So I may be old, my dear, but I can understand. John's an enormous drain, isn't he?"

"John is all right. He's taken care of."

"I understand that. But you're broke."

Nothing like calling a spade a spade. Evelyn

shrugged again. "Just about."

"I've felt it was coming. It's worried me. One hates to see things like this happen to one's children. You know you feel rather betrayed—like reading a good book then suddenly the plot goes wrong." She was knitting her hands together. The fingers were thin, and rings in old-fashioned settings flashed as they moved; as she watched them, she went on thoughtfully, "There has to be some solution. I've really been thinking about it."

For some reason Evelyn went on alert. She didn't know why—except that Jessie was suddenly looking her most school-marmish. She said, "There is. It's called going to work—something I should have done right at the very beginning. I got myself into this, Jessie, by being an ostrich."

"A what?"

She explained Jane's theory as Romeo jumped up in her lap. Jessie nodded.

"She's right," she said. "It's your generation. We didn't have time to be ostriches. We had the Depression, and believe me, lady, it was dig or die, and we dug. Brenda, now. Her crowd had their own depression but it was in the soul. They had causes, great moral crises—they marched to save the world and found it didn't want to be saved. Poor kids. I suppose in their own way they were ostriches, too. At least I don't think Brenda's pulled her head out yet. But you girls—Jane has hit you all on the button. Of course, I like Jane, so I'm prejudiced. There. Coffee's made. Goodness, it's slow; do you suppose you need to run some white vinegar through it?"

"Probably."

They were both distracted by the clicking of the gate. Brenda came inside, holding Poo's hand. He cried, " 'Oo-mo!" and hurled himself to Evelyn's side, reaching up for Romeo who audibly sighed and submitted. Brenda didn't move; her large, slanted eyes went anxiously from her stepmother to her grandmother.

"You!" said her grandmother.

"You!" said her stepmother at the same time. They both laughed, and she relaxed visibly.

"Oh God," she said. "It's okay, isn't it? I thought if I stayed back long enough you'd fix it up between you—and you have . . . haven't you?"

"What you have," said Jessie, "is the spine of a wet noodle. You promised me!"

"I know, Gram, I know," said Brenda. She moved swiftly, stooping to kiss the thin cheek, hug the spare, erect shoulders. "But you're so much better with words—Oh, well. Hi, Mom. Am I in the doghouse?"

"I haven't decided," Evelyn said, but there was no sting in it. "Certainly not for bringing Jessie."

"No one minds Jessie," said Brenda. She perched herself on the arm of her grandmother's chair, pushing back the long hair that swung forward and kissing the top of Jessie's fluffy head. "I think it will work out swell. She can help you with so many things—"

Had there been a slight pressure from the old, ringed hand on Brenda's? And if so, why?

Evelyn inexplicably went on alert again, but Jessie only said, "Now if you think I came to do Susy Homemaker—either of you—you may think again. As long as I can kick my way through to the bedroom, the refrigerator, and the potty, I have more important things to do with my time than keep house. With age one learns a better sense of priority. Speaking of which, Brenda darling, you have younger legs. Go bring out the coffee pot."

Romeo expertly slithered himself from Poo's grasp and followed. Poo, ever insouciant, pushed himself up into his grandmother's lap and leaned back, sighing comfortably. She hugged him and said to her mother-in-law, "I haven't meant to keep things from you. Not really. I wanted to straighten myself out before you knew." It was, in a way, an apology.

Jessie nodded. "I can appreciate that. How are you doing?"

Evelyn still didn't have quite enough courage

to say she was selling Jessie's house—although it wasn't Jessie's house, damn it! It hadn't been Jessie's for years. But no one could miss the proprietary air with which Jessie had eyed the crack in the patio floor, the downspout gone awry, and the split in the bottom step where Jessie had told John it would split. Old conditioning dies hard. She equivocated. "Better. Slow. But I'll make it. I'm getting thirty-six hours or more at Bunny Burger, and tomorrow morning I start at the library working for Karen Marsh. That's temporary, but it will help."

"So you're gone—"

"Until noon, then from five to eleven."

"Ears," said Poo, and stuck two fat fingers up on either side of Evelyn's head. Jessie looked startled.

"We wear plush ears," her daughter-in-law explained flatly.

"Oh. Well, it's better than ostrich feathers. How are the other girls—Liz and what's the airhead's name—Mary Lou?"

"Fine. They gave me a lovely birthday party. And—by the way—thank you for the check." All my sins, Evelyn thought uncomfortably, including those of omission seem to be catching up with me today. But Jessie merely nodded. Her eyes were on Brenda maneuvering through the doorway with the coffee pot.

"That child is too thin."

"She drinks rather than eats."

"Poo doesn't seem to suffer."

"No. I'll give her that. He's the one stable thing in her life now. She does miss her dad," Evelyn added.

"He doesn't know her either?"

"No more than you or I." No point in saying Brenda had not tried recently to find out. "Thank you, hon. Pour for Gram. I'm floating. Jessie, I do have to go see John shortly. Would you like to ride with me?"

"Tomorrow. You run along. I'll visit with Bren."

Poo twisted his slender neck and looked up at his grandmother. "Poo go?"

"If Mother says okay." John paid very little attention to his grandchild but Charley and Ed loved him. They also sneaked him candy which Poo remembered very well.

"Sure. If he's no bother."

"Of course not. Come along, Shortstuff, let's wash your face."

As she went into the house Evelyn saw Brenda drop onto the sun-warmed patio floor by her grandmother. When she and Poo left they were still sitting close, talking earnestly, waving their hands absently as Poo yelled, "Bye! See you!"

Of course they'd always been close, Evelyn reminded herself, and decided not to borrow trouble. She had quite enough of her own. If Jessie chose to spend her money financing Bren at the Springfield clinic, marvelous. It was one burden less for her. Also, she envisioned no problem having Jessie as a live-in for a couple of weeks. Jessie always carried her share wherever she was. Besides, she had enough friends locally to keep her entertained. If they even saw each other in passing they might be lucky.

As a matter of fact, Monday morning when Evelyn left for the library Jessie was still in bed. After three hours of dirt and grime delving in the library basement bookstacks that Karen said hadn't been inventoried since they quit using pit lamps, she returned home and found lunch ready. Nice. She really appreciated it.

The first reversal of the day didn't happen until she went to work at Bunny Burger. Margaret Daniels beckoned from the door of her miniscule office. Her glasses were thrust up on top of her head and she looked harried.

"Good. You're early. Come in a minute."

Puzzled, Evelyn followed her.

"Shut the door."

Even more puzzled, Evelyn shut it.

Leaning against her desk, Margaret pulled her glasses down, looked at the folded sheet of paper in her hand, shoved the glasses back up again, and directed her gaze at Evelyn.

"Somebody," she said soberly, "dislikes you. No—let me change that. Somebody hates your guts. Do you know who?"

Evelyn swallowed. "Good God. I don't think so. I mean—everyone dislikes someone, like that man who always orders 'qwish'—"

"I said 'hates your guts,' because this is vindictive. Listen to what it says." *It* was the sheet in her hand. " 'It is my duty to inform you'—" She stopped abruptly, muttered, "Oh, hell," and balled the sheet up, dropping it into the wastecan. "Basically, my dear, the writer says they saw you—saw you, mind—soliciting and engaging in licentious activity on the Bunny Burger parking lot. They request your immediate dismissal as a moral deterrent to our youth."

Stunned, Evelyn could only gape. She looked so completely incredulous Margaret suddenly giggled.

"Honey," she said, "if I were your age I'd take it as a compliment."

"Who wrote such a thing? That's awful!"

"It's not signed. That's why I filed it in the can. I hate those things—they're cowardly and vicious. And since it's anonymous I'm not officially compelled to do anything more than warn you. Evelyn—what in the blue-eyed world *were* you doing on our parking lot?"

Evelyn shook her head. "Going home," she said. Then she remembered Bob Marsh. She blushed and said faintly, "Oh dear."

Margaret waited, her eyebrows high over eyes that looked amused.

Evelyn said, "A friend gave me a ride home. He—he has sickness in the family. He looked so tired and worn I—I hugged him."

"That was it?"

"That was it." Evelyn felt the heat rising, and fumbled in her bag for tissue. "Then we went home. As I said."

"My jurisdiction ends at the parking lot," Margaret said, and grinned. "No more hugging on company property, okay?"

"Okay. I'm sorry—"

"Don't be sorry. But don't forget, either. Some-one wants to get you canned. Bunny Burger Cor-poration is pretty savvy about local pettiness so it didn't work. This time. And you're a good em-ployee, Evelyn; I'd hate to lose you. Yet it ap-pears you're really going to have to watch out. Would you rather work kitchen today? I had you down for drive-up."

Evelyn shook her head. She suddenly felt very angry.

"No," she said.

"Good girl. Run along, then. Sorry I had to tell you."

Shield time again, Evelyn told herself grimly as she trudged into the lounge, put her bag away, and adjusted her ears. With it, or on it, and that time I was almost on it. If it hadn't been for Margaret, I would have been! Who tried to do that to me? And why?

It bothered her all evening. She searched every face as it appeared at the drive-up window and found nothing. Her minister came through, laughing sheepishly about ordering Diet Coke and a double-fudge-nut sundae. Mary Lou collected two Danish and two coffees and said, "Well, hi! I thought you weren't here anymore."

"Every night but Sunday," Evelyn said. The significance of the remark totally escaped her. "Watch that coffee; the lid doesn't look tight. 'Bye. Welcome to Bunny Burger. May I help you?"

As she cleaned the last table at eleven she was so tired she could only nod gratefully when Marva offered to run her home. She slammed the car door, said "G' night, see you," and walked up her front walk on leaden feet.

The portico light was on. A light wind rattled the drying scarlet wisps of ivy as she reached for the door knob, turned it, and stepped inside.

From the living room Jessie's voice said, "There we are! I told you it was time! Hi, darling. Welcome home. Look who's here!"

Turning to hang her jacket on the oak hall tree, Evelyn froze in mid-gesture. Slowly she turned as though her neck were glass and might splinter. What she had glimpsed in the beveled mirror would not change, no matter how she turned.

Jessie stood in the doorway, smiling brightly. At her side, looking puzzled and a bit confused in his wheelchair, sat John.

Twenty-six

The first thing that swept over her was a sense of impending tragedy she was powerless to avert—for herself, because she'd brought John home before and it didn't work; for Jessie, who had to learn the painful way that sometimes mother love was not enough; and for John, who was already peering beyond her at someone or something he could not see.

She whispered, "Oh, Jessie."

There was pleading in Jessie's blue eyes but determination in the set of her jaw. "Give us a chance, Evie. Please give us a chance. I'll be here all the time. I can do it. And he's home. In his house. Not among strangers."

There it was: the echo of Brenda's voice. Home. His house. Evelyn thought, I'm going to kill that girl! I may kill them both! Desperately she said out loud, "Jessie, I've tried it."

"I know. But not for a while. Not with me. Please."

She was hooked. She knew it. At least for tonight. She was so tired she wasn't thinking straight. That meeting with Margaret hung over her like a threatening cloud; Bob's voice, his face lingered in the back of her mind attacking the weary reason in her mind with small needles of guilt; and on the first of November this was not going to be John's home.

She surrendered. More succinctly, she caved in. It was too late tonight to do anything anyway, she told herself, knowing all the time it was mere self-deception. She said, "All right, Jessie. All right."

John broke the skein of misery binding them together. In a querulous voice he said, "Where is she? This lady said my wife was coming."

Jessie bent over him and pointed. "Darling John, there she is. That's your wife."

His eyes swept Evelyn, dismissed her. "That's not Pat. I don't understand. Where is she?"

Evelyn sighed. Then, slipping into a role she'd become so terribly accustomed to playing, she said calmly, "I'm Evelyn, John."

"Have I see you before?"

"Yes."

"Is this your house?"

"Yes, it is."

380

"It's very nice. We hope to have one like this some day. But if Pat's not coming, I'd like to go home now."

Jessie began, "But John, this is —" and Evelyn overrode her, shaking her head negatively.

"In the morning. It's quite late. We can make you comfortable until then."

"Thank you. I'll try not to be any trouble. Take me to my room, please."

Her face a blank, Jessie turned the chair and wheeled it toward the stairs. Reality hit Evelyn like cold water.

"Jessie, you didn't get a hospital bed!"

"Of course not."

"But the stairs —"

"There's nothing wrong with his legs. We've already been up and down once, quite nicely. Come along, John."

It was the schoolteacher's no-nonsense voice. John stood and reached for the banister. Weak with concern, Evelyn said, "You could have fallen! You both could have fallen!"

"Pish. It's a good, easy staircase; you know that. Here we go."

"Wait!" Evelyn pitched the plastic bag of bunny ears onto the hall tree and almost ran. She put herself on John's other side, saying nothing more, only an unwilling prop in a venture over which she had no immediate control.

381

"There we are!" Jessie said shortly at the top in a voice that Evelyn suspected meant she was a bit breathless. With no obvious design and a face that mirrored only pity and concern, she reached inside Evelyn's bedroom and snapped on the ceiling light.

Sheer, irrational dismay swept over Evelyn. But Jessie either would not or could not look at her. She said to her son cheerily, "Delivered safe and sound. There are your pajamas on the bed. May I help you undress?"

"Certainly not. Thank you."

He'd walked inside, glanced around, and sighed. Then his finger beckoned to Evelyn. "You may. Please."

Jessie's face lit up. Gently Evelyn said, "No, no — it's nothing. Don't think it's anything else. I'm not me. I'm just the type of person who's been helping him for months." As Jessie hesitated further, she went on with a grimness she really tried to conceal, "Go to bed. You must be tired, too. I can handle it now."

John had sat on the side of the bed and was neatly removing his shoes. Jessie watched him, wringing her old hands, the rings sparkling. She was almost in tears, and Evelyn knew it. She tried to swallow the resentment surging inside her.

She touched the erect old shoulder that stood

382

higher than hers. She said, "Go on. We'll be fine. And I expect it will be an early morning."

Jessie's voice was choked. "Oh Evie, I hope I'm right. I pray I'm right."

"Good night," Evelyn said, and shut the door behind her.

Putting John into his pajamas was rote. She fished in a drawer, found the little Care Bear night light they'd used when Poo was younger, and stuck it into a socket in the bathroom. Behind her, John was climbing into bed, lying back with a soft sound of weariness. He called out, "Turn on the TV, please."

"It's awfully late tonight, John. Tomorrow."

"Very well."

She heard him turn on his side, the sheets rustling.

Then she faced herself in the mirror, desperately trying to examine her own feelings.

She hadn't slept with John since he'd had his stroke, and for long, lonely weeks she'd missed the warmth, the affectionate presence beside her. John's presence. Not this man's—this man was a stranger. The idea of putting her body next to his and touching him made her shiver.

But last night she'd lain naked next to another man and entered with him into the most exultant of intimacies and been glad, been joyous in their sharing. Was that the reason for her sick stomach, her cold hands now? Was she comparing them, and did John fall short?

No. She couldn't accept that. She wouldn't. She had to blot Bob from her mind for one last, desperate try with John — for thirty years of loyalty and companionship and laughter, she had to try.

And what if he responded — not as John, but as any man might to a woman in his bed? She had never been raped. Could she keep from screaming, could she swallow the violation, could she endure it? John would hate this. John would never have put her through it — good, kind, gentle John. Yet — if this might be what it took to bring him back — if Jessie was even a little bit right . . .

She turned from the frozen face in the mirror, and moving like an automaton she stripped, putting on the old nightgown that hung behind the bathroom door. It was one John knew well. They'd laughed when it washed to a totally different color from the matching robe that now lay across the slipper chair by the bed. "Throw-up green," he'd called it.

On bare, chilly feet she crossed the carpet and snapped off the ceiling lamp at the switch by the door. The room fell black with a few scant bars of light, lace-patterned by oak leaves, barely reaching John's side of the bed.

He lay on his side, knees drawn up, eyes shut. Thinning hair made a soft wing across his forehead. He still put one hand behind his head, the other beneath his chin. That much had not changed.

She went silently to her side, sat down, and swung her feet beneath the sheets.

Priorities, he'd always told his children. Place your priorities . . .

And her priority was, and would always be, John Cass.

He stirred. The one bedspring squeaked as it had for ten years. Flooded with memory, caught up suddenly in a tide of hope, she reached out, touched his shoulder, slid her hand down his thin flank, so shrunken beneath the loose pajamas. She felt him stiffen. She said, "John?"

Then he was sitting bolt upright, clutching at the blankets, crying out in enormous outrage, "Young woman, what do you think you're doing?"

"John—"

"Get out of my bed! Get out before I ring for help and have you thrown out! My God, what sort of place is this?"

He was out of bed, fumbling for a lamp switch, putting the slipper chair between them. The light glared and in it his face was a mask of anger although he was shaking.

385

"Get out! Get out! Get out!"

She scrambled from the bed, stumbled around it, and reached for her robe, seeing him shrink from her as she grabbed it. When she began crying she had no idea, but as she ran into the hall the tears were streaming down her cheeks.

She heard the door slam behind her, heard the click of the lock. Panting, trying not to pant so she could hear more, she listened. He was muttering to himself, but after what seemed an eternity the bed creaked again and silence fell.

Thank God. Thank God.

Swallowing, mopping at her wet cheeks with the hem of her nightgown, Evelyn turned blindly and almost knocked Jessie down.

Jessie caught at her daughter-in-law, steadying herself. She said in a broken whisper, "Oh my dear, I'm so sorry—so sorry—"

Evelyn actually, physically could have struck her. Anger burgeoned like a balloon inside her chest, anger at the world, at Jessie, at herself, anger that was so tangible she could have squeezed it with her fingers and thrown it at her mother-in-law. Through her teeth she said savagely, "Are you satisfied? Are you?"

"Evelyn—"

"No more—no more, no more—just go to bed!"

She stumbled away, leaving Jessie in the hall,

yanked open the door to Jack's room and fell on his bunk, sobbing into the one hard pillow John had permitted his son.

Jessie must have obeyed. When at last Evelyn fell silent, with a swollen face and blurry vision, the older lady was no longer in the hallway.

All right. She'd deal with it tomorrow.

Tomorrow always came. And she needed rest. She had to get some rest. She'd never be able to keep up if she didn't.

The hall clock struck one and two and three before she did.

At seven she opened her eyes. Seeing Jessie, fully clad, standing in the door of Jack's room, it all came back.

Jessie said hesitantly, "He's awake. I can hear him. But the door's locked."

"He'll unlock it. If not, I have a key. Somewhere."

She sat up, smacking her head sharply on the upper bunk. "Damn. I forgot about that. Jessie —"

Her mother-in-law had never looked so old, so frail. So beaten. Evelyn took another deep breath — the sort at which she was becoming so proficient. "Jessie, I'm sorry — whatever I said last night, I didn't mean to hurt you."

Jessie was still waiting, expectantly. Kicking herself for helplessly being good old agreeable

Evelyn, she went on, "We'll try. I'll try. For at least a week. But it's not going to be roses keeping him here and I can't afford to quit my jobs."

"I can manage. I know I can manage. Brenda says she'll help."

Evelyn swallowed that with difficulty.

"Bren's working days. At least until she goes to Springfield. That's next week."

"I know. But you'll be home in the afternoon and she says she'll come over at night. And it will save you money, Evie—that fortune they charge at the nursing place."

As yesterday she'd heard the echo of Brenda's voice, now she heard the echo of John's. And she knew it was useless to say that keeping John here might just possibly put the two of them back in the nursing home with him. Jessie had yet to realize the constant surveillance her son required—the unremitting attention. She was so accustomed now to having her time as her own—how long could she take having none?

John looked so healthy. Except for the slight hesitation in his speech and the thinness, there was no sign of the disease that had vacuumed his mind.

It might be better if he gibbered, she thought, then was ashamed. Standing up, she said, "Why don't you start breakfast? I'll figure out how to get him dressed and going. If he'll spend the morning on the patio that will be routine for him and easier for you while I'm gone."

Jessie nodded and went downstairs. In her neat slacks and cardigan sweater she looked very thin and her shoulders stooped. She paused as the telephone rang.

"I'll get it here," Evelyn said, and picked up the one in the hall. "Cass residence."

"Good morning, gorgeous! I hope you're not dressed yet. I know I'm going to prefer you that way."

She gritted her teeth. "Porter, I want a bill for the car."

"I'll give you a bill, gorgeous. On our weekend in November. I was just thinking a minute ago — since you probably won't be working, perhaps we could spend more than a weekend. Mary Lou's going to her mom's and I —"

Evelyn simply hung up.

She waited, braced. It didn't ring again.

Since John had locked her away from her closet, she dressed herself from the dirty clothes hamper in the hall. Something Porter had said struck her suddenly like a bolt of lightning: " — since you probably won't be working — "

Why should he think that?

Unless —

Unless Porter had been the one to write that vicious note!

The moment she thought the words she knew they were true. Porter. It had been Porter. Porter had seen her in Bob Marsh's arms.

Cold with anger, she shut her eyes and clenched her teeth, trying to master it. Anger without action was no good. Porter had been angry and he'd acted. So would she. Somewhere, some way she'd get back at him . . .

She slammed down the hamper lid and was trying to smooth out wrinkles on Saturday's brown slacks when a second idea penetrated — why had Porter been where he could see her and Bob, at almost midnight?

He was watching her!

That bastard, she thought and was conscious, not of profanity, but of the truth.

As if she didn't have enough to worry about already, she now had an overweight watchdog with hot pants! A watchdog who was getting mean and nasty. Very nasty.

Somewhere, she thought wearily going into the children's bathroom to brush her teeth, there are ostriches with their heads still in the sand. I wish them well. It may be dull but it's certainly easier on the nervous system.

When she came back to the hall, John had unlocked his door and was standing in it. He had dressed himself although his shirt was off one button. He was smiling pleasantly but his eyes were wary. He said,

"Good morning. I seem to have lost my way."

"Good morning, John. Let me help you."

He allowed her to guide him carefully down the stairs, one step at a time — such a far, far cry from thirty years of tumultuous descent with perhaps a fanny pinch along the way.

Jessie was bustling in the kitchen, a towel wound around her middle in lieu of an apron. "Good morning, children! Eggs up and smiling, John dear, just the way you like them."

"Am I to stay for breakfast?"

"Of course! Coffee's made, Evie, and I do think I'll run vinegar through it today — it is everlastingly slow. John's medication is there on the counter, love — the nurse gave it to me yesterday but I forget which is which. Sit right here, son."

Jessie was bustling. It was a rather unremitting bustle, but Evelyn forgave her when she looked from the polite and distant smile on John's face to the hurt on Jessie's.

Jessie had to learn as she'd learned. The lesson was simple: when the brain is gone, it's gone. Nothing less than a miracle could bring it back. At this point Evelyn's life was a little short on miracles.

When she returned from the library at twelve-thirty, John was bedded on the couch for a nap, Jessie was watching her soaps, and her ebullience was a little diminished. She let Evelyn get almost all the way through a tuna fish sandwich before she confessed. "He was almost out the gate, Evie! And I'd just run inside to turn off the teakettle. Can we lock it?"

"Of course." Evelyn bit back the told-you-sos. The potential was too scary.

"Surely he'll settle down. This is his home!"

"I hope so."

"We sat on the patio rather nicely." Evelyn realized the "we" was editorial. "I got some pictures out—old snaps, and so on—you know."

"Did he recognize anyone?"

Jessie sighed. "I'd love to lie. But no. He didn't. He didn't even—John Cass, what are you doing?" The last was in pure indignation. John had risen from the couch, gone over and calmly switched the television to an old movie channel. Lying down again, he replied, "That stuff's crap. I watch this."

"Oh," said Jessie in dismay.

Evelyn rescued her. "Go upstairs and watch your story. I'll take this shift."

"There's nothing you need to do?"

"Not for a while."

Only half way up, Jessie paused. "Is that the fire whistle?"

Evelyn listened, nodded. "It must be. It's not time for the one o'clock to blow."

Jessie ascended out of sight. Evelyn waited until John seemed to be asleep again, then went quietly to the telephone on the desk. First she called the nursing home and ascertained that they'd hold John's room for him for two weeks. Next, she called Vic Bonnelli, who asked her if she'd like to arm wrestle Saturday night, then in a more businesslike tone said that he'd be able to discuss lease terms by Monday. Last of all, she called Jane Nixon who began by saying, "Hey, kid — you just almost lost your job, did you know that? Some idiot tried to burn down the Bunny Burger."

"What?"

"I'm serious. Didn't you hear the fire whistle?"

"Yes, but —"

"They caught it in good time — but they wouldn't have if one of the boys hadn't had to go to the supply room. I hear Jessie's in town. Want me to take her off your hands? I need to go shopping."

"She brought John home."

"What?"

"She brought John home."

"To stay?"

"She hopes so."

"Good God. You poor kid. Want me to find the Bunny Burger idiot and have him set fire to her? Sorry. But it won't work, you know it won't

393

work, and I hate to have you put through the wringer again in the name of Mother Love." Once more, Jane had put her finger on the nub. "Oh, well. What can I do to help?"

"You've done it. Bolstered my spirits."

"By confirming your intelligence with mine? Yea, team. Hey—I found a cot in the attic that will just fit that small bedroom in the apartment. With a table, a chair, and a typewriter I'm in business."

"A typewriter?"

"I've decided to write a book. *Memoirs of an Ostrich.*"

"You're kidding. Are you serious?"

"Maybe. Maybe not. I just know I'm going to do *something.* Oops—door bell. Shall I call you back?"

"No. We can talk later. See you."

Evelyn hung up. John had not stirred, and his face in repose was even more that of a stranger.

She looked at the last telephone number on her list. It was one Karen had given her that morning. She'd said with a quaver, "Mother is very bad. This is Daddy's phone; he said to give it to you, to call if you needed him. He—really needs to be needed, Evie. Mother—doesn't. Not any more."

Evelyn looked at the number a long, long time. What she wanted was almost indefinable, and she was afraid to define it.

But she didn't call.

Not then. Maybe never.

Twenty-seven

During her fifty-six years Evelyn had enjoyed many weeks better than this one. The fire left a faint tinge of smoke in the air at Bunny Burger and everyone jumped at shadows. The weather turned rainy and chill. As a result, her arthritis kicked up; massive doses of aspirin soothed her aching wrist but reminded her daily that her ulcer was alive and well. She got her overdue notice on the house insurance—a little matter of two hundred she didn't have. Worst of all, Jessie was playing the "Nice Carrots" game—"Won't Mother's big boy eat his nice carrots?"—with a frail, quiet stranger who was becoming more and more obdurately silent.

It was a desperate silence that worried Evelyn as she trudged through scuffles of wet leaves to work on Friday. John was not a child. He was a stranger. There were no conditioned family responses to reactivate because there were no family responses in a stranger. Furthermore, his increasing withdrawal scared her.

"He's eating well," Jessie said, hope springing eternal, "and he's walking with me every day. Each morning we walk clear down to the alley fence and back. He goes to bed earlier. I suppose that's all the fresh air."

Or to get away from his mother. Except, Evelyn thought wearily, stepping over a puddle, she isn't his mother—she's just a bossy stranger.

True to her word—and much to her stepmother's surprise—Brenda came over every day after work, bringing Poo. John still showed no interest in the child, but he would let his daughter help him get into bed.

"It's the bunny uniform," Brenda told Evelyn flatly. "He thinks I'm hired help. And I don't mind. Truly, Mom. I don't—I guess because he isn't my dad any more. He's a nice man, but he's not Daddy. Is that why you're sleeping in Jack's room?"

Zing.

"Yes," Evelyn had answered just as flatly.

As she waited for the lights to change at the intersection, she wiggled one aching shoulder. She wasn't sure how much longer she could survive in Jack's bed: it was like trying to rest on a mortuary slab.

Burdened with worry, she punched in, put on her ears, and went to work.

There was a football game in town that night. Not only did they unexpectedly get two school buses full of cheering kids from the rival school during the dinner hour, but—the rivals having won decisively—they got them again at ten. The place was a madhouse. Evelyn had never seen so many double-cheeseburgers in her life. With mayo. Without mayo. Lettuce and tomato. Without lettuce and tomato. Hold the mustard. Persuade the cheerleaders they could be seen without standing on the tables. Fish the coach's ballcap out of the fries. Clean up after the puppy mascot who made a puddle on the floor right through his small varsity sweater. Smile. They're kids. They're only kids.

A slight, older man in a corner table beckoned Evelyn as she went by, almost running.

He said something she couldn't catch. She bent, saying, "I'm sorry. There's too much noise."

"Just a question. I'm a stranger here. Is there more than one nursing home in town?"

"No, sir. Just the one on the east edge."

He looked relieved. "Good. I'd stopped to see if I had a flat when this man came along walking. He asked, and I said I'd just passed one. I'm glad I was right; he looked awfully tired. I probably should have turned around and taken him there—but you know—you're even afraid of the old guys any more. Oh—I almost forgot. Look out for the ear raid."

"The what?"

"Your bunny ears. I heard the kids talking. They're going to start to grab ears."

"Not mine," said Evelyn and hightailed it behind the counter. She told Margaret, who swiped a stray fringe of hair up into her topknot and said wearily, "Oh shit," just as the big, battered young quarterback leaped into the air, grabbed Marva's plush headgear and yelled, "Ear—"

That was as far as he got, vocally. Further, he got Marva's knee in his stomach and as he doubled up, dropping the ears, a hand-edge chop fell on the back of his neck. He hit his seat, stunned, and sudden awed silence fell at the sight of his face pushed into his cheeseburger.

Into this silence Marva announced cheerfully, "Next time, buster, I'll make you a soprano for sure. Listen—all you guys! Any ears we lose have to be paid for out of our paychecks—and that's not fun for us. So cool it, okay?"

From behind the counter, Margaret whispered in sheer admiration, "My God—that was beautiful! I couldn't have said it better myself!"

Marva was readjusting her ears on top of her

green-blond head. She winked. "You haven't had the experience I have," she murmured. "That's the first time I've fought for *ears,* for Chrissake! And with a kid. Hey, buster, you okay?"

Buster was fine, although a bit subdued, and the incident was closed with an apology from a rather embarrassed chaperon. As the fans filed out and got on their buses, Margaret locked the doors, turned off the street sign lights, and said, "Everyone relax a minute. Then we'll clean."

Twelve Bunny people removed their ears and fell like rocks into chairs. Eileen murmured, "And this happens every time there's a football game, guys."

Margaret said briskly, "Well, this was your first experience, team, and now you know what to expect. I think you did well."

"Especially Marva," said Kooky, and the others went "Yea!" with a weary spatter of applause.

Marva was taking a mock bow when behind her the telephone rang. She picked it up, said shortly, "We're closed," and banged it down again. "Some people! It's after eleven; what do they think we are? Yeah, I'll take a soda. Margaret, sweetie, I've a gentleman named Jack in the glove compartment of my car that would love to share a Coke with me if you didn't mind."

Margaret laughed but shook her head. "Keep

Mr. Daniels in your car," she said. "While we're sitting—any customer complaints?"

She was perched on the counter, swinging her feet as informally as any of the others. There was catsup on her blouse and her topknot was a little limp. She was smiling. But she was still Management, still utilizing Bunny Burger time.

Evelyn sipped her diet soda and marveled. The woman never seemed to let up.

Betty was answering her question. "Ice."

"Ice?"

The telephone rang again, and she raised her voice.

Betty nodded. "Too much."

"We hear that all the time. They did a study and found we gave ten percent less ice than the O G's, or other guys, but the customer still complains. Maybe we ought to post a sign." The phone stopped and she lowered her voice. "Anything else?"

They were discussing the thrill of limp lettuce when Eileen stiffened. "There's someone at the door."

All conversation stopped. Marva craned her neck.

She said, "There's nobody now."

"I know there was, though! I saw the shadow."

"Anybody expecting someone?"

Negative reaction all around.

Marva slid off her stool. "I'll see."

Uneasily Margaret said, "Stay in sight."

"Don't worry."

She unlocked the side door, peered out. "Nope."

"Try the other."

They watched her cross the tile floor, open that one, too.

"Nope."

They watched again, *en masse*, as she came back and sat down again. Margaret said, "Okay. When we leave tonight, everyone goes together. Finish your drinks and let's cl—"

The "clean" never quite made it, drowned by the reverberant smash of something that made an instant crystal spiderweb on the plate glass of the front window.

"Hit the floor!" Margaret yelled, and no one had to be told twice.

But after that, nothing happened. Nothing at all.

Evelyn crouched beneath the counter with Eileen, who was muttering, "Gawd. Gawd." Marva crawled around the corner, said, "Scootch over," and crowded in beside them lighting two cigarettes with a shaking hand. Handing one in front of Evelyn to Eileen, she muttered, "What the hell's goin' on—someone miss an alimony payment?"

Evelyn was watching an arm reach up over the counter and pluck the telephone off its cradle. A hand went up and dialed. Margaret Daniels's calm voice said, "This is the Bunny Burger manager at 1011 Sycamore and Cross. We seem to be under siege. Would you send a prowl car, please?"

They not only would, they did. The city police screeched in, along with a county cop car and two state troopers. The parking lot was full of red flashers and the Bunny Burger full of uniforms before five minute had elapsed.

Marva said dryly, "It must be the most excitement this burg has had since the hogs ate Gramma." Nonetheless, she fluffed her hair and patched her lipstick before she crawled out from beneath the counter. Evelyn followed a bit more stiffly and was grateful for the helping hand of a young patrolman. He asked, solicitously, "You okay?"

"Fine. Thank you."

She saw another policeman handing Margaret a sizeable rock. Apparently that was what had been thrown. Margaret was saying in a calm voice, "I think it's just harassment. Nevertheless—" She stopped when the telephone began to ring again. The policeman said, "Let me," and picked it up.

He frowned and listened. "Who? One moment," he said and put the receiver to his chest. "Anyone here named Evelyn? It's a lady and she sounds real upset."

Evelyn's heart shot into her mouth. She gulped. "Me."

He handed her the phone. Conscious of all eyes being upon her, she quavered, "Hello?"

"Evie, he's gone! I'm just frantic! I've looked everywhere and I've called and called until I'm exhausted but he's gone! Why haven't you answered? I rang and rang—I have no idea where he is, he's just gone—do you hear me?"

Evelyn sat down abruptly. Into the desperate spate of tumbling words she said, "Jessie, listen! Listen! It's John—right? John's gone. You've checked the bathroom—the kitchen—the patio— is the gate locked?"

"Oh God! I don't know. You don't think—"

"I don't know what I think. Just calm down, Jessie, please. What else is gone—his pajamas?"

"He had them on—he went to bed early to watch that old stuff he seems to like—I heard "The Beverly Hillbillies" when I came upstairs once so I didn't look in—oh Evelyn, where could he be, I'm so scared—"

404

No one was likely to kidnap a sixty-year-old nobody. Evelyn knew that. So if John was not kidnapped but he was gone, then he'd gone on his own. She also knew that, as unhappy as he'd been, it was very reasonable that he'd simply bailed out. If he had bailed out — where would he go?

Suddenly she knew the answer as surely as if it were written on the Bunny Burger menu. It didn't scare her any less but at least she knew where to start looking. She took a deep breath and said, "Jessie — listen — please listen. You sit tight. I'm going to find him. I think I know where he is. Make some coffee. I'll let you know as soon as I can."

She hung up decisively despite Jessie's anxiety, and turned around. To the waiting faces she said, "My husband's wandered off. He's not — well. Margaret, I have to go."

"Of course. You walked today? Drive my car."

"I'll take her." This was a young patrolman with curly hair. "Okay, Sarge? It's Mr. Cass, isn't it? I used to play Little League for him; he was a hell of a guy. Do you have any ideas?"

Evelyn hesitated. "I think toward the nursing home. A customer said something about a hiker asking where it was. I just never thought of John. But I'm sure that's where he'd head."

The sergeant said, "Oh, God, the highway. Tim, you'd better go, too. I'll call the home. If he didn't make it, you'll have to check the ditches. Both sides."

"It's raining again," said the curly-headed man. "I've got my slicker. Bring two more, Tim, in case we find him. Get an ambulance on standby. Is he there, Sarge?"

"No," said the sergeant, hanging up. "Sorry, Mrs. Cass. Move it, guys. Stay in touch."

The tires of the patrol car made hissing sounds on the street. The radio at Evelyn's knee sparkled with red lights and burbled softly. At the edge of town, the policeman slowed to a crawl, and put his searchlight so it flooded the right-of-way, glancing off the wet grass, the fence posts, the huddled rows of osage orange and cedar brush. The other young man, bundled into a shiny slicker, took to the left lane, walking along the crumbling blacktop and shining his huge flashlight into the meandering water of the drainage ditch. Huddled on her side of the patrol car, cold hands clinging to the edge of the open window and hair beginning to dampen against her cheek, Evelyn called time and time again, "John! John! Where are you?"

When the beaded lights of the nursing home came into view she started to cry softly, trying

406

hard not to. But the night was so wet, so chill, so dark . . .

Chuck Benning, the young patrolman, reached over and patted her hand. "Buck up," he said. "We always find them. We'll just go back again and keep looking."

But incredibly, as they made the driveway loop to return, they saw him. He was sitting calmly on the low front step, out of the rain and wind. He was fully dressed and had his pajamas neatly folded in a plastic apple bag, shaving gear on top, at his side. He rose as they stopped by him and said, "I can't seem to open the door. Could you help me?"

There was a buzzer, but of course John had never rung it. Chuck put a warning hand on Evelyn's, got out, and said cheerfully, "Hello, Mr. Cass. Of course. It'll be warmer inside."

The heavy portal creaked as it swung. John walked into the foyer. As usual, there was an empty wheelchair there. He climbed up in it and sat with a sigh. The policeman glanced back at Evelyn. His eyebrows were raised, questioning.

She made a decision—one she should never have had to make in the first place if she'd not had the spine of cooked spaghetti. Wiping the tears with a messy wad of Kleenex from her bag, she nodded in assent and climbed from the car.

407

Chuck took hold of the wheelchair handles.

He said jocularly, "All right, young man, where would you like to go?"

"Home," said John Cass firmly. "To my room."

And they took him there.

Twenty-eight

The male night nurse took over as though having patients turn up before dawn was an ordinary occurrence — which perhaps it was.

"Call us tomorrow," he said. "He'll be fine. Won't you, John?"

Her husband didn't even look back as he wheeled into his room. But Evelyn was far from hurt. In fact, she felt a serenity she hadn't felt in days. The second patrolman was waiting outside in his car.

"Everything A-okay, guys?"

"Everything. Check in for me, Tim. I'll run Mrs. Cass home."

"Right. Everything's cool at Bunny Burger. Whoever pitched the rock took off. 'Night, Mrs. Cass. Glad things turned out okay."

Okay being a flexible term, of course. On the way home Evelyn said, "I'm so grateful."

"No problem. Besides, as I said, your husband was a hell of a guy. May I park here? I'll see you to the door."

As soon as their steps sounded hollowly on the porch floor the door flew open. Jessie stood there backlighted, a gaunt figure in a bathrobe, wringing thin hands. Her voice was husky with tears. "John? John?"

"He's all right. We found him."

"Where? Where is he?"

"He'd gone to find the nursing home."

The words struck John's mother like a physical blow. She started back, made some unintelligible protestation — then her hands flew to her face and she turned away.

Evelyn said, "Thank you again, Chuck," closed the door and put her arms around the shaking old woman. "It's all right, Jessie. It's all right."

"I failed. I failed."

"You didn't fail, Jessie. You can't fail unless there's a hope of success. There wasn't."

"He was so unhappy. I knew he was so unhappy — but oh dear God, Evelyn, I'm his mother!"

"And I'm his wife — but it didn't work for me either."

After a few agonizing moments she felt Jessie take a deep breath and straighten.

"Isn't it awful," Jessie said, "that even at eighty-five one *still* has to learn! There ought to be a break-point after which you're home free!" She blew her nose on a crumpled wad in one hand. "I made the coffee. Would you like some? My dear, you must be so tired, but— he's all right? He *is* all right?"

"I think he's fine. He's in good hands. They know what to do." If there was sting in the words, sobeit. "Yes. I'll drink with you. I can't sleep. At least not for a while."

She followed the robed figure with the wild hair into the kitchen. Sitting on a bar stool she hoisted her feet to another, shed her shoes and rubbed swollen ankles with one hand—the right one. The left one ached too much.

Jessie came with two china cups and climbed up on the third stool at the other side of the bar. Her cheeks were stained and behind the glasses her eyes were blurry. Sighing, she reached back and twisted up the straying parti-colored hair, skewering it with the sort of wire hairpin one couldn't even buy any more.

"I feel as if a nightmare was over," she said. "A nightmare of my own making, I'm afraid. But one never believes one's children, Evie. They're so—young. What do they know?"

It was an apology of sorts.

411

Evelyn said, "There also ought to be a break-point on childhood." She sipped. It was good coffee. "I wonder where it is."

"When your parents die. Then there's no one to turn to anymore. *You* are the parents. Age doesn't enter into it at all." She sighed again. "I'm sorry I disrupted your household, Evie. Since it was for nothing."

If she felt better condemning herself, Evelyn didn't care. Perhaps it would be cathartic. "It's all right. Really. I guess maybe we both had to find out for sure."

"About John. Yes. Only—"

"Only what?"

"Those young people are still in my house. I'm homeless for another week."

Evelyn reached across and tugged at both ears beneath the calico hair. "You idiot!" she said. "As if I cared about that! You can stay here until the cows come home and you know it. When does Bren go to Springfield?"

"Tomorrow."

"We don't have to take her?"

"No. She's going with a friend."

"You didn't just hand her the money!"

"No, my dear, I'm brighter than that. I mailed it to the clinic—any refunds come to me. However, I do believe she's serious."

412

"I hope so. I love the girl but she drives me up the wall. Oh, lord—two-thirty. I'd better go to bed."

"When do you have to be at the library?"

"Nine." She was dumping her coffee into the sink, picking up her shoes. "It's later on Saturday. 'Night, Jessie."

Because she ached so miserably, she went into her own room. Jack's bunks were for kids.

The bed was neatly made. John had apparently never even gotten into it. There was nothing of him there at all—no sight, no smell, nothing in disarray. He'd left no personal imprint, because it had not been his room, and John was a polite man. She turned down the sheets, pulled on another ragged nightie, and climbed in.

Arriving at the library next morning, she found Karen Marsh in the middle of Saturday Story Hour. Because she was playing a *Winnie-the-Pooh* tape on the VCR, Karen whispered in Pooh language, "I have a *missage* for you."

Evelyn sat down beside her. Her grandson appeared and climbed up on her lap, never taking his eyes from the screen. She tried to pretend her heart hadn't leaped into her throat. "What?"

413

"It's from my father. He said tell her 'Eleven o'clock. Dog Pile.' I presume that's either code or he's certainly slipped in terms of elegance."

Evelyn felt her face burn fiery red and was enormously grateful for the darkness about her. She tousled Poo's soft hair, making him mutter, "Don't, Grammy!" and said as calmly as she could, "The man's a humorist. So he's coming over. How nice."

"You couldn't get off a little earlier?"

"No. That's my shift."

"Too bad. Hear you had a little excitement last night. What's the problem — someone put Thousand Island Dressing in a Reuben? I don't think Dad would throw rocks, but someone else might."

"We don't make Reubens. The boss says it's harassment because we're non-union."

"Oh boy. I hope they catch him. You guys don't need that and this town does need Bunny Burger. I hear that the Princess Dress Shoppe might be down the tube, and there goes — what — three jobs? Four?"

Evelyn was experiencing a sense of pure relief. She was sorry for Nan and the girls, but thank God she'd gone to Bunny! "I don't know," she murmured. "That's a shame."

The VCR ran out. Evelyn left Poo and his

twenty-four cohorts to their cookies and Kool-aid, and went back into the stacks to work. She was not ungrateful for the chance. When the lights had come on, Karen's eyes had been amused but rather penetrating.

The prospect of seeing Bob was like the sun at the end of the tunnel and she had to face that—plus a couple of extraneous things, such as how to explain Bob to Jessie.

The problem, she realized as she threw old magazines into discard with a force that puffed dust up in clouds, was guilt. She felt guilty again and she thought she was over that. Damn it! Not guilty about John. Guilty in the eyes of other people—and that was so unfair. John was the one supposedly hurt and John wasn't hurting.

A sneeze turned her around, and through a haze of gray gloom she saw Karen standing in the door. "Good gravy, Evelyn—what are you doing, starting your own dust bowl?"

"Oh. Sorry."

"Telephone."

Recently her telephone calls hadn't been all that great. Scared, she hurried through the Kool-aid crowd and picked it up. "Hello."

Jessie's voice came at her ear. "Darling, I just had the most delightful chat with Victor Bonnelli—and he's taking me to lunch. Do you mind? There's chicken salad in the fridge."

What was Vic up to? "No, I don't mind, Jessie. That's great. Enjoy yourself. And by the way—Karen tells me we have a friend in town. Don't worry if I'm late tonight—I'll see you tomorrow. Got to run," she added right over Jessie's, "Really, and who is that, dear?" and hung up.

She then felt not only guilty all over again but cowardly, too!

Already she regretted her words—but it was a bit late, now, to call and say, "It's Karen's father, Jessie." Then what? "We're enjoying a little adultery"?

What the hell was a *little* adultery? Either you did or you didn't. She did. She *was* enjoying it. Like a sixteen-year-old, she hoped to enjoy it again, to savor a feeling she used to laugh at when she read of it in Emma's books. She wanted to revel once more in the sensation that she—Evelyn Matthews Cass, incredibly aged fifty-six—could generate with a man who also enjoyed it enough to come over and do it some more!

But how does one explain that to one's beloved mother-in-law?

One didn't. One couldn't.

The cheese stood alone in a few things.

She fished Vic's business card from her bag and dialed.

"Vic? This is Evelyn Cass."

"Hi, doll. I just talked to Jessie."

"I know. I just talked to Jessie. Vic, I've been a coward. I haven't told her about listing the house."

She heard him laugh. "I guessed that. No problem, kiddo. We're going to lunch and hash over old times. I may run her out to visit my mama. That's all. Be cool. How long is she here?"

"A week. Or so."

"Then I hope you can start packing."

She made a face. "I'll have to tell her first. I owe her that. She's a nice lady."

"You're right. But it's your ballgame, doll, not mine. I just sell houses. Okay?"

"Okay. Thanks, Vic."

"Don't worry. I'll take it out in a home-cooked meal one of these days. In your new apartment."

"That's a deal. Are you still eating canned rigatoni?"

"Only when Mama doesn't give me care packages. Or when I can't find some nice girl sorry for a starving Italian boy. You still

417

wouldn't like to watch me arm wrestle tonight?"

"I would love to watch you arm wrestle. But not tonight."

"Oh, well. Win some, lose some. Call you Monday like I said. 'Bye."

" 'Bye."

She turned to face Karen Marsh's grin.

"Arm wrestling? Evie, you do have un-plumbed depths!"

"That was Vic Bonnelli." She almost said "An old friend of John's." But she didn't. The cheese was also not going to prop itself up with John's friends. "He's trying to move my house for me."

"Oh, I know him. He came back into town a couple of months ago and rented the apartment down the street from Tim's clinic. Owns a cream Lab. Nice man. Crazy. Here." She handed Evelyn a trashbag. "Collect the dixie cups. Then we'll see if we can finish at least J through K before lunch."

The children were filing up the stairs with assorted adults. Poo's small hand was in that of his other grandmother. He paused, said cheer-fully, " 'Bye, Grammy Cass. See you!"

" 'Bye, baby. See you."

"Now," said Karen, and picked up her file drawer. "J through K."

Actually they made it through K to the midpart of L before time ran out and the accumulated grime made them both look like chimneysweeps.

"And they say being a librarian is such nice clean work," Karen giggled. "You wash first. You have to go. I'll feed Daddy dinner," she called after Evelyn as she went upstairs toward the one small sink. "Then you're on your own."

Evelyn pondered that as she ate her chicken salad sandwich. Indeed she was on her own — more than anyone realized.

During the Jessie Incumbency, Romeo had taken up his abode on the back porch where the fireplace chimney angled. Evelyn fed him and chose not to think about what would happen when she moved to an apartment. She'd forgotten to ask about pets.

I should make a list, she thought as she hurried down Sycamore after doing laundry, changing sheets, raking leaves in the west yard, showering, and curling her hair. She tried to make mental notes as she walked, but only got as far as what to do about Romeo, when to tell Jessie, and talk to Vic on Monday because list-making was a diversionary tactic — and it wasn't working. Her mind was on Bob. She'd thought of him in the shower — she always thought of him in the shower now — and blushed and shivered. She thought of him while putting on lipstick, the only make-up hot flashes couldn't melt. She thought of him while fastening her best bra — the one softly lacy. She'd thought of him while folding the rose-colored robe into a grocery bag with her rabbit ears. She was thinking of him now, walking through fitful sunshine and counting the hours until eleven.

It was unreal. She was almost sixty! Yet she was acting like a girl of sixteen! Perhaps she was having a second childhood, she thought, and tried to laugh.

A car tootled at her cheerfully as it swept up the hill. It was a Datsun. Two people were in front and from the back window Labrador ears were blowing flappily. Vic and Jessie, on their way home.

She waved back, caught the lights, and went to work.

As she punched in she read the notice on the employee bulletin board: "We are now under 24-hour surveillance. Accord the police officers every courtesy. The Mgmt."

Well, at least everyone could breathe a little more easily. On that thought she slotted her card, adjusted her ears, and went on the floor.

Saturday night was slow. One church was

having a spaghetti dinner, there was a JayCee barbecue on the riverfront, and an Apple Festival in an adjoining town. It seemed they trashed more food than they sold. Margaret let them start cleaning floors, tables, and windows early. As Evelyn shined panes, she kept looking out for a certain car with a white-haired man in it but none came. The parking lot emptied until there was nothing left but a row of employees' vehicles and the squad car sitting by the fence.

A few more people came through drive-up. Margaret told eight more people to go including Marva, who emerged from the lounge in a skintight, low-cut jumpsuit with fringe and a cowboy hat.

She said cheerfully, "I'm auditioning. Cross your fingers. See you Monday."

Eileen murmured, "Since Buffalo Bill's girl singer is quitting next week, I can guess where."

Betty said, "Good. She sang like she had 'er tit in a wringer anyway." She wrung her mop expertly. "Can't seem to get away from cleanin', myself. I guess it's whatever the good Lord meant you to do. I see Jessie's in town, Evelyn. She stayin' long?"

"A week or so."

"Holds her age good. Nice teeth help. I always said the dentist that made my old man's worked for a vet. Is that a car turning in here? I hope he goes through drive-up."

It was a car. It was not a Datsun. It went through drive-up.

They finished, cut the lights. The patrolman with the dark moustache said, "Everyone accounted for? Okay. If you forget something identify yourselves."

Eileen sighed. "What a day! Me for a beer. Evie?"

"No. Not tonight."

"Need a ride, then?"

"No. Thank you."

There was no one in sight. No one.

She couldn't stand around waiting like a lovesick school girl. Something had happened. Something must have happened.

She said good night, crossed the intersection, and started up Sycamore. It was a witch's moon above her, round and pale, wandering fitfully in and out of ragged shadows. A chill breeze whined in the tree tops, causing Evelyn to clutch her light coat around her throat. Leaves skittered across the sidewalks, making dry, rasping noises, and somewhere behind Everett Morris's towered old house a cat yowled.

Halloween was next Friday. Bunny Burger already had cases of free witch hats and orange and black balloons to give away. Margaret had a crew going in tomorrow to decorate. The special menu would feature pumpkin shakes, ghost-toasty grills, and vampire sodas all next week. To Evelyn, at that particularly depressed point in time, it all sounded funny as a hearse.

She quickened her pace, the brown bag with its rose-colored robe batting against her legs and the damp wind taking the curl from her hair. Who the hell cared anyway?

Then the car slid to the curb behind her, its headlight throwing her shadow long and black up the street. A voice she knew, she knew so well, said, "Evelinda? I'm sorry. I'm so sorry."

She turned, but he was already getting out, coming toward her, the old air force jacket belling behind him. She ran like a child, and he caught her, holding her tightly, saying in her ear, "I can't stay. I've only a few minutes while Karen throws some gear together. They called. They said she may be dying, that we'd better come."

He turned, bundling her into his car. "I'll take you home. I have time for that."

But that was all. That was all there was time for.

And I can't help, she told herself, sick at heart, sick for him. His arm was around her, holding her as he drove. The now-familiar smell of fuel and grease filled the car, rivaled the musty scent of the ancient jacket against her face. He stopped in front of her house, put the gear in park, turned and gathered her closely, his cold cheek against hers. He whispered in a stricken voice, "Hold me. I need to be held. There are so many things I cannot remember if I'm to get through this thing—let me remember you, let me remember your warmth and love and happiness so I can come back to you, Evelinda. So I can come back to you . . ."

She clung to him. She kissed the rough line of his jaw, his nose, the curve of his cheek, she murmured things, she let him cry against her breast—dry, heaving sobs from a man in terrible pain.

He made himself stop. He straightened, reached beyond her to open the door, and gave her a last hug. He said quietly, "God bless."

"God bless," she answered, and stood on the sidewalk watching him drive away.

The car stopped at the intersection, then turned west to Karen's. She saw the spray of its

424

headlights as it made the sweep. Then it was gone.

She went quietly into the house. It was still. Jessie must be sound asleep.

It was not until she was lying awake at two in the morning that she suddenly realized she'd left the brown bag with its robe and its ears on the seat of his car.

Twenty-nine

The wind and rain had blown themselves out by Monday morning and the sun presented a smiling face for early risers—among them both Evelyn and Jessie, neither of whom had slept very well.

"It should be a nice week for the little Halloweeners," said Jessie. She'd already poured a selection of wrapped sweets into a bowl by the front door.

Evelyn hadn't had the heart to tell Jessie there were no children on Sycamore Street anymore, and very few others made it up the long rise from the main drag. She also made no comments as her mother-in-law thoroughly washed the breakfast dishes before putting them into the dishwasher.

Jessie pulled out the top rack and glanced at Evelyn. "Shall we run it?"

Evelyn gave the assembly a practiced eye. "We can get lunch in there."

"Okay."

Romeo strolled by and looked in the screen door, his tail like a question mark. Jessie sighed, said, "Oh, well," scraped the rest of the scrambled eggs into a bowl, and opened the screen. "Come on in, cat."

Romeo rubbed his massive head against Jessie's flannel nightgown in passing. She didn't even flinch. It was suddenly evident to Evelyn's amazement that the cat had gained at least three pounds in the last ten days.

She said, "Jessie!"

"Yes, dear?"

"How much have you been feeding him?"

Jessie was pouring herself some coffee. Guiltily she said, "Oh—not much. Just a scrap here and there. We do share some Snickers bars on occasion. That's all. Need a warm-up?"

Resigned, Evelyn held out her cup. "Just top it. He's fat!"

"That's new?"

"Well—fatter. Patio?"

"May as well."

Romeo accompanied them, hesitated between their laps, then decided old friends might be more judicious as well as capacious. He leaped heavily into Evelyn's, kneaded his paws briefly, and settled down. She tickled his chin and he accorded her a small rumbling purr of approval.

Before sitting down, Jessie inspected the coleus for illicit stalks of bloom, most of it having been severely pinched some days ago. She is, Evelyn was thinking, more supple in the back than I, when Jessie turned abruptly. "Evelyn!"

"Here. In the other chair."

"I've been thinking."

On that premise she seated herself, crossed her legs in the long red corduroy housecoat that fell open, showing a kelly green flannel nightie. "John is not coming home."

"No."

"Then you don't need this big house."

Evelyn slopped coffee on Romeo, who was not pleased. He changed laps, and neither of them noticed.

Evelyn said, "No. I really don't."

"Jack doesn't want it. He has that nice ranch-type in the new suburb."

"Yes."

"Brenda doesn't know what she wants. Nor will she for some time — and I suspect this place would always be too much for her."

"You're probably right."

"Then why don't you get off your duff and put it up for sale? I've been thinking about that," Jessie went on, serenely oblivious of her daughter-in-law's total astonishment, "since I had lunch with Victor the other day. He says he could possibly get a good price for it—the location, condition, and so forth. Or—maybe, he says—even lease it if you really didn't know what you wanted to do. I said I'd bring the subject up. He's a little shy, poor dear."

Victor, Evelyn was thinking in a state of shock, is about as shy as a brass band—and as clever as a cage of monkeys. He'll bear watching. But she did thank him in her heart.

"Would you care?"

"My dear girl, of course I'd care! I'd drive by and mourn whenever I came to town. But one has to move with the times—" and she suddenly laughed. "At the risk of being ostentatiously clever, I think it's time *you* moved."

"I *had* thought about it."

"I'm glad. I'd hate to believe you were that obtuse. I hope you've also thought about trading the Lincoln. You need that iron whale about as badly as you need the measles."

"I've thought of that, too."

"Then do it."

"Jane Nixon has been wanting me to go

halves on an apartment."

"Whatever does Jane want with an apartment?"

"She wants to write a book."

"Splendid. I'll read it. Jane is more literate than any of your friends. Porter DeKalb has always disturbed me — that beautiful, mellifluous voice saying 'I'm gonna get me a'. It's like — like Caruso singing Boop-boop-adoop. Incongruous."

"Jessie."

"What?"

"Stop rattling for a moment."

Jessie looked a little surprised. Then she laughed again and it was a bit shaky. "I thought I was so clever."

"You were clever. It's just that we both love this place. And it hurts us both. You really think I ought to move?"

Jessie was wiping tears with a corner of her red sleeve. "Yes."

"I also love you."

"I know you do, Evie. We've both been blessed. Pat, God rest her soul, could never have been half of what you have to John and me."

Evelyn got up, went over and hugged the older woman, arms around the frail erect body, cheek against the amazing calico hair. Snuffling, she said, "You're making me cry now."

"Go answer the phone. That will cure it."

Evelyn obeyed, plucking the kitchen phone from its cradle and sliding her now not-so-ample fanny up on a stool. She hoped it was Vic. Over the phone she wouldn't have the impulse to kiss him.

"Cass residence."

Then she heard the tinny, watery sound of long distance. Her heart shot into her throat. She pulled up the antenna.

"Cass residence!"

Plink, plink, plink. Coins in a pay phone.

"Evelyn?"

"Yes."

"This is Tim Evans. Bob wanted me to call."

Jessie shuffled by in her red and green, looking like Mother Christmas, and headed for the shower. Evelyn nodded, swallowing. "Yes, Tim."

"Sue-Ann died this morning."

"Oh, Tim. What may I do?"

"Call the library—if you would. I've already talked to my mom about Robby."

"Of course. Tell Karen not to worry."

"Right. She'll be cremated and buried in Indianapolis. That's the family cemetery. We'll be back about—Thursday, probably. Bob's going on to Florida. People will ask so tell them the mortuary is Brender's." He went ahead in the rote manner of someone functioning on two levels and gave the rest of the funeral information. Evelyn scrambled for a pen that worked and finally settled for a marking pencil of Poo's.

"All right, Tim. I have it. Tell them I love them."

"They know. It's tough, Evie. You're never really ready, I guess — even though you think you are. I knew her. She was a lovely lady. Independent as hell. Always concerned about other folks."

"I didn't know her. But she must have been like that — because I know Karen — and Bob. Take care."

"You, too."

He hung up. So did she. Then she simply sat, turning the red marking pencil with its small tooth marks around and around in her hand.

So. It was over. Or, was it just beginning?

Pushing the hair from her eyes she glanced about at her quiet, sunny kitchen with the fat pewter jugs shining in the sun. The sibilant hiss from the sink pipes as Jessie took her shower upstairs made a song in the back of her mind as she looked at the row of tomatoes ripening on the window ledge, the calico place mats, the dirty ashtray where Jessie had had a surreptitious cigarette and forgotten the evidence, and the assorted smiling faces stuck to the front of the fridge.

Had Sue-Ann Marsh had a fridge with snaps stuck on it, tomatoes on the window ledge, country-patterned mats, dirty ash trays? Had Sue-Ann been a member of the ostrich generation too?

She'd never know.

What she did know—know with a terrible, blatantly selfish sense of desolation—was that the frail balance between herself and Bob Marsh had just tipped.

In the deepest recesses of her mind where the very seed of life fought like a tiger for survival she had considered herself and Bob equals. They both had partners who, for all purposes of human emotion, were gone away forever. Now that equality was shot. Sue-Ann Marsh was dead. Dead. A word the world understood in all its unquestionable finality.

Further, Bob was "free"—another worldly euphemism. Not free of pain; he was expected to feel pain. But free of guilt. Ah. There was the rub. Bob was free. He could have his cotton candy anywhere he liked now, without making a mess. He could return to Florida without a single backward look.

Tim had indicated he was doing just that. He had not said by any word or phrase that Bob was going south by way of here.

Dismayed at the despondency that descended on her like black night, Evelyn made herself slide off the stool, rinse the coffee cups and put them in the washer. She was acting like a jilted teenager! Wasn't she a little old for that?

She'd better get her perspective back. She knew what she was—a chubby, gray-haired broad with a poochy stomach, raised in a midwestern town where responsibilities were not taken lightly. She was a Cheese that had lapsed again, had started depending on a man once more instead of standing alone.

Well—damn it!

She could handle responsibility, and she could also stand alone! She was going to get her bills paid by herself, and she had found a job by herself—even if it was a trifle low class for an ex-colonel in the air force!

Now that is petty, she acknowledged grimly, and knew it was petty because she hurt. And why did she hurt, damn it? Bob Marsh had never promised her anything. She should be glad for him, that his trauma was over.

434

She was glad.

She also hurt.

Deciding that she was too old to learn to be completely reasonable, and musing, too, that age had some awfully strange compensations, she got dressed and went to the library.

It was odd without Karen, troubling her almost as much as it did the children whose small faces fell when they saw a different person behind the familiar desk. However, she did finish another file card drawer, and back home, she found a belated birthday card from Jack— all hearts and roses, which meant Michelle had chosen it. Jack usually went like a shot to the rack of weird or funny ones with fat turtles doing aerobics. It also contained a twenty dollar bill which meant that if her Bunny Burger ears hadn't turned up by Friday, the cost of new ones wouldn't have to come out of her paycheck. Eventually, if she could only stop doing jackass things, she might be able to afford a haircut.

Also, if she'd quit mooning over a man who'd never promised anything, perhaps she could get on with her life!

Of course he said he'd come back, she argued with herself as she trudged down the leaf-carpeted hill to work. But his wife has died—and now it's a whole new ballgame with different rules. For him. Not me. Now he can play anywhere he wants to play, including back in the world he shared with Sue-Ann and their friends.

Face up to reality, Evie. Be a lady. Smile.

What she actually did was mutter the agricultural word, catch her heel in the employee door, and almost break her neck—a lovely way to start a work day, especially as she fell on her arthritic shoulder and put one knee on a wad of bubble gum.

They had a team meeting before going out front during which Margaret suggested they appear Thursday and Friday in Halloween costume.

"Great suggestion," Eileen murmured as she punched in. "Kooky, let's you and me tie our hair up on top and come as the two ends of a sausage."

Kooky grinned but shook her head. "My brother's got a gorilla suit. I can wear that. What about you, Evie?"

"Evelyn shook her head. So far she couldn't feel much holiday enthusiasm. "I have no idea. John had a clown outfit once for a Rotary carnival, but even if I could find it, I'd be so hot I'd die."

Both Porter DeKalb and Charles Nixon were Shriners, and owned any number of sultanic robes and tarbooshes, but she was not likely to ask for help from either of them. She sighed and went on in exasperation, "I guess I'm getting a little old for Halloween. I'll come up with something, I suppose. Maybe a sheet . . ."

"You have white sheets?"

"Oh." Times had changed. Plaid or flowered ghosts wouldn't really cut it.

Maybe that's my problem, she thought drearily: a white sheet mentality in a patterned world.

On that cheery thought she went to work in drive-up.

At least on her shift the surly man didn't come through complaining about his ham quiche. One learns to be grateful for small favors.

Thirty

The week progressed. That was about all Evelyn could say for it. In their infinite wisdom, the city council had allowed *two* official Beggar's Nights. That didn't preclude the little darlings' exploding their orange and black balloons into the drive-up microphone all week nor quietly letting the air out of all the employees' tires while their ringleader engaged the attention of the attendant policeman with a tale of woe.

By Tuesday Evelyn had had enough, by Wednesday she had had more than enough, and on Thursday she went to work with all the enthusiasm of Marie Antoinette mounting the steps to the guillotine.

To be totally fair, the rites of Halloween were not contributing a hundred percent to her morale problem. Thursday was when the Evans family was to return, and she had jumped at the ringing telephone all day. Nothing. No word from Karen. More pertinently, no word from Karen's father. Vic's couple seemed to be dragging their feet on leasing the house, and she'd had a polite inquiry from the meat processor about his bill. Polite, but an inquiry nonetheless.

None of these things would ordinarily raise her spirits anyway, but adding them to the shaving cream on the windows of the Lincoln and the discovery of mice in the blanket closet hardly helped.

Mice were not on Romeo's diet. She and Jessie discovered this when they shut him in the closet. He not only wailed his displeasure nonstop for forty-five minutes, on release he left home and wasn't seen again until the neighbor started buying a cheaper brand of cat food.

They then went through six traps, as Jessie believed in tossing away the trap with the deceased. She'd rather, she said, pay for the traps. Evelyn was in no mood to argue.

It was a shock to realize how very much, in just a few weeks, she'd allowed Bob Marsh to be the sunshine on her path. Delayed adolescence, she decided grimly. Or second childhood. She'd heard of sensible women going all giggly as they went through menopause but she didn't even have *that* excuse. She'd already been there, and hadn't felt like giggling in the least.

Nor did she now. She was going to miss his warmth and his support. He'd made her realize she was still alive, that there was still magic to be had — and for that she'd never forget him.

That's what she argued during the day. At night she cried. She cried for John, for the more tender, passionate lover he might have been, had she only known how to help him. She cried for the idealistic, narrow-visioned, cliché-ridden young wife she had been. She cried because it was all too late for John, and possibly too late for her. She cried because a door that seemed to be opening was the wrong one.

It was all very tiring and totally useless. It made her grumpy and pale. At the nursing home, Charley said she looked like death warmed over. John didn't notice.

Going to work at Bunny as a witch seemed singularly appropriate. She found her old black church choir robe in a box in the attic with four hymnals, a crumbled palm leaf and — inexplicably — an ancient jar of grape jam. Or it was inexplicable until Jessie remembered old Mrs. Michaels, who gave away dozens of jars, explaining cheerfully that she crushed her grapes with her galoshes on. A rummage through Jack's drawers turned up a false and bulbous nose that rubber-banded to her ears. Jessie located a black straw breton hat that had been terribly fashionable until Jackie Kennedy had come along with her little poufs and pill-boxes; she attached a tall black cone crown to it with super glue, and made a tie for beneath the chin. The basement scrub broom completed the ensemble. Jessie was pleased. Evelyn felt like an idiot, but then, her sense of humor had been somewhat obscured for a few days.

She drove the Lincoln to work, first because it was safer there under police surveillance, and second, because she didn't much relish walking along carrying a peaked hat and a broom. If she was more sensitive than usual and someone wanted to fight about it, welcome—although she didn't know who it would be. Only the Bunny gang—she hadn't seen Mary Lou, Jane, and Liz for days. This was the madhouse season for organizing the church bazaar, a project in which she was ordinarily up to her ears. This year she hadn't even been asked. They *knew* she couldn't have helped because of working; still, it would have been nice of them to inquire.

It was, she conceded grudgingly, a case of "damned if you do and damned if you don't" as far as her friends were concerned. She couldn't

441

blame them. But it was also another example of the gap widening between herself and the others. She wasn't an ostrich anymore.

She was a cheese.

She locked the Lincoln, picked up her broom, crossed the parking lot, and went through the employees' door into a madhouse. A cat burglar wearing Margaret Daniels's round eyeglasses paused in mid-flight, seized Evelyn's shoulder, said, "You look great! Thank God you're here. Punch in and relieve Angie in drive-up; she's had the brats all evening and she's about ready to kill!"

Out front, two cowgirls, two tramps, a gorilla, and an astronaut were trying to handle the clamoring public. As Evelyn pushed by adjusting her hat, one of the cowgirls said in Eileen's voice, "Keep the broom; you'll need it. There's a ten-minute wait on grill."

The geisha girl at the drive-up window slid off her stool on to the floor where she fanned herself with the wide ends of her *obi*. "I'll stay and bag," she said. "Margaret's the back-up but she had to go order more buns. Look out for the double cheeseburger just driving around. I think I had him earlier, and if I did he's got a water pistol."

He did. He was also Ben Swan's oldest son. Evelyn raised her false nose and said calmly,

"You squirt me, Roger Bennett Swan, and you're dead meat. Pass the word."

It worked. There were still a few advantages in having well-placed friends, even if one didn't see much of them anymore. The rowdyism generated by Roger's high school mob departed to greener fields, and the worst Evelyn got from then on was a dollar and twenty-two cents dropped in her hand accompanied by a cold chunk of raw liver. Her reaction had to be satisfactory. She knocked over two sodas, one of which popped open and drained into the fries, and got the hiccups.

Closing time came two centuries later. By that time the bulbous nose had softened into a genuine hook. Evelyn pulled it down to hang around her neck like an obscene necklace, hung the witch hat on the rack, and stood briefly beneath the ceiling fan fluffing damp gray hair. Around her the clean-up crew was moving like robots. She got her squirt bottle and cloth and joined them. Sloshing scrub water, Marva said wearily, "Comin' out with us, Evie?"

Evelyn squirted the upper window panes. Her arms hurt, and she grimaced as she polished. "I'd die on your hands."

"No, you wouldn't. C'mon."

"Yeah, c'mon. We're just going out to Buffalo Bill's for a beer. Do you good."

That was from Eileen, wiping tables. She stopped, mopping at acne-scarred cheeks where the sweat was still running, and hitched at her brief, fringed cowgirl skirt. Evelyn met her eyes and found genuine welcome. They really wanted her to go with them.

She glanced out at the emptying parking lot. The Lincoln was there, shining wet and black. Eileen's yellow Trans Am. Betty's Chevy. A few other vehicles including a heavy Harley-Davidson road hog, and a beat-up jeep. No old Datsun.

Of course there wasn't. The gaps in her world were widening everywhere.

Eileen was continuing persuasively, "I saw your mother-in-law come through with the kid. Weren't they going out of town?"

Jessie had come to the drive-up window with Poo in his outer-space costume—Boltron or Snarf or something. Poo knew. He'd destroyed his grammy with a laser toy and said, "Bye. See you." They had decided to go to Springfield and stay overnight with Brenda.

Evelyn nodded. "Yes. They were going to my daughter's. All right. I'll go for a little. Had I better take my own car?"

"No. None of us can stay too late. Kook, you goin'?"

A gorilla was wandering by carrying garbage.

From inside a hollow voice said, "Sure. Wait for me."

"Why don't you take that damned head off?"

"It's stuck."

"C'mere."

With one smart tug of Eileen's hefty forearm, Kooky's damply frizzed and freckle-faced head appeared. "Thanks," she said, and retrieved the garbage. "Yell when you're ready."

Margaret came out of her small office. She pulled off the black stocking cap. With a thin, nervous hand, she combed at the light hair tumbling down on her shoulders.

"Good work, gang," she said. "I'm going to apply to Corp for combat pay. I'm serious. This town is wild, and you guys have run your tails off; you deserve it. Can you come early again tomorrow? It's the last day of Halloween and it may be a dilly."

They all said sure they could. They put away their cleaning gear. She dimmed the lights, handed Kooky her head, and herded them out, locking the door behind them. "Good night."

Everyone echoed, "Good night."

It suddenly occurred to Evelyn that no one had asked Margaret to go out and have a beer. She looked a little lonely getting into her car and driving off.

Musing the fine line between labor and management, Evelyn climbed into the back of Eileen's Trans Am next to the gorilla. Up front, Marva and Eileen were making cosmetic repairs by the dome light. A cowboy hat and a bra came sailing into Evelyn's lap. The hat was Marva's; she wasn't certain about the bra.

"Let's roll," said Eileen cheerfully, tapped a "How Dry I Am" on the car horn for the patrolman dozing in his car at the drive-up chain, and spun rubber out into the street.

It was the same place they'd gone before, and they got the same back booth. The crowd was smaller, the noise higher, and there was no sign of Vic Bonnelli. Evelyn ordered a Busch Light, and suddenly missed someone.

"Why didn't Betty come?"

"Her old man's not too good," Eileen said, pulling off her boots. She set them at the end of the booth where they lopped over like tired soldiers, stretched out long slim legs and wiggled the toes inside their nylon cover. "Oh, that feels nice! How's yours?"

"John? The same."

"That's tough. Doesn't he know anybody?"

"No."

"I'd go ape if I had a man like that. Jesus. It's kind of a cleft stick, ain't it? You know what I mean."

Evelyn knew very well what Eileen meant.

Better, perhaps, than Eileen realized.

Marva raised her can of Stroh's and drank deeply. Her western shirt was now unbuttoned three down, and Evelyn recognized the owner of the bra from the untrammeled amplitude thus displayed. Evelyn also recognized that Marva had become a regular, as two good ol' boys were already lined up asking her to dance.

Kooky was asked, but declined. "It isn't any fun dancin' belly rub in a gorilla suit," she explained calmly. "And I can't take it off. The thing's too damned hot to wear anything underneath."

She'd put the head on the table before her. Now she stuck an unlit cigarette over one simian ear and laughed. "Looks like my first husband," she said. "Hairy as hell, but a real sweetie. I loved that man." She glanced at Evelyn briefly. "He died," she said.

"I'm sorry."

"Don't be. He had cancer. It was bad." She took a drink of her beer and added soberly, "I don't know which would be worse—losing him like I did, or losing him like you have. I think dead is better. Then you know where you are."

It was such an unexpected but precise bit of philosophy that Evelyn was caught totally unprepared.

"Kooky," she said in amazement and agreement, "you're right. Because I *don't* know where I am. I really don't."

The younger girl was lighting the cigarette. She blew out the match, and put it in the ashtray. "Well," she said, "just remember one thing—you're not dead. Because I think here comes someone looking for you."

"For me?"

Puzzled, Evelyn leaned out of the booth and glanced toward the door. At first through the smoky gloom and the shifting customers she saw nothing. Then her heart leaped up into her throat.

Just inside the threshold a tall, thin, white-haired man was standing. And Evelyn understood what Kooky meant: In a world of blue jeans, boots, and tractor caps—even with a loosened tie—in his immaculate white shirt, the dark slacks and the London Fog top coat, Bob Marsh stood out like a sore thumb.

Then he saw her. He grinned. And came over.

"Told ya'," said Kooky into her beer.

The world was blurred before Evelyn's eyes, and her spine was a length of yarn. But she knew he was towering over her, and she heard him say, "The cop said I'd find you here with your wild friends. Scootch." He was peeling off his coat, hanging it over the back.

448

She scootched. He leaned around her. "Bob."
"Kooky."

A sixth sense was bringing Marva and Eileen back, trailed by their plaid-shirted swains. Eileen slid in with hers, leaving Marva and the lanky young man in jackboots to pull up chairs. The atmosphere was thick with Marva's perfume, heated by dancing, tobacco, beer, and men's deodorant. Eileen said, "Hi," and both she and Marva turned bright, steady eyes on Bob. Suddenly Evelyn realized they'd come to protect her. To be sure she was okay. In a warm surge of affection she said, "Guys, this is Bob Marsh. Eileen. Marva."

"Billy Gene."

"Hershel."

The men shook. Bob said, "Beer all around." He paid, and paid the second time, interrupting an animated discussion with Hershel about redbone hounds. Evelyn said very little, but watching him, she saw the worn, tight lines about his eyes fade, the laughter come back. And he had found her hand beneath the table and was holding it tightly. Her fingers hurt; they were, in fact, going dead. But she didn't care.

He was saying, "You'll notice I've very carefully not mentioned the head on the table—although neither have I bought it a beer. I suppose there's some explanation."

"My head," said Kooky and put it on. Her muffled voice added, "Halloween."

"Good God. So it is! Okay. I did think the fur coat was a little unusual."

"Hot, too."

"Then take it off," said Hershel.

"I haven't got anything on underneath."

"Do take it off," said Billy Gene and everyone laughed, Marva giving him a teasing poke in the ribs with her fist.

Bob stood up. He was still holding Evelyn's hand. "Before the party gets any rougher, I'm going to take this lady home."

Hershel said, "Do you know if *she's* got anything on underneath?"

"He'll find out," said Billy Gene and they both almost fell off their chairs.

"Boys, be good," said Marva a little crisply, and Evelyn, though blushing, heard the distinct maternal note. "Nice meeting you, Bob. We'll see you tomorrow, Evie."

As they pushed their way through the smoke and bar patrons to the door, Kooky's high voice followed them clearly:

"Evie! Remember what I said!"

Outside it was cool and clean, the yellow pole light casting black stripes across the gravel parking lot. Bob's Datsun was at the end of the row in the shadows of the scrubby cedar trees. They crunched toward it in silence. He was holding her hand again. As he opened the door he asked quietly, "What did she say?"

That I wasn't dead, she remembered.

But how could she answer that? It would intimate too many things, things that were already trembling inside her. She replied a different truth: "That you were looking for me."

"And wasn't I just!" he muttered, a sound deep in his throat. Suddenly he pulled her up into his arms, holding her tightly, his lean cheek against the top of her head, his heart pounding in her ear. "I was looking for you. I was looking for the one sane thing in my world right now. If I hadn't found you, I don't know what I would have done."

"I'm sorry." Her voice was muffled. "I didn't know you were coming back."

"Coming back! Christ, woman, I told you! Don't you listen?"

"Tim said you were going to Florida."

"I am going to Florida. Tomorrow. Not tonight! Damn that Tim—I love him dearly but I'm going to break his neck!"

Now he was putting her into his car, going around making long black leg shadows across the gravel, sliding in on his side and reaching out for her again. "Evie, Evie," he said thickly into her ear, "You're warm, you're real, you can unfreeze me. God, I've been frozen for days, just hanging on."

Then he choked it back. She could feel him physically choking it back, withdrawing, sitting erect, starting the car.

"God damn," he said, his voice strained. "I must seem like a barbarian. *Man rushes from wife's funeral to arms of paramour!* Isn't that what the scandal sheets would say? But it's not like that, Evie. It's not like that at all. How can I explain?"

She took a deep breath, reached out and put her hand on his, clenched around the steering wheel. She said steadily, "We've never required explanations of each other, Bob. We don't require them now."

"Bless you, love. Perhaps later I can find words. Perhaps you'll help me find them. They're there. She gave them to me. Two long years ago. It's just that—that in this ritual travesty of life and death they've got lost."

"Whatever I can do."

He turned, looked at her. His face was in shadow; hers was not, and she knew it. He said, "Come with me? Tonight?"

"Yes."

She heard his breath escape in a sound very like a sob.

"My apartment? No ghosts there."

"Yes."

His answer was to reach out, pull her tight against him, and hold her as he drove. Hers was not to move away.

She'd never known where he lived. It was a ground floor unit in one of the apartment complexes she and Jane had looked at but couldn't afford. He drove into the garage, pulled down the overhead, unlocked the kitchen door, turned on the inside light, then suddenly looked shy.

"I'm not much of a housekeeper."

"I'm not hiring you. I don't need a housekeeper."

"What do you need, Evelinda?"

She was getting out of the car. She straightened and held out her hand. "I think," she said and despite everything she could do, her voice shook. "I think the same as you."

Hand in hand they went quietly through a living room where a night lamp threw an obscure pool across dim carpet. Moonlight filtered between the slats of Venetian blinds in the bedroom, throwing silver bars across the bed.

Evelyn stopped and turned toward him. She felt his hands touch the top of her costume. He asked, "What *is* this thing?"

"A choir robe."

"Lord!"

"A witch's robe, this year. I left my broom, hat, and funny nose at Bunny Burger."

"You *are* a witch. You don't need a broom, and your nose isn't funny." He touched it lightly. "Take the thing off, my witch."

It was all as she'd remembered. She let the robe go into a pool at her feet. He turned her, unfastened her bra, and reached around to stroke her soft warm breasts before easing her panties to the floor and turning her to him again, lifting her. Loving her.

He was taller than ever, leaner than ever, and the warm, hard power of his thrusting shivered her body into a million shimmering pieces of joyous fire until—the fires quenched— he held her against him in contented serenity, his cheek pillowed on the top of her head.

She moved with a sigh. He loosed his hold, let her do what she would, and to her surprise and his pleasure, she found herself stroking him, following the lean lines of his flanks, his strong thighs until his tender mouth sought the round succulence of her breasts again and once more they locked together in soaring, loving, rhythmic passion.

They made love until the gray light of dawn slipped through the window slats, and still lay together, exhausted, calm, incredibly at peace.

She couldn't believe that she was here, that

she had done the things she had, that she had *known* to do them, that such latent sensuality could spring to life and so please the man beside her. Only from a dim roseate distance had she heard his voice in the soft silky gray that twined her ear: "Go with me."

She surely had heard it wrong. "What?"

"Go with me. Not today. I'll be back a week from Saturday; this is a business trip. When I move. Go with me, Evelinda."

"Bob—I'm married!" She said it with anguish. He answered in anguish, "No more than I! In Florida it won't matter. We'll start new—both of us. We can. Think about it."

She shut her eyes, but they couldn't close out the images, the thoughts that clamored inside her head.

He lifted himself on one elbow, and gently pushed the fringe of hair from her forehead. His shoulder was broad, his fingers long and hard. Capable fingers. He was saying, "With luck we've twenty years ahead of us. Twenty years, Evelinda—too much time to spend alone."

Alone. That was the word that had always frightened her.

"Think about it," he said gently. "I'll be back in a week. We'll talk then."

As they dressed, after a fashion—she still had

455

only her absurd choir robe—he talked about Florida. He was going to sell his condo, he said, and buy another around the cove where some friends were building an airstrip. And an old buddy had asked him to teach some classes at Air Guard. Did she play golf? There was a fine eighteen-hole course just down the road.

Evelyn admitted to playing very poorly. Sue-Ann, she knew from Karen, had won trophies.

No matter, he said. In the spring they'd take the old Stearman down. If she'd like to learn to fly, he'd teach her.

Sue-Ann had been a private pilot. But she hadn't liked old airplanes. Evelyn knew that, too.

Suddenly she realized she was drawing the parallels, not Bob!

Things were happening too fast. She said, "I'd better go."

"Okay. Shall we pick up the Lincoln or shall I drive you home?"

Suddenly she envisioned the patrolman's face at Bunny should she show up at four in the morning in her choir robe. "I think I'd better just go home," she said.

Bob grinned. He wasn't feeling guilty. She was the one. Damn it to hell!

He saw her face and the grin disappeared. "Hey," he said. "There's two of us here. You.

Me. Don't try to grab all the problems for yourself."

At her house, parked in the driveway, he held her tightly for a moment, then leaned across and opened the door. "Listen to a piece of statistical information," he said. "In the retirement areas forty-two per cent of the senior citizens living together are not married. They can't afford it. And who are they hurting, Evelinda? Think on that. I'll see you sometime a week from Saturday. Oh—and here."

Into her hands he put a plastic bag containing a rose robe and bunny ears. "I found them too late to give back—but they held me together for eight days, and they were about the only thing—especially the robe," he added, and drove away while she stood there in the morning sun, blushing.

Thirty-one

To say that Evelyn spent her Friday morning before work in a quandary was a ridiculous understatement.

She paced the floor. She clutched her head. She alternately hugged herself in shivering remembrance and pounded her fist on any handy surface. She punched the "hot water" button on the washing machine and subsequently extracted two sweaters that would fit Minnie Mouse. She reached blindly for the ulcer tablets and swallowed them for her aching stomach before she realized that the jar depicting Fred Flintstone contained Poo's vitamin and didn't do much for pain. At last, conceding that she was simply an accident waiting to happen, she made herself sit down at John's oak desk, shut her eyes, and attempt to organize the thoughts that were running around inside her head like a Chinese firedrill.

Evelyn Matthews Cass had the astonishing opportunity to spend the rest of her life with a loving, charming man. He had given her the opportunity, one certainly not offered to many women nearing sixty, of leaving her worries and troubles behind and starting again.

It seemed so simple, but it was really so complicated it had given her a miserable headache.

She knew he was loving and charming. What else about him did she really know? So far they'd lived in a clandestine world of fantasy, each giving their best. What would happen in the normal abrasion of day-to-day life?

Those were the easy questions.

The harder ones were about going away and leaving her family—and leaving John. Lesser matters concerning the house, her job, her financial obligations got lost in the morass.

As far as *knowing* each other—besides in the Biblical sense—their generation had mostly begun marriage not knowing many practical things about each other. She certainly had. It either worked or it didn't. Hers had worked because both she and John had been the purest stereotype of the married couple. Inside her little pin-curled head had been an orderly file of rigid clichés and they matched John's. They'd been happy ostriches.

As a cheese, she could handle not being married to Bob. There would certainly be no embarrassing pregnancies; that was one of the real benefits of being sixty. And, as Bob said, who would they be hurting? Not John. Not now. Not ever.

Certainly not Karen. She'd made that obvious weeks ago.

Her kids, then. Would they hurt them?

Brenda's freedom-philosophies of the seventies had been mob slogans. Her daddy had been in a different sphere. Her daddy had been, also, her touchstone. Brenda might be a problem, but then, when wasn't she?

Jack would understand. And, from a newly-acquired point of view, so might Jessie.

Her friends, then. But who were they, now that she was a cheese? Jane, really. And Jane would commend her. As for the rest, they could approve or not. She'd be in Florida, far away, and she wouldn't care.

Quitting her job would be easy, without a backward glance. Vic could go ahead and lease her house. A sore spot would be telling Janey she wouldn't need the apartment; she hated to disappoint Jane.

But the very bottom line, the heart of the matter, was John. Financially secure, John wouldn't care. John wouldn't even know she was gone.

She leaned back in his chair, hearing its familiar squeak. She looked at her comfortable living room with its leaded window panes and gracious staircase with the trailing fronds of the fern on the landing. She swivelled to see the pictures, the cartoons, all the family *graffiti* on the fridge. She realized with amazement, with a sudden childish delight: I'm going!

I'm going to say yes. I'm going to Florida with Bob. In effect: Damn the torpedoes! Full speed ahead!

She had been turning her wedding band around and around. She stopped. She thrust the fingers of both hands wildly through her hair, not believing, feeling no real sense of truth, but knowing it was decided, wherever the chips might fall. Inside her fifty-six-year-old head a young girl was dancing to meet her lover—And Live Happily Ever After.

Dear God. Could it be so?

She could do nothing yet. It was too soon even to give Margaret notice. Bob wouldn't be back for a week, and even then there would be time. She needn't hurry. She had the rest of her life. All she could do now was make secret plans and hug her joy to herself.

She two-stepped into the kitchen, poured cold coffee into the HOG cup, shoved it into the microwave. Looking out the window, she saw Romeo gazing at her distantly from atop the neighbor's rock garden. He was sedately curled in a very becoming nest of red mossrose. She forgave him and waved.

The microwave buzzed. She took the coffee out, scooted up on her stool, and let the hot cup warm her hands.

How many years had she done that? Many years of being a comfortable ostrich, secure in her own kitchen. Insulated. It hit her suddenly, stopping the coffee mid-way to her mouth.

Was she going back to being an ostrich?

No. No, she could never do that. She learned too much. She doubted that she could, or that Bob would want her to go back. He'd never known her as an ostrich.

But on the other hand, she surely hadn't enjoyed being a cheese standing alone! Of course she hadn't. Of course!

The telephone rang. She slopped hot coffee, said "Ouch!" rather crossly, and answered it. Karen Evans' nice voice said, "Good morning.

462

Shall I see you at the library today?"

"Yes. How are you?"

"Tired. But okay. Dad got off. He says he'll see us in about a week. Did you get your ears back?"

Was there laughter in the voice? Evelyn said, "Yes. I did."

"I thought you might. He sort of dumped us and left."

"Oh."

It was rather a dismayed sound. Then Karen did laugh.

"Silly," she said. "I'll meet you at eight. We need to talk."

She hung up. Evelyn ate two pieces of jelly toast to assuage the hollow ache in her stomach, got dressed, and went to work. She walked. She thought the air might do her good.

It didn't. Not really. Nothing was going to until she'd had her "talk" with Karen.

The janitor was piling leaves with dry swishes of his rake, making fluttering mounds of gold and red and brown on grass burgeoning falsely green from the rains. That's me, Evelyn thought wryly, burgeoning green in my old age. She waved, went inside.

Karen looked like an autumn leaf herself, in russet slacks and sweater. She was standing on a chair, hanging orange and black balloons.

"A little late," she said, "but the kids won't care. Staple the tail on that black cat, would you, then go plug in the hot pot. There's some Earl Grey teabags in the drawer. I feel the need of a "cuppa" before we go to work."

The last Halloween streamer secured, the last tissue-paper ghost pinned on the bulletin board, she sat down at last, stretching her long legs. She was thinner, looking more than ever like her father, and there were violet circles beneath her eyes. But they smiled at Evelyn and she was somehow heartened.

"I'll take you off the hook," Karen said. "Dad told me."

"Oh," said Evelyn. Her cup rattled on the desk as she lifted it.

"Are you going to go?"

"Karen, I—"

"I hope you are. I think it's super. Daddy is going to need someone, and I'd rather it be you than anybody. He's always had good taste."

A bit severely Evelyn said, "He didn't find me. You did."

"Don't you believe it. My father never does anything he doesn't want to do!" She pushed at the smooth brown wave of hair against her cheek and doused her teabag up and down, up and down. "A lot of our old friends came up for my mother's services," she said. "It was so good of them. They'd been a rather tight group for about ten years and it was really nice to sit and talk to everyone. Mom would have been pleased. Dad was touched beyond words."

"I'm sure he was."

"They all—kind of—live down there in Florida together—within a certain radius. And see each other. All the time. There are a few changes. But—not much."

Karen's words usually flowed more smoothly. She was searching for phrases—for the right phrase. She looked up at Evelyn and pushed at her hair again. "Dad's changed," she said. "He doesn't realize it yet. But he has. It's going to be a—a bit tight—getting back into the swing. Finding his niche again. He—he needs you, Evie."

Why did she suddenly feel like a sacrificial lamb? For that wasn't what Karen meant. That wasn't it at all.

Karen was stretching her back, digging into her slacks pocket. She pulled out an envelope. It was small, unsealed, and a bit scrunched. She handed it to Evelyn. She said, shakily,

"That's for you." Pushing back her chair, she stood up, holding her tea cup. "It's from my mom," she added. There were tears in her eyes as she walked away to the other side of the room and stood with her back to Evelyn. "Read it," she said over her shoulder. "Mom gave it to me two years ago. When she—she knew. I think you're the one to have it."

Evelyn's hands were cold. They shook. For a moment she couldn't even focus on the folded note paper. At last she put it flat on the desk, holding it still with stiff fingers.

It was written in a careful, rounded hand. It was brief. It said, "To the next woman in my husband's life—because there must be another or Bob will be only half a man. Cherish him. He is good, he is loving, he is constant. He has given me thirty precious, exclusive years. As he is so deserving of another woman's love, I bequeath him to you with all my heart."

It was signed "Sue-Ann Marsh."

And Evelyn remembered Bob's voice last night—about words he'd been given. Over a year ago. These were the words.

Damp spots were spreading over the note paper, and suddenly she realized they were her tears, that she was crying. She brushed them away, tried to speak, could not, tried again.

"Karen, I—I don't know what to say. Your mother was—a remarkable lady."

"I was with her when she wrote it."

Karen turned, came back, and sat down. Her eyes were dry now, and steady. She drank from her cup, put it on the desk and laughed a little. Shakily. "She gave it to me to read. I was furious. I didn't understand. I didn't see how she could just simply hand her man over to—to some stranger. And Mom reminded me that Daddy had been raised with four sisters, he'd always had women around, he needed their support, he needed me, he needed her—and when she was gone, he'd need someone else. She understood him very well. She did love him, Evie."

"I can see that she did."

"She loved him enough to let him go—when she was gone. When she could no longer respond, when she became the stranger."

When she became the stranger. Like John. John is the stranger, now.

Suddenly comforted, Evelyn folded the note. "May I keep it?"

"It's yours. She wrote it for you."

"It may be the—the loveliest gift I've ever had."

Karen suddenly held out her arms. Like her

467

father, she said, "I need a hug."

She got her hug. She returned it. When they finally got to work they were a little soggier but much more cheerful.

Thirty-two

When Evelyn got home for lunch, she found Jessie there, packing. Brenda was fine, she said, and Poo was at his other grandmother's and her housing unit had become empty this morning.

Evelyn said, "I'm going to miss you," and meant it.

"I'll miss you, too. But the Senior Citizen's Bazaar starts tomorrow, and if I'm not there they'll never sell that cutesy stuff."

"Cutesy stuff?"

"Darling, there are only so many clever things one can make out of bleach bottles and clothespins. If I'm not around to make some woman think she's a social failure without a door ornament carved from mulberry root they'll never sell that garbage—and we need the money. We want a tennis court by spring. How did they like the witch outfit?"

"Fine. I'll wear it again tonight." Absently Evelyn dipped into the trick-or-treat bowl on the hall table and unwrapped a mini-Snickers bar. It was notable, she thought, that though few Beggars made it up the hill the bowl was considerably less full.

"Got you another gadget."

Jessie was digging in her purse. She fished out a Wal-Mart bag and said, "Here. This ought to complete the picture."

Evelyn shook out the contents, and turned it curiously. Two small white hollow plastic prongs were connected by a soft pouch. "Dandy. What is it?"

"Teeth."

"Teeth?"

"As in vampire, but I didn't see why witches couldn't have them, too. Come on in the kitchen; I'll show you."

Evelyn followed, thinking that in her tweed fall suit and the smooth puff of calico hair Jessie looked very nice. She had good legs and neat feet in high-heeled pumps. Jessie had conceded a number of things to being eighty-five, but high heels were not one of them.

"Now watch," her mother-in-law said. She had busied herself at the table and at the fridge. She turned and smiled. Two sharp fangs gleamed and after a brief second also dripped blood.

Evelyn said, "Good God."

"Isn't that neat? You fill the little thingy in the middle with catsup and then just press it with your tongue."

Blithely she whipped the contrivance out, ran it beneath the tap and handed it over. "You try."

Evelyn tried. It worked. Gorily—if there was such a word. It crowded her partial plate a little, but didn't noticeably impede her speech. She said, "The kids will love it."

"Kids! *I* loved it! That's why I bought it. Have fun, dear. I have to gas the Dodge and get moving."

Then she said suddenly, "Oh."

"Oh what?"

"One more thing. I've been thinking—" She stopped. "Sit down a minute, can you, dear?"

Evelyn sat. Jessie sat, also. For a moment she only turned the old rings on her fingers. Then she said uncertainly, "I don't know quite how to put this. I don't want to hurt your feelings. You've been such a good wife—and the dearest daughter-in-law anyone could have."

"Jessie."

"Yes."

"We're also friends. Say it. Have you changed your mind about the house?"

"No. About John."

Evelyn felt a distinct chill. Jessie was too busy twiddling her fingers to notice; she went on hesitantly, "This is what I wish someone had told me fifty years ago. They didn't. So I've wasted fifty years. I don't want you to do that, too." She lifted her head, looked Evelyn straight in the eye. "John's father died. So has John. You haven't died, Evie. Find somebody. Find a good man to share things with. They're out there—I know. I had a chance for one and I was too—too hide-bound—too middle-class moral and I let him go. If you do that I'll wring your neck. Okay?"

Jessie the realist! Evelyn was too stunned to do other than faintly echo, "Okay." Briskly, as though a load had gone from her shoulders, Jessie got up again. "Now I'm ready," she said.

Evelyn helped put her bags in the trunk, and a new sack of Snickers on the front seat, then got a hug and a kiss.

"Promise," said Jessie, looking up at her daughter-in-law, "that if you need something, call me. Also, let me know what you decide to do about the house."

"I may lease it like we talked about."

"Fine. Whatever. Now—anything else?"

"Not just yet," said Evelyn in a funny voice, but Jessie didn't notice. Her eyes were scanning the coleus, whipped into orderly rows and the line of the back fence. "Have you seen that cat?"

"This morning. At the neighbor's."

"If you lease the house I suppose I could take

472

him. Although I'm sure I don't know why. A worthless bag of fur if I ever met one. Well. I'll stop by and see John on the way out." She sighed. "Goodbye, dear. Happy Halloween. I'll call you next week. And remember what I said."

The little Dodge Dart out of sight, Evelyn went slowly back into the kitchen and found a twenty-dollar bill on the table. The note beside it said, "Brenda and I beat the socks off the clinic night shift playing gin rummy. Keep this for emergencies. Love, J."

Talk about guilt trips! Evelyn suddenly was on one the size of a world cruise! Yet how in the world does one tell the nicest mother-in-law in the world that future plans did include going to live with another guy—even though she'd recommended it! But I will, she promised herself. Perhaps she'll think it's because she told me to! I will tell her. When I'm feeling brave . . .

She walked to work with her choir robe over her arm and got her revenge on three rather smug-looking co-workers by suddenly whipping around and smiling with fangs that dripped blood.

Marva said, "Gawd!"

Eileen said something more pungent. "I hope that snotty kid with the squirt gun comes through tonight. You'll scare the be-jesus out of him."

"She scares the be-jesus out of me," said Margaret Daniels from the door of her little office. "Evie, come show me how those things work."

But once inside, she said, "I really wanted to talk to you a minute."

Evelyn's heart sank. "Again?" What had Port come up with now?

"Again? Oh—no, no, no problem. Sit down a minute."

Margaret sat at her desk, took off the round glasses, and rubbed tired eyes. "I'm simply beat. This working a double shift plus that hassle with the rock through the window is getting to me." She laid the glasses down, clasped her hands around them, and looked across at Evelyn. "The Corp wants me in Moline in three weeks. They have a problem, too. I know it's sooner than we expected, Evie, but I think you can handle it. Congratulations, New Manager."

Evelyn caught her breath in sheer dismay. Margaret interpreted it as surprise. She said earnestly, "You *can* handle it, Evie. I've watched. I know you can. Just think positive. You've earned yourself a good rep with the crew."

"I will," Evelyn promised, of the "positive."

She went back out into the hall feeling both guilty and torn. Perhaps the cheese hadn't been doing too badly after all! Not only did she have a job for the first time in her life, but she had earned a promotion!

The evening went fairly swiftly. Because of last night's rowdyism, Margaret put one of the guys on drive-up and Evelyn worked a register up front. The Rotarians came in, hale and hearty, with six men from the nursing home. John was not among them. He wouldn't, Ed said, even get in a car. Evelyn understood that. A car had betrayed him. John was taking no more chances.

She was staying clear of Porter, whose deep voice could be heard all over the place. Marva murmured, "Who is that guy? He's got a voice like a church organ!"

"He's got one all right, but he don't use it in my church," said Betty rudely. She slid four wrapped ghost-toasty grills across to Eileen. "It will be a minute on the fish. Get your shakes and I'll be done."

Marva asked, "Does he sing? He should."

Porter answered her question by pulling Kooky over onto his lap and warbling melodiously, "Gorill-a-my dreams . . ."

"Oh, cute," said Eileen and looked at Evelyn, who made a face. "One of those. Funny as a hearse. Somehow I get the feeling that you'd rather I took the tray over. A friend of yours?"

"No," said Evelyn shortly.

"As in 'not anymore'!"

"As in."

475

"Gotcha."

To Evelyn's intense relief, Porter left without even attempting to make any contact. The idea of his even touching her hand made her shiver. Before Bob Marsh she'd found him merely repugnant. After Bob Marsh, she found him fat, ridiculous, and nasty.

At close, after cleaning, she shucked her choir robe in the Ladies, pulled her slacks and shirt back on, and was trying to take out the fangs when Eileen appeared behind her.

Eileen said, "Hi. Seen Kook? I know she wanted to go out with us."

"She was out there a minute ago. Doing her garbage bags."

Evelyn's voice was muffled. Eileen looked closely. "Got a problem?"

"These dumb teeth. No matter. I'll just wear them home. I think it's going to take a manicure scissors to get them off my partial."

Eileen fluffed her hair. "Sure you don't want to go with us?"

"No. Thank you. And don't look so smug. Bob's out of town." Giving up on the fangs, she pulled Jack's varsity jacket over her shirt, picked up the robe, broom and hat, and followed Eileen out into the cool night air.

Eileen asked, "Need a ride?"

"I've got my car."

"Oh, yeah. From last night."

"Don't get smart either. I'll fang you."

Marva came out with Margaret who locked the door and said "Good night, girls."

They chorused, "Good night."

Eileen said, "Wow. You look neat."

Marva, who'd changed into the lamé jumpsuit with the fringe, murmured "Thanks. I can't find Kook. She said she wanted to hear me sing."

"Maybe she took her own car."

"She didn't say anything."

Evelyn slid into her Lincoln, tossing the hat and robe into the back seat. The broom clattered to the pavement and Marva retrieved it. "Hi yo, Silver!" she said, straddled it and galloped in a circle past the patrol car, slapping her shining fanny. "Good night, officer. Happy Halloween!"

He grinned and nodded.

Evelyn was not grinning. The Lincoln wouldn't start. The Lincoln was, in fact, out of gas.

"No problem," said Eileen cheerfully. "Get in. We'll run you home. Or get you some gas. Whichever."

"Just take me home," Evelyn said, disgusted at herself. "I'll haul some gas down tomorrow."

At her own driveway she climbed out and said, "Thanks, kids. Good luck, Marva. I know you'll be a real hit. I'll come out and hear you next week when my knees aren't dragging."

They drove away. She turned, walked up her drive in the waning moonlight — and suddenly realized one very pertinent fact: her house keys were with her car keys and her car keys were still in the Lincoln, and she'd forgotten to lock the Lincoln.

Also, there was no way in hell she could get into the house *without* keys. John had seen to that some years ago. Back down the hill! Get the keys! Lock the Lincoln!

She turned and went back down her drive — and down the hill.

As she trudged, jacket zipped against the chill, she heard police sirens wailing on the main street and glimpsed red lights whipping by the intersection. There must be a wreck on the south side.

The Trans Am had gone north. She was glad. And Kooky would have driven north, too. Not that she wished anyone ill but it was nice not to have the police going to help somebody she valued.

Valued.

Now there was a change in attitude, she thought, scuffing leaves like a little child. Valued. A third-rate chanteuse, an eighth grade drop-out with an illegitimate child, and a teenager already married twice. And she did value them. They were good, hard-working kids.

478

The lights were red at the intersection, but no one was in sight and she ran across it noiselessly in her sneakers. The police car was gone, Bunny Burger silent. Her scrub broom was leaning against the Lincoln where Marva had left it. Picking it up, she reached in, got the keys, punched the lock, turned around and stopped still in her tracks.

There was something obscure but bulky moving in the dark, coming around the corner of Bunny Burger. It was weaving. No—not weaving. Spilling something. From a red can. Almost at the same time she caught the penetrating smell of gasoline, the bulk stepped into the light. A gorilla.

"Kooky?" she said in disbelief.

The gorilla stopped.

They stared at each other.

The gorilla said something muffled. Then it started toward her at a lumbering run, leaving the can to gurgle out on the pavement. And it was not Kooky. It was not Kooky at all!

She did the first thing she could. She got him right in the crotch with the broom handle. He doubled up with a horrible gasp. She started to run. Then looking back in terror she saw him on one knee with a cigarette lighter, flicking it, flicking it, and cursing.

All terror fled and she was madder than hell.

Yelling in a voice hardly even hers she said, "You son of a bitch!", ran and stomped his wrist. The lighter skittered away. He grabbed her ankle with one hand and the broom with the other. Just as car lights suddenly flashed across the lot from the street he started to twist and she screamed, knowing she was falling. She did fall, across the smelly, hairy chest, but strangely — at the same time — he yelled, "Jesus God!" and went oddly still.

The Trans-Am came to a screeching halt only feet away, and two efficient Amazons scrambled out, one pinioning the fallen miscreant with the broom across his throat, and the other hauling Evelyn aside and sitting on his hairy legs.

Panting, Eileen said, "It sure ain't Kooky!"

Marva said, "You bastard! Trying to burn down the place, weren't you! Where's Kooky? What did you do with her? Speak up!" she snarled, adding that if he didn't what she was going to do with his balls. "Where the hell are the cops?"

A wailing siren announced their arrival. A policeman shot out from each side of the patrol car like two blue peas from a pod. "What's going on here? First we get a false alarm, then this yellow Trans-Am shoots by like it's trying to break the sound barrier, then — what the hell is that?"

Both younger girls stood up, revealing the

somewhat mussy remains of a gorilla suit which was beginning to reek as the wearer had inadvertently relieved himself.

Everyone began to talk at once:

"Kooky wasn't at Bill's so we knew she was here—"

"He was spraying gas; I knew what was next—"

"We saw Evie wrestling this thing—"

"He was coming at me and I didn't know what to do—"

During the chatter, the form in the gorilla suit rose, weaving, to a sitting posture. They turned and looked at him. He looked at Evelyn. She said, "Where's Kooky?" thrusting her face at him angrily. He gargled and dropped again. Everyone looked at Evelyn. One of the policemen said, "Holy Christ!" and Marva began to laugh hysterically.

"The teeth!" she giggled. "The teeth!"

Evelyn put her hand to her lips. It came away catsupy.

"Every time you opened your mouth!" Marva choked, "you showed bloody fangs! No wonder you scared the shit out of him!"

Everything else was rather anticlimactic. Pulling off the gorilla head, they found the surly man who always complained about his "quish", and had to forcibly separate him from the Bunny crew again—a real tussle, until he finally admitted to knocking Kooky out and tying her up in the garbage enclosure.

"Not hurt!" he screeched, cowering from Marva's ten red false nails.

The word "hurt", of course, was arguable. Kooky was immediately retrieved in a disgruntled and rather cold condition, having been only basically clad beneath the gorilla suit. She willingly accepted the coat of the young patrolman who was covertly admiring her "basics" and glared at her attacker.

"I shoulda known!" she gritted. "I shoulda! Bitch, bitch, bitch, all you ever did!"

Grinning, the police led him away with Kooky, who was going to file a complaint. Over her shoulder she yelled, "Meet you guys at Buffalo Bill's!"

Not Evelyn. When they took her home, she unlocked her door, cut the fangs from her partial plate, went upstairs and fell into bed. Enough was enough. She'd think about everything tomorrow.

Thirty-three

"Tomorrow" came too soon. She awakened to the pale gray light of early morning sifting itself across the rumpled covers. The soft cheep of the summer birds had given way to the organized stridency of starlings. She lay inert, listening to them blearily and wondering why she was so much more stiff and sore than usual.

Then she remembered. And for the first time she realized with tardy hindsight that besides being a heroine of sorts she had also been a congenital idiot. The man might have killed her—just when she was least ready to die!

Why had she been so angry? She could still feel the fury lying latent beneath her skin. She had exploded like a mother hen defending her chick and for what? Bunny Burger?

She stared at the still-dark ceiling and the answer came—Yes. Bunny Burger. For people who had been good to her, for her friends, for the whole outfit who would suffer from one crank's idiocy.

She cared about Bunny and the gang there.

Two starlings in a territorial battle banged against the windowpane, lit on the sill, and glared in at her with fierce yellow eyes as though it was her fault. She got up stiffly, shuffled over, and pushed up the sash.

The entire flock flew away in a whoosh of black satin wings but the icy air that poured inside cut the warm stuffiness like a knife. She hustled back to bed, pulling the covers up around her chin but breathing deeply. The air smelled good and fresh, even with the faint smoky tinge of her neighbor's burning puppy papers.

Wide awake, she tried to uncrumple the untidy edges of her mind, straighten things up a bit. So much had happened in the last two days . . .

Could she be the same woman who had awakened in this bedroom for over thirty years with only a change of drapery to mark the time? There had been other changes. Jack's voice had deepened, the noises in Brenda's room veered from a little girl's prattling to her dollbabies to a young woman surreptitiously creeping home at dawn, John's lithe trimness

484

had gone to bulk, taking more room on the bed. Her hair had grayed, her waistline acceded to the blessings of elastic.

She was the same woman. Outwardly. Inwardly, if not going completely aboutface, she'd done at least a full half turn. It was going to affect everybody. She had to be careful. Not that she couldn't turn back. She probably could, but she didn't want to. Turning back just to make the people in her family comfortable again would be folly to the self she had become—and it was, after all, her life. Her last twenty years. Wasn't that, in effect, what Jessie had said?

Heavy stuff, she thought ruefully, and wanted a cigarette. There were none in the bedtable drawers. She knew there was no use pawing through the tangle of paperbacks, tissues, pencil stubs, half-done crosswords, and elderly sticks of gum. She'd done that before.

Maybe in the bureau . . .

She shivered her way to the big double dresser, found one bent Kent filter, ran back, pulled up the covers, lit it, coughed, and squashed it out. Awful.

The old gum wasn't too bad once she softened it. I sound like a cow, she thought, but persevered, leaning against stacked pillows and trying to resume her thought process.

Her last twenty years. Incredible. In twenty years she'd be seventy-six. Of course, Jessie was ten years older than that and going strong — but one couldn't count on it.

And, of course, what this was all leading to was Bob Marsh. She wanted to spend those twenty years with him.

In twenty years Bob would be eighty-two. A hale, hearty eighty-two? Or not?

She'd already had the "or not." At fifty-six. With John.

It was not a lesson in romance her brain was trying to get through to her this morning. It was a lesson in economics. The lesson was not designed to exclude Bob. It was meant to embrace him sensibly.

Embracing him sensibly meant not dumping all her obligations in his lap and running off to Magic Land expecting to live happily ever after while he coped and she floated.

She'd done that once and it had worked for thirty years — before the roof fell in. They didn't have thirty years. And she wasn't going to be crazy enough to try it again.

Place your priorities. How many times had she heard John say that! He was saying it to her now — dear John, the man she had known, the man she loved. Place your priorities, Evie.

Bring this lovely thing with Bob Marsh out into the cold light of day. Pray it doesn't wither and die. Pray hard.

Let Brenda know him, and Jack and Michelle. And Jessie. And while you are doing that, get your feet on the ground. Lease your house, take the apartment, trade the car—accept the management job from Margaret Daniels. Learn to cope without leaning. Learn to stand alone so if you *have* to, you *can!*

Bob was right. They didn't need marriage. They'd both had marriages—good ones. What they needed now was each other—but not like blind Sybarites indulging themselves. Like two lonely people who had found a magic that would live in the sun.

And if it didn't work? If he couldn't accept it? If he left her?

My heart will break, Evelyn thought painfully. But it's broken before. And I can't walk three paces behind my man anymore, either. If that's what Bob wants, and if that's what he expects, then I'd better find out now.

She got up, grimacing, closed the window, and trailed into the bathroom. She turned the shower on as hot as she could bear it and let the warm needles flatten her hair, massage her face, run in soothing torrents down her naked body. Inevitably she thought of Bob and clung to the thought, trying to push away the menacing ghosts of all the beautiful women in Florida who knew a desirable man when they saw one. Who knew a lonely one . . .

God. Could she really do it? Could she stay here and let him go back alone? What if she lost him to one of those women who played golf well, flew their own planes, had beautiful tans all over lithe and yielding bodies?

She had the desire to scream, and since she was *not* the same person who'd showered in this bathroom for thirty years, and because she was growing inside and growth when it burst the seed sheath was painful, she *did* scream — long and loud, letting all the frustrations and fears pour out, and almost drowning when she lifted her head to howl like a coyote.

But it felt wonderful.

As she got out, the phone rang. Wrapping a towel about her middle and with water dripping into her eyes from her hair, she padded into the bedroom and answered it.

Her neighbor said anxiously, "Evelyn, are you all right? I was just out burning garbage and heard the strangest noise."

Evelyn Matthews Cass replied in the most

innocent of voices, "Really? I was in the shower. I'm fine."

"I wonder whatever it was."

"Maybe kids going by."

"Maybe." This was said dubiously. "Well—if you're okay."

"Yes. I'm dandy. Thanks for calling, anyway."

"We should have coffee sometime. Jessie says you're working."

"Yes. I am."

"How nice. I suppose time does hang heavy with your children gone. Perhaps you could start coming to the Senior Citizen Activities Center. We have the nicest man slated to talk about blood pressure today, and it's free."

"Some other time," Evelyn answered, extricated herself, and hung up, grinning.

She went to towel her head and was heating the curling iron when the phone rang again.

Brenda's voice asked anxiously, "Mom, are you okay? The papers say you wrestled a man to the ground—in a gorilla suit! What's going on over there?"

"Oh. That."

"That! It doesn't sound like *that!* Are you sure you're all right?"

Evelyn explained. Pacified, Brenda said, "Mom, for God's sake—he could have nailed you good!"

"I didn't think of that at the time."

"I have to go to class. Will you stay out of trouble now until I get back? I only have six more days."

"I'll try."

"I love you, Mom." That was unexpected. "Kiss Poo for me. See you."

"I love you, too, Bren. I will. See you."

Perhaps Brenda was changing, too.

Evelyn went downstairs, holding that thought, taking with her the pale ghost of the willful little girl in ruffled dresses who wept for her "real mommy." The little girl had grown into a pale, willful *big* girl with straight straggling hair still obdurately searching for a Pat who never was. Still, she'd had her moments of bitter sweetness, and they did love each other, although it had been more, Evelyn realized, like battling sisters — competing for John.

John had never accepted that, no more than he'd accepted Jack's struggling inability to be a first-string quarterback.

Evelyn sighed over remembered ghosts, poked two slices of bread into the toaster, noticed they were her last and rejoiced that today was payday. She had a dollar and sixty cents in her purse and probably would have to break

Jessie's twenty to put gas in the Lincoln.

The telephone rang again just as—of course—she buttered the toast. She laid it on top of the toaster to stay warm.

"Evie! Are you okay? You're a heroine!" Mary Lou.

She explained again, learning also that there was this marvelous new spa at Hot Springs and Mary Lou's thighs were sagging so Porter said she could go and wasn't he just marvelous, the old Teddybear. She was leaving next week.

Bingo, Evelyn thought to herself. The second weekend in November. The old Teddybear certainly arranged things well.

Between the first piece of toast and the second, Jane called. That she could handle. Liz was next, and she also wanted to know if Evie had anything to donate to the Bazaar. Promising to leave three outgrown shirts and the new gray slacks that still wouldn't zip on the kitchen porch before work, Evelyn hung up again and put the bread heel in the toaster. She'd already eaten the two slices—or she guessed she had, they were gone—and she was still hungry. She scrambled two eggs. When there was a knock at the kitchen door. She almost answered the phone.

Vic was standing there. He entered breezily,

telling Baron to "stay" on the porch.

Evelyn said, "He can come in!"

"If you don't mind."

She didn't mind, and Baron was delighted. He entered, sloppily drank Romeo's stale water, and collapsed under the kitchen table with a noisy sigh. He also eyed her eggs.

"Coffee," said Vic. "My God, woman. Don't you ever get dressed? Not that I mind, but I think I've found you fully clad about once."

"I go to work at nine," Evelyn answered snappishly and poured. Her eggs were cold. She gave them to Baron.

"Sugar. And whatever controlled substance you have that passes for cream. As I say—not that I mind. But since I know what nice accessories you have on top, it would ease my mind to coordinate them with legs. I suspect they're nice, too."

He was grinning; beneath the salt-sprinkled tangle of black curls his eyes sparkled. Suddenly Evelyn realized a very pertinent fact: Vic Bonnelli found her attractive. Perhaps increasingly so. After thirty years of staid married life she couldn't believe this was happening!

Why?

She'd come alive. Maybe she looked it.

The telephone rang again. Gratefully she

turned to answer and lost some of the gratitude fast. Porter's rich voice asked, "Evie, are you all right?"

"Yes. I'm fine."

"God damn. If anything happened to you—" Appalled, she heard the shake in his voice, knew he was serious. She certainly needed *that* burden! She went on swiftly, "It wasn't anything. Everyone seems to be hyping it. We're all just relieved they finally caught the guy. Porter, I want my bill."

"You'll get it, honey, you'll get it," he said and hung up.

She did, too, with a heartfelt "Damn that man!"

Vic's good foot was stroking his dog's long cream back, but his eyes were on her. He grinned. "I don't believe it. After all these years!"

"After all these years what?"

"Old Port is still at it! Lord, lord. In high school he was trying to lay the coach's wife and half the cheerleader squad. Not that he did—he was just trying. I hear he married money. That hasn't slowed him down?"

Evelyn gave up pretending. "Not noticeably."

"Now he just gets it out of town."

"Whatever. He's not getting mine," she said

crudely and he applauded, clapping big hands.

"Yea, team. Got a cookie?"

She handed him the jar. It was fat, ceramic, and in the shape of a beehive. Jack had given it to her for Christmas when he was in sixth grade and Brenda dropped the lid, breaking off the decorative honeybee.

"My mama has one like this."

"It's old."

"The cookies aren't."

"Jessie was here."

"Oh, yeah. That's what I came about. The house. You distracted me."

"You distracted yourself, Buster."

"Whatever." He was munching chocolate-chip. He gave her a crumby grin. "I found the hold-up. Somebody was bad-mouthing this place to our client. I think I've straightened him out. It wasn't his job he was worried about; I think he's pretty secure with Porter, but—"

"What?"

"Porter. He's his new shop foreman."

"You just said the operative word." Evelyn gritted her teeth and smacked her doubled fist on the table so hard the cookie jar jumped.

"What do you mean?"

"Never mind. It doesn't matter—not if the man is going to take the house."

494

Vic shrugged and went back to eating cookies, but his eyes stayed curious. "Oh, he is. First of December. A thousand dollars if you pay utilities, seven hundred if you don't. It's no bargain for you but it's all the traffic will bear."

Seven hundred. Three would pay her apartment rent, and four would catch the insurance, taxes, bills, and whatever. Her Bunny Burger check could buy groceries. She said fervently,

"Vic, I could kiss you!"

"Any time, kid."

Fortunately, there was another knock at the door. She went toward it tolerating the cheerful smack on her fanny in passing but reminding herself very soberly that she needed to mind her mouth. She didn't want any misunderstandings with this nice man.

Eileen stood on the porch, the Trans-Am an exotic yellow craft behind Vic's ratty old Datsun. She wore tight jeans and a shrunken sweatshirt that said "Surf's Up," and carried on one arm a little girl with tight black curls and a finger in her mouth.

"Hi," she said. "I just wanted to be sure you were okay. This is my kid. Tina."

"Come in. Tina, you're a doll."

Tina was struggling to get down. When Eileen let her go, she ran across to Vic and wrapped her arms around his knee. Eileen said, "Sorry. She misses her daddy. It's been so long she thinks any guy with curly hair is him." Then she narrowed her eyes, adjusting to the dim kitchen. "Oh—it's you."

Vic was lifting the little girl up on his lap. "Well, hi, Tina. You want a cookie?" Over her head he glanced at Eileen. "Yeah—you're Marva's friend. Eleanor? Elaine?"

"Eileen." She sat down on the chair Evelyn pulled out. "How about last night, Evie? Pretty wild."

"I guess. It happened so fast." Evelyn was looking at the little girl leaning back comfortably in the curve of Vic's massive arm and noting that neither of them looked discontented. And although next to Marva, Eileen seemed ordinary, by herself—even with the poor clothes of a girl not able to afford much else—she had a pleasant face and nice figure. This fact was not missed by Vic.

He was saying, "From the papers, you girls certainly took care of the situation."

"Sure we did. We're a team, damn it."

Long earrings jingling, she took out cigarettes, looked around for the ashtray, and bent her head to the immediate flick of Vic's lighter. Her long dark hair swung down and she

496

pushed it back again as she straightened, inhaling. The hair was rich brown and silky clean. Vic was noticing it, too.

Playing devil's advocate, Evelyn observed impishly, "I thought you didn't smoke, Vic."

"I do not," he answered severely, "push my personal convictions on the world. But you're not going to smoke, are you, sweetheart?" he said to the small child snuggling against his bulky shoulder. Tina raised her chin and smacked his square, bluish jaw, leaving cookie crumbs on it.

"Wike you," she said.

"Wike you, too, kid."

"What I came for," said Eileen, calmly interrupting, "was to see if I could help you haul gas to your car. I have a five-gallon can in the back of the Trans-Am."

"Oh, Lord," said Evelyn, suddenly remembering. "Thank you. I didn't know what I was going to do—short of calling the gas station. And they charge an arm and a leg, I'm sure. Eileen, you're a doll. I'll go change."

"What are friends for?" said Eileen—which struck Evelyn as more of a profound truth than Eileen could realize. They *were* friends. As she'd said earlier, they were also a team.

When she came back downstairs, Eileen was

still there but Vic was gone. And Tina. And the dog.

"He said he'd get the gas," Eileen told her, squashing out her cigarette. "He took my kid. He seems to like her."

"She seems to like him. Does he look like her father?"

"In a way. Tony was Italian and built like a brick shithouse. And just as full of it." Eileen sighed, running short-nailed fingers through her hair. "Your friend seems like a nice guy. Is he?"

"I think he is."

"Unattached?"

"As far as I know."

"What shall I do if he asks me out?"

"Go."

"Okay, Mom." Suddenly Eileen grinned. "I've had enough of guys who only want to go to bed."

Suddenly Evelyn knew Vic had made his Speech. She said, "But I don't think he's dead, Eileen."

"No—but it will slow him down. Besides—my God—there's more to it than four bare legs. Everybody knows that."

Except me, Evelyn thought. And I'm just learning. She didn't say those words aloud, only hugged them to herself. And the telephone rang again.

"I'll go on out," Eileen said.

Evelyn nodded and heard the click of the door as she said, "Cass residence."

"Evelinda, are you all right? My God, I can't even turn my back—"

At the sound of Bob's voice, her knees went weak and she sat down.

"I'm fine. Truly. No one was hurt and they got the man."

"You're sure."

"I'm positive. How are you doing?"

Was there a hesitation before he said, "Okay. Could you possibly get off early next Saturday? I'm going to make reservations at a place I know, and I want your whole damned weekend."

"I'll see. I'll try."

"I have—a lot to tell you." There had been a hesitation there. She answered, "I have a lot to tell *you*. We need to talk."

"I know. We will. If there's time, with whatever else I have in mind." Now that was the Bob she knew. "Got to go. I'll call again this week if I can. I love you."

It was the first time he'd ever said that.

Stunned, she put the telephone down, not really knowing what she'd said in return.

"I love you." He could say it. Freely.

Could she? Oh, God. If she couldn't what could she say?

Just — let it be the right thing, she thought soberly, and went out the door to join Eileen.

Thirty-four

Someone had once said wryly, "Time goes so fast when you're having fun."

Perhaps that was Evelyn's problem. Time was not going fast, and she wasn't having fun. They all had to appear in court, which was not exactly riotous. Bob didn't call which, in her vulnerable state of mind, was frightening. Visions of all those "old friends" and Floridian beauties danced in her head. The washing machine quit cold, which sucked up the rest of her paycheck. And Betty's husband died, which not only required chipping in for flowers and making sympathy calls, but put some additional long thoughts into Evelyn's head about being able to stand alone.

In the "Good News" department, the Princess Dress Shoppe had re-opened its doors, and Margaret granted Evelyn Saturday off. If she needed it. If Bob called and said he was still coming. If Bob called and said he wasn't coming—in which case she'd need it even more—probably for the time to go and shoot herself.

She wasn't serious, of course. Yet the doubt was there. She kept remembering that small hesitation in his voice. His agreeing they had to talk. She'd said it first. She knew they had to talk, and the subject. But—what did he have in mind?

Guiltily, she used the last of Jessie's twenty on a haircut and felt enormously improved. Her hairdresser clucked silently at the shag, but worked her usual magic so well in restoring the smooth, brisk, curling swing that Evelyn walked out feeling like a new woman—faced with one more problem: what to wear?

She couldn't afford much, but she wanted *something*.

The Princess Dress Shoppe was holding a re-opening sale. Checkbook in hand, she went inside. She was welcomed warmly as she chatted with Nan, who looked thinner and worn and whose eyes were unaccountably sad. She found nothing she could afford—a "sale" being relevant to the state of one's bank account. She left and went to Wal-Mart. She found a pretty, soft, rose-colored dress with a neckline

502

that could be low or not and wrote a check for it, leaving herself six dollars. Fortunately she already had matching shoes.

She felt elated—if only Bob would call.

He did, but due to the court session she missed him. He talked to Karen instead, and sent word he'd be in Saturday morning and would pick her up about one o'clock. Karen was rather reticent about the rest of their conversation. Being a lady, Evelyn didn't push, but wished she had. There were times when being a lady was less comfortable than being pushy.

Friday at Bunny Burger she endured the results of a local football win, tripped over her cleaning bucket, and went home so nervous she threw up. All in all, despite the haircut, it had been a really dandy week, and she'd be pleased never to see it again.

Saturday morning lasted, conservatively, a year and a half. In truth, it was only long enough to shower and change, because she didn't know what to pack or what to pack it in. The suitcase seemed overly large, and made her blush at its intimation. The small, soft-sided one looked shabby. Her traincase was too little.

Suddenly she realized that this was the old

Evelyn, the proper Evelyn, obsessed with "doing the right thing"—which very probably was a lost cause from the outset. Appearances weren't what mattered. Nothing she was doing this weekend was designed to "look right" with the neighborhood, anyway.

She found a neat gray suitcase of Brenda's, abandoned early in its career when Brenda took to backpacks. She filled it with obvious necessities and set it by the door. Its sides were still dusty. With grim humor she took her finger and traced a large, eloquent A in the dust.

Then she showered quickly, blow-dried her hair, and put on what make-up she could, standing before the open window. Donning one of her three remaining wearable pairs of panty hose, she selected the gray, tailored standard utility dress that every woman has, noticed that there were now two remaining wearable pairs of pantyhose, changed, added Grandmother Matthews' brooch and called it a day. There was no need to further tempt the gods.

At one o'clock Bob hadn't come, which gave her time to throw up again, hurt her stomach, and down some Maalox.

When she came drearily out of the bathroom he was standing in the kitchen door. He said, "Hi," and opened his arms.

That part, at least, was all right.

Shortly after, he picked up her suitcase and grinned. "Ready, Hester?"

Among other things they shared, she realized, was a literary background. She took a paper towel and rubbed off the A, murmuring "That was silly."

"Not if you feel adulterous." He did have a way of laying it out, looking her right in the eye.

She looked back. "I don't," she said. "Not like that. It's a—an ambivalent feeling."

"Damned if you do and damned if you don't?"

"Not damned even. Scared mostly."

"Me, too."

That startled her. Soberly he said, "I told you, Evelinda. I'm not a tomcat. This is pretty momentous on my part also. We really have to mean it. I do. Do you?"

She knew the answer to that. "Yes," she said firmly, and followed him out the door. Win or lose, she was going to have this to remember.

He was more tanned than he had been, and looked a little less gaunt. Florida had obviously been good for him.

But it's not going to be good for me, she

thought soberly, not yet. Not for a while. And I have to tell him so.

But not now.

She hadn't realized she was turning her wedding band around and around before he reached over and laid his hand on hers. "Stop that."

"Sorry."

"Don't be sorry. Just don't do it."

He must have spoken like that to the young men in his command — and also he must have known it — because he brought her hand to his mouth, kissed the palm and laid it back in her lap. "Now *I'm* sorry. It's been a — a long week."

She wanted to hear about it. "A good one?"

They'd gotten to the highway and he was looking ahead down the straight, open road between the shorn grain fields.

"Different."

Not exactly a revealing answer. He added, "I expected something else. We'll talk about it later. How was your week — other than wrestling a gorilla?"

"Different." She could play, also, though she wasn't going to add that she threw up a lot. He glanced at her sharply, but he said only, "I missed you. I needed you."

"I think that was my problem, too."

"I could use a hug. But holding hands will do."

They held hands. Seemingly from a distance, he said, "You have no idea how important small things are to me now. Like holding a hand. I take yours. You take mine back. It's a response between you and me. That's—that's very precious, Evelinda."

She said nothing, only held his more tightly. She understood and he knew it. That was the important part.

They had crossed the harvested prairie and were now winding down the gap between towering rock and barren trees toward the river valley. She had been admiring the lean discipline of his blunt profile. He turned to her and grinned.

"You've never asked where we're going."

"I haven't, have I?"

"I could be whirling you away to durance vile."

"I was chancing it."

"Good girl. But ask."

"Where are we going?"

"Lost Harbor."

Her mouth flew open. She'd certainly never been there. She knew about it. Renowned for its privacy, it was a very expensive retreat for

507

people of unlimited means, and it was very definitely members only.

He laughed. "One shot, kid," he said. "That's all we get. I have an old commanding officer who owed me a favor. This is it. We're his guests." He stopped suddenly. "You don't look pleased."

"I'm in shock. Bob, I may not have brought the right clothes."

His grin was relieved. "We'll only see as many people as we want to see. That's what Lost Harbor is for."

She still looked sober, thinking of her Wal-Mart dress.

He added, "I promise. This is our weekend. When we want to be social we'll go to Las Vegas. Okay?"

"Okay."

They crossed the leaden waters of the river, sheathed in the lacy ironwork of the old bridge. Below them a few vagrant herons stalked solemnly along the marshland.

Bob said, "They'd better get their tails south."

"I should put out my winter bird feeder." Then she stopped, arrested by the intimation of her own words—if she was going to Florida she wouldn't need to think of it.

But she wasn't.

A tiny sense of discomfort pervaded them both, like a cold finger on a spine. They each felt it and started talking at once:

"Did I tell you—" and "How was it at Bunny—" ran smack together.

They stopped. He said, "Okay. You first."

"Did I tell you—" She started to say that Margaret had offered her a management job, but she didn't want to tell him that. Instead, she finished with "—that Vic Bonnelli found the problem with the guy leasing my house?"

"No. What was the problem?"

"He works for Porter DeKalb." Then she realized, looking at his suddenly-set face, that the subject of Porter hadn't been the best one to introduce. He muttered, "That bastard . . ." and she went on hastily, "It's all right. Vic convinced him the house is fine. He's going to take it."

"When?"

"The first of December."

She didn't get the reaction she had expected. He said, "Good," in a blank tone that indicated it wasn't of major importance to him. She felt deflated. She was such a creature of contradiction. She was going to tell this man she couldn't go to Florida with him, but on the other hand she wanted him to be — what? Upset? Concerned about the obstacles in her path? As if he hadn't had enough upsets, enough concerns of his own!

He was glancing sharply at the line of bluffs pointing their rocky scrub-cedar fastness at the blue-gray sky.

"Damn. I hope I didn't miss the turn. Open that notebook, will you? There between us on the seat. Don said there wasn't any marker and he drew me a map. Flip the pages."

She flipped, past rows of figures and scratches of notes, to a diagram drawn with a different-colored pen and resembling an agitated turtle — humped at the top and wiggly on the bottom. Bob said, "That's it. How many miles past the bridge?"

He took it from her, reading it in rapid glances from the highway. Two sycamores by an historical marker. There we go — that's the sucker up ahead."

They turned north off the highway onto a neatly-kept but characterless gravel road. Leafless wild grape vines tangled the bare trees on the bluff side. Beyond skeins of multiflora, marshy battalions of crumpled brown reeds lay jackstrawed, bordering gray mudbanks cross-stitched by the skittering feet of waterbirds.

Evelyn said, "All right, buster. If we suddenly drive into someone's still, it's your fault!" and he laughed, turning toward her with crinkled gray eyes and the quick grin she'd been looking for.

"They do still have them?"

"You'd better believe. Those guys at Buffalo Bill's weren't drinking water out of those glasses."

"Moonshine?"

"White lightnin'. All that stuff curling up above the timber early in the morning isn't mist."

"That's why I got shot at!"

"What?"

"A few months ago. I was just cruising in the Stearman and fiddling with my altimeter. I wasn't watching and guess I got a little low. Whammy comes this shot right by my wing tip. Scared the shit out of me. I poured the coals to her and got out pronto."

"Someone warned you off."

"It worked. My sense of survival is far stronger than my curiosity anymore. Look for stonework on your right, now. There'll be a checkpoint."

"Checkpoint! Why do I get the idea Lost Harbor might be run by retired military?"

511

"Because you're smart. As well as good-looking. And have a neat new haircut. I like it. Hey—there's the place!"

The road banked sharply around rather carefully nondescript shrubbery and dead-ended against two massive limestone corner-posts and a double gate which was almost medieval.

Bob slid out, took a small brass key from his jacket pocket, and used it. The gates groaned as they slowly opened.

"Voila!" he said cheerfully, climbing back in.

The gates, Evelyn noticed, also closed behind them. Ahead was more road, still winding but now not nondescript. The massed shrubbery assumed pleasant striata of light and dark green juniper behind which the trees rose bare-branched like sculpture, and ferns had been carefully set to trail down the rough facing of the rocky bluff. Unexpectedly, a water fall spun a slender thread into a pool from which silver rivulets trickled across the road before them.

Evelyn said, "Oh my."

"Not precisely Ladies' Garden Club?"

"Not unless the ladies own Fort Knox."

"We're not buying it, just enjoying it."

"In that case, it's beautiful." They were

rounding another corner, and Evelyn found herself echoing her mother-in-law: "Wahoo!"

Twelve rough-limestone, two-story units radiated from another central gateway, tied to it by short drives like the sticks of a lady's fan. Beyond, the unexpected sheen of a lead blue harbor sparkled beneath the pallid sun. At the closed gateway stood a pleasantly smiling young man in mufti with a clipboard in his hand. As they nosed toward the classic ironwork barricade he said, "Colonel Marsh, and lady. Guests of General Johnson, I believe."

He took the plastic card Bob handed across the gate, glanced at it, and thrust it into a selection of slots in a discreetly recessed control panel. The gate opened, and so did the garage door on one of the limestone houses.

"Unit two, sir. This card will also close your door, sir. You're expected. The service phone is the red one—You'll find it by the stairs. It may be plugged into the jack in any room. Enjoy your stay."

He was right. The garage door silently lowered behind them and a light came on inside.

Evelyn and Bob looked at each other. His silver brows were raised expectantly. She giggled.

"Total anonymity."

"That's the game. You can hole up. You can socialize. If you don't want anyone to know you're here, no one will see you but the staff. It's up to you. Us."

"And the staff is as mum as posts."

"Or they lose their jobs. Or—if I know Don—strung up by their thumbs. He learned some effective tricks in Korean prison camp. And so, as a matter of fact, did I. I hope you realize, madam, that you are my prisoner."

"I shall scream," she said, murmuring a very quiet "Help." They both laughed, and suddenly everything was all right, everything was lovely—at least for the moment.

He helped her out. Hand in hand, like children, they climbed the stairs, letting themselves in by way of a cubicle containing a bar, a refrigerator, and a microwave to a spacious living room and bedroom, both of which opened through glass doors onto a stone-rimmed balcony fronting the harbor. It was like a fan of English rowhouses, sharing inner walls. The right and left sides of each terrace rose high and solid, excluding sight of the neighboring area and showcasing the foam-tipped expanse of harbor, lazy beneath the autumn sun.

They walked to the edge of the stone balustrade and looked down on beds of dahlias and late asters, crimson and golden against the blue-green cedar branches further dividing each province. They went back in from the limpid air to the cozy warmth of a fireplace already leaping through showers of sparks up a blackened chimney. They looked at each other.

Evelyn said softly, "I'm Myrna Loy and you're Cary Grant. Right?"

"Wrong. You're Evelinda. And just now I'm the luckiest guy in the world."

Evelyn remembered thinking once—the old Evelyn—*but it's broad daylight*—and realized very quickly as his tender hands molded themselves to the soft shape of her breasts and his lean body searched hers that time did not matter, that even possibly in this place time might stop and not go again until one of them commanded it so.

She was wrong, of course. When later shadows began to cross the balcony and throw tentative bars to stripe the deep, soft carpet, she said lazily against his warm arm, "Tan becomes you."

It was patently obvious he'd spent some time in swimming trunks, but he turned and pulled the huge fur hearth rug across them both as if he didn't want to see. Once more she had the cold sensation of something wrong, something askew. All he said was "Down there it's almost a law." Yet she felt the sudden fear of those ghostly lissome Florida women in the brief swimsuits that merely outlined how desirable they were.

He was sitting up, tousling her hair. "Myrna—as crass as it may seem—I'm hungry. Did we have lunch?"

"I didn't. Did you?"

"Damned if I remember. Tell you what. I'll bring up the bags and you hustle something out of the fridge."

His voice had gone wrong. It was as if he was suddenly making himself play a game he didn't like. Whatever had come between them was as tangible as a coolness in the air. Yet he wasn't cool. That part hadn't changed . . .

She was still huddled in the fur rug when he came back, carrying both bags. He was now wearing a wine-colored, hooded robe, and in his new thinness he looked like an ascetic monk.

"Chilly down there," he said briefly, padding on bare feet into the bedroom. She followed him, trailing the bulky fur. Looking around, he grinned. "What do you want, little girl? Don't you know you shouldn't follow old men into their bedrooms?"

She was right. He definitely wasn't cool. That had nothing to do with the problem. He just didn't seem to want to talk about Florida . . .

Later, as he carved a slab of aged cheese and heaped it on a tray with thin-sliced ham and crusty bread and turned the bottle of wine in its frosty container she wandered out onto the terrace.

The unit looked toward the west. The sun was a molten ball caught in the fringe of the farther trees, the water a placid mirror. Tiny lights had come on and were lining the edge of the shore beneath her. As replete and sensuously content as a tabby cat, yet still feeling the thin edge of concern that would not go away, she leaned against the stone. She was wrapped in her rose-colored robe. The light breeze fanned soft hair against her cheek. She hardly dared breathe lest she break the spell of serenity that enfolded her. Deep in her subconscious she was grateful to General Johnson, whoever he might be, for this one golden point in time. It might not happen again. She was beginning to suspect that this was so.

The voice from the right terrace penetrated slowly. It was not directed to her, so her mind

517

rejected the intrusion—then suddenly, like a dash of cold water, rejection was no longer possible. What she was hearing was merely a sound, nothing intelligible, accompanied by a softer, feminine voice pleasant in its timbre. The feminine voice was not the difficulty. It was the man's voice—deep, caramel tones rumbling through the twilight breeze like the rich chords of a cathedral organ.

Porter DeKalb.

Thirty-five

She knew it was Porter. This was verified as the light, pleasant feminine voice laughed and said, "Oh, Porter, something—" The rest was unintelligible but the "Porter" was clear. She also knew the feminine voice if she could only put a mental finger on it. Of one thing she was positive: it was not Mary Lou.

Evelyn went quietly to the separating wall. Its construction precluded a view, but it did not totally prevent hearing. Evelyn frankly meant to listen with all her might as she clutched her robe around her throat against the chill of the November dusk and held her breath.

The woman said she was cold. Porter offered to warm her. She replied that she already had, besides she was hungry. Porter observed they hadn't come here to eat and reminded her

519

with warm crudeness what they had come for. She answered that it wasn't much fun if one caught pneumonia. The rest of her words faded into a small scream and other muffled noises relative to the basic reason Porter said they were there. But by that time, quite satisfied and not a little stunned, Evelyn had moved away.

She hardly admired her choice, but Nan's personal preferences didn't concern Evelyn. At least she was entitled to her privacy.

Besides, two things had just become patently clear to Evelyn. Three, really: who had bought controlling interest in the Princess Dress Shoppe; why Evelyn had not gotten a job there; and why it had recently re-opened — or rather why Nan, beggared and with two other employees also out of work, had felt she'd had no choice.

Perhaps she really hadn't. Or perhaps she even liked Porter, although, remembering Nan's worn face and sad eyes, Evelyn grimly thought that part a bit far-fetched. Anyway, the top line said it was plainly none of Evelyn's business.

The bottom line was Evelyn's business.

Porter DeKalb was dallying at a very expensive retreat on Mary Lou's money with another woman—and that fact Evelyn expected to find very useful indeed. It should put an end to all Porter's nonsense in regard to one Evelyn Matthews Cass. Nan was on her own.

Shivering but terribly pleased—wickedly pleased—Evelyn reached out to open the sliding glass doors and stopped. Inside, Bob had wheeled the small trolley of goodies into the living room. Turning to poke up the scarlet embers, he had lost himself in deep reverie. She could see his face in profile. It was saddened. Worried. Caught in some terrible indecision.

It was also what had been hovering over the two of them all day, a black crow flapping its funereal wings. The thing must be dealt with, and now. They were, after all, adults, although whoever had said children hurt worse than grownups had been dead wrong. She didn't think she'd ever hurt worse in her life.

Bob was a good man. He'd simply gotten his perspective back and discovered the woman he had needed in the Midwest was not the woman he needed among his friends in Florida.

There. She'd admitted the truth to herself. That was a start. Now, Mrs. Cheese, go take that good man off the hook. Set him free.

The slide of the door made a whispery noise on the soft carpet. He glanced up, and the crimson flames backlighted him, silhouetting the broad shoulders, the spare tall frame, turning the white hair on that fine head to a cap of silver. Incongruously she remembered the early time when she'd seen him slouched in despair on a garbage can, long legs stuck out in front — and she'd wryly hoped he could afford the expensive jogging shoes on his feet.

How far they'd come from there!

Must this be the end? She thought it in a sort of muffled agony, recalling Sue-Ann Marsh's words: "He is a constant man," knowing full well there could be no trailing edges, no half-way goodbyes. Whoever it was to be, wherever she was, the woman in Bob's life deserved all of him.

He saw something on her face. His seemed set in iron. He said, "Evelinda?" and the fear in his voice almost broke her heart because she recognized it. She knew it as the fear of hurt, of more hurt when there had already been enough.

With your shield or on it, Evelyn.

She leaned for support against the glass door, feeling it cold on her back. In her ears her voice sounded like that black crow in her head. She said, "I can't go to Florida with you."

He didn't move. Only the fists balled, dug deep into the pockets of his monkish robe. Quietly he answered, "I thought you were going to say that. I've felt it. All day."

He'd felt it! What had she felt? A wall between them, a reluctance to talk. Well, reluctance was over, talking time was here.

Neither had moved. A flame shot up the flue behind him, and the end of the log fell, shooting crackling sparks. The distance between them was twelve feet, yet she thought it was also the distance between two worlds.

He was saying, in a courtly voice, like a gentleman, "May I ask why?"

The tone was so cool that abruptly, childlike, she wanted to hurt. She said, "Probably the same reason you were going to give me."

Now the sparks were not in the fire. "What the hell are you talking about?"

"You know you've been trying to tell me something ever since you walked into my kitchen!"

"All right. What have I been trying to tell you?"

They were quarreling! They were squared off like two dirty-faced little kids, daring each other to cross a line! And that wasn't what she'd meant to happen! Not at all.

Near tears, she said, "Please, Bob. Just let me say I understand!"

"Well, I don't! Yes, I've been trying to tell you something, and yes, it was going to take understanding, but I also think one of us has got the wrong end of the stick!"

"Yes. You have!"

"The hell! You started first, you finish first! Why won't you go to Florida with me—and if the answer is what I'm beginning to gather, then what I was going to tell you has no relevance anyway!"

"I—don't—belong—there!" she said firmly, spacing every word between gritted teeth.

He roared back, "What?"

"I don't play golf, I don't swim, I don't fly my own airplane, I don't do aerobics—or anything! Your friends would hate me. You'd be miserable."

"You've decided these things without asking me."

"I didn't decide them. They're obvious."

"Thanks for the lesson in observation. Would it do any earthly good to say you still have the wrong end of the god-damned stick?"

"I can't have. I know."

"You're sure that's all? You're sure that it doesn't also have something to do with your own morally upright and small-minded friends?"

"That's not fair!"

"I don't feel fair. Answer me!"

"No! It doesn't have anything to do with anyone else! Just me. Me! I have debts to pay, obligations I am *not* going to dump on you, and besides, I'm small-town, home-made, wear Lane Bryant sizes, and eat green apples! It wouldn't work!"

"You've decided this all by yourself."

"Yes!"

He looked at her a long moment, unmoving. Then suddenly, unexpectedly, he laughed. Real, genuine laughter. It made her so furious she screamed. "I DON'T BELONG IN FLORIDA!"

"NEITHER DO I!"

The silence was so thick it could have been sliced. Through it at last in a shaking voice she said, "What?"

"I don't belong there either."

"Why? Not because of me! Bob, I couldn't let you do that—they're your friends! Karen's told me how close you all were, how many years you've spent together—"

525

He cut her off. "You're jumping to conclusions again. Will you listen?"

As chastened as a child, she said, "Yes," but had to add, "Have they changed that much?"

"No, love. That's the problem. They haven't changed at all. I'm the one."

Karen had said that, too. Why was it so important?

"I don't understand."

"Do you want to understand?"

It was a rather terrible question. It said, in effect, get on or get off. She said, "Yes. Yes!"

"Come here."

She didn't care whether it was a concession or not. She went, the soft rose-colored robe belling out behind her. She stood before him, looking up but not touching. Nor did he reach out. He merely looked down, catching her eyes with his, holding them. Behind him the fire hissed as heat found the last wet seam of sap in the old hickory log.

Soberly he told her, "My friends are just the way I left them two years ago. Two years ago! Christ! When you're there, when you're with them all the time you don't realize it — you don't realize they're also the same as they were two years before that. It's scary. At least it scared the shit out of me."

"How can they do that?"

"By living in the past."

"That can't be done."

"They're doing it. They're damn well doing it. The guys talk about nothing but their golf scores and what they lost at the races—and that last sweep across the MeKong Delta. The girls only entertain each other, no strangers allowed, as though they were still on base somewhere. And in the background are the aerobics, the jogging, the tummy-tucks, the face lifts—no gray hair, Evelinda. They even dye their eyebrows."

"The guys too?"

"Probably. I was afraid to look."

He wasn't being funny. He turned to stare at the fire, and turned her with him, holding her inside one long arm, the other jammed into the robe pocket. He went on, "You may talk about your kids. That's okay. But for God's sake, don't mention grand-kids! I said something about Robby and it was like I'd committed incest. Jesus! They're lemmings. And they're just as self-destructive. I found myself sitting poolside, listening to them—and I thought—these are the guys I spent half my life with, the guys who saved my ass time after time, I love these guys—but they've turned into silly old men in varsity sweaters and I can't hack it! I can't play by their rules anymore. I—I couldn't wait to come home."

She said, "Oh, Bob," and put her arms around him, around the warmth of his chest beneath the robe, holding him tightly. She was crying again, but they were different tears.

He put his cheek on top of her head. Huskily he said, "That's what was bugging me. I don't like making promises I can't keep. I was afraid you'd be so disappointed."

"And I was afraid you'd be disappointed."

"I may be yet. I think it's your turn to do a little clarifying, love. What the hell is a Lane Bryant, and how do green apples enter into this?"

She sighed deeply and turned her face to the hollow of his shoulder. "I just—knew I couldn't go. Beyond the fact of—of belonging. Beyond that."

"One question." His voice sounded strained. "Was it me?"

"Oh, no. No. Never."

"Two questions, then. Was it John?"

She raised her head and looked at him. She knew she must, and she was right. They were the eyes of a man who was going to hurt badly if she didn't tell the truth. She said,

"I've reached my peace with John, Bob. And to his friends who may think he's been betrayed I can only say, 'Go out there and see for yourselves. Talk to the stranger in John's body.' If they still don't understand, then I don't care. It's not worth my time."

He put a hand up, gently stroked the gray hair from her forehead. "What *do* you care about, Evelinda?"

"You. And my daughter. My son. Poo. John's mother. My job. How about that? I've learned that I do care about Bunny Burger—and the kids there. Last of all—myself. I care about myself. Too much to be an ostrich again."

His eyes crinkled at the corners. "Ostrich. Does that go with green apples and **Lane** Whatever?"

She told him about ostriches. He said, "Jane's right. But I never knew you as an ostrich, and I like you fine the way you are. Ask me what I care about."

She did.

He said, "You. Karen. Tim. Rob. My Air Guard classes and the chance to teach some more of them. Proving to myself that I am not a glitch in time as my old friends are. You know what I think we both did, Evelinda?"

529

"What did we do?"

"We lost our perspective after all. We let ourselves get in a toot, we tried to hurry. Hell. What's the rush? We're not kids."

"Speak for yourself. I feel like one."

"I've been acting like one so we're even. I apologize."

"For what?"

"For even thinking I could take you away from your family. For believing that I wanted to go, myself, taking you. I want them to like me, not put out a contract on my life."

Standing close to him, in the circle of his arm, Evelyn was feeling an enormous burden slip from her shoulders. Quietly she said, "They will like you," knowing it was true, that Jack would be pleased beyond measure—for her, for his mom—that Jessie would have private twinges, but first be smug, then charmed, and that Brenda—having learned a little recently—could learn some more.

He was saying, "I do have to go back down. I promised Don two weeks of Air Guard tactics classes, and he'll come get my hide if I don't. Besides, he says he'll recommend me up here at the University afterwards. Okay? Worth it?"

"Worth it. Two weeks I can handle. It was

forever I wasn't dealing with very well."

He laughed, and said she was sweet, and did a few things to prove his point that she found satisfactory.

Eventually they got around to eating the snacks on the tray by the fire, but as the evening deepened, it was not enough—especially for Bob, who had eaten sparsely since his Continental breakfast in flight.

"I ordered beef bourguignon when I made reservations," he said. "We can eat it here, or we can go down to the dining room."

It was an unconscious test, but she recognized it.

Well, world—she was ready. She said, "Oh, let's go down! I'd like to see the rest of this place."

"That's my girl," was all he answered, but she knew he was pleased.

She put on her make-up, watching him in the mirror as he shaved, and there were no ghosts there. John had used an electric shaver for years. She'd forgotten the small dextrous flip of shaving-cream-and-stubble-mixed globs on paper towel, the hoisted chin, the fingers searching the jawline. But when he came to zip her dress, there was a ghost—and he had one, too.

Gently he turned her to face him.

"They were good times," he said soberly. "Sue loved me. John loved you. What would they wish for us now?"

She blinked, but answered only a bit shakily, "To love each other. And not to forget the good times — with them."

"Nor mourn them."

"No. Just to remember. And be glad. For them. For us."

He nodded. Then kissing her lightly, he twirled her so her hair sprayed in a soft fan, and the silky skirts of the new rose dress flared. "Classy," he said.

She laughed. Standing on tiptoe, she kissed him back. She said, "Shall I tell you something? Will you let it go to your head?"

"Probably."

"You are the handsomest man I have ever seen."

She meant it. The dark gray suit fitted with the expertise of a master tailor across his broad shoulders, the white shirt gleamed, silhouetting the subtly striped, precisely tied tie — but that wasn't it. What counted was the way his proud head sat on those shoulders, the steady, steel-gray eyes above that blunt nose and Bristol white moustache, the erect, military carriage of all six feet of him.

It was a far cry from dirty sneakers and patched blue jeans and he knew it. He grinned. "My mother always said I cleaned up good," he said. "Well, Myrna. Shall we go?"

"Well, Cary," she answered. "Let's."

They were almost to the dining room before she remembered Porter DeKalb.

Thirty-six

Graceful masonry arches led from the guest houses to the soaring, vaulted ceiling, the vast beams, and the tapestry-covered limestone of a baronial dining hall. They'd hardly stepped inside its cool and disciplined brilliance when Evelyn said suddenly, "Damn!" Fortunately, she kept her voice low.

Bob had just handed his magic plastic card to a blank-faced *maître d'* who murmured, "General Johnson's guests. Of course. We've been expecting you. This way, please."

Their table was set, along with a few others, on a slightly raised stone platform along one side of the hall. It could be discreetly shielded by a brisk tug of beautiful tapestry hung to glide silently on brass rods, or left as it was so the diners had a view of the tinkling fountain in the center of the floor. There were brief glittering flashes of quick, darting fish in the pool at the foot of the fountain. At the far end of the hall gaped a large fireplace and small cocktail tables scattered on its immense hearth. From the walls floated the musical strains of something lightly Hungarian, pleasant enough to be cheerful, faint enough to be unobtrusive.

Bob declined the shelter of the tapestry, ordered two gin and tonics, and leaned forward, clasping his hands. His expression was severe.

"What was that you said, young lady? You are to mind your mouth when I take you to dine!"

He was grinning. She made a face.

"I forgot to tell you. Porter DeKalb is here."

"Porter—"

He stopped, his face set. "You're sure? You saw him?"

"I heard him. That's enough."

"When?"

"Back at the guest house. When I was on the balcony—before—" Then her face grew pink. "Anyway. He's next door. On the right."

He grinned briefly again, at her color. "You should have told me."

"I forgot. We did get—involved."

"And may again. We also could leave. There are other places."

"I wouldn't think of leaving. He is not," she

535

added succinctly, "with Mary Lou."

His eyebrows peaked. "Ah. That's why I distinctly heard the little wheels turning. Wouldst like me to challenge him with duelling pistols on behalf of the current injured husband?"

Firmly she said, "No, I wouldst not. I know the lady. There isn't an injured husband, but she's very nice. I think he just has her in a cleft stick as he's tried to have me. What I do want is for you to stay strictly out of it, Lochinvar."

Now he was serious. "Only if it's feasible."

The drinks came and they sipped as she said, "No one is going to start anything here—not even Porter. All I want—all I really need—is to have him know I saw him."

"You think that would get him off your back?"

"I'm positive it would. The magic word is *Mary Lou.*"

"She'd leave him?"

"No. She wouldn't leave him. And he can't afford to leave her. She'd just make his life a living hell and he'd have to take it."

"You're not a nice lady, Evelyn."

"He's not a nice man."

Bob said grimly, "I'll drink to that," and they both did.

The beef bourguignon was superb, as was the clear, rich ruby wine that accompanied it. The last crumb of a satisfying cheesecake was just being coaxed onto Evelyn's fork when Bob said softly, "Goal."

"What?"

"Goal. They just came in. Tall, golden lady with cheekbones, right? Sit tight, honey; they're going to go by us in just a minute."

Evelyn was conscious of her rapid breathing. With an effort she forced a pleasant smile and sealed it there. Bob laid his hand on hers, curling their fingers together. She appreciated his support but honestly wished he hadn't. This was one of the moments during which the cheese really wanted to stand alone.

The waiter went first, then Nan, tall and regal in a cream-colored gown that draped softly and showed her long lovely legs as she walked. She was looking neither to the right nor to the left. Porter was doing both—admiring the hall and glancing curiously at the diners.

He saw Bob first, registered surprise, then opened his mouth to say something as he slid his eyes to Bob's companion. Whatever he meant to say was never said. His jaw froze in position—not unlike a largemouth bass. Somehow his legs carried him right on by.

537

They were given the second table down. The tapestry slid shut. Bob and Evelyn distinctly heard a chair slide and some table service clatter to the floor. Then a muffled curse.

"He's rattled," said Evelyn.

"Now what will he do?"

"Come back. He has to come back. He can't *not* come back. You'll see." But she raised her wine glass to her lips and drank unsteadily. "I'm really not enjoying this. I hate it. I do, Bob. I just know it has to be done."

"What do you want me to do?"

"Leave."

"Evelyn, for God's sake—you can't be serious."

"I *am* serious. Leave. Just for a few minutes. Then come back. Please come back. You may have to carry me out in a basket."

"As long as you go home with the guy what brung you."

"I always do that."

He stood up, towering over her, then stooped to gently kiss her cheek. "I'll be lurking around the nearest corner. One good loud holler will do it."

He was making fun but he meant it. She nodded, and watched him go, wondering if she was totally out of her mind. Bob could have handled it so neatly. Just a few words would have done it. She wouldn't be sitting here alone with cold hands and cold feet and a rock in her throat the size of a goose egg.

A cheese with a shield. With it or on it, one or the other, she thought ruefully and downed the last few ruby drops of wine. When the shadow fell across the table linen she knew without looking that it was Porter.

He sat down in Bob's chair. His heavy face was the color of putty, and every red, thread-like vein showed. Looking at him, meeting his eyes, finding them not the clear sharp gray of the man who'd just left but smudged with yellowing whites, she suddenly wasn't uneasy any more.

The mellow bell of his voice was uneven. He said, "All right. So we're both getting it on the side."

That was the wrong way to start—trying to dirty her along with him. She said quietly, "John doesn't care."

"You think Mary Lou cares?"

"Doesn't she?"

If he'd thought of bluffing, he dropped it as useless. "Yes. She'd care. Okay, Evie. In a way, I guess you win. What do you want me to do?"

That was easy. That was pie. "Two things.

Get off my back. I mean—totally off! Send me a bill for the Lincoln, no more smarmy phone calls, no nasty little notes trying to lose me my job."

He'd winced at the "smarmy." His voice sounded thick, like cold syrup. "All right. What else? Money? I know you're short—unless the ex-fly boy, there, is paying your bills—"

"Watch it, Port!" And she hadn't known her own voice could be so icy. "No one is paying my bills but me." She almost added, "If I wanted money I'd borrow from Mary Lou," but she really didn't care much for going at it toe to toe.

"Sorry. You said two things."

"Right. The second one is this—give Nan a fair shake or I'll have your hide."

"Nan!" Incredulously she realized he was almost laughing. "Nan! You're kidding! She's a slut—a lay! Why are you worrying about Nan?"

Evelyn knew she was angrier than she'd ever been in her life.

She leaned forward and said softly, "Listen, Buster. You think you have Nan on the same cleft stick you wanted me. She's broke, she has obligations, you own her livelihood. Here's a piece of news—I care about Nan. If I hear so much as a whisper from her that you're not treating her right you will be the sorriest tom-cat in town. Have you got that?"

"You're serious!"

"Try me."

He leaned back, working at keeping a casual look on his face. But he was sweating. "God," he said. "The last thing I expected—the last person I ever thought to see here—"

It was as if he was talking to himself; she answered anyway.

"Sometimes you're just due."

He turned his bleary eyes on her. He said, "And you're the only one I ever wanted. All those others—just substitutes for you. Yet, look at us now—not even friends. It's crazy."

"I didn't do it, Port. I needed a friend, but you couldn't stay with that. You couldn't let well enough alone."

"Because it wasn't well enough."

He lumbered to his feet. He looked down, and put out a chunky, tanned hand. He almost touched her shoulder.

"I loved you," he said. "I really loved you."

He went away slowly, almost shuffling like an old man. She felt no compunction. She knew Porter. He'd think of something tomorrow, something to buck up his ego. That would be fine with her—as long as he obeyed the rules.

And she really thought he would. This time the shadow falling across the linen was long and thin. Bob was smiling down at her, but the smile was anxious. "No fireworks."

"I defused him. I hope."

He sat down again, taking her cold hand in his and warming it. "Do you really think his wife doesn't know about his catting?"

"Of course she knows. She's always known. The important thing is that he doesn't *realize* she knows."

"And on such frail threads are marriages preserved."

"Yes. Some are. Mine wasn't."

"Nor mine."

They looked at each other, and the question was obvious: How frail, then, are we? The two of us?

She said painfully, "We can only try."

"I'm willing. I was standing back there, thinking—thinking about being up here permanently. Close to everyone. About living in my apartment. You, living in yours. Because that's the way it has to be—for a while, anyway. Doesn't it?"

"Yes. Probably. But there doesn't have to be total lack of communication, you know."

He stood up, pulling her up also by the cold

542

hand he'd warmed. He was smiling again. "Shall we send secret notes back and forth by Poo and Robby—until they learn to read, that is."

"They're pretty bright. It won't be long. Perhaps we'd better just—talk. Spend time together. Right in front of everyone."

"Or other forms of—communication?"

"There are other forms?"

"One or two. Would you like to hear about them?"

"Do you demonstrate?"

"On request."

They went out into the clear night air and stood in the shelter of the arcade, looking at the black enamel sky glittering with tiny diamonds. Slowly across its shiny patina traveled a small, red, flashing point of light as a high and purposeful airplane cut its way through time and space.

They were holding hands like children. Bob was saying, "We'll go to Florida eventually. All of us. I've found a little piece of land on the Gulf with good hard white sand to land on. Robby and Poo can play in the water. Our girls can get a tan. The guys can help me build a place to winter in. Sound okay?"

It sounded beautiful. Of course it might not

ever happen. Evelyn had learned that the hard way. Don't wait too long for tomorrow. John had waited — and what he'd waited for never came. The young can dally a while — if they don't push their luck.

But when one has only twenty years or so, one had better not wait. She'd already gone from ostrich to cheese. She'd never really made Wonder Woman, but truthfully she wasn't the type. She didn't mind being a cheese. In fact, she rather liked it.

"Bob."

He'd been watching the airplane disappear. Whatever had been his own long thoughts, his hand tightened on hers, not letting go. His voice was quiet and very far away.

"What?"

"You like cheese, don't you?"

"Only old cheese," he said, and was surprised when she laughed. Monday she'd be a cheese again, old *and* good. Tonight she was as young as her dreams. They both were. It was a nice way, she thought as she responded to the warm hand holding hers, to begin the next twenty years — or so.

Whatever happened, whatever came, she could handle it. Now.